33 PLACE BRUGMANN

33 PLACE BRUGMANN

A NOVEL

ALICE AUSTEN

Grove Press
New York

FIRST EDITION

Published simultaneously in Canada
Printed in the United States of America

First Grove Atlantic hardcover edition: March 2025

The interior of this book was designed by Norman E. Tuttle
at Alpha Design & Composition.
This book is set in 11-pt. Scala Pro at
Alpha Design & Composition of Pittsfield, NH.

Library of Congress Cataloging-in-Publication data is available for this title.

ISBN 978-0-8021-6408-7
eISBN 978-0-8021-6409-4

Grove Press
an imprint of Grove Atlantic
154 West 14th Street
New York, NY 10011

Distributed by Publishers Group West

groveatlantic.com

25 26 27   10 9 8 7 6 5 4 3 2 1

for Guy

What is thinkable is also possible.
Ludwig Wittgenstein

BUILDING RESIDENTS

5th Floor Maid's Room
Miss Masha Balyayeva, refugee–Nansen Passport, seamstress

Apartment 4L:
Mr. Francois G. Sauvin, architect
Miss Charlotte E. Sauvin (daughter), student, Royal Academy of Fine Arts
   Antwerp

Apartment 4R:
Mr. Leo Raphaël, fine art dealer
Mrs. Sophia Raphaël (spouse), housewife
Miss Esther Raphaël (daughter)
Mr. Julian Raphaël (son), student, Cambridge University

Apartment 3L:
Colonel Herman Warlemont, Belgian Armed Forces (widower)

Apartment 3R:
Miss Agathe Hobert, former café proprietor

Apartment 2L:
~~**Mrs. Mathilde Boudrot**, (widow)~~ **deceased, 13 April 1939**

Apartment 2R:
Mr. Martin DeBaerre, attorney
Mrs. Katrin DeBaerre (spouse), housewife
Mr. Dirk DeBaerre (son), student, Katholieke Universiteit Leuven

Ground Floor
Mr. Jan Everard, notary
Mrs. Annick Everard (spouse), housewife
(two children below age of mandatory registration)

All residents are Belgian citizens unless otherwise noted and duly registered
in the Commune d'Ixelles.

Sworn and attested, this 2d day of April 1939

The Raphaëls leave in the middle of the night, and they leave everything behind.

The sofas and chairs and beds and lamps and heavy carpets and the dining table. The films we made are in a box together with the projector, a set of oil paints, and a blank canvas. On it is a note that reads, *For Charlotte*. I gasp, the air coming in tight and sharp. I might have thought I was dreaming, but for that note. When I see it, I know the Raphaëls are truly gone.

In their wake, rumors swirl through the building. The Raphaëls haven't left *everything*. They took their silver. And the paintings? The paintings simply disappear.

Brussels, Belgium
August 1939

Before

CHARLOTTE SAUVIN, 4L

The pounding on our apartment door wakes me early Saturday morning. Throwing back the covers, I jump out of bed and run down the long terrazzo hallway. But I know who it is. I can hear them.

We hear every sound in this building.

Through thin, rippled window glass, gaps between frames and doors, crude holes around pipes and wires, up and down the broad echoing stone staircase, up and down the narrow echoing elevator shaft, every sound travels. The squeaks and groans and sighs, the thumping of taps calling water up, the flush and flow of water falling, the clank of radiators, the squawk of Dirk's saxophone, the thudding fall of stockinged footsteps, the clop of stacked leather heels on soft wood floors, the turning of keys in locks, slamming of doors, sharp click of latches, and the voices. Miss Hobert shouting at her deaf aunt through the telephone receiver, the Colonel barking commands at Zipper, his hard-headed Bouvier, and Annick on the ground floor berating her husband, Mr. Everard, the notary who manages the building.

Father is already up and making coffee in our simple Italian pot, and I catch a glimpse of his slim, straight back and the flash of his smile as I fly past the kitchen door and around the corner, feeling the slap of cool stone on my bare feet, past three sets of double French doors—to Father's study on one side and our living and dining rooms on the other—finally reaching the massive paneled front door and throwing it open to see Julian, amused expression on his pale face, camera in hand, leaning against the heavy oak balustrade. Esther is beside him.

The sun through the hall window turns her mass of curls to a burning bush, and a smell of sweet yeast floats up from the basket she holds. Mrs. Raphaël has sent over bread for our breakfast.

The Raphaëls' door is ajar and from across the expansive landing, I catch a glimpse of their hall. Our two apartments are architectural mirror images. But this is where any likeness ends. Our apartment is spare and restrained, with simple furniture and elegant lines, while the Raphaëls' is a jumble of pattern and complexity and treasures. A museum. Their long front hall is lined with paintings, and these paintings are my good friends too. I've spent time with them, studied them, absorbed every brushstroke, form, shape, and shift in tone. I have been intoxicated by their energy. I could describe each in near-perfect detail.

I hear a swish and bump as Incarna, their thumb-bodied cleaning woman comes into view. Mumbling under her breath in Spanish, she glares at the three of us as she mops her way to the door then shuts it with a bang.

"Hurry." Julian steps through our doorway with Esther close behind. "The light."

*

I've thrown on clothes, passed a comb through my fine, tangled hair, and joined Father and Esther and Julian at the table, where we sip coffee and eat bread in that lucid morning light.

Father is asking questions about the camera, which Julian answers with great earnestness, Julian being the most intelligent and serious person I've ever met. How is it possible he's only eighteen and a year older than me? I'm looking at him now. Deep, knowing eyes. My dear one, I understand you when you speak. I read your silences. Like the paintings, you are known to me. You are the closest to a brother I'll ever have.

"And using a camera on the Sabbath?" Father asks with a wink at Esther, who is my age.

Father knows the Raphaëls aren't religious, not like that, nor for that matter is Father, who believes only in the divinity of nature and the capricious cruelty of God and man. But, as always, he's trying to get a smile or a rise out of Julian. He rarely succeeds.

"I'll leave resting to the dead." Julian isn't smiling, but he's amused.

"Who better?" Father laughs.

Julian turns to me. "The light."

Julian and Esther and I go out into the square as we did nearly every Saturday morning when we were younger. For the camera has made us children again and for a brief time it has freed us from the weight of the falling world.

*

Mr. Raphaël brought the movie camera back from America on one of those rare, perfect days in a Belgian summer, a day of such intensity and contrast that even I could see the clouds floating across the sky. The camera is a prototype made by an American company. Mr. Raphaël told us it was a gift from the owner of the company, a man called Bellow, who hails from Chicago, and that he, Mr. Raphaël, tried it out on the crossing back to Europe and nearly dropped it in the ocean when a big swell rocked the ship.

"Actually, Bellow isn't a belower at all," Mr. Raphaël began—his face beaming, a face like Julian's. Or, rather, Julian takes after his father, only slimmer with his mother's elegant bones—Mrs. Raphaël still being quite beautiful.

"He's soft-voiced, and his name is really Belov. Moreover, he isn't from Chicago. He's from Russia, and when he arrived in America, by boat as well, he only spoke Russian. And some Yiddish."

All this Mr. Raphaël learned over a beer and some sausages at the Berghoff restaurant in Chicago.

"The little ironies," Mr. Raphaël said in that expansive voice he uses when he knows he has an audience, "make life delicious and appalling.

Don't you know, it was the best and undoubtedly the last German sausage I'll ever eat."

It wasn't long after this that Mrs. Raphaël firmly banned all German products, be they music or food or language. She said simply that she wouldn't allow them. "And anyway," she added, "sausage makes me fat."

And what did Mr. Raphaël do with his collection of Wagner recordings in the wake of this pronouncement? I never learn.

*

We have filmed almost every day since Mr. Raphaël brought the camera home, and this morning I have a yearning for life to stay in one place a little longer. Julian will be leaving within the week to England where he's studying maths at Cambridge.

"And it wasn't even a lecture," he's saying with admiration. "It was an argument."

I see the familiar look of concentration on his face as his hands delve into the dark folds of the makeshift tent where we load film.

"Wittgenstein was sitting there, just sitting in the midst of us. As though he was one of us."

Wittgenstein being a philosopher and mathematician Father also greatly admires.

"You were arguing with Wittgenstein?" I ask.

I hear the whirr of the film winding. Julian's skin looks even paler in the shadow of the church.

"Never. Another fellow was. Turing. Brilliant chap. Odd, but they all are. We all are. I was taking mad notes. They were arguing about the liar's paradox. Do you know it?"

"Not sure."

"If I'm a liar, and I say I'm a liar, I must not be a liar because if I say I'm lying, I must be telling the truth, ergo I'm not a liar."

"Or you're a liar telling the truth this one time," I say.

I move closer, the smell of him mingling with acid from the film. I couldn't describe Julian's smell if I wanted to, and there would be no point, other than to say it, too, is known to me.

"Then I'm not really a liar, am I? But if I say I'm telling the truth, I must be lying unless I say I'm a liar in which case, once again, I'm telling the truth," he says doggedly.

"The whole thing is silly. The fact is you can't pay attention to what people say. What matters is what they do. And in this case, no one has done anything. They've said things. I don't think it's illuminating."

"You and Wittgenstein agree on that."

The mechanism catches, the film stops. Julian adjusts his hand in the tent, and I hear a whir as the winding starts up again.

"Are you finished?" Esther calls from across the square where she's petting a stray cat on a stoop to keep it there until Julian can film it.

"Almost," Julian says.

I could lick Julian's ear, bite it, like kittens do when they're playing. A lock of hair falls over his eye, and I brush it back for him. I'd like to think I'm the only person Julian confides in, but I'm sure that's hubris on my part and that I am as susceptible as the next of putting myself at the center of a story having little to do with me.

"Done. You can unfasten it."

I unbutton the flap, Julian pulls out the camera, newly loaded with film, and I put the reel he's just tinned into my bag.

Julian presses one eye to the camera lens, squeezes the other shut, and begins to film.

The filming has been a beautiful distraction. It has taken my mind off Philippe.

*

Philippe saw me off at the train station in June. The semester had just ended at the academy in Antwerp where we both study, and I had thought he would come to Brussels and meet Father and the Raphaëls, but he told me he had no time for all that. He was traveling home to Paris and then taking his parents across the Pyrenees and on to Spain. He was brusque and preoccupied and didn't seem to have a thought for me, and I admit I felt a stinging hurt. Not that I showed it. All I said was that it sounded like a lot of strenuous travel for a vacation.

"It is. And please don't mention it to anyone. Not even your father."

How could I not feel offended? But I didn't ask questions or let on that I felt hurt. It isn't my way. I don't show emotions like that. I can't. I was raised to be strong, and I can't be both strong and emotional. Maybe a better person could, but I'm not that better person, and I can't pretend to be someone else. Even if I could, I wouldn't.

Philippe insisted on sitting with me in the station waiting room, an echoing cathedral of space. Amid the bustle and the voices bouncing off walls around us, ours were silent. When my train was called, he carried my bag, and we walked under the iron-and-glass-domed central terminal and down the platform.

"It's an indignity," he burst out.

I thought he was talking about the fact of carrying my bag, so I tried to take it from him.

"What on earth are you doing?"

"If it's an indignity to you, I'll carry the damn bag."

"Not the bag. This mishmash." He waved his free arm around indicating the station. "It's an architectural spoonerism."

"You think it's a joke?"

"To me."

I understood that Philippe was objecting to the collection of architectural styles in the station, an assemblage praised by many. But Philippe's a purist, a minimalist. And he was in a contentious mood.

"Anyone who says otherwise is a pretender hoping to be mistaken for an intellectual. Don't tell me you disagree," he added.

"Antwerp's a dark place."

"What does that have to do with it?"

"Here. There's light. So much light."

He stopped walking and turned to face me. "You think it's beautiful?"

"If light is beauty, yes. I do."

"I don't know anymore."

I was looking for the light in Philippe's eyes, but all I saw was his troubled brow, the tense line of his jaw. He dropped my bag, clutched me to him, and kissed me. I could feel the energy and fury in his body as his arms tightened around me. I kissed him back, feeling the same energy and fury in my body. It was a contagion. I wanted him. In that moment, I think we both understood that we had to have each other.

We didn't say a word after that. He picked up my bag and carried it the rest of the way down the platform, helped me to my seat, kissed me again, and got off the train. As it pulled away, I could see him waiting there, hands in the pockets of his linen pants, looking up at the ceiling as if he were seeing death itself through all that glass. I watched until I could no longer see him, and only then did I realize that my whole body was shaking.

*

On his way back from America, Mr. Raphaël stopped in London where he found a projector. He told us that screens were few and far between, so when Mrs. Raphaël was out one afternoon, Mr. Raphaël helped Julian take down the largest painting in the living room, leaving a bare rectangle a shade paler than the rest of the room and in it an uneven circle where the wall had been replastered. Upon her return, Mrs. Raphaël insisted that the hanger be left and the painting replaced between viewings and so in every film we watch, there's a brass ring in the upper middle of the image.

Mrs. Raphaël was so adamant it made me wonder if there was something more than met the eye to that circle of plaster.

We've watched the films over and over, and then we've watched them in reverse. Julian especially loves to see them backward.

We filmed the Colonel who lives below our apartment on the third floor with Zipper, the dog he bought after his wife died. Julian filmed Zipper gulping down food then vomiting great unmasticated chunks of it on the speckled terrazzo floor. On our plaster screen, Zipper's mouth became a vacuum that sucked the vomited food back in.

We filmed a monsoon of a summer rain, and we saw God draw the rain up from the ground like a stage curtain.

*

The stray cat is still lazing in the sun when Julian starts filming it. It yawns. A yawn in reverse is not so interesting, I think.

I'm facing our building and standing far enough across the square so I can see all of it. I love this building. To me it looks modest and confident, noble yet indifferent to the opinions of others. Prepossessing. I know that the symmetry of it appealed to Father—the two identical apartments on each of the three upper floors, an apartment on the ground floor facing a large, high-ceilinged but austere lobby, and the maid's room at the center of the fifth level at the top. The brick facade, stone balconies, and thick exterior walls give it the feel of a fortress that's impervious to anything beyond, and in a way it is. Number 33 is a world unto herself.

I don't know if it's the whir of the camera or our intrusion into its nap, but the cat springs up and dashes across the street just as a car rounds the corner. The driver swerves, too late, and the car hits the cat with a thud. The car doesn't stop. It screeches away. And Julian doesn't stop filming.

Esther runs to the cat and crouches beside it, trying to stay the bleeding, but there's nothing to be done. Tears flow down Esther's cheeks as Julian films the cat bleeding out on the pavement.

I watch all of it. The tide of blood flowing over the cat's poor crushed skull and soft fur. Water over sand.

I glance back at the massive church doors behind me and see that blood is seeping out under them, too, flowing from the church and flooding the square. Blood is everywhere. The passersby wade through blood, and it spatters their pant legs and skirts, but they take no notice. I grip the iron railing that frames the now-bloodied concrete steps, feeling the chipped edges of old paint, the cool metal pressing against my palm. I look up at the brilliant sky for a moment, staring at the sun, and then down at the square where Julian is comforting Esther on the dry sidewalk stones.

*

We're all in a somber mood as we walk back to the building and step into the lobby that smells of pine soap and petrichor. Julian runs ahead, slipping, nearly falling, on the newly mopped floor.

"Careful!" he calls behind.

"I want to be a nurse," Esther says softly as we start up the stairs behind him.

"You should."

"I might have saved it, if I knew more."

"You couldn't have. No one could have."

I'm watching Julian above as he makes the turns of ascending rectangles of stairs.

"Still. It's what I want. You know what you want. You're already doing it."

"So should you."

"Mama's against it. She thinks I don't understand what I'm getting into."

"Remind her that you were the only one who could change Julian's dressing after his appendix surgery," I say.

"She said that doesn't count because Julian is my brother and one of the people I love most, and the real test will be when it's a stranger. Or a person I don't like."

"She might be right."

From above, I hear the Raphaëls' door opening. Julian is already inside. I walk faster.

"And I thought you were my friend." Esther pulls on my skirt.

"Only if you'll take care of me when I'm old and sick."

"I'll be older—"

"By a month."

"And likely sicker, so maybe not."

We reach the third-floor landing, and Esther hugs me. It's impulsive of her. I understand the gesture, and I try not to show my impatience with it. Instead, I concentrate on the view of the courtyard, cheerless even in summer, through the octagonal landing window. I remember how Julian and his friends used to play in the courtyard. The time one of them, a boy called Guy, climbed out Julian's window in his underwear on a dare and walked along the narrow stone ledge. We all thought Guy would fall and die, but he climbed in my window bare legged and grinning. Later, I remember Dirk telling me that Guy wouldn't have died because he's a trickster and tricksters don't die. They simply change shape.

"You mean he's Jewish," I said, narrowing my eyes at him.

Dirk didn't reply. He turned on his heel and walked away.

Esther's trembling. I can feel the vibration in her soft, slender body. Her hair smells like roses, and I look down at the thin waxy part in her curls. I'm nearly a head taller than she is. It's Julian who inherited his father's height, a great relief to Mr. Raphaël, who has a cousin with a giant daughter and a diminutive son.

"Make a promise," Esther says.

"What's that?"

"No matter what happens, we don't cry. Unless it's an ending."

"Yes." I pull away and run up after Julian.

*

I slide back the long, dark velvet curtain and rap on the utility room door.

"Hold on."

I drop the curtain and stand in darkness waiting until Julian opens the door for me to step inside.

The tiny room is hot and damp. Julian already has the film soaking in water so the gelatine will swell.

"Gloves!" he orders as he takes the film out of the water and plunges it in a bucket of developer.

The darkroom bulb is a dropping sun, and in its faint glow I can just make out my gloves hanging over the edge of the sink. I put them on as Julian swirls the liquid in the bucket, making sure every frame of the celluloid is covered.

"Ready."

I rinse the film at the sink as Julian prepares the bleach bath. We're standing so close I feel his breath on my ear.

The reversal film requires more steps, more precision. We arrived at this process after two ruined reels and one that made all the people in the frame cellophane ghosts. But it's worth the trouble. We don't have to send the film off to be printed and we can project it right away.

We work in our usual quietude. Unlike the rest of his family, Julian's never been a talker and I treasure our silence. But today he breaks it.

"If there's a war, I'll fight," he says.

"For the Belgians?"

"For anyone who's against the Nazis. Light!"

I snap on the bright overhead lamp. Julian opens the door and holds back the curtains to illuminate the tiny room. I notice a wild intensity on his face that I've never seen before.

"I want you to think of me," he says.

"Think of you?"

"Like a prayer," he admonishes.

Julian's eyes are blinding. I look away.

"I thought you didn't believe in praying," I say.

"I never said that. Thoughts are energy. Energy transforms matter. Light is energy. You of all people understand how light can change everything, even our film. Light!"

He drops the curtains and I yank the chain to click off the lamp. We complete the last two steps in tense darkness. I sense there's something more he's trying to tell me that I don't understand, and I feel the weight of my incomprehension. The taste of bitter acid drifts to my tongue. And now it's me breaking the silence.

"I'll think of you. How could I not? But there isn't going to be a war here."

"Charlotte. You're not stupid, so don't say stupid things please."

*

As I walk across the hall to my apartment, I have an impulse to run upstairs and tell Masha about the cat and the blood in the square, for it was Masha who told me that the mystical holds hands with the ordinary. From the time I was small, I've spent countless hours with Masha. She's the keeper of my secrets. But as I make the turn around the newel post, I remember that Masha has gone away.

I saw her when I was home from the academy on Easter break. I went up to her studio, my place of mystery and comfort. She welcomed me with a cup of tea, a freshly opened box of tender Turkish delight. After, we cleaned the powdered sugar from her table, and she took out a beautiful piece of fabric and shook it. We watched as it rippled and fell in waves.

"It's blue," she said, "the palest blue."

"A winter sky," I said.

"Yes."

As we considered where to make the first cut, I told her about Philippe.

Masha listened but said nothing in response. I don't know what I expected, but I think I wanted her to tell me what to do. We had begun to pin a tissue paper pattern to the fabric and in my frustration, I pricked my finger, and it bled on the wool. Masha quickly cleaned it off, then folded the fabric and handed it to me.

"Why?"

"It was meant to be yours. You marked it."

"But the stain came out."

"It was a sign. Blood always is."

MASHA BALYAYEVA, 5TH FLOOR

Listen.

All men are dogs. They can't help it. And this is why men love dogs, sometimes more than their wives and children.

I'm the one who persuaded Colonel Warlemont to get the dog after his wife died. Zipper. That's what the Colonel called him.

Listen to me.

Please. Listen.

I was there. I was there the whole time, one way or another. And in the interests of setting everything on the table and as a matter of record, I never officially had an apartment in the building, but I did live there. I'm not a leech or a parasite or a beggar, G-d forbid. I've never begged. Or pleaded. I don't like to ask favors, nor do I take them unless there's no choice.

And let me tell you something else. When I was a small child, they called me the bold one. I had to live up to my name, didn't I? Lest it become another source of ridicule. So, I'm the bold one. If I don't speak up, someone else, some man, will. He'll steal my story and he'll change it, making me seem worse and him better. But don't think for a moment that I'm justifying my presence here. I belong here. It is meant to be.

*

I came to Brussels in 1924 with a list of three names given to me by the rabbi, though I myself was nameless. The first name was of a priest, who right away tried to sleep with me, confirming everything my poor dead mother had warned me about the Christian clergy. The second was that of a tailor, who like me had once lived in a settlement calling itself a town east of the Urals. I found him in his large but cheap shop near the Gare Central in Brussels where train workers and waiters had their uniforms made and mended. I have nothing against workingmen, but after a day in that establishment, my ass had bruises from all the pinching. The third name was Sophia Raphaël. I never knew how the rabbi came upon her name and address. But I do know that if I had asked, he would say, as he often did, "We have our ways, don't we?"

When I arrived at 33 Place Brugmann, I took a deep breath. I had never been inside a building of its standing before. Oh, how I loved the pale stone and brick, the tall windows, the heavy doors. A small fortress for those lucky enough to live within its thick walls.

*

Mrs. Raphaël took in my blue eyes and blond hair, not unlike her own eyes and hair, and then she did the most noble thing of all. She named me.

"Call yourself Masha Balyayeva. The blond one. And be careful. You're pretty."

She decided to have me alter one of her dresses, a simple wool day dress. We both understood this would be a test. When she put it on, I saw that it hung on her like a sack, even though the wool was expensive—the sort of wool you can't buy in Russia, finely woven, not scratchy at all, with a soft sheen to it—and a deep Prussian blue that brought out the blue in her eyes. *This is no test,* I thought. *It's a pleasure.* But I didn't tell her that.

"Not tight, please. Don't need to show it all. After I gave birth to my bunnies, well, they seem to have left some little bunnies behind. There's a bunny here." She indicated her slim waist. "And here." She patted her somewhat more ample derriere. "And here." She pointed to her back where a too-tight bra strap cut into the soft flesh of her shoulder.

"Let's loosen that."

"They'll fall down," she laughed.

I adjusted the bra strap and stepped back, looking at her with a critical eye.

"You're slim," I told her sternly. "And you have wonderful breasts. That's not the issue."

I saw that she liked my impudence. My confidence. I knew she was hoping it translated to know-how.

I took out my pins and began. A little taken in here and a little something adjusted there. The trick is to make the person look as if they were born in the clothes they're wearing. Effortless and smooth. No bunching of fabric. Not too tight or too loose.

I looked into Mrs. Raphaël's eyes—a cerulean reflection of my own, with the same intense black pupils that seem to have a light shining from within their orbs. I've been called a witch because of my eyes. People in my village said it was a trick of Satan to give me blue eyes with that strange, intense light coming out of the darkness. This was one of many reasons I left.

"I have no place to sew," I told her.

"Where are you living?"

"With a group of people who made it out."

I didn't tell her how we were all in one room with a bucket to bathe. How most of them were uneducated people who had nothing to do with me, some had been wealthy, but fate and circumstance had thrown us together and we had drawn the same lot regardless of what we did or who we were before. This, too, is a fact of living. All the money in the world won't insulate anyone from anything when G-d rolls his dice.

"Maybe you can use the maid's room upstairs," she said thoughtfully, seeming to glean the misery of my circumstances from my omission. "No one's living there now. It's small, but there's a window and a sink."

Her eyes remind me of the Aegean. I would have stayed there—in Turkey—the sea was so beautiful. But the rabbi insisted that I go west. And go west I did. As I looked into her eyes, I understood that if the dress came back as she liked it, I would have a place to live for as long as I needed.

This was fifteen years ago and nearly a year after I fled the place I once called home. I don't like to think of that place. When I do, I see the blood on my mama's face, and I remember a soldier on our side, whatever side that was, telling me Mama had been caught in the crossfire.

"I didn't hear of bayonets going in the other direction," I said, for Mama had been stabbed clean through. I was fourteen years old.

The soldier looked at me and then looked away. It was no secret that in the midst of the revolution, the Red Guard was carrying out pogroms where we lived. He had the grace to feel shame about it. I can't say that of most people these days.

Mud and troops. Men were fighting the Germans one moment and the White Russian army the next. Years of fighting before it was over, the royal family dead, and the idea of aristocracy, of anyone being born better, supposedly dead with them. The tailor, the tinker, the farrier, the railway workers, they were all sure the tide had turned and the people had won. There would be no more pogroms. The only person I knew who wasn't convinced everything would go our way was the rabbi.

I wanted him to be wrong, and at first I didn't listen to him, even though I had no one else. I never knew my father; it was rumored that he was gentile. Maybe he was. Mama never said. She only told me I looked like him. I had no siblings, and my grandparents were dead. The rabbi, may his memory be a blessing, was my uncle, and he was as stubborn as my mama.

I stayed until I was twenty-one. Lenin had died, Stalin had come to power, and the League of Militant Atheists was founded. There was a push to resettle our village farther east.

"Get out now, while you're able," the rabbi said, looking not at all pleased that his instincts had been right. He jotted down the three names. "America would be better."

"I don't have enough money for America."

"Go as far west as you can afford. Don't stop until you're out of money or train track."

"Thank you," I said.

*

Several years after I moved into the Raphaëls' attic room, I happened to run into that tailor, the one with the shop near the Gare Central. He told me the rabbi had been sent to gulag for teaching Hebrew rather than Yiddish. There was pleasure on his face as he gave me the news.

"I hear he's feeble. We all know Stalin takes no prisoners. That's why people try to escape the gulag. It's the only hope. And they always take an extra person along, you know."

I could see a flicker of malice at the corners of his mouth.

"I don't know."

"A weakling. A *carcass*. It's cold. They're on the lam. No food in the snow. You get my drift?"

I admit I was speechless, a rare state for me, but only for a moment. "The rabbi believes one must sit in the chair fate pulls up to the table. If he's in gulag, he'll stay in gulag."

"He might not have a choice."

"There's always a choice," I replied, not sure I had yet lived long enough to say it with conviction.

"You should have worked for me. That was a poor choice, and now there's no one to take care of you."

He'd have taken care of me all right.

Men are dogs. Men are death. I have always known this.

Back to the dress—Mrs. Raphaël loved what I did with it. She told me that simple wool dress had become her favorite.

"Strangers compliment me on this dress," she said. "All because of you."

"It was in the fabric all along," I told her. "It needed only a bit of adjustment in the seams."

"As for the room upstairs," she continued, "it's yours. Be unobtrusive. And learn better French."

I set up my atelier in the cramped attic room in Number 33. I had two small dormers with a view of the clunky church steeple in the square and one skylight that flooded the room with light, even on cloudy days, and I covered the old plaster walls with shimmering white cloth to reflect it. I cleaned and polished the wood floor, and I set up my little cot. This was where I slept for many years. When I wasn't in someone else's bed.

But it was the women who flocked to me at first. They had noticed Mrs. Raphaël's clothes. Where was she buying? Who was her tailor? Mrs. Raphaël is a generous woman with certain exceptions, and she generously shared my name. Before long, I was seamstress to all the socialites in Brussels. In those days, money was flowing and thanks to Mrs. Raphaël, some of it flowed to me. I would go to the homes of these women—tall ceilinged, lavishly furnished, ornate, and gilded where it made sense and didn't, as if painted gold fools anyone—then take their clothes back to my little room under the stars to make magic. There is magic in dressmaking. It's conjuring to understand how the body moves and how clothes should flow around it to create an illusion of grace and symmetry.

You see, my uncle taught me geometry and astronomy. There were no boys in the family, and even if there had been, I like to believe he would have done the same. He said if books were water, I had gills behind my ears the way I took to them. Thanks to him, I understood the movement of the spheres, and from this I learned how to change people with their clothes.

All of that proved useful in ways I would never have imagined.

I kept to myself in the building in those early days. The Colonel's wife was still alive, a charming if forceful woman, and when she learned

I was a seamstress, well, that was more money. And company. They often would invite me in for tea or supper.

And of course, there was Charlotte. She was a strange child, a girl who didn't look of this world, tall for her age, slender, with deep-gray eyes and flaxen hair. There was almost no color in her, only light.

To me, she was an angel.

One day, while her father was away at work, Charlotte and Esther, Mrs. Raphaël's daughter, climbed up to my atelier and watched me sew. Charlotte was transfixed by the fabrics, the dresses, the pinning, the stitching. But Esther was used to me and not interested at all, so they left.

After that, Charlotte came up on her own almost every afternoon, and we would talk as I worked—about her father, the building, Esther, Julian, the paintings, Brussels, her school, the boy Dirk on the second floor who had taken up the saxophone and played it so badly. How the notary on the ground floor used cologne that smelled like skunk and his wife looked like an eel.

Charlotte would watch me sew for hours. As she became more comfortable with me, she would make suggestions. What about that fabric or this trim? Widen the skirt, narrow the waist. She was seeing it with an artist's eye.

Sometimes she would bring a notebook and draw. Her father taught her well, for she drew with great precision, the lack of which color so often compensates for and hides. Charlotte also brought something of her own to the sketches. I didn't know at first what it was. And then I saw it.

You see, there were no straight lines in Charlotte's sketches. Only the illusion of straight lines.

Those afternoons with Charlotte were some of the best of my life, and I can't tell you how I looked forward to her visits. How I missed her when my life took an unexpected turn and my absences from the building became more and more frequent.

Charlotte was the closest I've had to a daughter. She was my angel. And I will be hers.

*

Back to the Colonel. I know what you're thinking. I didn't sleep with him—not before his wife died and not after. And I tell you, he was as appealing as some of the men I've slept with. Even the spikey gray hairs growing like weeds out of his nose wouldn't have put me off. It wasn't like that between us, that's all. He and his wife were childless and after her death, I gave him a shoulder to cry on. You might even say we were friends. The Colonel is one of the most upright men I've met, and he's old enough to be my father. For me, there are fathers. And there are lovers.

It was the Colonel who introduced me to Harry. Younger than the Colonel, older than me, Harry never told me his age, he was cloaked about those kinds of details, about his past. But when in a room with others he was boldly present, telling stories, making jokes, filling it with energy and life: his life.

LEO RAPHAËL, 4R

So, I didn't tell them everything, not exactly. I entertained them! With stories of sausages and beer made in the German style and of a particularly choppy sail back across the Atlantic.

It *is* true that Bellow and I ate and drank together in a German restaurant in Chicago. It is also true that we confided in one another as much as men who trust no one can. This is when I learned that Bellow lost two daughters more than a decade before amid fleeing Russia and arriving in America.

"Thanks be to G-d," Bellow added, "that I have four other children."

When Bellow learned that I have only one boy and one girl and that my plan to move the family to America had been torpedoed by U.S. government quotas that no amount of money or influence seems to be able to circumvent, we had a moment of silence together.

Amusing, isn't it? The two of us mourning the past and future as tuxedoed waiters drifted across the sawdust-covered floor, serving beer to the incessant thud of a lederhosen-clad oompah band? What a place to contemplate America's upcoming failure to save the Jews.

The next day, as I was about to depart for the ship, a package was delivered to my hotel. Bellow had given me a movie camera, perhaps in the hope that it would keep us alive, if only on film.

Before returning home, I stopped off in London to meet with a cousin of mine who is closely affiliated with one of the museums and rather well-connected to the international art world as, I like to think, am I.

We met in his office, a stuffy room that smelled of mothballs and cleaning wax, with a poor view of a gray street through an immaculate clear-paned window. You'd think it was the office of a struggling functionary. But I happen to know that he draws a comfortable salary, and I have in turn kept him flush with art sales, as we've continually shared information and insights over the years.

The desk was piled with books and papers. Bookshelves lined the walls. There was no space for art, but why would there be given that the office was in the museum? A short walk down a long hall and you were in a gallery. I perched on a stack of boxes and waited.

My cousin's face was guarded, as if he were afraid I would ask a favor he couldn't accommodate.

"Not everyone here is persuaded that Hitler is a monster," he began. This out of the blue.

"Here as in . . . ?"

"England."

"Still holdouts?"

"The Duke of Windsor did us no service." My cousin shrugged.

He was referring to the former king who abdicated to marry the American woman.

"The duke made a tour of the continent that included a jaunt around Germany, where he was spotted rehearsing the Sieg heil! salute. With much enthusiasm. So the rumor goes."

"I have a proposal."

"Well, make it a good one. Nothing's easy."

I began by reminding him of how many paintings had been lost to German looters between 1914 and 1918. I studied him as I spoke. He's a cousin on my mother's side and takes after her family, with a long and dour countenance, deep-set eyes, and broad forehead. It's a face that's hard to read, but as I talked, I caught an encouraging glimmer in his eye.

*

These weeks since returning home, I have been waiting for that glimmer to manifest. And today in my office, I received a telegram containing my cousin's counter-proposal. I read and pocketed the cryptic message. I was going to lunch with one of my buyers and before I left, I took a moment to look around my office. Belgian, of an era, spacious, high ceilinged, with crown moldings and tall windows overlooking the Parc de Bruxelles. Through the wavy glass, I could see the chestnut trees in full leaf shading narrow gravel paths that cut through the lawn. People strolling in the dappled late summer light. Women wearing swinging skirts, sticky-handed small children, men in shirtsleeves, jackets slung over shoulders, out for a midday jaunt before returning to hot offices. All so familiar. Did they know what was coming? Or were they holding on to a past that was gone and never coming back?

*

My buyer, Mats, and I lunch at a charming restaurant on the Rue des Bouchers, amid the clatter of plates and the clink of silver, the hum of voices. The waiter has delivered a plate to amuse our appetites, on which is a pile of miniscule gray shrimp, the ones they haul in from Knokke and serve with straight pins so flesh can be better excavated from shell. I prick my thumb, swear under my breath, and look up to see Mats watching me closely.

"What?"

"You eat those?"

"I'd rather have bigger shrimp and no pins."

It takes me a moment to understand that Mats, like everyone else of late, has become aware of what could be called my Jewishness.

Mats is from Antwerp. He is not the most or the least cultivated man I've encountered. My son, Julian, would call him a Flem. Or a pig. And I would tell Julian in turn not to say such things. We must be better than they are.

And then Mats surprises me by ordering caviar and a bottle of champagne.

You see, Julian? You're young. What do you know?

"To our Russian émigrés and their caviar connections!" Mats says, raising his glass. "And the occasional utility of politics for giving us what we want."

I give his glass a solid clink. I'm more than happy to trade the shrimp for the salty crunch of good caviar.

It's a pleasant lunch. We discuss the state of the art world, and I mention Magritte's latest comment, that Nazi idiots are creating more pandemonium than the surrealists did.

"A devastating revelation to our national treasure. Magritte loathes being unseated as the king of chaos. By Hitler of all people. And he's worried he'll be sent to the asylum for his paintings," I add.

I'm spreading butter on my bread more thickly than Sophia would ever approve. I take a lusty bite, tasting the salt and cream and sour yeast. Inspired, I order a good bottle of wine, a crisp white to accompany the sole mousseline we've both picked as our main, and it's after I order the wine that Mats insists he'll be picking up the check.

Things that don't make sense at first blush often do with time. Take Mats, a notoriously cheap Dutchman, offering to buy what is shaping up to be an expensive meal. Mats has never bought me a drink, let alone lunch. I'm sure there's a catch.

There are questions of trust in all transactions and, over the years, I have gained the trust of both sides in the art world. No easy task, but not as difficult as it might seem. I don't gouge buyers and I don't under-sell artists. I have sympathy for both and I'm not an idiot, at least not a common one. My father was a mathematician, his father a merchant. I take after them. My mother's father was an artist ousted from Moscow for being a Jew, but he painted on, dying of a case of tuberculosis more vigorous than he. His works survived him and are now considered no-table if minor. My brother was a brilliant pianist. Like my grandfather, he died young. Julian looks like my brother, that same black hair and blue eyes. The resemblance is so strong I sometimes wonder if the reincarnationists are right.

The caviar plates are removed by our most efficient waiter, and the sole is served. The sommelier pours our wine, and I raise my glass again.

"To art," I say warmly.

"Hear, hear," Mats responds, on his face the certainty that he's making headway with me. About what, I still have no idea.

We drink, and I dive into my sole.

Biding his time, treading carefully, Mats tiptoes in. "It would be a shame if the painters were no longer able to support themselves."

"Indeed," I say.

"In this regard . . ."

He takes an overlarge bite that he's forced to maneuver into his mouth with both fish fork and fish knife, a process that leaves a dribble of sauce on his chin. I discreetly point it out, and he wipes it with the linen napkin.

"I may be able to help," he continues.

I smile at him and shrug. "Very kind of you to offer, but how? You've sold only from your gallery. It's small, regional. Or are you hoping to expand in wartime?"

Mats pauses, a subtle discomfort on his face, and I take another bite of my sole. It really is delicious, the delicacy of the sauce, the tenderness of the fish.

"Wartime. That's a bit exaggerated, don't you think?"

"I do not. Russia and Germany have just aligned. Or did you miss yesterday's announcement?"

"A trade agreement. Good! Consequently, my business is expanding across the border."

"Germans?"

"They're quite flush. The Weimar days are over, which will affect you, given what's happening, and this brings me to my proposal. If you share your clients with me, I will be able to represent their work freely in the open marketplace."

"You'll be the front man?"

"I don't like that expression. I find it insufficient, demeaning. But yes, buyers would see and deal with me. I'll give you a commission of course."

"So generous."

"Is that sarcasm?"

"Never!"

"Leo, be realistic. It's only a matter of time before you will be prevented from working . . . in this way."

"Or any other?"

"I didn't say that."

"I suppose labor camps will be an option. You see, I am being realistic, and I have few illusions about what is to come."

I put down my fork and knife and look at him with what I hope is genuine sympathy.

"There was a group of buyers in Paris, years ago now," I begin. I confess I take no small delight in the confusion on Mats's face, for now he has no idea where I'm going.

"These buyers were among the first to invest in works by contemporaneous artists, Picasso for one, who had not yet been given the blessing of legitimacy by the French Academy or some other pretentious institution. These investors called themselves the Bearskin."

"Ah yes, I've heard of them," Mats says, relieved he has.

"Do you know why they called themselves the Bearskin?"

"No."

"It's from an old fable about the man who sold a bearskin before killing the bear. You understand? The business of investing in art is all risk, and they knew it."

"As do we," Mats smiles—what a straightforward explanation! He raises his glass.

We clink again and I notice a chip in the rim of his glass. I don't mention it, but I would have asked for another.

"The Bearskin was known for two notable things," I continue. "They gave artists the right to a twenty percent fee on all resales, which as you know I insist upon. And they had taste."

I pause seeing a nervous tic on Mats's face. He waits.

"The trouble is the art market has gone underground." I pivot, intentionally taking the circuitous route.

"Underground?"

"What choice do they have, given the times? Failed artists are dangerous. They're left with nothing but to criticize those who didn't fail."

"I suppose." Disgruntled, Mats takes another messy bite.

I happen to know Mats was rejected from art school, so instead of becoming a painter, he joined his father's modest import-export company. He deals in caviar and rubber and the like. Dirty businesses all.

I continue. "Everyone is aware of Hitler's artistic aspirations and his failures, and this is why artists who have not already been disappeared by the regime are disappearing themselves."

"Ah," Mats says. "But I have no doubt you can show me the doors to their bunkers."

"How could I? No one has shown them to me."

This is true but incomplete. I may not know the precise whereabouts of my clients. But I do know how to get in touch with them.

For the first time that afternoon, Mats, my former—yes *former*—buyer looks dour. He's doubtless contemplating the money he's throwing away on our lunch, since I am not cooperating.

We finish our meal in silence, and I become aware of two couples seated at the next table. The women are comparing stones. Diamonds. Discussing grades, colors, flaws. One of the women, the tilt of her head reminding of a magpie, is scolding her husband for refusing to bargain more and better with a seller recently arrived in Antwerp from Prague.

"Should have tried elsewhere," she says to the other woman, big-eyed, long faced, making me think of a horse. I catch snatches of their conversation as I watch her valiantly keeping pace with her husband at moving food from table to mouth.

"Farther down," Magpie says.

"The street?" Horse asks, revealing a turbid nugget of half-chewed food behind prominent front teeth.

"Warsaw. Illicit number of children. Ten! Consequently desperate. Don't go up."

"The street?" Horse asks.

"Berlin," Magpie shrieks.

"Berliners. Profiteers," her husband agrees.

As the waiter takes my plate—I finished every bite, mind you—I wonder if the difference between profiteering and surviving is retrospective.

"If De Beers knew of this influx of stones in Antwerp," Horse's husband muses.

"Price-fixing!" Magpie exclaims with a triumphant slap of her hand on the table.

"Never in wartime," Horse's husband corrects.

"Always in wartime," Magpie's husband argues.

From this, I understand that neither man has experienced war or anything like it.

"Making a killing for years off poor women like us who just want one decent stone apiece," Magpie says.

"I thought you wanted more," her husband says drily.

Magpie's bird eyes fix on me. I look away.

This is when it happens. The strangest phenomenon I have ever experienced. I see people eating and drinking at linen-clothed tables, marble counters, crumbs falling on the worn stone floor. It's an old establishment. People have come here for a century. More. They will continue to come. I don't know how I understand this, but I do, and for a terrifying moment, I am unfixed from time and filled with dread and vengeance. I'm seething with it, and I know that only I see the moment in context. But it's too much for me. I breathe faster. I'm shivering and sweating. I grip the edge of the table. I don't want to see everything I'm seeing, and I'm afraid if I don't stay fixed in time, I will disappear in a flow of life and death, the sluice pipe of humanity passing before me. And this? It is unbearable.

My eyes settle on narrow-skulled Magpie, the collector of shiny things, as I try to place myself firmly in history: 1939.

Anyone with money bought diamonds eight years ago after the market collapsed and before De Beers closed its mines.

Do I say this to her? Or only think it?

The prices have been going up since.

I turn to look at Magpie's husband and his friend, both large jawed and chewing on bread between courses.

It's only a matter of time.

Again, I'm not sure if I say it or think it. I'm acutely aware of time moving. I tighten my grip on the table.

Time will reduce all of us, grind us to bone and blood.

I don't want to see the future, not that future.

Hold on, I tell myself. *Hold on.*

I can hear all the chewing and smacking, the click of bad teeth, Belgian dentistry being a step below veterinary medicine.

Hold on.

August 1939.

Mats catches my eye with his watery one and below it—shocking—the man has grown a snout!

Mats *is* a pig.

I look around and see animals dressed in skins of their kind.

I look back at Mats. There's no fear in those pig eyes. And because he has no idea of what is happening, in other words, of *what is to come*, it is a supreme irony that those eyes moor me in time.

He is watching me, hopeful, holding on to the possibility that I might change my mind.

"And so, we must act," Mats continues with great enthusiasm. Has he been talking this whole time? "Before the world to come—"

"That world has arrived," I interrupt. "Most people are hoping to wait it out in silence and comfort."

"Hear, hear!" he cries. "And why not?"

I'm spent, breathing hard, returned from my nightmarish reverie. I stare at the rough linen cloth.

"Well? What do you say? To my proposal."

"I'm afraid that under the circumstances, it is impossible for me to accept."

The waiter passes by to crumb the table, and I watch his hairy knuckles adroitly flick a steel blade over the rough white linen.

"A crème brûlée, a coffee, and a glass of cognac," I tell him.

Mats orders a coffee. He's still biding his time, perhaps imagining I'll sweeten with dessert. I eat it slowly, savouring the rich cream under the browned caramel. After I take my last bite, I say to him, "You're no Bearskin. You have no taste. You won't pay the artists. And we have no further business to discuss."

*

As I leave the restaurant, I look back and see Mats, hat in hand, standing in front of a crate of iced oysters, as if he doesn't know what to do next.

Put on your hat and leave, Pig!

I walk down the street to the Grand-Place—the square Victor Hugo called the most beautiful in Europe. Who can say if he was wrong or right? I've never believed in objectivity when it comes to art, once it's at a certain level, that is. Cream rises but the flavor of the cream—grassy or sweet—that's a question of taste. I make my way across the brick paving stones, taking in the vista of ornate buildings. I reach in my pocket and the sharp corners of my cousin's telegram provoke a surge of gratitude. Thanks to Mats, I've made my decision. I know what I must do. I shall accept my cousin's counter-proposal without delay.

It's a long walk back to the apartment but a good day for walking, and Francois won't be home from his office for an hour or two at least.

FRANCOIS SAUVIN, 4L

I've always respected Leo Raphaël, but his visit caught me off my guard. Rattled me. The first thing he mentioned was that he'd lunched in a barnyard. A curious beginning to an unexpected conversation over a beer and an even more unexpected business proposal. Later, after Leo left, with the usual invitation for Charlotte and me to join the family for dinner, I sat. I needed to be still in myself. To feel my heart beating. To understand what I'm willing to do.

I'm convinced we will have to choose. All of us. How far we will go. I said as much to Leo after he made his proposal.

"I want to disagree," he replied.

"Even though you know I'm right. It's your nature. You can't help it."

"Why is that?" he asked. It took me a moment to realize this wasn't a rhetorical question.

"Through disagreement, one hopes to find truth."

"That's putting a laudatory spin on it. For once, I won't. Disagree, that is."

"About the choosing?"

"Yes," Leo said, and he looked irritable, probably as a function of all the agreeing. "I trust your work will be infected as well."

"Oh yes," I said. "Viruses rarely discriminate."

I was thinking of my studio, a converted stable beyond the Bois de la Cambre with an open-air courtyard that's host to a large chestnut tree or, rather, the tree is host to us, and next to it, a fountain that once provided water to horses, now bringing a kind of music to the architects who work there. All of them in my employ.

"The question being, can you bring yourself to design buildings for the Nazis? Mark my words, they'll be the only buyers."

Leo was expecting an answer. I knew this because I have known him for years. I took my time.

"My colleagues would say art takes the real and makes it abstract but architecture does the reverse. I think that's pedestrian and missing the point."

Leo looked pleased at my expression of contrarian spirit.

"To me, architecture is an idea about how we should live. A good architect creates a system of communication and relationships."

"You're saying it's philosophy not art?"

"Insofar as it shapes society. What do we value? What is order? What are the rules? Man bending nature to his will has been the push of the twentieth century. I'm not sure it's been for the best."

"Again. I want to disagree. You still haven't answered my question."

"I won't design buildings for the Nazis. I don't like their version of society. They have no morals and less taste."

Leo finished his beer and got up. He's a restless, practical man. It's good he buys and sells. A man like Leo would feel trapped in the inevitable cul-de-sac of creating.

"I was in the Grand-Place this afternoon," he said.

"Each building points to heaven."

"A strange afternoon. I had visions."

"You're not ill?"

Leo looked fine. Robust, somewhat stout. A face that manages to seem amused and pugilistic. I've always thought Leo is the sort who'd have my back in battle, and I know from experience this is far from inconsequential.

"If the Grand-Place were bombed—"

"By whom?"

"The Luftwaffe, most likely. Would it be rebuilt?" he asks.

"Rebuilt again, you mean. Remember, it was destroyed in the seventeenth century."

"Was it?"

"Yes. Granted, a different time. But as to your question, it would come down to money."

"Doesn't everything?"

"I wish it didn't."

"And I wish for you to be less of a dreamer."

We were quiet a moment, for already there was the question of money between us. He hadn't given me a moment to contemplate his proposal as a favor. From the start, it was business.

"Well? Are you coming to dinner?"

I nodded and got to my feet with some effort, my leg of late being more of a nuisance, and I saw him to the door.

"I remember. When Hitler first came to power. We were at your table, and it was all we talked about. But no one else was, not much," I said.

Leo shrugged as if to say, *How not to talk about it?*

"As rumors floated across the border, people talked even less. It was considered tedious to ruin a dinner party with talk of Nazis."

"And rightly so," Leo said. "Unfortunately, the most tedious subjects need to be beaten and aired like laundry."

I opened the door for him.

"Don't be late. We have a brisket," he said and stepped out.

*

I closed the door and turned back to the apartment. The French doors to the living room were wide open, and the light that evening was particular, allowing me to see a landscape of lines and dimensions, every bevel in the crown moldings, each trowel swipe in the plaster, the drop from the black-bordered Venetian terrazzo in the hall to the pine floorboards in the living room—a flaw that had always bothered me. In that light it seemed strange I hadn't rectified it. But how? And then, as quickly, a solution presented itself. A client was pulling an old parquet floor out of his house. I recalled that he was putting in slate instead and we had intended to send the parquet to salvage. I changed my mind.

I sat in my chair and looked out at the church; I knew the architect. He designed some of the most hideous buildings I've seen, our massive, graceless church being one of them. Even the brick is ugly—dried blood with a sheen. Bakelite. Had the church been built before I acquired the apartment, I wouldn't have. But the ground for it was broken when Charlotte was a child and by then, I had no intention of moving. Ever again.

I raised my sights to the sky, seeing the warming clouds float across the blue as the glow of evening set in. Charlotte would never see this the way I could. In that moment, I doubted anyone could see exactly what I saw. Or understand it. And if we were all seeing and understanding everything differently, how could there not be wars?

*

Charlotte was three and we were in the Flemish shop, the one around the corner and down the street. I asked her to pick out two red apples and one green. She looked at the apples and back at me, a question on her face. I realized she couldn't tell which apple was which. Smets, the shopkeeper, was watching us. If eyes could gossip, his dark eyes would. I scooped up my child, feeling her little bones, her warmth and gentle flesh. I smelled her sweet breath as we left the shop, my heart pounding almost as fast as hers. As I hurried up the street, past the pharmacy and across the square, I thought it must have been a trick of the light in that cramped dumpster of a place.

At home, I took out a set of brightly colored blocks and watched Charlotte play with them. She kept glancing at me. She knew I was worried. I asked her to tell me which block was yellow. She couldn't.

"And the blue one?"

Charlotte had no idea. I asked her if the square red block was the same as the square green block. She shook her head no. But she couldn't tell me which was which. She didn't understand yellow or blue or green or red. She knew only that the differently colored blocks weren't identical, even if their shapes and sizes were. I was mystified, and I felt a familiar fear creep in, a seasick queasy in the base of my stomach, rising like sour bread.

There was no trick of the light in the apartment. How had I not noticed before? What else might I have overlooked?

I put the blocks away and sat down, trying not to cry. Charlotte climbed into my lap, and we sat together in silence for maybe an hour. She put her small hand on my cheek and let it rest there. From this, I knew we would find our way.

*

Charlotte was born early—one month to be precise. She was a chick, a bunny, a tiny *almost*, and the doctor wasn't sure he could save her. In fact, he was sure he couldn't. She was on one floor of the hospital, my wife on another, and I ran up and down between them, aware that the limp I acquired in the war slowed me. I forced myself to run faster, feeling a burning in my lungs that reminded me of that first whiff of gas in the trenches. *Faster! Faster!*

Even after the doctor told me my wife was dead, I ran, up and down, as if the running might reverse time and bring her back.

Another doctor saw what I was doing. He ran up and down the stairs with me a few times, and then he took my hand and pulled me through the double doors to a corridor where there was a bench, and we sat together outside the nursery. Through the window, we could see little Charlotte Emilie, named for my mother and my wife, now both dead. But Charlotte was very much alive, red and squirming in a heated rectangle the nurse called an incubator. Finally, I cried, and the doctor cried with me. He told me he was exhausted, for he had been up two nights delivering babies.

Everyone was being saved or dying.

The doctors saved Charlotte, and it was Sophia Raphaël who in turn saved me. She was a constant presence through the overwhelming days of confusion and sadness with my tiny colicky fury, one who the entire building could hear screaming at night. It was Sophia who taught me to swaddle Charlotte, how to give her a bottle and keep her doll head from flopping back. She insisted I leave Charlotte under the watchful eyes of their nanny for a few hours during the day so I could work. I insisted on paying part of the nanny's wages. Sophia and Leo didn't object. Everything in life is a transaction of one sort or another and, over time, I'd come around to Leo's view that the best deeds become better when accounts are square.

Still, Charlotte cried. And she didn't fall into her fitful sleep until dawn when rays of sun had already begun to shoot into the bedroom I once shared with my wife. Charlotte slept only when I couldn't.

Whenever I passed Miss Hobert—the nosy and dour woman who lives alone on the third floor—she would glare at me and finally one day she grabbed my wrist. "What's wrong with that baby?" she burst out.

But really, she was asking, *What's wrong with you?*

"She has come to this world and found it too great a shock. But then, haven't we all? Good day, Miss Hobert."

I was furious with Miss Hobert. Nothing was wrong with Charlotte. It was me. I had become a stranger in my own building, with that vertiginous tilt one has upon arriving in a foreign country to find that night is day and day is night. Secretly, I resented it. I resented her, the baby who came when my wife left. The child I wasn't sure I had wanted in the first place. I began to resent my entire life. All I wanted was to reverse time, but I knew that was impossible. Until one day, I realized that Charlotte, my tiny whatsit, was cleverer than I was and that I had spawned a future more hopeful than it would be if there were only me to show for my life. For it was Charlotte with all her crying who had made day night and night day. She had unknowingly performed a magic trick and reversed time.

*

I watch the glow of the clouds recede and the sky darken into a deep Magritte blue.

I've made up my mind, and I'll tell Leo tonight. Without Leo and Sophia, Julian and Esther—and Masha of course—Charlotte would have had no family to speak of. Only me. And I would have been far from sufficient.

AGATHE HOBERT, 3R

I brought the Colonel cakes after his wife died, and he was grateful. Kind. Well, he's a kind man, isn't he? We'd chat in the doorway to his apartment. I never went inside, and he never invited me. He's too much of a gentleman for that. Anyway, I could see a bit of the apartment from the hall. Enough to know there wasn't much to see. His wife's taste was in her mouth, and he left it all as is where is. Who can blame the poor fellow?

I would have invited him into mine, but I would have had to ask my aunt to come along, wouldn't I? I don't want to ask anything of her, the lazy bitch. So, I didn't ask him in. Not once. Propriety! I wasn't raised in a barn.

Prune cake. Nut cake. Butter cake. My specialties. My recipes, and I never share them. Cakes yes, recipes no. I'm happy to ask for yours, but please don't think I'll show you mine. Loaf cakes. Not fancy. Slice and eat with a cup of tea. The Colonel had begun to look thin you see. He needed a woman's hand to keep him in form. You know. How women do.

*

A few days ago, I was in my apartment, and I heard footsteps in the hall. The sound of knocking on the Colonel's door. Voices. I admit I hurried to my door and listened from the other side. It's normal. I am a woman living alone, and I need to be aware of what's happening around me. This was when I heard the words *butter cake*.

Who on earth was talking to the Colonel about my butter cake? I had taken a cake to the Colonel just that morning. Two voices—a woman's and a man's. Hand poised on the brass handle, I waited. I heard the Colonel say goodbye and shut his door in that way he does. Military man. Decisive.

There was no sound of footsteps in the hall. That was odd. I could hear the Colonel's footsteps as he retreated into his apartment; he wears shoes. Most people do. Wear shoes. That woman in the attic—Masha—I remember the Colonel saying she was shocked by that when she first came. People wearing shoes inside.

I will say, I was aware that Masha visited the Colonel regularly before she went away in the spring. I don't know where she went and I haven't asked. It isn't my way. Masha left her shoes outside his door. I've always maintained that she's beneath all of us, and yet she lives above. That's life for you. Masha is a trollop and a poor excuse for a seamstress. I think she must be related to Sophia Raphaël. Putting up a poor tramp of a cousin in the attic, that's the Raphaëls for you.

And there's the swarthy man who visited the Colonel and Masha, always on Wednesdays. They didn't know I knew. But I did. I know everything because I hear everything—and not because I'm listening.

Masha would leave first.

"Goodbye, hope to see you sometime soon," she'd say.

Slip on her shoes in the hallway—isn't that the surest sign of what a peasant she is? Higher-born people, well they just wear their shoes in and out knowing others will clean up after them.

Masha's shoes made a distinctive click. Taloned heels—no decent woman could walk properly or far in heels like that. The sidewalk stones would skin them in three steps.

I would hear her door open in the attic, and a little later the squeak of the Colonel's door opening then closing.

The Colonel was in on it; he had to be. Not a word spoken. And nothing like the usual decisive shutting of the door, only the drop of the latch. I think the Colonel went back down his hall on tiptoes, that's what I think.

The man with the dark skin, he was stealthy as a cat too. Stocking feet. How do I know?

One Wednesday evening before Masha went away, I left my door unlatched but shut far enough that it looked closed. I heard the Colonel's friend arrive as usual. A few minutes later, Masha came tripping down the stairs.

Don't think I'm a common voyeur. Far from it. I was making sure we were safe. That it was indeed the Colonel's friend I was hearing, not some unknown and dangerous man being let into the building late at night.

When I finished my supper, I moved to a chair in my front hall. There's a good lamp there, and I keep a glass—for water—and a book. I read all the time.

I'm not reading now, I confess. I'm listening at my door, and I would swear I hear whispers and the sound of breathing from the hall. *Butter cake.* Who are they?

Look, one must be vigilant in these times. The world is closing in; we're oranges in a juicer. Fate hinges on comings and goings. For all I know, this building is at the center of everything.

"Never underestimate the peculiarity of the common man," as my departed daddy used to say.

*

It was Daddy who bought the apartment for me. He said I took after my aunt, his sister, who aged early and not well. By the time she considered marriage, no one was considering her. Thanks for that, Daddy. At least I didn't inherit my aunt's mad gaze—head down, eyes up, staring beyond me at who-knows-what. It gives me a shiver to think of her. These days, we speak only over the telephone.

Mum never liked my aunt, who lived with us for as long as I can remember. Mum wanted her out, but Daddy wouldn't hear of it. One evening, they had a spat about everything but my aunt, who we all knew was the real subject of the argument. It was after dinner and Mum was playing cards as she liked to do. She threw an entire deck at Daddy and said she'd had enough, his sister had to leave immediately, and that was when Mum's artery blew. *Pop!* There she went, face down on her solitaire game. Like the Colonel's wife—dead! I could see from the look on my aunt's face that she understood this to be her golden opportunity. Tilted and askew, the cards scattered around, gazing at her future. And then she looked at Daddy, and he looked at her, and that was that. Daddy left my aunt the apartment on Avenue Molière—with the proviso that it was to go to me when she died. I laughed. What else to do when you want to cry and are too proud? I told him she would outlive us all. Two out of three and counting.

But what I distinctly remember about the apartment on Molière was Daddy putting a glass to the wall so he could listen to the neighbors. This was when I was a child and before the Great War. Belgium was more unified then, but still. As Daddy said, "You never know." He should have taken that to heart for himself.

I visited his grave the other day. I don't like to drive my car, but I did, past the university, beyond the Bois, all the way to the cemetery. I didn't leave flowers. I don't believe in such nonsense, and I wouldn't leave flowers for Daddy anyway. No, I went to tell him that my aunt is leaving the apartment to a cousin on her mother's side—who is unrelated to us. My patrimony and his estate now being pissed away, handed down to a family of illiterates. My aunt doesn't read you see. She sits. And she's quite fat. Daddy should have written it down. What he wanted. Unless that wasn't what he wanted, and he was afraid to tell me. You understand, I force myself to see the truth at every turn. In the end, truth is all that matters.

In full disclosure, Daddy didn't leave his entire estate to my aunt. He had a golden goose of a café in the Grand-Place that I ran for some years after Daddy became too weak to stand. There was a time when I loved that café, when I saw each man who came in as a possibility, and I still had hope for a different kind of life. Never mind, that life wouldn't have suited me at all.

They called me Diva, and I quite liked that.

I understand everything. I'm self-aware. No, really, I am! Line me up with a group of beautiful women of class and standing and no one would call me Diva. Not then, and certainly not now. Especially if I had opened my mouth to speak. I have an alarming voice, a grating voice. Not throaty. Phlegmy. I'm horrified by the sound of my own laughter. I overheard my aunt once say I had the voice of a pig squealing.

You see? She really is a bitch.

But at the café, that voice was useful. The staff could hear me through the din. I was Diva. I was the queen.

I was hard on the people who worked for me. I expected much and they delivered. Not fear. Respect! I paid attention to money, and I told the truth. Food costs cut by a third. Daddy, the old fool, bought produce and meat from farmers who overcharged, passing along their own inefficiencies. No need to use fresh butter when you have lard leftover from cooking. You understand? I invented a *salade folle* everyone loved. Leftovers and no one knew! A question of planning. And the cakes brought in a whole new clientele. People who wanted a coffee, a tea, a dram of sherry, a slice of cake instead of the usual beer and sausages.

What was the secret of my butter cake? Can you guess? Guess! I'm not telling.

The truth is, I don't think about the café much. I don't miss it.

It was a marvelous place. Dark wood-paneled walls, polished tables worn from years of use, leaded glass windows illuminating it so everyone looked as though they'd stepped out of a Rembrandt. Wonderful light that took years off my face.

Well, even candlelight only goes so far.

I saw it like a bad dream. Everything moving slowly, but I couldn't stop it. Not time. No. My face was falling. I could see it falling! The men who had looked at me, chatted with me, the men who had sought my company. They could see it too. How do I know this? They stopped looking and they stopped talking.

I watched as the gray crept in around my temples, above my ears. And my skin, too, was turning gray. Even that beautiful, *beautiful* light in the café betrayed me. I didn't look like I could have stepped out of a Rembrandt. I looked like that corpse he painted. You know the one. Lying down about to be dissected.

Diva?

A joke. What people used to call me. They probably laughed about it when I wasn't there.

Don't think I'm paranoid, please. I'm a realist, that's all.

Anyway, when Daddy died, he left the place to me, and I sold it right away. I bought some cheap apartments down near the Gare du Midi that I rent to people passing through. Currently I'm renting to a fellow called Putzeis. He seems pleasant enough, but that's not the point—no questions asked and all on the up-and-up. So little is these days.

Truth. It's all that counts.

Daddy also left me his puzzles. I've never liked puzzles and he knew it, but now they're on my shelf taking up space. I should get rid of them. The Colonel saw me bringing those puzzles up the stairs and into my apartment, and he told me he loves a good jigsaw. I could invite him over. But I feel it's too forward. Shouldn't he invite me first? And what about a chaperone. Who but my aunt? You see the dilemma.

*

I took a sip of water. I was engrossed in my book and had all but forgotten about the Colonel when I heard the soft click of his door closing. Masha had already gone upstairs. I put my book down and listened to the faint thud of a stockinged foot on the stone, and then another. I jumped up, ran to the door, pushing it open enough to see who it was. As I had surmised, it was *not* the Colonel but his odd visitor. I only saw him from behind, but I was certain. He was walking up the stairs, shoes in hand. I waited until I heard the attic door opening and closing. He had gone up to Masha's.

I shut my door and locked it. I didn't want to hear more. But please, feel free. Extrapolate as much as you wish about what exactly they were doing up there. I did.

*

So that was then. But the other night after I heard the Colonel utter the words *butter cake* and then retreat into his apartment, I made a bold choice and I opened the door fearlessly and wide. There they were—the Raphaël children, not children anymore—whispering like thieves as they waited for the elevator. Not taking the stairs as young people should and what did they have but my butter cake. The Colonel gave it to them.

Those Raphaëls have never fooled me. Not for a moment. Always sneaking around, getting an advantage. I'm not fond of them, and that's an understatement.

I didn't smile. I didn't say a word. I went back in my apartment, and I bided my time. I know how delicious that butter cake is. I had no doubt they would eat it.

I waited a day, and I dressed for the occasion. In black. Pastels turn me into an old rug. Bright colors clash with my hair. Yes, I color it with henna. Yes, I'm vain enough to do that. Does it mean I have hope? I don't think you lose hope until you're frozen in a box like a side of beef. Even Daddy on his deathbed asked if I would make him a cake. Minutes left and he wanted my butter cake tomorrow.

How could the Colonel have given it away to those spoiled, privileged Raphaëls?

I knew Leo and Sophia were both home. I heard Sophia go out and come in. Sensible shoes, her heels make a strong report on the stone. And Leo has a heavy tread. Only leather-soled shoes are good enough for Leo Raphaël.

I put on lipstick, not enough to look like I have, but a touch, as though having put it on earlier in the evening for some other occasion after which it wore off.

I took the stairs and was winded after the one flight up, for heaven's sake. A long flight. I knocked boldly and Leo opened the door, but I could see Sophia behind him. I could smell roasting meat and onions. I imagined the browned crisp of fat. Beef. It smelled divine.

"Yes?" Leo asked.

He looked dour. Not because of me, or not only because of me. I could tell that his mind had been on something or maybe they had been discussing something. I had heard a hum of conversation from downstairs.

"It came to my attention," I gasped, still winded, but nonetheless getting right to it. No need for niceties.

"Yes?" Leo asked again.

"That your family has been given one of my butter cakes," I blurted out.

"Oh it was delectable," Sophia said, stepping forward.

She had no idea what was coming.

"Do you need to sit down?" Sophia asked me, noticing I was still out of breath.

"Yes . . . No!" I said, "I know people quite like the cake. I used to make it for the café."

I hated myself for saying it. It made me seem a working woman in a cheap cafeteria.

"In the Grand-Place," I added.

"I was there just today," Leo said.

"We sold it."

"The Grand-Place?" He looked confused.

"No, no, the café."

For the love of heaven, stop talking about the café.

"Ah," Sophia said. "We never went. To the café. Had we known—"

"The trouble is," I interrupted, "it's made with butter."

"Yes," Leo said. And he seemed to brighten at this.

"And also with lard." I was croaking like a damn frog.

Honestly, I thought it would be a bombshell. Butter and meat fat in the same cake. But they only looked confused.

"Oh," Sophia said. "Interesting."

"Do you know English ice cream is made with lard too? Pig fat, even," Leo said. "Coats the top of your mouth for hours."

Sophia looked saddened by this. Why on earth did this fact of all facts make her look sad? As for me, I admit, I was completely at sea. Lost. What to say?

"I didn't know about the ice cream," I began.

Idiot. Why did you come upstairs?

I focused my attention on the paintings in the hall. I had seen them before. The time the old lady who lived in 2L caught her apartment on fire—shortly before she died, though the fire had nothing to do with her dying, and I don't remember how I found myself at the Raphaëls' then. But I did and I noticed the paintings. How could one not? I knew then that Leo was some kind of thief. No one comes upon work like that—owns it!—without stealing. Truth will win out!

But that night as I caught my breath and grappled with the Raphaëls' complete lack of distress over the butter-cake revelation, I saw that the paintings looked different. It was something I couldn't put my finger on. But I did notice.

The apartment door across the hall opened, and Francois Sauvin stepped out. I've always appreciated Francois. He wouldn't hurt a mouse.

No, no, no, no. I don't have feelings for him. Not like *that*. But I do appreciate him. And here he was saving me from a supreme moment of inconsequential discomfiture.

"There you are," Leo called out to Francois. "Charlotte's set a lovely table."

All of them having dinner together. A roast.

"Well, thank you," Leo said to me.

But what he really meant? *Please, go home you silly twit.*

I wouldn't have wanted to join them. Onions make me itch.

"I don't suppose you eat butter and meat or *lard* in the same sitting," I blurted out. "But that is my cake."

I could see a dark look pass over Leo's face.

"Mentioned twice in one day," Leo said, "as though we've ever kept kosher. It's a sign."

In that moment, I was, truly, rudderless.

"A sign of what?"

"That it's better not to suppose anything," he said.

FRANCOIS SAUVIN, 4L

Martin DeBaerre stopped in after Leo left the apartment. He's a kind man, gentle, with a sense of decency, otherwise undistinguished but for a large mole on the tip of his cheekbone, a mark his son Dirk inherited. I'll never forget how he apologized for Dirk's behavior when the children were small. I told him then that Charlotte was stronger for it. And since, we've made a point of chatting in the lobby and exchanging pleasantries.

There was time for a stroll down the avenue with Martin before Charlotte and I went to dinner at the Raphaëls', and so we set off across the square together. I took in everything with an acuity that was almost painful—the fresh salt air blown in from the sea combined with the tobacco smoke from Martin's pipe. Sweet and rough in my nose and throat. I could feel the dampness of the pocked building stone as we walked past. How tired those buildings looked. Elders whose time had come. *If it's all destroyed*, I thought, *something new and fresh will rise in its place*. What a horrible thought.

"I have a question for you," Martin began.

"Yes?"

"I might need your help."

"Of course. I'm always here."

How careless of me. First Leo and now Martin. One of these days, I'll have to put my foot down and say no. But as soon as I heard what he had to say, I was moved almost to tears.

Charlotte would not approve; she doesn't feel things the way I do. Sometimes I think we've switched places, and I've become the weaker one. Charlotte is firm. She has expectations of people. I see her watching, calculating, deciding. She's making sure. That's my girl. We should all be ruthless for the good.

*

It didn't occur to me that Charlotte was unusually even tempered, but then, I had never raised a child before, let alone a daughter. Once past the colic, she was remarkably even-keeled. And she didn't like it when others were angry or sad or demonstrative. Charlotte allowed three people to hug her—Sophia, Masha, and me. I thought this was all very rational. But even I had to admit there was something more to it.

Sophia said it was lucky that Charlotte was so sanguine and that she had gotten it all out of her system with the colic. I thought perhaps it was because Charlotte had experienced the worst. She had lost the most important person in her life as a baby, and this gave her a preternatural calm and a fearlessness.

Over time, I understood that Charlotte feels the world as she sees it. For her, there are no vivid bursts of color. Everything, even her emotions, is in gray scale. This is fundamental. I've also come to believe that Charlotte feels things no less strongly or profoundly than anyone else, however subtle her reactions may be. She holds her emotions close, but they are no less deep. And I see her doing everything in her power to keep those around her in that same steady counterpoise she herself displays.

Charlotte is remarkable.

When she was small, I was determined to help her adapt to a life she inhabited differently and to protect her, for the world does not accommodate remarkable people—rather, it punishes them.

I'm an architect. I deal with form and structure. My work has little to do with color. And then there was the fact of the last war, which will always remind me that color is no saving grace.

I was in the trenches when news that a line of Algerian and Canadian troops at the Salient were gassed. They'd been under heavy machine-gun fire when they heard something sizzle like wet fish in a hot pan. A yellow-green cloud floated overhead that quickly fell and settled into the trenches. The gas falls, you see, and the trench becomes a burning vat. You get out as fast as you can, and that's when they would shoot you.

This was the beginning.

I saw comrades with red, oozing skin, eyes streaming, many of them blinded.

After that, we were given masks—wool pads with gauze. You couldn't get any air with the damn things on, and men had to decide whether to breathe gas or not to breathe at all. Still later, we had helmets that looked like grazing muzzles, the ones they put on horses.

It was a war in sepia. The trenches, the dirt, the uniforms, the faces. I remember popping my head up from a trench for a moment, long enough to see the shimmering azure sky above. A few minutes after that, a soldier developed a sore throat and a kind of contagious hysteria set in, my comrades one by one falling prey to imagined symptoms. There was a move to another trench we were also holding. I told my commander that I had seen the color of the sky and there was no cloud of gas. He looked and he saw I was right. We stayed on. It was in that trench a few hours later that a shell blew up part of my leg. So, you see, in the end, color betrayed me.

I vowed not to let color betray Charlotte. I swore to myself that with my damaged leg and ruined heart, I would teach Charlotte to make sense of the world as she saw it.

When it came time for Charlotte to go to school, I enlisted Masha to help me devise a plan. Masha agreed that not telling the school might save Charlotte from the inevitable teasing and ridicule that would follow should the children find out she was color-blind. Charlotte could read by then, so Masha helped me label Charlotte's clothes by color, and we marked all of Charlotte's pens and pencils. The scheme seemed to work. But one day, Martin DeBaerre's son, Dirk—who was in Charlotte's class—switched out her pencils for his. How did he know she was color-blind? The same way everyone knows everything in this damn building. He must have overheard. The other children found out and how they teased her. Brutally. When Charlotte came home that afternoon, she didn't cry. And she didn't speak. Not a word. That night, when I tucked her into bed, she finally broke her silence.

"Everyone knows about me," she said with calm gravitas.

I had the same feeling I had in the war when I would hear the enemy guns begin to fire. A cold shiver through my limbs, a gnawing hole in my stomach. I sat on Charlotte's bed, trying to think of a salve, something I could say that would give her comfort. I reached out to hold her hand. She pulled hers away and closed her eyes.

I followed Charlotte's lead. I shut off the light and let her sleep. But I didn't sleep at all that night. The next morning, I walked her to school as usual, but instead of leaving, I went in and talked to the headmistress.

"You should have told us. We could have protected her," she said.

I wasn't sure I believed her, even though she was a nun and we're disposed to believe what nuns say. When I told Charlotte this later, she said only, "It has to do with their hats."

"They're not exactly hats, are they?" I asked.

"That's just it," Charlotte replied.

I knew she was on to something I didn't quite fathom.

But I did believe what the nun told me next.

"I've not seen anything like these children," she said.

"What do you mean?"

"They're heartless. Cruel. They find the wound and salt it. They think nothing of tattling. For us, tattling was worse than being an outcast. If you tattled, you were a traitor. They tattle and they push and scratch when they play games. I've seen children bite each other. Not small children. The older ones. I even saw a big boy hit his teacher."

We were in her cell of an office. No frills. Only a black-and-white photograph of the *Madonna of Bruges*, the one by Michelangelo that's in the Church of Our Lady.

Before the war, when I was in art school in Brussels, we would joke that if you didn't have enough money to go to Rome and see the Vatican and all the art in it, you could go to Bruges instead. We were always making fun of the Flemish. How they used the Flemish name for the city—"Brugge" pronounced with a hard "*g*"—and called it the "Venice of the north." And what about Petersburg? Isn't that city grander? More Venetian? Not that anyone goes there anymore, not since the revolution renamed it Leningrad. As I think about it, we always made fun of the Flemish. In retrospect, it was unwise. You hold people down long enough and they'll find a way to take revenge.

"Are the children like this because of the war, do you think?" I asked.

"They're like this because of what their parents have taught them. Maybe because of their parents' experience during the war. I don't know. I do know that they make me feel afraid."

"Why?"

"It's a sign of things to come."

I was surprised to hear a nun talk like that, but one should never underestimate others.

"It's better if Charlotte understands the truth sooner than later," she added, as if reading my thoughts.

"And what is that truth?"

"No one sees anything the same way. When we stop trying to understand how others see the world, when we lose our compassion, our empathy, we become animals. Worse than animals."

*

After my wife died, friends and colleagues told me I needed to move on. To let myself forget so I could remember how to live. The trouble was,

I had already forgotten her. I couldn't picture her. I couldn't remember
her smell. Her voice. I would look at photographs and I would think,
Yes, there she is. That's her. My wife. But it was all notional, abstract,
two-dimensional. I had no recollection of her, nothing to hold on to.
Nothing but Charlotte.

*

The night after I spoke to the headmistress, I told Charlotte a story.

"Once upon a time, there was a harbor and fishing village in the
Place Sainte-Catherine."

"In Brussels? That's not a harbor. It's a square."

"Before you were born."

Charlotte settled back to listen, her gray gaze directed out the window at the kitchen balconies and bedroom windows circling our drab
courtyard, but I knew she wasn't looking there either.

"A beautiful harbor with tall ships."

I could tell Charlotte wanted to argue, but she held her tongue.

"It wasn't a wide or deep harbor, but it was connected to the river
via canals, and all around it were houses with stairstep roofs. Ships
came and went, bringing food and carpets and dishes. Small boats
came too."

"How small?"

"Rowing boats. Like the one you and I took out on the pond in the
summer. On the afternoon in question, there was one small boat among
the tall ships. Clouds covered the sky, and the water in the harbor was as
dark as the river Styx. The captain of the small boat held his daughter's
hand tightly, for he feared dark water."

"Couldn't she swim?"

"Even so . . . it was her father who was afraid."

A hint of a smile danced on Charlotte's lips.

"They were dressed in what I would call green."

Charlotte shrugged. Almost imperceptible. A disdain for green.

"Not clothes. Leaves."

Another hint of a smile.

"There was a rumble in the sky. The girl felt a drop of rain, but she wasn't concerned as leaves make the best raincoats. The proud, tall-masted ships were already anchored for the night by their proud complacent captains. But the father didn't want to stay. He told the girl they would row to the canal. As they stepped into their boat, there was an enormous clap of thunder, and the water began to undulate. He knew there was no time to spare."

"How did he know?"

"His stomach told him."

Charlotte once told me she listened to her stomach because it knew better.

"The girl took up her small oar, the father his bigger one, and they rowed hard and fast to the edge of the harbor as the sky became a raging, swirling beast. The father worried they had made a mistake in leaving, but it was too late to turn back, and they continued on. With one last mighty pull, the little boat surged into the canal. In its wake, there were great cracking sounds. The father looked back to see the tall masts fall, one by one, and beat the water in the harbor into a whirlpool of foam that sucked every ship into it.

The father and daughter dragged their boat to shore and slept under it for a night. After that, they had a strong desire to be on dry land, so they abandoned the boat and found a home. And this, my dear, is why there is no longer a harbor in Brussels."

"What happened to it?"

"It was bricked over."

"So the painting in the Raphaëls' hall is from when there was a harbor?"

My clever girl. She figured it out.

"And they're wearing green? The two people next to the little boat in the painting?" Charlotte's voice was sleepy.

"Yes," I said.

"Then green is a color I understand."

"We have that in common," I said, and she drifted off to sleep.

*

I taught Charlotte mathematics. Philosophy. Latin. How to catch a fish and shoot a gun. Charlotte was patient with me. When she was thirteen, she told me she didn't like fishing any more than she liked philosophy. I asked why, and she said, "There's something rubbery about them. You're waiting for the idea or the fish. And then you're forced to digest it."

She didn't mind the shooting lessons. She liked going into fields where I taught her to load and shoot the old army gun I keep at the bottom of my wardrobe. Useless now as it's missing the bolt.

"Should everything really go to hell, my darling," I told her, "I want you to go down shooting."

Hindenburg appointed Hitler as chancellor, this after the Nazi party began to win elections. *Elections.* The meaning of the word has changed for me since. Or else my understanding of my fellow humans' basic intelligence has changed. I don't know if it will come to shooting, but I know it might.

Above all, I taught Charlotte to draw. She has a gift, a rare eye, for composition. She understands form. And light. Of course she does. It's what she sees. Charlotte was determined to attend the Royal Academy of Fine Arts in Antwerp, not in Brussels where I studied architecture. I suppose she wanted to differentiate. To have something that was entirely hers. She didn't talk about it much, but I saw how she worked on drawing after drawing. I helped her assemble a portfolio, a remarkable collection. I decided early on that I couldn't allow myself bias with Charlotte. I had to be honest with her. If she were talentless, I would have had to find a way to tell her.

Some of the drawings were in color. We talked about color all the time, Charlotte and I. For example, after I told her the story of the harbor and the tall ships, I found her staring at the Boudin painting in the Raphaëls' hallway. She was teaching herself something. But it wasn't until I saw Charlotte's color drawings that I understood. While she might not see pigments, she sees subtle differences between them. One might even say—although such a comparison is of course impossible—that Charlotte has a more discerning ability to see what is commonly called color than the rest of us. I wasn't the only one who came to this conclusion.

One evening, I was stepping into the building, just home from my firm. Masha was in the lobby and I held the door, thinking she was going out.

"Not yet, I'm waiting for someone who's late," she said.

"Shame on them. No one should keep you waiting."

"I've been meaning to tell you that Charlotte and I have been talking about her study plans. I've urged her to go forward with her application. To paint. I have faith in Charlotte."

"Thank you."

"Don't thank me. Thank her. Well? Do you agree?"

"I think we've always agreed about Charlotte."

Masha gave me a quick kiss on the cheek.

At that moment, the Colonel's friend—I think his name is Harry—opened the door.

"So sorry," he said to Masha. "I was held up." He was full of energy and he had that easy confidence I've observed in very handsome men.

He looked at me curiously for a moment, but he didn't seem jealous or sorry, and Masha wasn't upset. She linked arms with him, and the way they looked at each other—I could see they were in love.

Masha is protective of Charlotte. She doesn't want her to be alone like she was. Together with the Raphaëls, Masha has created a family for my daughter. Charlotte once asked me why Masha and I hadn't married. I didn't have much of an answer, only that it wasn't that way between us and it's something you can't explain.

Charlotte was admitted to the academy, and she has become known there for the unusual and stunning color combinations she brings to her work, combinations rarely if ever seen in nature, and then only in the most exotic and extreme environments.

I don't know if she tells anyone that she's color-blind. It's her life now. And I hope she's equipped to live it.

*

I can't sleep and I find myself in one of those useless loops. Do I lie here thinking or get up and make a cup of tea and read a dull book in hopes of tricking myself into sleeping? Either way, I won't sleep much and it's because of Dirk's father, Martin DeBaerre. The last person I would expect to keep me up at night.

CHARLOTTE SAUVIN, 4L

Esther fastens a stray ringlet back with a hairpin.

"No! Leave it."

"Too late."

"It looks better when it isn't tidy. And don't smile!"

I move my pencil on the paper, seeing the curves of Esther's face emerge in dark arcs. She adjusts her posture to seem taller and slimmer in the velvet chair. We're in the Raphaëls' study. The light isn't as good as it is in Father's study at this time of day, but Father's laying a parquet floor in our living room, and the apartment is filled with noise and workers. Father's so preoccupied with the project he forgot to make my coffee this morning.

The noise of our construction must have rattled Mrs. Raphaël. She's left and returned twice—for money and a sweater—since I began to draw Esther.

I work quickly, trying to capture something I'm seeing in Esther's face. What is it? She looks older and she's preoccupied too. I won't ask. I'll let her tell me.

I shade in faint hollows under her large round eyes. I want the sketch to be true. Always the dilemma.

Julian won't let me sketch him. He's angry about what he learned at dinner last night when Mr. Raphaël asked if my painting was still on display in Antwerp.

"Yes," I said.

"Don't forget, that painting is mine," Mr. Raphaël said.

"Ours," Mrs. Raphaël corrected.

"It goes without saying."

"Nothing does." Mrs. Raphaël turned to Esther. "Please pass the butter."

"Don't forget, the painting is *ours*," Mr. Raphaël said with a smile.

"Charlotte never forgets anything," Julian said.

"Of course not, and I do hope you'll convince her to let me pay in advance. She's refused money until she can hand over the work. There's something prophetic in it, the truest sign in my view. Don't you need to buy supplies? You are continuing to paint?" Mr. Raphaël peered at me over his wineglass.

"I'm working with fabric as well," I said.

"What? No! Impudent girl."

"Clothing?" Mrs. Raphaël brightened.

"Hats."

"You must make me one," she said smiling. I could see the lovely curve of her cheekbones, her aquiline nose. Such an elegant face. The face of a woman who is almost a mother to me.

"I insist that you keep on with the painting! Look at that young woman from Mexico." Mr. Raphaël reached for the butter plate.

"What young woman from Mexico?" Mrs. Raphaël moved the plate away from him.

"The one who wears the costumes. The *dresses*."

"Oh yes," Mrs. Raphaël said. "Also Mexican, the *dresses*."

"And sublime, as is she. Rather like Lautrec she uses her infirmities to shape her work in a brilliant way. Breton got her in that show in Paris. Kahlo. That's her name. All of which is to say, Charlotte, I'm being selfish and practical, as always. If you continue to paint, and you must, we'll have acquired an early and potentially valuable work."

"But I want her to make me a hat. So. There you are," Mrs. Raphaël said.

"Butter, please."

Mr. and Mrs. Raphaël's eyes locked.

"I'd be very pleased to make you a hat," I said.

Mrs. Raphaël passed the butter to Mr. Raphaël.

I could feel Julian watching me from across the table. I looked at him, seeing his even features, framed by his mother's cheekbones, his father's long-lobed ears. It was on the tip of my tongue to say I wanted to sketch him when Mr. Raphaël asked, "And has some young artist swept you off your feet? Come, Charlotte, don't be shy."

"Not exactly. He's a little older. An architect. And he paints."

"Perfect!" Mr. Raphaël said with a nod at Father. "What is his name?"

"Philippe Kahn."

"Even better." Mr. Raphaël spread butter on his bread. Thickly.

I heard a clatter of silverware and glanced at Julian. His face was tight, and he was sawing at his meat with clumsy vigor. He abandoned the knife with another clatter and jammed an overlarge piece of roast in his mouth, this followed by a hard swallow and a sputter as he washed it down with wine.

"Julian!" Mrs. Raphaël exclaimed.

I was irritated. What did Julian think? Nothing would change between us. Not fundamentally. Didn't he understand that we were a bulwark, he and I? We would have our lives and we would have each other. Always.

Earlier in the evening, Julian and Father had been talking about parabolic arches and why they're strongest and how it all boiled down to a quadratic function. Father mercifully returned to the subject, and after dinner they moved into the living room, where Julian wrote out an equation for Father. The lamp illuminated the curve of Julian's lashes on that rise of cheekbone.

"Can I sketch you?" I blurted out.

"No," he said, and he didn't look up.

He was gripping the pencil so tightly that his knucklebone was visible under the skin.

Julian hasn't spoken to me since.

*

This afternoon, I went to the bakery for bread, and I saw Julian walking down the avenue. The wind had come in from the coast in great gusts and a few dry leaves were dancing across the paving stones. Julian was alone, filming the tops of the trees, fluttering and shimmering in the late summer sun, the branches waving with the wind. I began to walk in his direction, but then the truck that delivers grain to the bakery in the afternoon drove past, reminding me of my errand. I turned back and continued on to buy my bread.

Dirk was stepping out of the bakery as I arrived. He held the door for me with one hand, a bag filled with croissants was grasped in the other, and he had to scrunch aside to make room so I could pass. He's always been large-bodied; the children used to tease him about it when we were at school. "Fat floats! Jump in the water!" they'd scream, and now the layer of fat makes him seem muscleless and tender-fleshed. I thanked him and approached the counter. I considered taking a croissant to Julian but decided against. I don't need to placate Julian; he'll come around.

*

Mr. Raphaël stopped in to look at my sketch of Esther. "I want to commission a proper portrait. In oils. But when? Over the winter holiday?"

"I could do it now," I said.

"Let's see if I can find a good canvas. You have paints here?"

"A few."

"A canvas and paints," Mr. Raphaël said. "Saturday?"

"Perfect."

"Canvas and paints," he repeated.

*

Today, I've locked myself in Father's study to work at his drafting table, and I'm trying to ignore the pounding of nails into boards as I draw up a plan for the portrait. Every sound chafes, even the ticking of the bronze clock, one Victor Horta designed, its enameled face perched in twisting bronze branches, giving it the look of a timepiece lost in a forest. I sit back from the table and look over the courtyard. It's dreary and raining. Summer's end.

I saw Mr. Raphaël in the hall this morning when I was getting our mail from the mailbox.

"Canvas and paints! On the job." He pushed open the door and stepped out. "The ladies are going to the shops this afternoon to get their minds off the situation in Poland."

"Situation in Poland?"

"The Soviets and Germans have announced a pact. Rumor has it they plan to divvy up Poland."

"But . . . how?" I asked, my naiveté apparent to both of us.

"That," Mr. Raphaël said grimly, "remains to be seen. Sophia and Esther would love to have you along. Why don't you join them?"

"All right." I followed Mr. Raphaël out of the building and bought a few newspapers from the Flemish newsboy in the square. And now I've locked myself in Father's study to read as much as I can about the Molotov–Ribbentrop Pact. There's no mention in the papers about the two countries partitioning Poland, only their agreement not to side with each other's enemies. But the cartoons, like Mr. Raphaël, suggest a deeper alliance: Hitler as a groom with Stalin in a wedding dress, Ribbentrop kissing Stalin's hand beside a smiling grandfatherly Molotov. A mood settles over me, the feeling of going to the dentist or a funeral. No wonder everyone's distracted and preoccupied and Father's looking inward, making the apartment a sanctuary. A worker walks past the glass-paned French doors with what looks like a large vacuum. What does Father think? That we'll be trapped here, staring at the floor? We're going to Italy for Christmas. The only decision is whether to invite Philippe along.

I try to think of Philippe, but I struggle to remember him. How is that possible? It's only been two months. I think of how I once saw him on a tram and from a distance. It was nighttime, and now the memory is shadow. It's because Philippe abandoned me, that's what it is. I'm not letting myself remember him. And then I think of how Julian is abandoning me because of Philippe, and I could scream.

I want to talk with Masha, but I don't know when she'll be back. She's gone more and more, and I feel her absence. I realize how much I've depended on her. I suppose I assumed she would always be there for me, upstairs, ready to make a cup of tea and advise me on the angle of a seam, the nature of desire.

I have taken Masha for granted.

And it is this thought above all that makes me feel small and needy and ungrateful. I'll tell her when I see her next how I've depended on her advice. Especially on subjects I can't or don't want to talk to Mrs. Raphaël about—Julian being one of them. I'll tell Masha she's like a sister or an aunt. That she's family and I love her and I hope in some way she depends on me. I *am* small and needy and ungrateful, but despite that, I do know family is not when you want them but when you need them or they need you.

*

In the afternoon, Mr. Raphaël stops in to remind me about the shopping expedition.

"They're heading out." He squeezes his bulky torso between stacks of chairs and tables. Seeing my sketch, he nods approval. "Canvas and paints!"

I shouldn't have agreed to go with Mrs. Raphaël and Esther. I don't like shopping, and I can't find my shoes in the mess of furniture and rolled carpets. I hunt around in the bottom of the wardrobe and sneeze. What I took for a vacuum turned out to be a sanding machine and dust is everywhere.

"Truly, a brilliant move, Francois," Mr. Raphaël is saying. "I've always liked a good herringbone pattern. And what a fine border. It echoes the terrazzo, elevates the room."

"By four centimeters." Father laughs. "If I have to see that infernal church out the windows, at least I can look down at the floor and feel better."

"I can walk on it?"

"Be my guest. It's being varnished tomorrow."

I spot my shoes under a stack of end tables. As I retrieve them, the Colonel knocks on the door and squeezes in to look at the floor.

"I was wondering what all the ruckus was. Oak?" he asks appreciatively, bending down to give the new floor a knock.

"Walnut and maple in the border squares," Father says.

"Would you mind giving me the name of your contractor?" Mr. Raphaël asks.

"Of course. I'll write it down for you."

Father steps into the study as I hunt in the wardrobe for a sweater and the Colonel launches into a tale about how he once saw a tiger sitting in a walnut tree in India.

"As we might sit in a chair, and he looked exceedingly comfortable."

"How do you know it was *he*?" I call out.

"You can always tell by the face," the Colonel shouts back.

"And what was *he* doing?"

"He seemed to be contemplating the view, but unfortunately that view was me."

"Were you afraid?"

"Good God no. I had a gun, although no desire to use it. The creature was spectacular. I've often thought of that book of yours, Francois."

"I didn't write it," Father calls back.

"If you didn't write it, how do you know which one?"

"I haven't written any book."

"If the tiger could talk. You know the one I mean?" The Colonel is bellowing.

"I do and it's a lion."

"I can't remember the damn title," the Colonel says.

I find my sweater. It, too, covered in dust. I shake the sweater and sneeze again.

"Charlotte?" Mr. Raphaël calls out.

"My handbag."

It's in the study where Father is still searching through tall shelves that line the walls.

"What are you looking for?"

"Wittgenstein," Father says.

"It's under *w*. I organized the books, remember?"

"Aha." Father pulls out the thin volume.

The book reminds me of Julian, making me feel even more out of sorts. I find my handbag behind a chair cushion and follow Father into the living room. He gives a card with the contractor's number to Mr. Raphaël and the book to the Colonel.

"*Tractatus*, etcetera, etcetera. That's the one. Incomprehensible," declares the Colonel cheerfully as he leafs through it.

"Unreadable," Mr. Raphaël concurs, realizing too late he's agreed with the Colonel. "Julian admires that book. I thought you were posted in Africa," he adds.

Mr. Raphaël has little use for the Colonel, who he describes as a retired military man with an unmanageable dog.

"And India." The Colonel is undaunted. "During the Great War, helping the Brits recruit. Wonderful soldiers, those Punjabis. You know there were a staggering number of them who fought on our side. Here. In Europe."

"We might need them again. Now," Mr. Raphaël says.

The Colonel doesn't respond to this, but from the sober look in his eyes, I know he heard and doesn't disagree. He hands the book back to Father, who puts it on a table in the hall next to a pile of keys and coins and a petal-shaped ceramic vase that he uses for flowers.

"Africa weakened my constitution, and India finished the job. I still sweat through my sheets every night. Sorry, Charlotte, you didn't need to hear that. And I dream of lions and tigers."

"Ready," I say to Mr. Raphaël.

"Finally." He steers me out of the living room and into the hall, calling behind him, "Don't be surprised if you hear thumping and bumping from our apartment next. I think the floor is first rate."

"Wait until it's varnished. Then, you'll see," Father says.

"I'll stop back tomorrow."

*

The day does not improve. I spend the afternoon with Esther and Mrs. Raphaël in the tedium of small errands—from the tailor to retrieve a suit for Mr. Raphaël, to the post office where Mrs. Raphaël sends four enormous boxes off to Cambridge for Julian, to the shoemaker where a pair of Mrs. Raphaël's more practical walking shoes have been reheeled. We stop in a tea shop for a biscuit. The tea is too strong, the biscuit too sweet. I remember hearing that after the Great War, Americans came to Brussels and flocked to the pastry shops with oversweetened chocolates and less buttery cookies that we Belgians consider less desirable. This must be one of those. I feel restless and want to be home, brush in hand, painting.

"Are you going to eat your other biscuit?" Esther asks. She's been distant all afternoon, and I wonder if she's taking Julian's side and not telling.

I push my plate over to her. "Have it."

Mrs. Raphaël watches Esther nibble the biscuit. She opens her mouth to say something then closes it and sighs. She looks weary.

"Julian's sick," Esther says as we leave the shop. "Don't worry, he'll be fine. But Mama doesn't want anyone else in the apartment. In case he's contagious."

Next to the tea shop is a hat shop I've never seen before.

"Our last stop." Mrs. Raphaël smiles and I notice again how tired she looks. It's uncommon for her to look like that, and I hope she hasn't caught Julian's cold.

Mrs. Raphaël introduces me to the hat-shop owner, a woman with inquisitive eyes and a symmetrical, strong-featured face. Mrs. Raphaël moves off to browse, leaving me to talk to the owner. Mrs. Raphaël isn't buying hats; she isn't there for herself or for Esther. She's making a connection for me.

*

The next morning, I hear a familiar pounding, and I run down the hall, expecting to see Julian on our threshold. I don't want him to be contrite. I want him to be there. But when I open the door, the only person I see is Incarna, the Raphaëls' cleaning lady. In her nearly incomprehensible mix of Spanish and French, she tells me the Raphaëls aren't answering the door, and they never gave her a key.

"Trust. Not me. No trust for me," she says resentfully.

I follow her across the landing, knock on the door, and wait.

"Esther? Julian?" I knock again and again.

Incarna's angry. Lips pursed, she shakes her head and tells me she doesn't like to travel far for nothing. She turns to leave, mumbling under her breath—the only word I hear clearly is *Jews*—trundles downstairs to the notary's apartment, and knocks on his door. I lean over the balustrade, straining to hear.

"Did they leave. Anything. For me?" Incarna is asking.

"For you?" the notary asks.

"Raphaëls away."

"Not there?"

"No. Gone. Did they leave money? For me!"

"No. There's nothing for you."

I go back in our apartment and shut the door.

*

I feel betrayed. They gave no hint they were leaving. Father tells me that it was the only way, and if they had told us anything, we would have been complicit.

"They haven't committed a crime."

We're in the kitchen. Father has made a fresh pot of coffee.

"Would you like a cup?" He doesn't look at me as he asks.

"No thank you."

As I watch him pour a demitasse for himself, I think of Julian and how he wouldn't look at me that last night.

"There's no reason they had to go now."

"I think there's every reason."

"No one else is leaving."

"I wouldn't be so sure. And if they hadn't left now, at some point in the future they would say they should have left then, meaning now. And they would be right."

"But Julian was sick."

"I doubt it. He was probably packing."

I'm disgusted by Father's sense of logic, and by how easily he accepts their departure. He's infuriatingly calm. When he asks how I like the new floor, I tell him I liked the old one better. It was familiar. My feet knew it.

"But this is walnut."

"Yes, I know. The Colonel's tiger."

"And look at the pattern. The old floor was soft pine. It took varnish poorly."

"I suppose."

"And how many people tripped on the edge of the terrazzo when they stepped into the hall?"

"You tell me."

What I want to know is how they left in the night without a sound. I have trouble falling asleep early. I stay up and look at the stars; they comfort me. I'm not a deep sleeper. I would have heard them go.

Maybe they left early in the morning.

Father's watching me closely.

"I would have helped them sneak away, and I could have said goodbye."

"Goodbyes are inconsequential," Father says softly. He steps out of the kitchen with his coffee. I see the catch in his leg as he walks, and I hear it in his tread as he moves out of sight. He must have overdone it, dragging all that furniture about.

He's making me feel like a bad person, a nasty and mean person. Selfish.

Goodbyes are not inconsequential. They're essential.

                                *

It's late morning and I'm in bed. It's been two days since the Raphaëls left. I'm not *not* speaking to Father. I'm in bed. That's all.

Father never said goodbye to my mother. She died too fast for that.

I get out of bed and go into the living room. The windows are open and Father has set bowls of vinegar around, but the stink of varnish bites my nose.

Father's in his chair sketching. He puts down his pencil and gives me a hard look of disappointment.

"You'll see them again. And you might not have otherwise."

I pick up the book from the table in the hall and plop on the sofa. I'm scowling at Father from behind the book. Childish, I know.

The volume feels unsubstantial, thin. The cloth of the cover is worn, and when I open it, I smell eggshells.

It is the book of secrets.

"Are you reading it?" Father asks.

"I don't know if I can. I have a headache. The varnish."

I am pretending to have a headache. I do have a headache.

"I leave tomorrow for school," I add.

"I thought the next day," Father says mildly.

"You're wrong," I say. A blanket condemnation.

I regret it right away. Peeking at him from behind the book, I can see the sadness in his eyes. Without the Raphaëls, without me, Father will have only the Colonel.

That night, I watch the films. All of them. I've been told they're in black and white. I don't know what that means. To me there are infinite shades between.

*

Fall comes early to Antwerp, the leaves thin, letting light through in defiance of the dark times. On the third of September, France declares war on Germany, and two of my new classmates, just arrived, must already leave to fight. One is French. The other's German, and he says he doesn't want to fight. But a lot of young men are being called, him included, and he's afraid his parents will be ostracized or punished if he doesn't return.

Before they go, Professor Weiss holds his annual welcome for the students in his home, one of those great brick houses built for the tapestry barons, with tall, thin windows that give it the elegance of a slender woman in a discreetly revealing gown.

"Did you know that the pope paid more for a set of Flemish tapestries than he paid Michelangelo to paint the ceiling of the Sistine Chapel?" Professor Weiss asks.

He's flushed with pride—for his house and his students—and he looks happy, despite the somber news of the day. The French with what military experts had believed to be the best army in the world have been forced to beat a hasty and humiliating retreat after their failed invasion of Germany.

I'm standing apart from the group under a large chandelier that dapples the ornate plaster ceiling with sparkling jewels. Philippe is late.

"As for the statues and the paintings, what can I say? We're collectors. My father, my grandfather before him, who was an Egyptologist.

But if you poke around, you'll also see plenty of work by students who were once just like you."

I step into the next room and notice the floor, an inlaid parquet, that reminds me of our new floor at home and makes me think of Father and how lonely he must be without the Raphaëls and without me and how badly he was limping, and I feel the creeping guilt of my meanness.

In a room farther on where Professor Weiss has set up a makeshift bar, I hear the German student who's leaving making fun of the French army. "An offensive move at the start that backfired, forcing them to an early retreat."

He's talking about it like a soccer match, but I'm distracted by a stir near the door. It's Philippe making his entrance. Though he comes in quiet like a fugitive, everyone notices him. He doesn't say a word; he's waiting. You might call him unobtrusive, but that would be mistaken. He's a magnet, the way he attracts attention, and he knows it. Philippe is aware of his allure.

He doesn't let on that he sees me, but he moves toward me. I smell musk and tobacco as he links his arm in mine, and we stroll together through the lower rooms of the house looking at paintings.

Philippe has been working long hours on a model of an apartment building. I don't see him much unless I go to his studio, but I'm used to that. Father often took me to his office. When I was small, I would watch him sketch and build models late into the evening, and when I grew older, I helped him.

I haven't offered to help Philippe.

I have my own work.

I tug on Philippe's arm and stop before a painting of a woman with a noble face wearing a peasant's dress. A Flemish Madonna, she holds her secrets close, other than the one she can't hide. Her hand rests on her swollen belly.

"Can we move on?" Philippe asks.

"But I know her," I say. I do know her. I don't resemble this woman, but I'm looking in a mirror.

Philippe is staring at me with that near cross-eyed gaze he has. He doesn't understand. The truth is, while my attraction to him is a mystery to me, I'm also a mystery to him. I think we both like that.

The moment is broken by an enormous crash from the next room and shouting. We hurry in to see two students wrestling and straining. At first, I think they're playing like big stupid boys do.

"Stop! Please. Stop at once!" Professor Weiss is shouting.

They don't stop. It's the French and German students, and they're not playing. Rope-veined necks, red faces, deadlocked in an embrace, they crash into a chair, knock an ancient statue off the mantel, and overturn the drinks cart in an explosion of glass and liquor. They separate a moment, and another man grabs the German from behind and holds him, I suppose believing the French student will see it as unsportsmanlike to hit the German when he can't hit back. But the Frenchman—being French, as Philippe later says—smashes the German in the nose and there's a terrible cracking sound and another small explosion, this time of blood. The German breaks free, shouting and swearing and spitting red as he tackles the French student. They wrestle like dogs—shards crunching—and roll around, once again locked in each other's arms.

Philippe grabs a full bottle of *genever* that somehow didn't break. "The police are on the way," he announces in a calm, loud voice that pierces the hullaballoo. "But I'll bash you both on the head with this bottle if you don't stop, and I won't care if it kills you."

There's something in the tone of his voice—it's both clinical and commanding—that silences the room. For a moment, it's dead quiet. The two men pull apart and sit up and look around, dazed, as if they had been overcome by a temporary madness and are only now coming to their senses. They understand that Philippe means it, that he might kill them.

As I watch, I remember my promise to Julian—that I'll think of him if it comes to war. Julian has nothing in common with men like these. He's at Cambridge where he must stay. He's too good and too young to go to war.

The police come and take the French student into the station. It's decided that the German must first go to hospital for his broken nose.

As they lead the French student out, he shouts at the German, "Next time, we'll have a proper duel with rules of the game, and I'll shoot you dead."

The German's too drunk for words and he begins to ribbit like a frog.

I'm watching Philippe, still holding the *genever* bottle, seeing the darkness in his eyes, the rumpled mess of his hair, loathing and amusement on his mouth, his straight spine as he stands with both feet planted. He puts the bottle down and offers to help clean up the mess.

Professor Weiss has picked up the statue. It's a woman with the head of a lioness. He fingers a crescent-shaped chip on her bare shoulder.

"She who dances on blood. Not the goddess whose repose one wants to disrupt," he says softly as he replaces it on the mantel. "Thank you for stopping those idiots," he tells Philippe.

A couple of servants begin to sweep and mop up the mess of alcohol and broken glass.

"If all idiots could be stopped with a bottle—" Philippe begins.

"Sadly, not."

Philippe turns to me and offers his arm. For the second time that evening, I slip my hand in the crook of his elbow, and we leave together.

*

The night is cold, a damp cold that seeps in through seams and buttonholes. When we reach my flat, it is only natural that I would invite Philippe in to warm up before his homeward trek.

He's standing close as I put a pot on to boil and set out cups. I feel the rise of nerve and heat in my body at every brush of his sleeve, his hand.

I pour the tea, steam rising from cracked cups, both of us waiting to see what will happen.

But I know what will happen. Do I decide to sleep with him? Not exactly, but somewhere in the little hard nub of brain that keeps itself apart from the rest of me, observing, weighing in, knowing what I should do, and telling me to go ahead, I do decide.

His breath is hot on my neck. His body, the firm fit to mine. He yanks off my clothes and looks at me, notwithstanding the cold, he observes me as he takes off his clothes and pulls me to the bed.

How we sweat through that cold night. The sheets are drenched. We throw them off and wrap ourselves in the quilt to stay warm.

And when I awaken? My face is clasped between Philippe's hands. I see him sleeping like a child, whistling softly with each exhale, and I know that it is right.

*

A few weeks later, Father visits. I can sense he has an instinct to come, to meet Philippe, even though he says it's to see my painting, and we do see it. With Philippe.

Father stands before the painting for a long time, memorizing it. When we step out of the gallery, I see him brush a hand over his eyes to wipe the tears.

"Shall we get a bite to eat?" Philippe suggests.

"I would like that," Father says.

A gentle rain falls and the streets are quiet. In the café, Philippe asks for a table next to the fireplace. It's cozy, the food is warm and filling, and Philippe charms Father with stories and anecdotes. As for me, I'm memorizing this moment with the two of them.

Philippe waits until we've finished our food to tell Father our decision. "We intend to marry. It would make us happy to have your blessing. More than happy. But please know, we're going ahead, no matter what."

Father's expression doesn't change. He sips his beer, clears his throat. "I think highly of you," he says to Philippe. "I think you're a good and fine man and you'll make a good and fine husband for my daughter, but of course, that's for her to decide, and it seems she has.

And I would be honored to have you as a son-in-law. But I worry it's rushed. These things should take time, shouldn't they?"

"Yes," Philippe says. "But we have no time."

Father, of all people, understands the problem. He tried to outrun time on the day I was born. He has been trying to change time for my entire life.

I tell Father he won't lose me when I marry Philippe. He'll gain a son, and I promise him I'll finish my studies. And that this is my choice.

*

I have come to understand why Philippe went to Spain in such secrecy, why the Raphaëls left the way they did. I also understand that Julian was right, and he was wrong. There will be a war, but I wasn't being stupid. If Julian fights, it won't be for Belgium; this country hasn't the will or the strength to fight a long battle. And I'm not being stupid now. I know what I want, what I need, what I desire. I believe I knew from the moment I first saw Philippe.

It was at a critique—Philippe's. A professor whose own work is not brilliant or exceptional was castigating Philippe for his use of color in a painting. The attack was vicious, and Philippe seemed to take it in stride, but there was a look in his eyes that said otherwise. When the professor opened the critique to students, I spoke. Not about Philippe's use of color. But about light and form. Philippe tried not to let on that he was grateful. I wasn't looking for gratitude. I was describing what I saw.

That night, I caught the tram to my flat and saw a solitary figure in the back. Philippe. I didn't sit beside or near him. I sat where he could see me. I was looking out the window at the starless sky when I felt a bump and turned to see him beside me.

"You found me," he said.

"It was only a question of time."

*

I knew it would go like this. I know myself. I understand how to shape my world so I can live and that world doesn't exist without Philippe in it. It sounds strange, but I have the sense he's always been there and I've always loved him.

*

Late winter gloom seeps in the windows of Professor Weiss's drawing room as I help him take down paintings. We remove them from their frames, roll and slip them into long tubes. There are stacks of crates on the floor, false bottomed, that will be filled to the top with tins of herring once they're loaded.

"G-d help the canvases if oil leaks out of the tins," Professor Weiss says.

I imagine these crates in deep tunnels that smell of oysters and rusted chains. I don't ask Professor Weiss where he intends to send the crates or where he'll be. What I do know: he's saving the art before he saves himself and this is perfectly consistent with his character. But he looks so sad. He's been abandoned by most of his students.

"Everyone's afraid of being caught in the sorting machine of history, ending up in the wrong pile. It's hard to blame them. The way it's going, it won't matter what you believe, what you do. It will be a question of what someone in charge decides you did. Witch trials in this century . . . I didn't imagine we'd go backward so fast. When those buffoons started fighting in my drawing room, I understood." He picks up the statue they damaged a few months before. "More newspapers, dear."

I find a stack in the corner of the room. "What did you understand?" I ask.

"All the science, all the advancement, it's not progress. It's accelerated regression. We're giving men better weapons to fight, that's all. So much for the future . . . What? You disagree?"

"About the future? Not sure. All I know is we have this moment." I pull apart the newspapers, putting sheets in a stack on the table. "That's Egyptian, isn't it?"

"Indeed."

"When they knocked it over, you said something about disturbing the wrong goddess."

"Did I?"

"Yes. Who is she?"

"The goddess of divine retribution, Sekhmet. The eye of the sun. Her tears created man and then she nearly destroyed him. Egyptian warriors believed she accompanied them into battle. Our Belgian lion's a modern variant, resistance against occupiers and all that." He shrugs. "But being Catholic and patriarchal, they made him male. You see, Sekhmet balances light and darkness. She guides spirits of the dead to the afterlife. And she's worth a small fortune. Thirteenth century BC or thereabouts."

I help him wrap the statue in the old newspapers. "Does the chip devalue it much?"

"I'm not selling her now. And we're agreeing not to let all these worries about the future tarnish this moment, isn't that right?"

But it's impossible not to. He's going into hiding, and we might never see each other again.

*

"He's not religious. Maybe no one knows he's Jewish," I say.

Philippe and I are at the train station, but this time we're waiting to board the train together to visit Father. And Philippe isn't looking at the building. He's looking at me.

"It's good he went into hiding. They know everything. They know about him, and they know about me."

"Who knows?"

"Remember the German student who got his nose broken? He told everyone Weiss is Jewish. And homosexual. Too many people know and someone will inform on him."

"To whom? Belgium isn't a Nazi regime."

"Yet. If the Nazis get to Weiss, he's lost. His only hope is to disappear and pray he's forgotten. If he's caught, he won't fight to save himself. He's only ruthless for the art, and now it's gone."

I know Philippe is right. Professor Weiss shipped out his will to live with the art.

*

We marry in secret. Father is our only witness other than the priest, and we don't register the marriage. It's safer this way. We sign a ketubah, and the priest reads the seven blessings. He tells Philippe that the rabbi he's been hiding helped him with all this.

We have no honeymoon. This is not a time for honeymoons. The school has closed, but Philippe keeps his apartment and we stay in Antwerp, visiting Father almost every weekend.

*

It turns out that Philippe and Father share three idiosyncratic obsessions.

They are both obsessed with the book—that thin volume written by Wittgenstein. Philippe is convinced it contains the world and insists I should read it.

I don't argue. I don't explain that if I read the book and don't find it transformative, I'll wonder about me, and I might wonder even more about Philippe and Father. Or, if I read the book and find it problematic, I'll be forced to argue with them. And if I find it as transformative as they do, I'll always wonder if that's because I want it to be so.

And then I remember that Julian loves the book too. I can't let myself think about Julian. Not when I'm with Philippe and anyway, Julian isn't at war. He isn't old enough. Father told me the British aren't sending men overseas into battle unless they're twenty.

The second obsession Philippe and Father share is Django Reinhart, the Belgian guitar player with burned hands.

"Django's a gypsy," Father says. "He has a limp and walks with a cane, but he says he'll keep playing in Paris even if the Nazis invade."

"A gypsy and a hero," Philippe agrees.

We're at the table in our apartment. It's spring and a few brave blossoms have ventured out on the trees that frame the church door. Other than the fact that the apartment across the hall is empty, and I'm now married, it seems almost normal.

The third obsession they share, of course, is me.

*

I have no intention of reading that annoying little book. Men invented philosophy to explain how the world they see in black and white could be so gray. I don't need philosophy to understand the world as I have always seen it.

SOPHIA RAPHAËL, 4R

I don't like that man. Harry. The one Masha has taken up with, the Colonel's friend. He's too old for her. She needs younger blood. She needs a husband with a warmth and vitality to match her own. But maybe that ship has sailed, and she's always told me she's not the marrying kind.

The Outer Hebrides. Not my idea, and as my mama used to say, "Not exactly Gan Eden." But there's a family home there, on Leo's side, and we're driving to it now. Even though we have provisional papers thanks to his cousin, who I will never criticize again for being a skinflint, Leo felt driving was safer than taking the train. Good. I'll never get on another train given what I've been hearing.

Exhaust is seeping through the rear window and I taste it on my tongue, caustic and bitter. Esther has fallen asleep; her head bumps on my shoulder. The roads in Scotland are filled with potholes and only a few are tarred. Leo tells me to sleep. How? I haven't slept since we left. Boats terrify me and the channel was choppy.

"Why such a small boat?" I asked Leo.

"Why such a large channel?" he replied.

What can I say? The gloom of this landscape matches my mood. But then, if it were bright and cheerful, I might go mad. I must keep telling myself that I am grateful and we are fortunate.

*

That Harry fellow claims to be English. I don't know what he is and
I don't care about that. It's that he isn't telling Masha. Or maybe he *is*
telling her and I'm becoming paranoid and distrustful. Still, I don't
trust Harry, but then I can't allow myself to trust anyone these days.
Not even the English.

*

Leo tells me we're nearing the house and that we'll be safe here. I'm
worried we won't, that it isn't the impenetrable crag he thinks it is, and
the Nazis will get through. And living in this cold, miserable chunk of
stone will have been for naught.

I would never tell Leo any of this; he'd say I'm ungrateful. That's
not it at all. It isn't a question of gratitude but of recalibration. I was
convinced Europe wouldn't fall to the Nazis, and I argued with Leo. I
told him he was being bleak but I was wrong. And now I'm the one
being bleak not Leo; he's so confident the English won't fall to the Nazis
and I have to ask, what makes them any different from everyone else?

*

But then again, Harry might be in a position where one must be careful about whom to trust and he doesn't yet know if he can trust Masha.
Or else he doesn't want her to have knowledge that could put her in
danger. Or maybe Masha knows, he has told her, and she isn't telling
me. People don't always blurt out what they know. Masha has always
been discreet.

*

That old snoop knew we were leaving. Miss Hobert. She asked too
many questions. I ran into her days before we left as I was coming up
the stairs and she was waiting for the elevator.

"Oh, you're becoming such an active group, aren't you? I saw your daughter take the stairs too. Yesterday. And it struck me . . . Your children always took the elevator. Esther, is it?"

"Yes, Esther." She knew perfectly well what Esther is called.

"A pity Esther doesn't look like you. She's so recognizably Leo's."

A couple of days later as I was going down the stairs, I found Miss Hobert at the mailboxes.

"Trying to take off some kilos, are you?"

The notary's wife was in their doorway, watching us—the way she was looking at me, the distrust in her eyes. There was danger in those eyes. She's ignorant, afraid of difference.

I'm not afraid for Masha because Harry is different. I'm afraid because he has too much ego. Self-interest. Masha has told me enough about him that I know everything will always come down to him.

Leo was right. We didn't leave early. We left just in time.

We were rehearsing. Ergo the stairs. We couldn't risk the noise of the elevator in the middle of the night or turning on the hall lights. We had to practice taking the stairs. They're terrazzo. Stone. They echo. We would descend in stocking feet and darkness. You understand how careful we had to be?

I should have been taking the stairs all along. I was winded going up and down. The trouble with someone like Miss Hobert is she puts her finger right on the pulse and takes it. I should have stayed slimmer.

I could blame Masha. I put on weight, and she let out seams.

"No matter. You're beautiful no matter," she would say.

Flattery. Who's immune? I don't blame her. I blame myself for not taking a good hard look in the mirror. Naked.

*

I'm staring at the sea. The blue-green water has turned to gray under the overcast sky. Cold. I wouldn't want to escape across that water, although I've no doubt that's Leo's next big plan.

An odd sensation comes over me, a feeling I've never experienced. I feel fidgety. Numb. I pinch my hand and I feel the sharpness of my nails. Good. I'm fine. I'm sure I'm fine.

It's rattling about in this big stone box alone for a fortnight, that's all. The cleaning girl doesn't come until tomorrow, Leo's gone to London for his work, Esther's volunteering at the local hospital, and Julian is in his castle of a college at Cambridge. I dreamed of it the other night. I was on the lawn, no, at the gate. But I couldn't open it. So I flew, over the wall and above the college—slate roof needs fixing, too many pigeons. Dirty birds. There was a small boat on that stream that goes through the city. Punting, is that what they call it? I couldn't get in Julian's window and instead found myself in the bun shop down the street.

Oh dear, sugar buns, delightful, but I should not eat buns. Or sugar.

I must have drifted off. I'm awake now, still staring at the sea, still thinking of Julian. How he loves Cambridge—and Charlotte. My poor dear boy.

The sensation is still in my head. The strange lightness. My fingers are tingling. What on earth?

Esther is determined to be a nurse. Fine. But I tell her there will be plenty of soldiers to care for in Scotland when they're flown back, and she mustn't be foolish and return to the continent. She'd be found out right away. Her hair. Her eyes. Dark, dark eyes. Miss Hobert was right. Esther does look like Leo's family.

What do you do, but save your own in times like these?

I wanted to bring Charlotte. She'd be a candle in the room. She's unaware of herself, and that's what makes her so radiant. But Esther tells me Charlotte's in love. And Leo said it was impossible. We couldn't bring Francois too, and taking Charlotte away from him would put his heart at risk because he adores his daughter. And Charlotte's not in danger, not in the way we are. Leo's right of course. I was being selfish to think of it.

I'm still fidgety. I take off my shoes and stockings and plant my feet on the cool, smooth floor and I shiver. Stone. Why not wood? All right stone.

My mama used to say, "If you're feeling flighty or worried, take off your shoes, stand on earth, be naked, and understand you are part of something bigger."

It takes time to remove the layers. Didn't the Scots consider going farther south? Or the Vikings before? Or were they like us? Trapped. Leo said when we're feeling sorry for ourselves, we should remember those Celtic slaves the Danes dragged to Iceland.

"What about your relatives shipped out to Siberia?" I asked.

"Misery abounds," he replied.

Leo's in London for the paintings. London. The paintings.

Leo heard stories from Poland. About hair, among other things. He wouldn't tell me. He should tell me. It's worse imagining. Or maybe not.

I'm naked and looking at myself in the mirror. A film of dust over the glass. These old stone houses. Provocatively dusty. My mama gave me a coin for dusting when I was small. She would put on a glove and run two fingers over the piano or a picture frame or a shelf, and if they left a trail like skis in the snow, I had to give the coin back.

The dust on the mirror makes me look better. It's Julian's silk stocking over the camera lens.

And still, I can see the deepening lines in my face, gray streaks at the temples, neck crimpling like a plucked bird. Blue eyes anchor me a moment. Until they catch sight of my falling breasts. Masha can say all the kind things she wants, but they were once up here and now they're down there. Perhaps they're more useful like this. I could hide diamonds under them or coins, and they'd stay put. I turn to look at a side view and see a sandcastle after the sea has come in, all collapsing. I turn to the back and look over my shoulder. When did those arrive? Dimples and lumps? On my bottom. Another indignity. I liked my bottom, the old one. But with this new bottom, there's no line to the thigh, it all seems of one and I've got veins climbing my legs like vines—the ones you rip off a stone wall, so they don't destroy the mortar.

I'm shivering, the tears are flowing, I'm shaking. I feel so strange.

And now a crunch of gravel. A key in the door, the cheerful "hullo there" of the cleaning girl. *Oh dear,* I've gotten the day wrong. They all meld together. I'm throwing on clothes, my undergarments, stuck on my thighs, yanking fabric across breasts. Won't hook. Sweater, skirt, never mind the stockings, I bunch them up and stick them in my pocket.

The cleaning girl pokes her head in. "Hullo," she says again with a lopsided smile on her bun of a face. "Starting in the kitchen today," she adds.

I nod and force a smile. She leaves. I don't talk a lot to her. I hear how foreign I sound.

I'm shivering as I put on my stockings. Who cares how I look? It doesn't matter.

Masha would tell me it does matter, and so would Leo. He would say that our ability to see beauty is what makes us human. My dear Leo, what beauty?

And I'm not sure I agree. I think it's kindness. Doing things for people even when they're doing nothing for you. Not telling them you've done it. Leo doesn't believe in that. He doesn't believe anyone does something for nothing. I want to think he's wrong. The rabbi saved Masha. But then, he had no children. He was her uncle and she was the continuation of his family bloodline, so Leo would argue it was a question of genetic survival and not for nothing.

Would I have helped Masha if that first dress she altered hadn't fit? If she were ugly and her work matched her face?

And Charlotte. I felt for Francois. It was ideal to have a playmate for Esther across the hall, and we had a nanny. I was embarrassed when Francois gave us money to pay her. But Leo said it was better. He's a firm believer in the monetized social contract. In his view, it's what keeps people in line.

I step in the kitchen. The cleaning girl is polishing the stove.

"Do you like cake?" I ask. "Please, help yourself."

"After," she says with a bright nod that reflects on the bright stove. "I do like a bit of cake. Some tea for us both?"

She lights the stove and puts on a kettle.

I wonder if Leo will go to Cambridge and see Julian. He hasn't mentioned it. I think he's afraid of how I'll react if Julian joins up. But Julian warned me, and I know my son. I know he'll do it.

You raise a child. You see him grow and you grow too. If you're paying any attention at all, you develop an understanding of his possibility. You see the hair sprout on his chin, hear his voice deepen. And then? You let go. That's what Mama always told me. I wish she were alive and we could talk.

Detach. Let go. You won't be able to control anything but your tongue.

I'll write to Charlotte. And to Masha. I'll write letters. That's what I'll do.

MASHA BALYAYEVA, 5TH FLOOR

You know the feeling. *That feeling.* The tingling, the rising flush, stomach to cheeks, the pull. I used to believe it was proof that something could come out of nothing. That G-d's creation is possible. I'm sure doctors have explanations. That it's all about having babies. Keeping the species alive.

Had I known what was coming, I might have. Had a baby. But in truth, I can't imagine that. A baby from the two of us.

I still want to believe it's more than an animal urge but, under the circumstances, how can I?

I had that feeling when I met Harry. But not right away. First, I noticed his eyes—dark eyes. Blue, but not like mine. Harry's are the darkest blue I've ever seen in an iris. He has black hair, smooth tan skin. Beautiful skin for a man his age.

When I described Harry to Charlotte, she told me his coloring doesn't matter and not to pay attention to it and to please describe other characteristics. Of course she said that. And then she said, "If there's no light in his eyes, that worries me."

Such a rare creature, my darling Charlotte. I used to see her with Julian, and I wondered how she hadn't understood that he loves her. She never said it, but I think Julian was too familiar and Charlotte was looking for the unknown and something, someone, more dangerous. I understand too well.

It wasn't manufactured, Harry's attraction to me. He was sincere, and that's what I told Charlotte.

"How do you know?"

"I know Harry. I understand him. I know when he's faking and when he's being genuine. You get to know a man, even if he's a liar, because you get to know the boy inside him."

Did I mention that all men are dogs? It's true, but they're also boys. You see, Harry loved and hated me like he loved and hated a mother and a sister and a lover. It was true and real, all of it. Deep down, men are petulant and needy and all they want is to suck your breasts and be babies when no one's looking. All of them. And if they can't do it, if you don't let them, if you don't give them everything they want, or if you stand in the way of it. Well . . . That's when they turn into beasts.

I'm sure men have a rejoinder. They always do. I'm not interested.

The night I met Harry, the Colonel had invited me to his apartment. I was sitting on one of the floral sofas—pink, lavender, chartreuse, mercifully faded—and looking at the fit of the Colonel's new jacket. There was something off about the shoulders. The bell rang, the Colonel went to the door, and I looked around. He had changed nothing since his wife died, and it was sad to see him alone amid the frills and florid prints but also comical as he was forever digging about trying to find his things under all that fabric. He was such a dog in the flower garden.

When the Colonel returned to the living room, he had Harry with him. The story was that Harry happened to drop in for a visit. But I came to learn the occasion was orchestrated. By Harry.

What no one expected were emotions.

As the Colonel often said, "Complications."

A tack had come loose from the sofa skirt and it scratched my leg, leaving a hole in my silk stockings and a trail of blood trickling down my calf. Harry noticed right away. He used his handkerchief to stay the bleeding. Bright red on white linen. I remember wishing Charlotte could see those colors.

"The door to the ground floor flat was ajar and a woman in there was berating . . . who knows? Her husband? Her voice could grate a radish," Harry said as he dabbed the last of the blood from my leg.

"The notary's wife, yes," the Colonel said. He was pouring Harry a glass of whiskey. Turning to me, "Masha?"

"Please."

"That's my girl."

"I peeked in to make sure all was on the up-and-up. Saw a couple ghosts—children—in dirty nightclothes. Potato-faced indifference. They didn't seem to notice their mother's fit. I assume she's their mother," Harry continued.

"Never assume," the Colonel said sternly, handing me the whiskey.

"Does she scream all the time?"

"Every night," I said.

"And her husband takes it?"

"And he doesn't even drink," the Colonel said. "Cheers!"

We laughed at this. I took a small sip of my whiskey. It tasted like the bog where Mama and I once hid for three days when soldiers came through our village. I put down my glass and could see that my hand was trembling. Harry noticed.

"Shall we scare up some tea? I brought along a bit of food. Hungry?" he asked me.

"I didn't think so."

"Good," Harry said.

As we moved into the kitchen, Harry switched my glass for his empty one, downed my whiskey, and winked.

He was living in Paris at the time, and the way he talked about it, well it sounded alive in a way Brussels never had been. It reminded me of how Berlin used to be. I nearly moved there, but Mrs. Raphaël told me I would end up a prostitute or worse. She didn't trust the Germans. Not a surprise, as she trusts few people beyond her family. But she was right about Berlin.

We ate bacon and beans and toast and eggs, and the Colonel made us strong tea to swallow it all down. Harry and the Colonel joked that it was the kind of meal you'd have in England.

"I wouldn't know. I've never been," I said.

"Never been to the farm?" Harry exclaimed.

That's what they called England. The farm.

*

He was a strategist and what I didn't know is that he was courting me on two fronts. The rabbi told me not to mix work and love. I should have listened. But Harry was leisurely. He didn't rush; it wasn't his style. He took his time.

*

The beauty of my attic kingdom was that no one could see in, but I could see out.

It was months later, a dreary, wet October. Sheets of water were pouring from the sky, and Harry had walked from the station to the Colonel's. He was drenched. He didn't explain why he had walked instead of taking the tram, but I had the feeling he thought he was being followed, and the surest way to know—or to lose whomever it was—would be to walk. The Nazis had invaded Czechoslovakia earlier in the month. Harry told the Colonel and me that the Germans were deporting Jews to Poland.

"It's 1938," Harry told the Colonel, "a mere twenty years since the last war ended. No one wants to believe it will happen again. But it is happening."

Harry looked tired and troubled and I wanted to comfort him.

When he came to my room, I was ready. The sky had cleared for the night as it so often does in Brussels, and I was naked, waiting in the moonlight. I took off his damp clothes and asked if he wanted an apple. He laughed and said he would call me Eve from then on.

Eve was my code name. It's true. Eve was all anyone I met through Harry knew.

I was no virgin, but I finally understood what all the fuss was about. He didn't say a word, and neither did I. He was more than a little aggressive, but he didn't hurt me. He was overtaken by it, and I let myself be overtaken by him. I lost myself and tasted life in a way I never had before.

And this is why I have no bitterness. You can't be bitter about living.

*

I knew Harry was dangerous. This was obvious, to me at least, and to Charlotte. She has an instinct for these things. I hope she follows it. I'm here, insofar as I can be, to see that she does.

That night, when Harry fell asleep, I couldn't. I watched the rise and fall of his chest. I could see the strength of his chin, lips that were too thin for simple kindness. His face told me everything. He was so innocent and treacherous. I could have killed him then. Stabbed him in the heart. Maybe, in the end, that's what I did.

You don't stop living because of danger. And you can't always go back, especially if it means turning your back on life. It may be hard to believe that I understood all this then, but I think I did. I climbed onto my chair and stood over him, naked. I was not his murderer. I was his guardian. And then something outside caught my attention, a subtle movement in the shadows. I looked out the window and saw how in the moonlight the square looked black and white and gray. There was no color. I thought in that moment I was seeing it the way Charlotte always did.

Perhaps I was imagining it, but I could just make out the shape of a flaxen creature. I would swear it was a lioness stretched out on the pavement.

I'm not joking, and yes, I do joke sometimes.

Harry always said he taught me to tell a joke, that women don't understand humor. I don't agree. Women understand something men never will. That life is the big joke.

I was straining to see if it really was a lioness. Harry snored, and I glanced over as he turned on his side and pulled the covers around him in a cocoon, then settled into soft breathing.

When I looked back out to the square, she was gone.

The lioness was the color of Charlotte's hair. I wanted to tell Charlotte, but she was away at school. And I was superstitious about it. If I told her, I might never see my lioness again.

*

At first, I did small things to help Harry. We began to travel to Paris, where I would deliver a letter or a package. No contact. Simple tasks but I had to do something. I couldn't pretend it wasn't happening, could I? Word reached the tailor near the Gare Central that a man from my village who had settled in Prague had been sent by the Nazis to a work camp with his entire family, and no one had heard from them since. Everyone knew a story like this. And I mean *everyone*. Anyone who claims they didn't is a half-wit or a liar.

Harry never doubted he would be involved. He claimed to be English, but he had grown up mostly near Paris, and his accent was perfect when he spoke French. He had boxed, hunted, and fought in one war. In short, he could take care of himself, and so he was well situated to take care of others in the circumstances we found ourselves. For a time, I even thought he could take care of me.

I love Harry. Still. Nothing can change that. He was my fate, and I was his. I understand this better now.

We spent most of our time in Paris, but we traveled to the south as well. Marseille. Harry was forming a network there. He predicted the collapse of the French army, the army everyone said was the best in the world.

"It isn't the best. The Nazis with their efficiency and this *idea* they have of themselves . . . They'll walk right through France. It will be a garden stroll once they break the gate, and the gate is flimsy and old, so it will take no time," he said.

The Nazis didn't have to break any gate. They broke through the Maginot Line and Pétain handed them the key.

I had made a good living for all those years, and I had money saved up in a bank account in England that Mr. Raphaël set up for me. I could have afforded another flat, but I quite liked my room, and I loved the square and the building and my Charlotte. I had all I needed, and I had money so that one day I could travel. *Maybe*, I thought, *I would finally go to America.*

Harry was worried I was giving up my income to be with him, because he couldn't pay me.

"Not for that," he said. "Darling, I didn't mean that."

I didn't tell Harry about the letter from Mrs. Raphaël. She wrote pleading with me to leave Paris and come to Scotland, alone, that she could obtain papers for me as a domestic. But not with Harry, please. It was clear she doesn't trust him. I received the letter just before the Germans marched into Paris, and then it was too late to go.

But we were all right, Harry and I. We had money for food. That was taken care of—by whom, I never knew. Harry liked a good meal. He loved sausages, Bordeaux, apple tart. He said that had he stayed in England through his childhood, he supposed he would have liked sausages, port, and apple pudding. Harry was also a great believer in fate and how you can't shake your destiny, however hard you try.

If I had known what I know now, would I have tried to make it to Scotland? It wouldn't have been the worst plan.

*

Before Paris fell to the Germans, we went on a trip that took us near German territory. If we ran into Germans, we would pretend to panic about having crossed over, not that the lines were clear in France given how the countryside rolled and the Germans in turn rolled through.

Along the way, we stopped at French farms. The farmer would offer us refreshment, and we would take it, and when we handed back the jug or plate, there would be a message inside. It was simple.

We had a driver, a cheerful boy of a man who couldn't have been more than twenty-one or twenty-two. He had grown up just outside Strasbourg, so he had learned both French and German, and he had stories about his family farm. He told us he was going home after our little jaunt to have his mother's goose liver pâté—that we should stop by and try it. His family had been raising geese to make pâté for nearly three hundred years.

"I didn't know you could raise geese for that," I said, regretting it right away as I thought it made me sound provincial, and I don't like to expose my ignorance.

Harry didn't seem to mind. He was scanning the road and the fields, for what I didn't know. Harry never relaxed unless he was asleep. And he was never asleep unless he was certain we were safe.

"Oh yes," the driver said. "You see, the goose's liver is not nearly big enough. You'd have to slaughter twenty geese for a single tin."

"Oh," I said.

"It's ingenious, really, how they cracked the liver problem," he went on. "I didn't think of it. I don't know who did, but it's brilliant."

"I'm dying to hear," I said.

He smiled at this.

"What we do is we nail the goose's feet to a wood beam."

"When they're dead?"

"No, no. They're quite alive. We don't want to kill them. Not then. That's later."

Something in the ribbon of road ahead had caught Harry's attention.

"We keep them very upright, all lined up. And then you take a pin. You know, a pin? A dressmaker's pin."

"I'm familiar with those," I said.

"And stick it in the center of each eye. It blinds them, just like that, but you have to get it right in the center of the pupil."

"Why do you blind them?" I asked.

"Otherwise, they're panicky and they flap about. But blinded, they calm right down."

"How convenient," I said.

"Then we stuff them with nuts. You jam the food down far enough, they'll swallow it. And they're upright so gravity works for us, and they keep it down."

"How long do you do this?" I asked. I was feeling sick at the thought of blind, upright, stuffed geese with their feet tacked to a beam like a dress to a dummy.

"Three weeks . . . Bit more. Then we kill them."

"Turn around," Harry said. He was watching the driver with that gaze he has. "Now."

"But we're almost there," the driver said.

"I said turn around," Harry repeated.

The driver didn't turn around. Harry pulled his gun and shot the driver in the shoulder. But he didn't kill him.

Harry yanked on the injured arm and the driver screamed in pain and swerved. I could see then that he had been reaching into his pocket for a gun. Harry took the gun and grabbed the wheel to steady it.

"Turn around," Harry repeated.

The driver wasn't cheerful any longer. He had tears running down his face as he slowed the car and, one-handed, he turned the vehicle around.

"Stop the car," Harry said.

The driver stopped, and Harry ordered him to get out. The boy did.

"I imagine they'll come for your body when you don't show up," he said.

And then Harry shot the boy dead.

"We were his geese," Harry said.

Harry got in the driver's seat. I was staring at the blood on the driver's shirt—a white shirt—and as we sped off, I remembered the blood on the handkerchief in the Colonel's apartment.

I was holding tightly to the door handle, trying to keep my hand steady.

"If all was well, the farmer was going to leave his tractor in a particular spot. I could see that spot ahead but no tractor. Someone else had communicated with the farmer. Through another channel."

"How did you know the driver was in on it?"

"I didn't," Harry said. He was silent a moment, and then he added, "I watched his face when I told him to turn around. You watch the muscle in a man's jaw. The sinew of his neck. It tightens when he's about to reach for his gun and shoot you. Mine probably did the same. Everything flashes through your head when you reach for that gun. The possibility that you might die. He was probably thinking of all the foie gras left to eat. We know he was thinking about that."

"I'll never eat it again."

"Oh, you might."

We drove on in silence.

And then Harry said, "Or he was thinking of his mother. I saw that in the last war. All the men who lay dying. *Mama.* Last word. Or maybe he was thinking about how he wanted to live long enough to talk about his adventures with the Nazis. Poor chap. Decommissioned now."

Harry had no illusions. But you could never say he had no empathy.

Brussels, Belgium

May 1940

After

CHARLOTTE SAUVIN, 4L

Looking for eggs. Trading drawings for meat. The gray of the sky meets the gray of the fields.

I was in the countryside with Philippe, at the farm of Father's friend.

If the planes were hats, they would be Maysers. Elegant. Slim. Nothing superfluous in their design, even the engines exhibited a smooth restraint, a steady low-key hum that opened a register or two as they swept across the sky dropping dandelions that drifted to the ground. Not dandelions. Invaders. Men removing parachutes and dispersing.

*

The occupation of Brussels was immediate, but the constraints—the impositions, the curfews, the ostracizing, the marking, the bans, the roundups, the deportations, the murders—these happened so gradually they might be called cunning, for just as you got used to one thing, there was another. It was always happening to someone else, until it wasn't, and by then it was too late.

*

Philippe left right after the Nazis came. He understood how the fabric of the country would rot faster than old silk. He wasn't safe in Antwerp. Brussels would soon be as bad. And like Julian, he was convinced he had to fight.

I wanted to leave with him, but he wouldn't consider it. "You can't go where I will go. You can't fight. And your father will be alone," he said.

I helped him pack and I memorized him. What he looked like. How he smelled. I'd sketched Philippe more than once, but he doesn't like sitting still unless he's working, so in my sketches he's always gazing down, a pencil in one hand, the other propping up his forehead, and only part of his face can be seen.

"I don't need a sweater," he said, wiping sweat from his brow.

June was sweltering. Mrs. Raphaël wrote that after the coldest January on record, they were having the hottest June and that 1940 was not a good year, but she feared it wasn't yet the worst.

"It can get cold in the south and colder in the mountains," I said stubbornly, folding a sweater.

"Who said I'm going south? Or to the mountains?" Philippe was agitated, as if the knowledge of where he was going might be dangerous to me—or to him.

"You aren't going north. It's impossible to go west."

I tucked the sweater in his bag, he removed it, I put it in. He took it out and held my wrist and I looked at his hand. His nails were perfect horseshoes.

*

The month after Philippe left, I had trouble breathing again. Father said it was likely asthma.

"When you were born, it was touch and go for you and your mother. Her heart was a struggling bird, but she kept breathing until the end. Slow and steady. She was so calm, knowing you were here."

"And me?"

"Your heart was a bass drum. But you couldn't catch your breath."

Father, wondering at the two of us. How we seemed to be dividing the spoils of life. How it was that the tiny creature won.

*

Already six months since Philippe left, and my last day working at the shop where Mrs. Raphaël brought me over a year ago, a place that has been my refuge, where cheerful-voiced women with artful hands make clever hats of ribbon and felt, hats that are flowers and seashells. It is a place that can no longer exist in our bleak city. The owner is Jewish and she's closing its doors, maybe forever. As I step out, I try not to feel hopeless. My only consolation is the heavy wood hat form and the lengths of soft, gleaming wool in my bag.

To my astonishment, there's a parade in the street. It's so long I can't walk around it, and I'm forced to stand in a crowd of glum onlookers, most of them, like me, waiting for it to pass on this cold, sunless day.

I try not to look at the parade itself, but that makes me want to look. I look. Well-cut jackets, long tailored sleeves, arms swinging back and forth with energy. Precision. Jodhpurs and shiny black boots. The men look confident and fit. Well-fed. I'm thinking about how I'll describe the uniforms to Masha, and then I remember that Masha, too, has seemingly gone away for good.

*

The parade passes and I hurry across the street to the tram. It's a short wait, but then nearly anything feels short compared to a parade of Nazis. As I step onto the tram car, I hear a woman say to her husband, "Not the funeral march. Yet."

I barely see the woman's face, given the height of her scarf and the low brim of her hat, but a drooping nose and rumpled bags under her eyes tell me she has familiarity with funeral marches.

*

The German channel airs on the radio. The shop smells of molding fruit and cheese rinds. I resist an impulse to plug my nose as I slide my card across the marble counter, where it sits under the doughy Flemish nose of Smets, the proprietor, I pull myself up to stand as tall as I can, my mind flickering like a newsreel. Something Philippe told me.

Height, weight, gold teeth, good shoes.

I concentrate on butter.

"Two hundred and fifty grams a month each," I say in Flemish.

I don't think it matters, which language I speak. Not with this man. If I speak French, he'll think I'm a snob who needs taking down. If I speak Flemish, he'll think I'm being patronizing. There's no winning, and all I want is the butter he isn't giving me. I tap the paper, with the tip of my short fingernail. He doesn't look at it.

I'm giving him the benefit of the doubt. The possibility of being slow-witted rather than malicious.

"Two hundred and fifty grams," he responds stubbornly in Flemish, staring at his stubby fingertips.

What a malicious man.

To clarify, Smets and I aren't strangers. I've known him my entire life. This shop has been in his family for a generation, at least. My father and his father before him bought butter and eggs and lettuce and milk and sliced ham and tinned sardines here. But the past year has taught me that all bets are off when war is on. War is not evenhanded. It gives some the power to reinvent themselves and knocks others off their feet. I'm still standing, but just.

"Two hundred and fifty grams. Final. That's all. No more."

"Two hundred and fifty per person," I counter.

The evening curfew is minutes away and time is on his side.

He swipes a drip from his round tip of nose with the fuzzy back of his hand and glances at my card.

"Two hundred and fifty . . . It's a lot. These days . . . A lot."

He wipes another drip as the shop bell tinkles. I glance over to see a German soldier step in wearing the same dapper uniform I saw in the parade an hour before. He steps up to the counter and surveys a selection of cheeses that would have seemed beggarly only months before but is now an embarrassment of riches.

This is not a shop where anyone bought cheese except as an after-thought, having forgotten to buy it at the market or as a convenience, needing a quick hard chunk to grate over potatoes. Like almost every-thing else, this, too, has changed.

Smets and I are at an impasse, and we know it. It's a relief to watch the soldier, who has a plain, sober face and is taking his time as though the choice of cheese is the decision of his lifetime. Maybe it is. He can't be more than twenty-five. Philippe's age. On this closer view, I decide that the uniform is ugly. Silly trousers. Not elegant at all. Father has always said that civilizations are measured by art and ideas. I realize the man is no mere soldier. He's an officer. There's a patch with two stripes and a pair of leaves on his jacket. And he's obsessed with cheese. Does he take this much time before he kills? Surely a man with a gun at his head would sweat as much as that chunk of Emmenthal.

I turn back to Smets, who's leaning against the wall, arms folded, a smug half smile playing on his face.

"What color is my awning?" he asks.

Definitely malicious.

The officer looks up, puzzled. Seeing me, he smiles.

Reflexively, I smile back. It's natural. If he had yawned, I would have yawned. It's human.

God help me.

"Old," I say to Smets in French. "Please wrap my butter. Five hundred grams."

"Two hundred and fifty," Smets repeats in his slow, rolling Flemish. And louder, "Two hundred and fifty grams per ration card."

"I have my father's ration tickets—"

"But not his card." Smets digs in with a stubborn jerk of his chin.

I lean over the counter and whisper, "You have known my father all your life. He has his card with him at work."

"Then you can't get his butter, can you?"

I'm trembling with fury.

"No meat?" a voice asks in unsteady French.

We both look at the officer, who has finally decided on the terms of his sandwich.

"We might have a ham coming in tomorrow. Are you in the neighborhood?"

"Yes." The officer smiles.

"Give me your name. I'll put some aside."

"Schmidt," the officer says.

Smets writes it down. Turning back to me, he says, "I have to attend to my other customers."

"I was first."

I know I should be quiet, stand in line. That's what's expected.

"Please, go ahead," Schmidt says with absolute courtesy. And he clicks his heels.

"I'll wait," I say firmly.

Smets proceeds to make the sandwich that has been so long in the choosing. It is the Chimay that wins out in the end, with lettuce and butter.

"On the darkest bread you have, please. And two hundred and fifty grams of butter on the side," Schmidt says.

Smets is more than happy to oblige. Schmidt glances at me. He smiles again.

This time, I don't smile back.

"I've only arrived this afternoon, so I'm a bit hungry," he says in his broken French, but with exquisite and unexpected politeness. And then he adds, "I hope I'm not making you late for anything."

My life. You are making me late for my life. All of you.

Schmidt clicks his heels again—and he extends his hand.

I look at the hand. Tapered fingers, clipped nails, a brushing of hair on knuckles. I don't take it.

Smets quickly puts a bag in the outstretched hand and Schmidt thanks him, nods politely, and bumps past me on his way out.

"So sorry," he says.

The door shuts behind him.

Smets doesn't notice any of this. He's too busy slicing the thinnest 250-gram tranche of butter he can, closer to 249 grams, certainly not 251 grams. He weighs it with the paper, then wraps it carelessly and hands it to me. I refold the paper before dropping it in my bag.

"When this is over, and it will be over, we will remember everything."

The words come out before I can stop them. I try to slam the door on my way out, but there's a pump that slows it, so my gesture, like my words, pushes only air.

I step into the familiar side street leading to the square. There are half a dozen streets like it. When I was a girl, I thought all roads led to Number 33. I walk a few steps, then stop and look in my bag. Not one knob of butter, but two. That officer—Schmidt—must have slipped one in the bag when he bumped me. I have an urge to smear it on the shop window, the door handle, better yet, to give it to someone who needs it more than I do. But the street's empty, and Father could use the butter. I'll have to live with the guilt of my own weakness. I smiled back.

It's dusk and there's no one else on the narrow sidewalk. Streetlights are off, and windows have already been covered with dark fabric and paper for the nightly blackout. The windows remind me of the darkroom—and Julian. I promised I would think of him. I don't know if he thinks of me. It was his fault, needlessly rupturing our friendship right before leaving. Julian would like Philippe. He would! He should have understood me better. I was sure he did. I think of his chin, the hurt look on his face, his eyes, the arc of his cheekbone. Julian. He wanted to possess me. I walk along the dark street and I think of him. I tell him I'll always be with him, even if I'm not his.

I catch my toe on an uneven sidewalk stone and stumble, gripping a rough cement window ledge to catch myself. The smell of dog feces floats up from the pavement, and I see a flat slick ahead, scraped to a ganache by a careless heel. The city's gotten dirtier since the Nazis came. Father said that so long as the French run the city, the Flemish workers will do everything in their power to make the French look less competent than they are.

"The Flemish believe Brussels is theirs, and they want it back," he added.

"Is it theirs?"

"Probably."

I avoid the mess and another ahead. I can see better than most in the dark, almost as well as I do in bright daylight. When I was small, Father had shaded eyeglasses made for me.

"Why?"

"To keep you from squinting and blinking in the sun."

"I can't help it."

"I know."

"No, you don't."

"That's why I made you the glasses," he said.

"It's not that I don't like the sun. I *can't* like it."

"Why is that?"

"I'm a vampire."

"Don't ever say that again."

"I was joking."

"People believe anything. Everything. The less you tell them about yourself, the better. Remember that."

"So, I shouldn't tell anyone I'm a vampire?"

"No one but me."

I won't tell Father about the second knob of butter. It will make him feel bad or guilty or make me feel bad or guilty.

I pass the dark pharmacy window—an odd place run by an older Flemish couple who sell outdated pills, stale lozenges, dusty boxes of tea—and step into the square seeing the dark surround of rooftops and cupolas against the night sky. A tram screeches in the distance, and I hear voices from the other side of the church. I walk quickly in their direction, seeing a flicker as I draw closer.

It's the bakery door, opening and shutting as customers come and go, illuminating an arc of soldiers huddled outside.

I walk past them, not looking to the right or the left, dulling the expression on my face, and slouching a little.

I'm not interesting, don't look at me.

I push open the door, step inside, and smell the wood-sweet tang of browned crust. I used to think I could live on this smell. Now, I know better.

Maryanne, the owner, is a true Brussels woman—not French and not Flemish but rather a native of the city—and she's behind the counter now in front of shelves that are nearly bare. She adjusts her apron over breasts as large as the loaves and takes my ration ticket. With a brisk nod, she steps into the back room, returning a few moments later with a fresh, hot loaf. She cuts a half, not a quarter, and hands it to me.

"Whole wheat and rye, no beets. I'm supposed to save this one for *them* but they can have the damn beet loaves as far as I'm concerned. They're devilishly fond of sweets. All my beet sugar dumped in their damn coffees."

She speaks French with an accent that sounds like it's falling down a gentle slope. I'm sympathetic. I understand what I didn't before. A lack of sugar is a minor shortcoming until it's yours. The same goes for a lack of butter or meat or water or heat or socks or shoes or a scarf or a hat or mittens or a bed. Or a husband.

Thirteen weeks since Philippe made it across the sea.

A cardinal number, divine attributes, a prayer, God's mercy. Judas was the thirteenth disciple. A lucky number, an unlucky number, a card that brings the pale horse of death.

I'm forgetting Philippe again, bit by bit. Losing him. The texture of his skin, the sound of his laughter, the feel of his breath on my cheek at night.

That first time I saw Philippe at school, I felt a shock of recognition. I had never seen him before, but I had known him forever. I couldn't shake the feeling, and I didn't want to, but now I'm losing him, and the idea that I could know someone forever and still lose him, this mystery of love and forgetting that Father has mentioned when talking about my mother, is one of the many paradoxes of my new life.

We have been married less than a year, and I've had no news in a month.

I step out of the bakery, passing a soldier going in.

What if the soldier is Philippe? And I somehow don't recognize him.

I look through the bakery window and I see the soldier's face—pug nose, dull eyes.

I feel a pulse-in-my-ears surge of anticipation as I walk toward the press shop. It's closed for the night, but the sallow-faced Flemish boy in his moth-eaten cap is still out front selling newspapers. The boy collects coins from a soldier and hands him a copy of *Le Soir*, the French paper that's been taken over by the Nazis. I wait for the soldier to walk far enough down the street so he won't be able to hear a voice, let alone a whisper, before I turn to the newsboy and ask if he has any copies of *Le Figaro*.

Flicking a crust of snot from his nose, he shakes his head no.

I nod.

He nods.

No news.

I turn toward home, then impulsively I reach into my bag, pull out the packet of butter, and slip it in the newsboy's hand. He flicks another crust from his nose and calls out to an approaching soldier.

"*Le Soir!*"

*

I'm fighting to remember details.

We were sitting on a lawn. But I had things to do. I got up and Philippe pulled me down. He was damp from the sun and his sweat smelled of musk and onions.

"The grass has no meaning without you," he said.

Philippe is freer than anyone I know. He pays little attention to rules or etiquette, and he's often late, not because he's rude but because he's preoccupied. Yet he obsesses over details. Colors on a canvas. How pencils are arranged on a desk, each line of a drawing.

"Not drawings. Plans. I don't hope they'll be built. I shall build them."

Brick or stone? Oak or mahogany? Three floors or four? Square windows or Romanesque? A raised entry? A sunken lobby? Double doors? A side entrance?

And he obsesses over the fit of his clothes. They must be comfortable. Not dandyish. Linen pants. Philippe wears linen pants year-round. He says they keep him warm enough and cool enough. They're his signature. He wears them *no matter what.*

One rotation around the sun. All the no-matter-whats left behind.

People are giving up, giving in, trying not to stand out, pretending they don't know what they've lost. A few, like Smets, think they've gained—people who smell of rot and sulphur. They disgust me.

Philippe will not forsake anything. He will not forsake me. He is not giving in. He is wearing linen pants and standing out to spite them all.

COLONEL WARLEMONT, 3L

Shirt off, I'm looking in the mirror at flesh rolling over my belt like a loaf over the pan.

Let it out man, take your medicine! Can't fool your own self. Pretending the old gut isn't a collapsing pile of offal. No call for that.

Take a pork belly before it's sliced for frying. Then you'll get the idea of what a man's stomach will become without moderation.

Before the rationing kicked in, I was trying to slim down. I had lost three kilos with eight to go.

That infernal cake. The Jacob's ladder of the occupation was that Hobert wouldn't have the ingredients to make more of them. How did she wrangle butter? Let alone flour. God knows what else was in it, one of those sticky surprise cakes they sell around Christmas when people eat things they would not consider injesting at any other time of the year—dried fruits, bitter spices, sick-sweet syrup, tooth-cracking nuts. All of it leaving a skim of grease on tongue and throat. Although, these days, a lot of people would be grateful for a nasty slice of Christmas cake.

How did Hobert pull it off?

He's a good lad, Zipper is. Mind you, I keep him on the straight and narrow. Military style. He's got a mind of his own as the best of them do but I'm getting through. No easy task, especially these days without treats to reward good behavior. Used to give him horsemeat and vegetables. Now it's bread and cheese ends and he's always hungry. I was making such progress but Zipper got to the cake before I could. One gulp. Two. After, he had the runs all the way down the hall. Bad luck on timing as I was in the bath when I heard him yelping and, not understanding he had torqued his innards, I slipped and nearly cracked a rung on my spine when I got out to see why the hell, he was bellyaching. And no, I did not slip on water—so there was the damn mess on me to clean up as well. I knew right then I would have to take another bath. I scolded the lad but not very enthusiastically. He looked downtrodden and smelled like shit. I didn't have to tell him. He knew. I had to use both soap and vinegar to get the smell out of the floor. Washed Zipper in the tub. Washed the tub. Washed my own self again. I'm spent after all that damn washing.

Enough looking in the glass. I put on my shirt and check the floor to make sure I got it all up.

Where is he? "Zipper!"

Thump of a tail. Scuttered under the bed, that's where. Shame will do that. Hope he learned his lesson. He's looking at me. Contrition. Don't tell me Zipper has no feelings. He's as loyal as they come.

I'm reaching down to pet him when I hear the knock on the door. Hobert coming to ask how I liked the cake. Zipper and I freeze like bunnies with rabbit fever and wait in darkness for her to leave.

The knocks come harder and louder and then a man's voice shouts, "I know you're in there, open up, dammit!"

I go to the door and open it to see Harry standing there.

"Smells like vinegar."

"Only vinegar?"

"Yes, why?"

"Good."

I haven't seen Harry for months. He's terribly thin and his skin seems a size too big and darker, his nose larger. I suspect I'm the only one who knows the truth about Harry. I knew his father, who was a Brit. But his mother was half-Jewish and half-Indian. Harry's damned on three counts, should the Nazis figure it out.

Harry could use a couple of my spare kilos. And I'm wishing the bloody dog hadn't eaten the cake.

"Follow me," I say.

We go in the kitchen, and I poke through my meager provisions. I always assume Harry will stay for a meal, and he always does. I pull out some cheese and a bit of bread.

"How's Masha?"

"Fabulous. She's in Paris. We married you know."

"I didn't. Will there be a little Masha or Harry on the way?"

"Oh no. I don't think that makes sense. Not now."

I uncap a beer and hand it to him.

"And what are you up to these days?"

I regret the words as soon as they leave my mouth. I'm out of the game and I did my time. I went through all that in the Congo. Unspeakable. Sorting out that bastard King Leopold's messes. Baskets of hands, that's what people told me—missionaries, natives, Belgians who fancied they'd gone native—they had seen them. And then I saw too. Men who refused to work. The hands were proof they'd been shot. But not all were dead. Hands cut off anyway. How do you move beyond baskets of hands? You don't. They're rigid, those hands, and the Congo's damp enough that they don't dry out. They rot. And smell. I got the hell out, went from war to war, bad to worse. Saw sights that made those baskets seem like the work of tourists, not professionals. The professionals make people suffer longer and more. Those wars stole my youth. But I have nothing to complain about in the grand scheme. You take it seriously, you try to be decent, be the outlier, the person a native might trust not to stab him in the back, let alone cut off his hand. You lose sleep and hair. You drink and smoke and pretend you didn't see five men cut to pieces in one day, and you lose more sleep and hair. I'm an old man. I lost my wife. I lost my hair, other than in my nose and ears. I have a dog. I take walks and smoke my pipe when I find a bit of tobacco. If an old friend happens to stop by, I'll offer him a meal.

But Harry never happens to do anything. He's always thinking, Harry is. Wheels turning constantly. Makes sense knowing everything I know about him. We have an understanding, Harry and me. It comes from being in the trenches together. When you've gone through that experience with someone, it's even harder to say no.

Harry opens his satchel and pulls out three eggs.

"We can have these," he says casually.

I take the eggs, being careful not to drop one. "Those are scarce."

"Eggs are never scarce, just expensive."

"Some people figure out how to make money no matter the times. I'm not one of them," I say.

"I don't think you care about money."

"Are you about to ask a favor then?"

"Yes. No. Sort of."

I cook the eggs, dish up a plate of food for Harry, and a smaller one for me, and we sit at the kitchen table. Zipper slips out from under the bed and moves into the hall, where he can watch us eat.

"Good dog," Harry says.

"Not today. What's Masha doing?"

"Sewing."

"Really. She has business?"

"All the wives of the men running things in Paris adore her."

"Harry."

"What? Masha doesn't know a thing. She tells me about her days. And I glean from that."

"Harry!"

"You'd be surprised how much women talk among themselves."

"I would not."

I watch Harry eat. He's taking small bites, savoring them. I know from experience he's biding his time.

The kitchen is cozy if not large; it's an apartment kitchen. I spent my childhood in a farmhouse in England and we always had a big wood table, a lit stove that warmed the room. Cured meats hanging from the ceiling. My kitchen is warm because of heat pipes that run up the wall. It looks out over the courtyard, and I can see the glow from windows, or I used to before the blackouts, and then I don't feel alone, even though

I am. When I lost my wife, I thought I lost my life. Whether I liked that life wasn't the point; it was mine. I made another life with a dog and that is how I wish to finish my days. In as much peace as I can find given the damn Nazis. I would have to be firm with Harry.

"Harry . . ."

"Don't say anything. You don't have to decide now. I'll tell you all about it and come back in a month for an answer."

"Isn't it dangerous? Going and coming?"

"Everything is occupied now. It's all the same. My wife is white Russian and fled to Belgium when the Jews took over."

"People believe that?"

"Masha passes. And right now, I'm visiting my uncle in Brussels."

"Me?"

"Why not you?"

My vanity gets the better of me. "I'm old. But am I that old?"

"Yes."

And Harry proceeds to tell me how he got the idea, how he wasn't alone. It was springing up everywhere.

"It's a tree that knows it's dying and sends out seeds, cones, whatever, and little trees begin to come up in its place, so many that there will be at least one that survives to replace the dead tree. Maybe more."

"That's all very lyrical."

"It's not. It's essential."

"You never got over the thrill of being in wartime."

I'm watching Harry and he's watching me. Harry is one of the most perceptive men I've ever known.

But his face isn't revealing a damn thing. He's good at that too.

My god, I introduced Masha to this beast.

"I love Masha," he says.

Did I say something about her? I'm sure I didn't.

"I adore her," he continues. "I would never want anything to happen to her. My plan is to send her to the farm. Through the network."

"What network?"

"That's what I'm telling you. There's a network." He takes his last bite of eggs and wipes his mouth.

"I thought there were seeds of ideas."

"We've gone beyond that."

"How do you know it's reliable?"

"Good question."

He calls Zipper over and gives him a swig of beer before I can stop him.

"Don't do that. He's just shit all over the hall."

"Yes, I know. I smelled it. The beer's good for the stomach."

"I thought you only smelled vinegar."

"I lied."

"And how do you know the people in this network aren't lying? How are you verifying them?"

"As best I can. We can only verify the next link. No one can know the whole chain. That would be too risky."

Harry won't look me in the eye as he says it. Because he knows, and I know, there is risk everywhere. And what we also both know is that Harry hasn't always had the best instincts about whom to trust.

LEO RAPHAËL, 4R

The train rounds a bridge suspended across an unforested sweep of land, reminding me of a Roman aqueduct I once saw in France. Modest mountains, rain deepening the green and desaturating any other color. I understand why the English are devoted to this land, why they're fighting so hard for it. Unlike the Belgians for theirs.

Sophia didn't want me to take the train. She has a thing about trains these days.

"You never know," she said.

Sophia thought she'd had a stroke. The doctor said she was fine, but what do doctors know? Strokes are mysterious. I remember a great aunt who had a stroke and after that she could only say three words: *some poison ivy*. She got very good at saying it—as a directive, a lament, a kindness. We always knew more or less what she was trying to get across.

I turn and look back at the bridge. Roman? Impossible. The Romans did come here but not successfully. It's a hard country to occupy. Only the French did it by becoming more English than the natives. We round another bend, I settle in my seat, a hard seat for a long journey, and close my eyes as thoughts filter through.

Julian.

I open my eyes.

Can't think about Julian.

I look at the scattering of people in the car: soldiers returning to their bases from leaves, a group of young women talking with great intensity about their work for *the cause*—I gather with the government—and an elderly woman with a cavillous face across the aisle. Sensing I'm looking at her, she glares, ready to contradict anything I might say. I close my eyes again.

Julian.

Dammit. Eyes open, I crane my neck to look at the bridge, but it's too far back. Think about the Romans. The Greeks. Anything but Julian.

I can't tell Sophia that Julian has joined up. She might actually have a stroke or shoot me with that old hunting rifle we found in the house. I wouldn't blame her.

Think of guns.

I have it on good authority that the Nazis rounded up the guns first, which made it infinitely easier to round up the people. After Kristallnacht. You understand? We'll be holding on to that rifle, thank you very much.

I'm sure Julian has learned to shoot by now.

No, must go back to the Romans. Or the Greeks. The monuments. The people or the monuments? Monuments or the people?

We know which lasts longer.

Sophia would say, *The people, you idiot.*

But then, she's the one who insisted I leave her and continue with my work. So, there you are.

Here's what I'm thinking: if it's the idea that counts, and without it there's no civilization, no humanity, and if that idea is embodied in and carried forward by the monuments, then it's a bit tricky, isn't it?

The train's lulling me to sleep. I force my eyes open again. I'm wary of sleeping in waking places because of an odd phenomenon I've noticed of late. I can't seem to separate my dreams from my waking hours, and they're all mixed up in my memory. Sometimes I have no idea which is which.

What's the name of that damn book? *Tractatus.* Pretentious. Those of us who went to school learned Latin. My father was a professor, a mathematician like Julian. My brother and I were subjected to tutors who insisted we master our declension. We spoke German in our home even though we were born in Russia and grew up in France. Why not just call it *Tract* or *Treatise* or *Discussion*? As I recall, it has little to do with Romans or Rome. Yes, I did read it, years ago. Yes, I disagree with most of it. For instance, pictures aren't facts reaching up to reality as he says they are. I don't know whose reality that man was conjuring. To my mind, it's the opposite. Reality aspires to the picture, the *ideal*. Reality is the catastrophe. Don't we all understand this now?

Dammit, what's his name. He's the fellow who's been teaching Julian. I hope he knows more about maths than art. He was in the trenches too.

But then, many of us were. Francois had particularly bad luck for someone who lived, having a chunk of leg blown off. My brother, Isaac, was older. He had gone to America where we thought he was safe, but he caught that odious flu there and died of it. I came down with it in the trenches, was sent to hospital, and it probably saved my life. What to say, but you never know. Sophia tells me I'm lucky.

Collecting four-leaf clovers and evil eyes, spitting over my left shoulder, sitting before I leave the house. I've turned into a superstitious nut bag.

Wittgenstein! That's him.

I'm thinking of a painting . . . bouquet of flowers, a shell, a spiderweb. A simple piece, to my mind, notable. I'm sure it will gain value. Correction: can't be sure of that for reasons having nothing to do with the painting. The world as we know it might not exist in a decade. Less. We might go back to painting on cave walls.

It hangs in our hall . . . it did. Probably should be in a museum . . . undoubtedly should be in a museum. The point being—the flowers. Or the painting of the flowers? Which is reaching up to which?

Some say great artists add to reality. Others say they'd rather sit in a garden than a museum.

I've heard he's the reason Hitler hates the Jews. Wittgenstein. I don't believe it. Hitler didn't need a reason. People who want to hate will find a specific reason and make it general. Or a general reason and make it specific.

Hitler can fuck off.

This my last thought as I drift off.

I'm in the Parthenon among the Turks. I'm one of them, not sure how I know we've invaded Athens, but I do. We've captured the city, and we are sure—certain—that finally Greece is ours. Infernal Greeks. Staging a comeback. What the hell did they do to inspire themselves after losing so badly? Sit around mountain campfires and recite *The Iliad*?

We didn't imagine a picture that included a Greek revival.

They're ambushing us, firing guns, bullets flying. And we are out of ammunition.

There's one clever officer among us who knows, for reasons he doesn't share, that the columns of the Acropolis have lead cores and clamps. Those Greeks knew how to build things that last.

And now we're chipping away at the marble to get the lead out, stripping the columns.

Sun filters in. I feel the heat of it flicker across my face, illuminating our efforts to destroy the Greek idea.

But they can't bear it, those Greeks. The monument falling, the idea destroyed. It is so central to their understanding of themselves, of who they are, that they make a remarkable decision. They give us bullets. They do. They give us bullets in exchange for the understanding that we Turks won't topple the Parthenon by gutting the pillars, because what the Greeks understand and we don't is that so long as the idea lives and the monument that embodies it stands, a lot of people can die, and a civilization will carry on.

We all must die, it's a question of when.

It's something to ponder, that's for sure.

The train bumps, and my eyes fly open. The sun is flickering on my face through the dirty train window not the Parthenon columns, and I realize I've been in another of those waking slumbers that mix time and reality, leaving me with little grasp of either. Is this what it's like to grow old? Everything you've ever known or done or thought becomes an incomprehensible tangle. Maybe it's easier that way. There's no earthly point trying to untangle it, so you give in to the gentle departure from what we call reality. But I'm not that damn old. Not yet.

I feel the warmth of the sun again as it emerges from the clouds, and I realize I haven't seen the sun in months.

*

I do know I'm not a Turk.

*

No straight lines in the Parthenon. A miracle of engineering. When Francois realized there wasn't a straight line in anything Charlotte drew, I reminded him of this fact. He said he took solace from it.

*

I have a close friend who is a Turk, a man named Bekir. I haven't heard from him in over a year, and I wonder how he's weathering all this. He collects art in Istanbul and has a marvelous house overlooking the Bosporus with a large room in the center of each floor where people can gather and talk. I told Francois about those rooms and he was very taken with the idea of them. He's convinced talking can keep us from fighting. A few years ago, Bekir and I were sitting at a café a short distance from the Hagia Sophia drinking coffee from translucent blue-and-white porcelain cups that matched the sky. A tiny black kitten with eyes as blue as the cups, ergo the sky, jumped into the empty chair next to mine and was staring at me. It was disconcerting. And then I noticed that the kitten had tufts of hair coming out its ears, exactly like my father had. What if Father were watching me in the guise of a rare feline. Not many black cats have eyes that blue. Julian has blue eyes and black hair, like my father and my brother had, like the damn kitten. It was a hot afternoon, but there was a cool breeze, and we were sitting in the shade of a sycamore tree as we talked about how many Greeks were killed by their own bullets that day over a hundred years ago.

*

Hitler has an idea, and that idea has caught fire. It's not a good idea. It's not a clear idea. It's not factual. It is an idea that creates a picture that has very little to do with reality and nothing whatsoever to do with logic.

*

To me, the truly cogent notion Wittgenstein has—the only idea of his that makes good sense—is that ethics and aesthetics are one and the same.

I've seen some of the so-called art coming from the new regime, and I understand why they're stealing everyone else's art. It's because they can't make it themselves. But then art is a prophet, prophets have souls, they have none, ergo they have no art.

Julian would like my little syllogism.

I get up and stretch my legs. I grip the tops of seats as I make my way down the aisle to the dining car. We're out of Scotland, speeding through the countryside.

Julian loves trains.

Dammit, Julian again.

I've lost all mental discipline. I can't stop thinking about my son. When last I saw him, he told me that another Cambridge math man—a fellow called Turing—also a student of this Wittgenstein, is now in London trying to break the Nazi codes, and like Wittgenstein, he's rumored to be homosexual.

"Who cares about that?"

"I don't," Julian said.

If I knew where the hell this Turing lad was living, and if I had any paintings left, I'd send him one for his rooms. Don't tell me mathematics has nothing to do with art. Both seek perfection. One can inspire the other. I'm sure of it.

*

I should have packed a lunch. The train is jilting side to side so much that the beer in my glass looks like one of those German wave pools. I take a sandwich. The bread is dry, the watercress tired, the filling over-mayonnaised and under-egged.

The food in Wales won't be better.

When I told Julian what I'm doing with the art, he was dismayed we didn't use trains for the transport.

I told him trains these days have a mixed reputation when it comes to evacuation and transport. But the truth was, they were too much of a target should the Nazis have caught wind of it.

Lorries. We used lorries to get the paintings out of the museum and up to Wales. For the smaller paintings, we borrowed lorries from the Royal Mail—and from Cadbury. I have lived in Brussels most of my adult life, I'm a Belgian citizen, and, as such, I am a chocolate snob. How could I not be? What some call chocolate, I would describe as a sad excuse for a confection.

But I will never again sit on the sidelines with contempt when it comes to Cadbury.

The woman working the dining car, if you can call it that, stops by my table to ask if I want anything more.

"A Dairy Milk bar."

"Terribly sorry, sir, but we're out."

"That's all, then."

Rumor has it Cadbury will have to change up its formulas because milk is being rationed. Toward that end, I have a small stockpile of Dairy Milk bars waiting for me in Wales. I've been eating one a day. Another fact I can't share with Sophia. Marriage used to be about sharing everything, but these days, it's about hiding things. These days, every-thing is hidden. Julian joining up with the RAF, for example.

*

Back in my seat. No sleeping. Thinking only of the task before me. But the beer and hard-cooked egg are sloshing around in my stomach, and a soft belch escapes my lips before I can suppress it. The woman across the aisle looks at me with open disapproval. I smile blandly and look out the window to see that the train is edging along a ridge below a deepening blue sky and snow-patched emerald hills. We've reached the Welsh mountains. Only a couple more hours to go.

*

At first, the museum hid the art in multiple locations—a university, a library, a scattering of castles. As I told my cousin when we discussed the initial plan, I thought it best that the collection not all be in the same place, should the Nazis start bombing. I thought they would, and my cousin agreed. We had both heard enough from Prague and from Warsaw, where we have relatives. Some were able to save assets; others tried to save themselves. Now, they're all silent. What more to say? But my cousin's colleagues were skeptical at first. They hadn't believed the war would spread to England. How fast that worm turned.

I acknowledged to my cousin and his pusillanimous colleagues that the drawback of paintings being hidden in various locations was that storage conditions would be far from uniform, but to my mind, the risk of mold on a few paintings was outweighed by the possibility of the entire collection being destroyed in a single bombing.

We were forced to revisit the plan upon receipt of an alarming mis-sive from a museum employee telling us that the owner of one of the castles where we had stored paintings seemed to believe he could best support our troops by remaining in a constant state of drunkenness, that said owner possesses dogs, and he and a dog had a collision that nearly ripped a hole in a priceless canvas. The employee wouldn't say which one given that no real damage was done, sparing us the heartburn he had on that occasion. He concluded his letter writing, "Happily, the Baron has been in a car accident that has put him out of commission long enough for us to seek a better venue for the art."

After what felt like an endless charette of discussing and reevaluating, we set forth into the wilds of Wales to scout—a fancy term for a lot of mucking about on foot in Wellies given that many of the roads have been made impassable by the appalling weather—in search of that better venue.

And this was when my waking hours began to feel like dreams, and my dreams began to seem as real as my waking life. I found myself walking at night on roads I had never seen before, and I couldn't for the life of me work out how I'd taken them. I remembered events that hadn't happened. Experiences that weren't my own. At night I had visions, unspeakable visitations from emaciated guests who turned to skeletons and dust in the course of conversations. Cut-off noses, and fingers, hands, and heads, of people known and unknown to me. The dreams bookended my days, causing me to comment on a severed ear three times—twice when I seemed to have been dreaming and once when I was not. Happily the ear in question was intact. You see how confusing it is?

Maybe it's all the travel—the detachment from a consistent frame of reference—from Brussels to London to Wales to Scotland and back and forth and now back again and to the mine. Literally.

You see, we found no building that could accommodate the entire collection safely, and as we searched, it became clear to a few of us that one of the mines, a slate quarry really, might accommodate. The cool temperature with some care to make sure nothing froze, the modest humidity with more care to make sure nothing got wet, and we'd have our underground museum.

We had to blast out the opening to get the larger paintings in. And we've built brick bungalows down below that will hold temperatures steady and humidity down. We're preparing to load in, and I must say I find it inspiring when so little else is.

But here's a fact. Around the time we began to construct our Daedalian village in the mine, I told my cousin we should be sure we had considered allocation of resources. Shouldn't we make better planes? Parachutes? Flight suits?

My cousin was surprised I had cold feet. "You're thinking of Julian obviously," he said.

"Not only Julian," I told him.

"We considered moving the collection to Canada but the prime minister put the kibosh on it. There was a concern about U-boats."

"Julian knows a chap who's trying to break the damn code."

"Yes, well. In the meantime, we've been instructed not to let a single painting leave this island. We're otherwise free to hide the paintings as we see fit. And we have the means to do it in no small measure thanks to your vision."

The first and last compliment my cousin gave me, but then I'm not looking for laurels.

*

The Nazis pummeled Cardiff as we were building out the mine. They were after the coal but on the way out decided to deconstruct the cathedral as well. We were 150 miles north in the snowy mountains, but it was sobering. What if the Nazi reach is indeed unstoppable?

I try not to think about that either. But clearly, I'm a failed cognitive didact.

*

I wear three pairs of socks to keep my feet from turning blue. Legacy of the trenches, but the cold and damp in Wales has tipped the balance. At night, we've blackouts, and thanks to Baron Von Hun and the fact that so many miners have signed up for service, there's precious little coal for the hearth. If Esther and Sophia knew, they'd be sending more socks, and instructing me to rub my feet with smelly ointment. They're more proactive about these things than I. My dear, good women.

I won't be surprised if women are allowed to go down and work in the mines soon. Children. That one man has caused this worldwide catastrophe. It still astounds.

*

When the train pulls into the station, I disembark, stepping around troops lining up for food—train stations these days being feeding posts—and I head straight to the quarry.

There, I make my way down the new wood staircase to a tunnel that smells like spoiled beer, earthy and sour. Carts have been set on old tracks and they've already begun to roll in paintings. A man who came up from London to oversee the load-in is showing me around. They've even set up a dorm with bunks where he's been sleeping. He's generous with his time, not that there's so much else for him to do right now.

Someone calls him over to advise on where in a brick house to put a painting, leaving me to wander through the mine alone. This is when I see the shadow of a man ahead of me, always ahead of me. He's painting, but there's no canvas. As we go, the mine fills with naked women, statues, and trees so dark they look black not green.

The man steps behind one of the carts and moves quickly toward the stairs. I hurry after him. He turns and looks at me, paintbrush in hand. It's Paul—Paul Delvaux! He's smiling and making a gesture as if to say, *Look what I've done.*

I turn to look at the quarry, and I see that all the women are skeletons.

For a moment, I can't breathe. Gasping, I turn back. But Paul is gone.

"Leo? Are you all right?"

It's my cousin.

"Oh yes. Needing a breather, that's all."

*

Outside, I suck in raw sulfurous air. It's damp, a sore throat in the making.

*

Delvaux isn't here. As far as I know, he's still in his studio in Brussels. Delvaux and Francois studied architecture together before the last war. And after, Delvaux began to paint. I used to go to his studio and watch him. He didn't mind and for me, it was pure pleasure. Better than going to the symphony, the ballet, even my beloved opera.

I remember one wet afternoon in winter, the rain was swashing down so the window looked like glass over a river.

"I have something to show you," Delvaux said.

It was a painting I hadn't seen before, not the one he was working on but another, unfinished, that he had put aside. The painting was of a woman and a man embracing or perhaps dancing in abstract surroundings that looked vaguely Delphic—a sort of garden, the deep blue of which might have been a sky. The man's back was to me, so I couldn't see his face, and he was wearing a dark jacket, but the woman was facing me. She was naked, and I could see her bare shoulder, the soft line between belly and thigh, an eye, strong nose, full lips. It affected me and I sat down.

"Not finished. I think this"—Delvaux pointed his brush end at the blue—"should be a room. And that"—he pointed at the garden—"should be viewed through the window."

"What window?"

"You can't see it yet, but it's there."

A month later, Delvaux stopped in with a thin square package.

"Open it," he urged.

It was the finished painting. Delvaux had made the deep blue a room as he said he would, but he'd added wainscoting, a pink bow fallen on the plank floor. The garden had faded into an autumn field and a naked girl sat in it playing a lute.

"The man is looking at their daughter," I said, pointing at the girl in the field.

"But she's not a child, is she? It's for you," he added.

"Only as a loan. I'll help you place it."

Delvaux laughed. He has a child's eyes and a man's forehead that swoops back on either side of the midline making his face a heart. I've heard his paintings are filled with skeletons these days. Like the ones I saw in the mine.

I did see the skeletons. Even though they weren't there.

As he left that afternoon, one hand on the door, Delvaux hesitated a moment. "Or he's looking for the woman of his life. His one love."

Delvaux had one love, and it wasn't his wife. Life is like that sometimes.

The next day, I came home from my office to find Charlotte in our hall looking at Delvaux's painting. She had come to see Esther and Julian. Charlotte is strange in the best way, and I love her almost as much as my own children. Sophia considers her to be one of the children. If Charlotte were a man, they'd call her a genius. Life is like that too.

"A friend painted that. What do you think?" I asked her.

"I feel it."

"What is the first thing you noticed?"

"The girl playing the lute."

This girl is so in the background I considered her a detail in the larger work. "Not the woman hugging the man?" I asked.

"They're the same," Charlotte said.

"What do you mean?"

"It's what it is to be in one place and also another. I think Father will appreciate it very much."

"He knows the painter," I told her. "They're old friends."

"That makes sense."

It comforts me to think of that conversation, because it, too, made sense, and I'm trying to remember everything that does.

JULIAN RAPHAËL, 4R

The fellows tell me they like the fact that I'm quiet. Given what I do on the plane, it's reassuring to them. The only thing they want me to tell them, other than the coordinates of us and the others and *them*, are the odds.

I never tell them the odds.

It isn't because I don't know them.

The boys talk about odds all the time. They banter about odds as if they know what they're saying and 99 times out of 100, they don't. Somehow this idea of 50/50 floated. I don't know where it came from. But everyone latched on to it, and I'm sad to say, it's dead wrong. I don't tell them this either.

The other day, we were climbing into the plane, and one of the boys who's organizing takeoffs and landings, he runs up and says, "Counting on you to beat the fifty/fifty."

You see how wrong it is? There's no such thing as beating odds, not really. We can't beat them. We're part of them. What happens to us will become part of the computation.

Let me be precise.

It would be correct to talk about odds over a number of occurrences, basic Bayesian probabilities, how to factor the likelihood of dying on a mission. So far, given the number of planes downed and crews dead or thought to be, the current odds are at best awful.

I wouldn't want to tell the fellows that, not as we're climbing to twelve or eighteen thousand feet, would I?

And the variable that's most difficult to factor in is the human dimension. Error. Acumen.

I want to believe that a great pilot and a great navigator and a great engineer can bring a plane home almost every time.

So, what do I say to the boys? I tell them our odds aren't the same as everyone else's. Because we're going to do this brilliantly.

It's a bit of a cheat.

Because of variables. Other planes. Engine failure. Instrument failure. A sudden storm. A surprise hit. Parachutes failing.

A friend of mine—from Cambridge—his plane was shot up and he ejected, but his fucking parachute didn't open and he died. Splat on a beach somewhere in France. Didn't have to happen. He could have had a running chance on that beach.

When I heard, I confess I raced over to the equipment people, and the words poured out of me. I didn't know what I was saying, but they seemed to get the upshot and then Blake, a crewman who grew up on a farm and worked with tractors before they sent him along to fly on the planes, pulled me out of there and dragged me to a pub.

"Don't add injury to insult," he advised, ordering another round— and another after that.

I like spending time with Blake. He has a colorful grasp on the English language, and he makes me laugh. He calls our sorties "taking a teapot out in a tempest."

I didn't wake up for a full eighteen hours after that, and when I did, I could feel the scratch of the wiry wool blanket on my face from where I'd been clutching it like a child. My tongue seemed to have grown a coat of fur.

Here's another confession. I don't like flying. Some of the fellows, they love it. They tell me they would do it if the odds were 90/10, not in our favor. I don't tell them that the odds are often 90/10 and not in our favor.

They like the speed on the runway.

It's all physics, all math. The properties of a plane. It's made to fly in the air, not crash on earth. Things made with the idea that they might crash on earth with people in them—cars or tanks or trucks—have a different weight-to-volume ratio. Metallic exoskeletons. Whereas a small fighter plane is about as resilient as a piñata when it crashes. The flying suitcase I go up in is a bit more solid. I should write Papa and tell him that.

Or they tell me they love the climb. I focus on my instruments during that climb. They have no understanding of how precarious it is. If we don't crash on the ascent, we'll be in good shape for the rest of the flight, barring a dogfight or an unforeseen bit of weather, both of which are somewhat likely.

Or they say they love the feeling of floating up there in the blue. Just . . . floating. It's as close to heaven as any of them want to get because they figure in heaven there will be no fucking and no drinking, and life will be like Sunday when you were eleven years old.

When I hear this, I can't help but feel I missed out on something to dread. Sunday. Yes, we had our Saturday, but we didn't do much about it—lighting candles the night before, no work, no cooking until after sundown, but that was no hardship, and there was otherwise little distinction between Saturday and every other day. Papa thinks religion is primitive, and he's not fond of holidays generally. He says it's because he loves his work, and you don't need a holiday from the thing you love. I can't disagree, because I haven't experienced enough to know for myself. There was a time when I would have liked something more to fight about with Papa. It's natural. Boys need to become men. Fighting is part of it. Papa's family was religious and part of his becoming a man was not being. Mama holds on to tradition. Maybe women are different. I don't know.

When we're up there, and all is calm, I'm thinking about things I'd rather not—gray planes darting about, wave-tossed gray boats fighting hidden enemies under pelagic waters, countless men on the ground with boots and guns and helmets, the people who've lost everything, the people lost, smoke rising from the camps. An intelligence fellow I know told me about the smoke. The higher-ups forbade him from talking about it, but he told me because I'm Jewish and he thought I should know.

Sometimes, up there, I try to remember a boy lying on his back looking at the sky and wondering if it goes on forever. And if it does, what lies beyond forever.

And of course, I think of Charlotte. I try not to, but that's never worked before, and it doesn't work now.

There is the question of what exists to be discovered and conversely what is invented to explain what exists. Wittgenstein and Turing had that big row over it—whether we mathematicians are discovering or inventing math, finding truth or imposing a system on what we see. Confounding enough even leaving aside the greater ontological question of the unseen. Of what lies beyond infinity.

How could I not think of Charlotte? If I were to argue that everything exists, and we have only to see it and to name it, well, then there's Charlotte. She sees what I see but differently, and she would choose other names, unknowingly throwing a wrench in both camps. She doesn't need to invent a system to explain her view. And she sees things no one else can. She told me her way of seeing is most akin to a pattern of light put through a lens that reorganizes itself on the other side. I think this is why she's uninterested in philosophy. It's a question of communication. If we can each explain what we see and understand, does it matter whether an idea existed before? Or who invented it?

I shouldn't have been cold to her that last week. I should have told Charlotte how I feel. I should have kissed her.

*

The other day, an intelligence officer pulled me in to headquarters for the purpose of discussing my role.

"What role?" I asked. "I make sure the pilot knows how to take off and fly and land. I'm telling him where we are and where everyone else is. I can't do more than that."

"It's good to know your limits," the officer said. "There's someone here to see you."

I immediately thought it was Papa, and he had come because something had happened to Mama or Esther. Or Charlotte.

A man stepped into the cramped room—not Papa. He was about my age, and he was looking at me with an amused expression on his face. I knew him. But I didn't. He had blond hair and was wearing spectacles, and I was thinking he should have dark hair and no spectacles, and how that was silly because I didn't know him.

He turned his profile to me, and once again I was certain I'd never seen him before in my life. Why then was he so familiar?

He turned back, took off the spectacles, looked me in the eye, and said, "Julian."

"Who are you?" I asked.

"Wonderful," the officer said. "Brilliant. Perfect. Couldn't be more pleased."

The man started laughing. He was laughing so hard he had to sit down, and again, I found there was something completely familiar about him.

"Julian," he said again. "It's Guy."

"Oh my God," I said, and then I was laughing too. I couldn't help it. And the officer was laughing, and Guy—my oldest friend, my childhood mate—was laughing even harder. We were laughing like we might never laugh again, and the fact is we might not.

"What did they do to you?" I choked out, and then I sat beside him. I was laughing too much to stay on my feet.

"Carved me up a bit."

"Was it an accident?"

Guy was roaring. "Does it look like a bloody accident?"

"A very tidy one," I said.

"I don't have accidents," he said. "Remember the mortar?"

"Mortar?"

"Yes, mortar."

That was when an air raid siren went off. We shut up and hurried to the basement.

"I'm working with the SOE," Guy whispered.

"Of course you are." The Special Operations Executive or "SOE" being the elite spy bureau Churchill recently set up.

"They can't know I'm Jewish," Guy said.

"The SOE can't know?"

"No, no, no. The Nazis."

Someone had flicked on the lights and we could see each other better. Guy was looking critically at my face.

"Turn sideways."

"What?"

"You're lucky," he said. "That you have a pug nose."

"I do not have a pug nose."

"Do you remember what my nose looked like?"

"Is that why they wanted me to see you? So you could decide if I need a nose job?"

"They figured if the smartest guy in the RAF who has known me all my life couldn't recognize me, no one would."

"Well," I said. "Glad to be of service. But why bob your nose?"

"I was captured, you see. I had this with me," he pulled a book out of his pocket. A copy of Stendahl's *The Red and the Black*. "Turned out it was my guard's favorite book. And that was the tip of our common iceberg. We talked every day. Wonderful chap. Don't make that face. You'd love him."

"He's German."

"Yes," Guy said. "And I can imagine his friend right now is saying the same about me. 'He's a Jew!'"

"No," I said. "Because he can't risk saying a kind word about you."

"More true than you know. He heard that another guard had figured out I was Jewish. The nose gave me away. My fellow risked his life to help me. I won't go into the nitty-gritty, but I was on the run, and they were shooting, and do you know what saved my ass?"

"No."

Guy turned the book over, and I saw the bullet hole in the back cover.

"Life is a series of accidents and miracles," Guy said.

*

Mortar. It came back to me as I was strapping in the plane.

When we were boys, Guy and I would dare each other to do something we thought no one had done. I never saw Guy turn down a dare. No matter how dangerous or foolish.

It was winter. Not a snowy day, but frigid. We were outside in the courtyard at Number 33—Guy, Dirk, some other boys, and me. Mama had taken Esther to her music lesson, and the apartment was empty. I had pulled one of the metal bins out of the basement, and we put a fire in it to warm our hands. Guy touched the wall and said it was warm and that was dangerous. We moved the can out, but Guy kept his hand on the wall. He was fiddling with it. I noticed that Dirk was watching him too. Dirk was an odd duck. He had told Guy he was an orphan, but when Guy saw Dirk with parents, Dirk changed his story and said he was adopted. I never knew if he was telling the truth about anything, but I always invited him to join us. Mama had taught me to include everybody, that it was the only way the world would become a better place, and I always thought Dirk was all right.

We couldn't have been more than ten or eleven. Twelve maybe. Boys. Stupid boys.

Upstairs, I could see Charlotte at her window looking down at us. Charlotte was always game to do things, and I could tell she wanted to join us.

I motioned at her to open the window. She did.

"Wait there," I called up. "And keep the window open."

Then I gave Guy the dare.

"Guy," I said. "I dare you to walk from my bedroom to Charlotte's."

Guy shrugged. He looked amused, as if to say, *What kind of dare is that? Child's play!*

"Outside," I said. There's a stone ledge on every level in the building that's at most two inches wide. The window ledges are deeper, but there's a good distance between windows.

"What do you mean outside?" Guy looked a bit less cocky.

"Go out my window, walk along the ledge to Charlotte's window, and then go in through it."

Guy looked up at the building and assessed. "Is her father home?"

"Not yet. In your underwear," I added quickly.

"That will be the least of my problems." Guy turned, jogged to the back door of the building, and went inside.

From where we stood, we could see him running up the stairs. At every landing, Guy pressed his face against the window and smashed that nose of his to one side. It was a macabre sight. I think he was showing us how he might look when all this was over. I was getting cold feet. So, when he got to my room, I shouted up, "I was joking. Never mind."

"Never you mind," Guy called back, stripping off his jacket, his shirt, his pants, and his shoes.

Guy jumped up and down. He stretched his arms. And then he climbed out the window, letting his body drop so his toes could find the ledge.

"It's perfect."

"Never mind," I repeated.

"Careful. Don't distract him. You won't stop him now."

It was Dirk who said it. His eyes were fixed on Guy.

My stomach became a churning acid bath. What if Guy fell? Died? What would Papa say? Charlotte would hate me forever.

I love Charlotte. This is the trouble. It's why I haven't found some other girl.

Guy began to scoot across the ledge, holding tightly to my bedroom windowsill. There's a good eight feet between my window and the kitchen window, then twice that distance between our kitchen window and Charlotte's kitchen window. And so forth.

I started to call out again, but Dirk put his hand on my shoulder and said, "It's more dangerous for him to go back at this point."

He left his hand there as if to comfort me and together we watched Guy move along the outside of the building, He had something stuck in the band of his underwear. It was Papa's oyster-shucking knife. Guy reached the edge of the windowsill, and, holding tightly with one hand, he took out the knife with the other hand and dug into the wide strip of mortar that was in a line with the window ledge. A big chunk fell to the courtyard where we stood.

"Hey!" one of the boys shouted.

Guy was laughing. He used the hole in the mortar as a handhold, and it got him to the next windowsill. He did this all along the side of the building until he reached Charlotte's window. Guy climbed in, and she slammed it shut behind him. But not before shouting down to us, "That was really stupid, and if Guy were any less smart, he might have died."

I felt like such a fool. I walked over to where Guy had been standing earlier, when we'd lit the trash-bin fire, and saw that he had been picking at the loose mortar in the wall. Dirk saw it too.

And this is why Guy is in the SOE, and I'm strapping into a glorified flying bucket readying my instruments.

CITY OF BRUSSELS

29 May 1942

German Military Authority Ordinance Regarding the Jews.

The Secretary General of the Ministry of the Interior of Public Health, under the authority of the German military, urgently demands the municipalities to publish the following notification:

The wearing of the Yellow Star is obligatory for all Jews six years of age and older.

Jews are required to register at the registry for Jews.

Jewish-owned hotels, restaurants, and cafés must register their businesses and post notices in accordance with municipal rules.

The Bourgmeister
DFG Van Maalbeek

FRANCOIS SAUVIN, 4L

I dream I design a garden that is a building and a building that is a garden. No one knows which is which—there's no inside and no outside. Only life. Everyone is crying tears of joy. I see rounded corners and soft landings. Feather beds and moss carpets. People sit in open spaces where they discuss ideas and politics without coming to blows. Staircases on hills and hills of staircases, and I climb on and on for the pleasure of the views.

"Dwell in my house," I say to each person I pass.

They smile at me through their tears. And I know my name will be remembered.

*

The truth is, I've lost all ambition. It happens at a certain age. You forget why you wanted more, and you don't even know what *more* means. There is only one question—do I live or die?

*

When the millinery shop where Charlotte worked designing hats was forced to shut, she took a sewing job in a factory that makes uniforms for train conductors and the like near the Gare du Midi in Saint-Gilles. The factory's owner happens to be Jewish. Or he *was* Jewish. Hopefully *is*.

Charlotte told me he was taken to the Nazi headquarters on Avenue Louise to be questioned and didn't return. Charlotte had been at the factory almost a year at that point. Now a Flemish man known to be a senior member of the Vlaamsch Nationaal Verbond or VNV, the Flemish party supporting the Nazi occupiers, is running the factory.

Charlotte saw the stars in the factory—not stars in the firmament. Stars meant to be sewn on clothes.

Charlotte didn't know they were yellow; she knew only that they were meant for all people of Jewish descent. This was in late April. She told me they were piled in boxes outside the factory manager's office. And then they disappeared. A little after that, we all saw them, on coats and jackets and shirts.

In my firm, there are two Jewish architects—David and Albert. And two Catholic architects—Jean and Christophe. And then there's me. Who was who or what was what—that's not something we ever discussed or considered. We design buildings. We aren't ideologues. At least, I didn't think we were. And we've gotten along for years. Each one of my architects has a different talent. I put the group together based only on that and because I have professional respect for them all.

I call the meeting on a spring morning in Brussels, one of those days that gives you the mistaken hope that summer is soon to arrive instead of the usual month or two of cool air and drizzle. The trees in our office courtyard are in late bloom, color faded, barely pink.

We sit on benches. A breeze kicks up, and I feel spray on my cheek from the fountain. How can everything be so bleak in this paradise I have created for us?

My colleagues sense we're about to discuss a serious matter, but then everything's serious these days. You can't make jokes about what's happening. People try, but it's stupid.

It's my obligation to tell them, these men I've worked with for years, about the stars. David and Albert and Christophe know about them. As for Jean—he's the most absent-minded person I know. It's a miracle he gets to work and home in a day. He's always got his notebook open, a pencil in hand, and he pays no attention to his surroundings. He's a dear mess of a human. At one time, I thought he might be a good man for Charlotte, but now I know better, and anyway, Charlotte's married to Philippe, so there you are.

Jean had no idea about the stars; he hadn't heard. He looks ill as he listens to what I have to say. He can't drink his coffee, and he steps away to take a cigarette alone. We wait in awkward silence for him to return and when he does, we carry on. It's a shameful conversation, dirtying all of us, and yet I know it pales in comparison to the horrors people elsewhere are enduring.

I tell them I won't comply. I won't make anyone wear a star. Not here.

"The alternative," I add, "is we all wear the damn things."

To my shock, David is furious with me.

"We have to go along with it, or we won't be able to feed our families."

"They're marking people," I say.

Albert agrees with me. "I'm ready to go underground," he says.

"Easy for you," David tells him. "You don't have children. Or a wife."

The Catholics are likewise split.

"We must carry on," Christophe says. "The Germans aren't devils. Think of Georg Falck. Richard Scheibner. Great architects. Germans."

"Both Jewish," David says. "And one of them has already disappeared. In a camp most likely."

We're all quiet a moment after that.

The most painful complexity is David. We are collaborative, and we work as a team. A few months ago, David asked for his name, and his alone, to be on a project.

"We aren't Communists. That project was my idea. Not yours, not Christophe's. Mine," he said.

In truth, the original idea was Jean's.

And now, David is pacing around the courtyard. He's furious with everything and everybody, most of all himself. I understand and I don't understand—and I realize there's a limit to empathy.

"It's our decision at the end of the day," he says.

"Of course, yes."

I add that there probably won't be much work, other than for the Nazis. I realize I'm echoing Leo as I say this.

"What's wrong with working for Nazis?" Christophe asks. "And you know perfectly well if we're inspected by the party and the Jews aren't wearing their yellow stars—"

"Not my yellow star—" Albert says.

"We'll be shut down," Christophe finishes. He's staring hard at Albert.

"I'll leave the firm if that makes you feel better," Albert says.

"It does," Christophe says.

How is this possible? How can these people, my colleagues, my friends, how can they disagree about something so fundamental?

"No, no!" Jean says. "We're all in this together."

"I would feel more comfortable if you both left the firm," Christophe tells David and Albert.

"Why don't you leave," I say to Christophe. "In fact, why don't you leave now. Immediately."

Christophe looks at Jean, who's leaning against the wall with his eyes squeezed shut.

"Jean?" Christophe asks.

"Get the hell out," Jean tells him without opening his eyes.

*

A week after our meeting, the firm is shut down by the authorities for noncompliance with the new building codes.

"What building codes?" Jean asks me.

"That the foundation of every structure be constructed on a lie," I tell him.

Albert promises he'll stay in touch. He's going to the south of France. "It's the only place people like me can put up a real fight," he says.

I tell him to look out for my son-in-law. "I don't know where he is, and I'm not supposed to know anything. But I've no doubt he's fighting."

David leaves without a word. It's the last time I see him.

That afternoon, I ride the tram to the Palais de Justice and get out, taking in the view for a moment before I walk down, choosing my route with intention—I haven't been in this part of the city in months—following the cobbled Rue de Rollebeek, flanked by fifteenth-century houses, some timbered, some with stair-step rooflines, all too ornate for my taste but something to behold nonetheless. The faint stench of sewage floats up from old drains as I continue to the Grand-Place. My leg aches when I reach it, the pain rising to my chest when I see the square filled with military vehicles—trucks and cars—and soldiers, some on horseback. And for the second time in my life, I can see a German flag flying from the town hall, though this flag is more menacing and sinister than the one that flew there a little over twenty years ago. It's small solace that Saint Michael is still slaying his dragon at the top of the lantern tower.

I have an urge to talk to Leo, to tell him. My old friend.

I walk along the edge of the Grand-Place and head north for a block or two before beginning my ascent to the upper city, my leg unstable as a bad tooth, and this is when I hear the music. It sounds like it's coming from above and when I look up at the clouds, I see every instrument in them and even walking I can't take my eyes off those cloud instruments. The sound of the playing grows louder, and I'm thinking how odd it is that the music is anything but heavenly, not what you'd expect from clouds. I hear the squawk of a saxophone and I look straight ahead expecting to see Dirk standing in front of me on the sidewalk. But instead, I see a group of players circled around the fountain in front of the Hotel Metropole and now I'm sure it's an hallucination and I want to tell Leo this too. But then I notice the uniforms—the hats, the jodhpurs, the boots. Dirk is not among them. I register a small sign—LUFTWAFFE ORCHESTRA. I quickly turn and walk up the hill. What a joke. To call that oompah band with its Octoberfest chorus an orchestra. Reaching the Rue Royale, I continue along the edge of the park where chestnut trees are in magnificent bloom, and I pass Leo's office. The big double doors are chained, the windows are shut tight, but I would swear I see a light on.

*

In the evening, I stop by the Colonel's for a drink. I sink onto his garish chintz sofa with a generous glass of whiskey in hand. Never let it be said that the Colonel is an abstemious pourer.

"I'm officially out of business," I tell him.

It takes the Colonel a moment.

"My firm," I say.

"Oh. I'm surprised you lasted this long," he says, a knowing grimace on his face as he right away tops up my drink. He sits across from me on a floral print chair that's undoubtedly meant to go with the sofa but doesn't, and I recount the story.

"Why don't you give me this Albert's telephone number," he says.

"He may already have left."

"You never know. Please. I insist!"

The Colonel's wife was Jewish. He doesn't talk about her much, but the other night, when I took some beer to him, he said, "It's a blessing she died before all this. It would have been a living hell for her one way or another. She didn't take things lightly, you know," he added with a chuckle.

*

Today, Martin DeBaerre, the lawyer from downstairs, pays me a visit and asks if we can take a stroll and smoke a pipe. The spring air is soft and you almost forget that the city's occupied. Or I do.

"I've been supporting a family. No one must know about it," Martin begins as he knocks his pipe against a tree to empty it. He refills it with a fresh bit of tobacco, strikes a match on the sidewalk stone, lights up, then offers me the first puff. "Can I trust you?" he asks.

"Trust me to what?" Tobacco enters my passages giving me a dizzying sensation.

"Not to tell."

"I won't tell a soul."

"You might have to tell the right soul. Can I drop off an envelope?"

"Of course."

"Should anything happen to me, you must give it to the baker in the square. Maryanne. The stout woman—"

"I know her."

This is a surprise. Again, my world divides. You can never predict who will do what.

"Give it to her when no one is around. Please. Off hours. I've observed that midafternoons on Saturdays are slow in the bakery. Please," he repeats.

"Yes, but I hope it won't come to that."

We've made one tour around the square and clouds have assembled in the sky. It's beginning to sprinkle, so we go inside.

A few minutes later, Martin is at my door with the envelope.

"Might I step in a moment?"

"Of course. Please."

He waits for me to shut the door. I indicate the table.

"Only a moment."

"No rush. I'm turning my hand at making beer, with hops instead of barley. An old friend grows the hops. I get the beet sugar from Maryanne."

"I see."

"Would you care to try it?"

"I'm not much of a drinker but please, you go ahead."

I pour a beer for myself, and Martin recounts the conversation he had with his son, Dirk, the day before. I suppose he's explaining why he's giving the envelope to me and not his son. Or his wife for that matter.

"Dirk says life is for the strong. But he's living off me, not earning his keep. You see the point."

I tell him I do.

"I changed my mind," Martin says.

"About?"

"I'd like that beer after all."

I fetch another glass and fill it with a modest sense of accomplishment seeing the rich amber liquid capped with a thick head of foam.

Martin takes a sip, savoring it like a condemned man. "Excellent," he says, then continues, "Dirk went on to tell me that we can't stand still in the wave of history. If we do, it will sweep us under. And so, we must ride it. I asked him, 'Then why aren't you riding this wave? Off fighting with the other big, brave lads?' He was furious. He stomped out not finishing his breakfast, which is something because the boy likes to eat. The rations might be the death of him."

"They might be the death of us all."

"And my wife is blind."

"I had no idea."

"Not here." He points to his eyes. "Here." He points to his heart. "She doesn't see what she's done to the boy. Raising him in this situation."

I don't ask him what situation that is. I'll listen to what he wants to tell me.

"Dirk stayed out all day. My wife was frantic, sure he'd been conscripted. She told me if so, it was my fault. My fault? Ha! I told her it might do Dirk good. He's fat and could use a little exercise. I'm joking of course. It will do no one good to fight on the side of the Nazis. 'My son is brilliant,' she said. 'Brilliant?' I asked. 'You don't see it because you aren't,' she told me. Even after that, I tried to reassure her, I told her that Dirk would be back. He'd plant himself on our sofa and play that infernal saxophone and she'd wish he had signed up for the army."

Martin is laughing now.

"But it didn't end there. She told me I had never understood Dirk, who has *imagination*. I told her Dirk should imagine some food and money, so we'd have enough to feed him. Oh, she was furious. She asked where all *my* money was going. I told her I didn't know what she was talking about. And of course, that's precisely when Dirk re-turned home from his little outing, unharmed and without a word of explanation for his poor mother. He plunked down on the sofa and began to play."

"That was yesterday?"

"Yes."

"I heard him."

"It's not that Dirk is for the new regime, but I can't say he's against it either."

We sip our beers in silence.

"I never liked the saxophone. Trumpet, piano, clarinet. Give me any one of those. But not the saxophone," Martin says sadly.

"The instrument asserts itself."

"He's unbearable. I don't know what's gotten into him. I told my wife, 'Nazis or no Nazis, I'll kick him out if he continues like this.' My wife thinks he needs to go to church. Church!"

Martin finishes his beer and gets up to leave.

"What sort of god protects his creation from the knowledge of evil?" I ask abruptly.

"No idea. But then, I don't believe in any god."

*

The smell set in soon after. Sharp. Rotting. Feces and urine, ammoniac, flesh turned pudding in bodies medics can't decamp, an odor that lines my nostrils like skin on an old fish. I can't get rid of it.

I look for a dead mouse or rat that got itself stuck under a cupboard or a piece of furniture.

Last night, I checked my body in the bath, wondering if I'd over-looked a festering wound. Nothing.

This morning, I ask Charlotte if she's well. If she has any malady or injury.

"No." She looks at me with curiosity, her breath sweet as milk.

Fickle, capricious, the smell wanes and intensifies with no logic, giving me visions of men wasting to skeletons, of meat falling from bones in yellow curds. The smell is always there.

Only the beer sends it away.

*

Charlotte was eight years old, and she'd had a nightmare and couldn't sleep.

"I want Masha," she demanded.

"It's the middle of the night. You can see her in the morning."

A moment went by in silence.

"Why don't I have a mother?"

"You do."

"You know what I mean."

She was angry. Would she have been less angry if I had married again? To a good woman?

During the last war, a soldier in another unit had his privates blown off. The story circulated around the troops, as the most awful stories did, but this one was true, and I've often thought of that man. How he lived. How he managed. For a time after Charlotte's mother died, I thought I might as well have been that man. Mine were hanging about, useless and unused. I had a dream that Charlotte asked if I ever had sex. "There's an operation," she said, "Do you need it?" But it wasn't me and finally I was on the telephone to the doctor who explained if I wasn't in a state of erection at the time of the operation, there was nothing he could do.

I've been with women since my wife died. I have needs. But fewer and fewer. I'm reconciled to that.

Charlotte's hair was clinging to her forehead and the well in her pillow was damp. I fetched another pillow and a clean case.

"Leave the light on," she ordered.

"As long as you're awake."

"You go to sleep too."

"All in good time."

She was still angry with me, or with her dream, or with her mother, Emilie. I remember telling Sophia that Charlotte's middle name is Emilie and seeing a look of pain on her face. Sophia was thinking maybe it was the naming that killed my wife—the idea that only one of them could live. Sophia is superstitious that way.

"Once there was a garden."

"Whose garden?" Charlotte asked imperiously.

"It belonged to itself."

"That's strange."

"Oh yes. This garden was a most unusual garden. And in it, there was one of each of the most exquisite flowers ever to grace the earth."

"Are there flowers on other planets?"

"I don't know, darling, but I doubt it."

"What about Mars?"

"Possibly."

"I thought you doubted it."

"This garden," I continued, "was not on Mars."

Charlotte lay back on the fresh pillow and closed her eyes. It had become harder to tell her stories. She had more questions.

"What made this garden so unusual and so delightful were the smells that came from the flowers, at once similar and yet distinctive. As were their shapes and sizes. Anyone who saw them would wonder why those shapes were not seen everywhere. Why windows and doors and rooftops were not in those shapes."

"What about hats?"

"Hats too. Anyone who stepped into the garden would take a deep breath and inhale the wild mix of perfumes and see those shapes that were in perfect harmony. The tall slender flowers in the back of the beds, the short round ones in the front, and explosions of delicate lace joining the two and making it a whole. There weren't only flowers in the garden. There were spiders. Grasshoppers. Even sea creatures in their shells that rolled in when the tide was high."

"Was the garden next to the sea, then?"

"Yes of course, darling. All the beautiful things are next to the sea."

"Why don't we live next to the sea?"

"A very good question . . . The creatures and the flowers in this garden knew one another. They would say good morning and good evening, quite politely too. The spiders would nibble on the aphids that tried to attach to blooms."

"What are aphids?"

"Tiny insects that suck the life out of flowers and destroy their beauty."

"Ah."

"All the plants and creatures lived together in harmony. But one day . . ."

I could see Charlotte snuggle down and smile. She had been waiting for something to happen. Aren't we all?

"One day a woman came to the garden and cut some of the flowers and took them away. This strange assortment of friends, the only kinds to have, followed her. They were a remarkably fast-moving lot for a couple of mollusks, a spider, and a grasshopper. They snuck into the woman's house and watched her put the flowers in a vase of water."

"But wasn't that selfish? She had to kill the flowers to do it."

"People are selfish, darling. That isn't the point. And she gave them water so they didn't suffer as much as they might have. The next morning, the woman came down and she saw a remarkable sight. There was a spider on one of the blooms that was shaped like a web, and there were two shells at the base of the vase. *How beautiful*, she thought, and she called her friend the artist to paint the tableau. So, you see, the flowers and their friends lived longer than they would have. And many people saw them."

"You mean the Raphaëls see them and anyone who goes in their apartment."

"Sometimes they send the painting to museums."

"But it always comes back?"

"Always."

"Esther told me everything in the painting but the flowers is in gray tones and that's why I see it so well."

"Esther is perceptive."

"She wants to be a nurse."

"It makes all the sense in the world."

"I don't want to be a nurse. I want to paint beautiful things that will last forever. Even after all the people we know are dead. But I would have painted the flowers in the garden. There was no need to take them away."

CHARLOTTE SAUVIN, 4L

This morning on my walk from the tram to the factory where I've worked for nearly two years, I see a woman selling bread. She has more children than seems possible. All of them are young and thinning with too-large eyes and too-small clothes, and I wonder why they aren't in school. Are children going to school? I realize I have no idea. Everything has changed so fast. This is not how I imagined November 1942. I should have finished my degree at the academy by now. Philippe and I should be living in a flat or a little house somewhere. England. But England is still being bombed by the Nazis. A few weeks ago, a boy's school in Sussex was hit with three bombs thought to be intended for Canadian troops housed nearby. The Nazis claim the English are using civilians to shield troops. The English say the Nazis did it on purpose to undermine civilian morale. But the fact is, when you drop bombs from the sky, you're never sure who will be killed on the earth.

I hear a door shut and look to see Mr. DeDecker, the factory manager, stepping out of a run-down apartment building. He's shapeless, a dirty puddle of a man I avoid. He's carrying a large satchel and as he steps away from the door, he looks up. A woman with a face as sharp as a peeling knife is leaning out the window and blowing a kiss down to him.

And these are the people who have power over me now, I think. I'm surprised they live in such a squalid place.

I walk fast up the sidewalk, hoping DeDecker hasn't seen me. Reaching the corner, I look back to see that the woman in the window has disappeared into the apartment, and DeDecker is talking to the bread seller, who's crying as she hands him loaves. All her loaves. DeDecker is stuffing loaves in his satchel, and he doesn't give her a penny. He glances in my direction, as though sensing I'm watching. I turn and run all the way to work.

*

I'm settling in at my sewing machine on the factory floor when DeDecker approaches my station. He stands close enough that I smell egg on his breath. He watches as I put in a new spool, thread the needle, and begin to sew a jacket.

"There's a loose thread." He points to the exposed inside of the jacket back.

"I haven't trimmed the threads yet."

"It's too long. Wasteful. Thread's at a premium. Follow me."

DeDecker turns and walks to his office at the end of the factory floor. I follow, feeling the eyes of my fellow workers on me as I step inside, and he bangs the door shut behind me.

He doesn't sit at his desk. He stands next to me. Burnt eggs.

"I saw you today. Were you buying bread illegally?"

"No. But you were taking bread illegally."

I've overstepped but I see a flicker of vulnerability on his face. He was planning to keep the bread.

"I may have to let you go," he says with a big sigh.

I step back.

"We have workers in Poland and Germany who are more efficient."

"Who has workers there?"

"The company."

"But this is a Belgian company."

"Not exactly. Wartime." He steps closer.

I move to the other side of the messy office—piles of papers everywhere. Germans are neat. Someone should report DeDecker. He should report himself. The satchel, stuffed with loaves of bread, is in a corner.

He sees where I'm looking. "Evidence. Reporting her," he says briskly.

"Better not eat the evidence," I say.

He's angry now. And smiling.

"We may be conscripting workers."

"Women?"

"Possibly."

Still smiling—it must hurt to force a smile for so long. He's taking his time. Giving me time to think. There's only one window, and it looks over the factory floor. I can see the workers glancing at me as they sew.

DeDecker yanks down the window shade.

"We're laying people off and you're on the list."

I don't need to think.

"Thank you for letting me know." I step to the door.

He steps in front of me.

"I understand how difficult it is. When your father isn't working."

"Who told you that?"

"Word travels."

"We're fine."

"I have an idea."

He puts his hand on mine.

I pull my hand back.

"I might be able to arrange for a promotion. Otherwise, I'll give your name to the labor authorities. We're also sending people to Germany. To work in factories. We find their efficiency improves after being sent to the homeland."

"I didn't know you were German."

"I'm not."

We stand there in angry silence.

Finally, he says, "Very well. You've expressed a clear preference to travel abroad—"

"I'm pregnant."

DeDecker stares at my bare ring finger.

"We couldn't afford a ring. We married before he went off to fight."

"Conscripted?" he asks.

"It's only a matter of time before we all are, don't you think?"

My hand curls around the door handle and begins to turn it.

"You're sure? That you're pregnant?" He puts his hand on my stomach, blasting me again with that breath.

This is when I vomit. Without warning, it spews out of me, hitting his wool vest, running down his trousers, and spattering his dusty shoes. Unintentional. But also, I mean to do it.

DeDecker jumps back, pulls out a dirty handkerchief, dabs at the wet, sticky mess. The handkerchief is useless.

"You wouldn't want anyone to know you propositioned a pregnant officer's wife. Would you? I'll be leaving the company immediately. And I won't report the bread. Unless I'm forced."

Pushing open the door, I run out.

*

Throwing everything that's mine in my basket, my hand hovers over a spool of dark thread and then moves to the stainless-steel bobbin that has almost as much thread as the spool. Flat, round. I could tuck it in my undergarments or knot my hair around it.

My next paycheck will not come unless the punch cards are processed in another more central place where DeDecker can't intervene. The Nazis are using American technology for the cards—some kind of counting machine.

"If efficiency were a horse race," Father said the other day as he peeled potatoes, "the Nazis are running neck and neck with the Americans, and they've both lapped the Belgians twice."

DeDecker has raised his office shade and he's watching me. I leave spool and bobbin in the machine. I lift a stray thread from my skirt and ceremoniously lay it on the sewing machine.

How does DeDecker know Father's not working? If he knows

that, he could find out I'm not married to an officer. I should have said *soldier*. Philippe is French. Are any French soldiers fighting for the Nazis?

Not officer. *Soldier.*

Who would ask? Germans? Belgians? What's the difference?

Six loaves of bread. No one will care about that, and now he'll probably report the poor woman who made them.

Basket in hand, I make my exit, head high, chin up, stepping over fabric scraps and around baskets, passing women at their machines. I reach the station of my one almost friend in the place, a girl called Beatrice—spun-candy hair, a large mouth with an unfortunate tendency to sneer when she's not smiling. She grew up in a coal-mining family in Charleroi. She came to Brussels for work.

Beatrice leaps up from her station, gives me an impulsive hug, and whispers, "I'm next, don't you know? DeDecker doesn't like me either."

"He doesn't like me?"

"He thinks you're full of yourself."

I didn't know.

The hug makes me feel trapped and uncomfortable. I'll never see Beatrice again. Why waste time on her? Unless she can help me. Father tells me we're all trying to stay human. I will care for myself, for Father, for my unborn child—for Philippe, if I ever see him again.

"Careful of DeDecker," I whisper to Beatrice in a wave of unwanted emotion.

"I'm not afraid. I know his wife. She and my mother are from the same town. How do you think I got the job?"

"He has bread in his office. Six loaves."

Why did I tell her that? She knows his wife. They're probably friends.

"His wife thinks he's taking food to a lover. If she finds out he is, she'll destroy his reputation with the party. The VNV."

I can see DeDecker still peering at me through the window.

"How?"

"He's been stealing from them. The VNV."

"I saw her this morning. His wife," I say.

"Where?"

Beatrice is still wrapped around me like a monkey.

"Their apartment, just down the street."

Beatrice pulls back and looks at me with that sneer. "But they live in Anderlecht."

Bless Beatrice. Bless the sneer. Bless her mother. Bless the coal.

I give her a last hug. "Tell his wife she'll find what she's looking for two blocks from here," and I whisper the name of the street where I saw DeDecker stepping out of another woman's apartment.

I escape the embrace and hurry across the factory floor, down the stairs, and outside. What else but to return to Number 33?

*

"Can you imagine? We used to shop," a woman is saying. "For amusement."

I'm in the tram line. It's mist that's dampened my face. I'm not crying.

I notice the woman's dress—altered to have a tighter waist and bigger shoulders. Fashion wants us to look like soldiers. The hem has been let down and Masha would tell me the tailor who did it is a hack because the alteration is visible.

"Everything is an illusion," Masha told me. "We hide flaws to create perfection. It is a question of what is unseen but exists and what doesn't exist but is seen."

*

People are selling possessions:

Boch Frères elephant vase, cloisonné

Italian men's shoes, leather

Patek Philippe watch, gold

Victor Horta drawings, pen and ink

But who's buying? Nazis take what they want. People who had money have lost it. People with any money left bury it in cellars, sew it into clothes, slip it under loose floor tiles.

We have no money to hide and not much to sell.

Father has a friend who grows hops and has sheep.

By the time the tram arrives, the mist has turned to a soft rain, dampening my clothes. The woman with the altered dress steps ahead and takes the last seat. An old woman reaches for the overhead strap as the tram lurches ahead. No one offers her a seat.

I brush droplets off my leather bag. As Father says, we're lucky to be in a place where there will always be good air and plenty of water. All other necessities have become luxuries. Soap. Food. Medicine. You can't imagine until it happens, how you can have plenty—not too much, but enough—and then nothing, forcing you to think about everything.

How to make the soap last. A candle. Butter.

The tram hurtles toward Avenue Louise. Through the dirty windows, I see the rows of brick and stone houses lining the treeless street, each house different from the next. Father once said that despite being a city with no architectural continuity, Brussels has pulled off the impossible, managing to look at once whimsical and bleak.

"The efficiency of Rome and the beauty of Manchester," Father told Philippe shortly before he left.

"There was an old woman in Brussels . . ." Philippe began.

He and Father raised their glasses at this.

"Who lived on brandy and mussels . . . When she rushed through the town, she knocked most people down . . ."

The tram screeches to an uneven stop, and I feel another wave of sick. I push forward. It's no time to vomit—or faint.

I step down to the street, take a deep breath as the tram rattles away, and walk the few short blocks to catch the corresponding tram home. The rain has stopped. Wet, clingy fog makes my throat hurt. What can you expect from a city where the river, too, has been forced to hide underground?

Must drink hot water. No lemons. No honey. The sick is a sign. Vomiting. A good sign.

I haven't let myself think of the baby. It's too much. I cross the wide avenue to avoid passing the Nazi headquarters. Miss Hobert claims the gestapo has a torture chamber in the basement. From the relative safety of the other side, I glance at the plain art deco building. Father describes it as a building without a soul, and he thinks that's why the Nazis were drawn to it. *As if buildings have souls,* I think. But Father and Philippe are both convinced some do, that the architect's soul inhabits a great building, and that's why it lasts and is remembered.

One thing I'm sure of, this building, a final stopping place for Jews and those who haven't learned the art of stepping aside or who were caught sidestepping, does not have a soul.

I turn the corner, my heart pounding as if the gestapo might see me on the street and pull me in for questioning.

Are you really married?

Yes.

Is your husband an officer?

Yes. No. I'm not sure.

In what division?

And this is where I would stumble. I would struggle for the right term. I would die before I would tell them about Philippe. Husband. Jew. Parachutist. SAS.

I feel the flush on my cheeks, from the walking, the nausea, the anxiety.

There's an open wooden seat on the next tram, and I take it as the car jolts up the avenue toward Number 33.

*

I saw Philippe a few months ago. I'm carrying his child. Will it look like Philippe? I try to remember his chin. The curve of his hand. The length of his earlobe. He has no idea I'm pregnant.

*

I hurry past Smets's shop and then remember we need endives. I turn back and step inside, feeling a wave of warm stuffy air. There's a short line today and when I reach the counter, I hold out my tickets and ration card and four endives.

"Ah," Smets says in Flemish. "Prices go up, up, up, but supplies go down, down, down. The tickets must be supplemented."

At first, I don't understand, and I have that feeling of being stuck in a dream I must fight my way out of, but instead I seem to go deeper in, and the fact that I know I'm going deeper means that I might never find my way out.

Don't cry. You have no right.

I put a hand on the counter for support.

"No, no! Dirty!" Smets sweeps my hand off the counter.

"You need more tickets?"

Smets rubs index finger on thumb, "*Handelszink*," he says.

It's the Flemish word for the occupation government's zinc coins.

"I gave you tickets."

Smets shrugs slowly, as if to underscore the fact that without something more, I won't get what I need.

"That's not right," I say.

"Right. What's right?"

I pull out my coin purse and give Smets the coins. I drop the endive in my bag and leave the shop.

*

"You look tired, dear. Pale." Maryanne takes my ticket.

"I've lost my job."

She gives me a larger chunk of bread than she should.

"Thank you," I say.

"Drink some hot tea and turn in early," she says.

No more going to the factory. It's a relief and a catastrophe.

*

The newsboy is in his usual spot. In the glow from the cigarette butt clenched in his mouth, I see his nose is running. As I approach, the boy tosses the cigarette in the gutter. He coughs, a rough cough.

"One copy of *Le Soir*, please."

The newsboy nods. He adjusts his cap—even more moth-eaten than a year ago—wipes snot with sleeve, and takes out the newspaper. I lean in to take it, and he whispers, "He's alive. England. Parachuting, probably Ringway, lucky bloke."

"Thank you." I hand him coins, tears welling in relief.

No crying.

I stick an endive in the boy's bag and consider giving him another but decide against it. Best to control expectations. I might not have anything next time.

A soldier is strolling toward us. I nod briskly to the newsboy and walk away.

He can't be more than eleven, this boy. Dutch courage incarnate, he's a Flem, and he's been handing out copies of the resistance paper, *La Libre Belgique*, right along with *Le Soir*, daring for a boy from Anderlecht whose father is a proud member of the VNV and, according to the Colonel, known to routinely tip off the gestapo at 453 Avenue Louise.

Just last week, Father said, "Boys like him don't come along every day, that's certain. Too many of these Flemish boys have flipped around the other way and begun to salute alongside the Huns."

I doubt Father has any idea the boy is a conduit for information. I haven't told Father where Philippe is, what he's doing. The telling of things, too, has become luxury. Information must be viewed in the context of necessity.

This is why I haven't told Philippe I'm pregnant, and I have no intention to do so. It's too dangerous for him to see me again.

I hurry across the avenue toward home with a copy of *Le Soir*, which we'll burn in the stove, and a copy of *La Libre Belgique* for Father to read, and I feel a burst of gratitude that Philippe is alive and in England. The way things are going, someone would have found out about Philippe. The Flemish hold the bureaucratic jobs in this country. They have always been the keepers of records—births, deaths, baptisms or not, marriages—and this is how they've been able to identify almost every person of Jewish ancestry in the country. And this in turn makes me think of Julian and the Raphaëls. And how Father was right. Had the Raphaëls stayed until now, we would say they should have left then.

DIRK DEBAERRE, 2R

They came for my father. The Belgians, not the Germans. We don't need Germans to have villains, see, we have plenty of our own.

This surprised Mother. I told her that all things considered, she shouldn't be surprised by anything. Mother sobbed all that day and into evening. I could have strangled her.

What did she think was going to happen?

Mother said there was one German—probably a gestapo. And then she set off to wailing again. A horrible sound, one that would provoke a better man to kill.

"Why weren't you here? What were you doing?" she sobbed.

"Your nose is running."

"You have to go down there!"

"Down *where?*"

"To the headquarters. On Avenue Louise. That's where they're set up." And how did she know that?

"Your nose," I repeated. I didn't offer my handkerchief.

"You have to go to Avenue Louise." She wiped her nose on the hem of her dress.

Yes, she did that.

"How do you know that's where they're headquartered?"

"Everyone knows." Mother started sobbing again.

"I didn't."

"Don't lie. Never lie to me." She couldn't even manage to point a finger at me.

You lied about me. I didn't say it. What would have been the point? A discreet tap on the door interrupted us.

"Don't open it," Mother hissed.

My god, she was hysterical.

I opened the door. It was Miss Hobert.

"Yes?"

Hobert looked unsure of herself but no less determined for it. I glared at her. I wanted to make her feel unsure, the old bat.

"Yes?" I asked again.

Mother was still crying in the next room but in a somewhat more subdued way.

"I couldn't help but hear," the old bat began.

"You want to know what it is?"

"If I can help—"

"You can't." I pushed the door to close it. Hobert stuck her boot in the opening before I could.

"I might"—she winced as the door squeezed her foot—"be of help."

"No. Mother will be distraught for the rest of her life."

"Oh dear!"

We eyed each other through the crack. I could see the wild curiosity in her eyes.

"And there's nothing you or I or anyone can do about it."

"I could make a cake."

"Don't bother."

I'm not saying another word to the old cunt. She can fish all she wants.

"Oh, aah . . . Is your father home?"

"No."

"Is anyone else here?"

"Mother."

"Besides your mother."

"I'm here."

"She's been crying all day."

"I wouldn't know."

"Are you working?"

"Are you?"

"Listen," she said. "People need to sleep."

"Maybe Mother will throw herself out the window and then we'll have some peace and quiet. And if you really want to know," I added, "it was a man. Mother suspected a woman. But it was a man, who also had a family."

Miss Hobert's eyes widened. Oh yes, let her think it was salacious. I opened the door wider to shut it hard. She pulled back her foot. I slammed the door and latched it.

*

What can I say? I'm living alone now, and I like it, better even than living in Leuven where I was studying. When the school closed, half my classmates joined up with the Nazi army, and the other half joined the Communists. But I couldn't do either—and certainly not the army. I even had a doctor's certificate attesting to the sad state of my lungs. They're weak. Sometimes, I can hardly breathe. I'd be dead of pneumonia if I were in the ranks. It's why I play the saxophone, for my lungs. To develop them just enough to stay alive.

I practice my saxophone on the couch, but sometimes I look in a mirror as I play to be sure my mouth—my embouchure—is in the correct position. I turn a bit to the left when I'm looking at myself, and I have a suspicion that the right side of my mouth isn't fitting as it should around the reed and maybe that's why it squeaks. But I can't bear to look at the mole on my right cheek. Hideous. Black. My father had one too.

What a fucking diabolical thing to do, Mother.

You think I'm a bastard, don't you? You're right about that.

I'm certain the music is salutary. When I play, my mind wanders about, letting the darkness inside come to the light.

I always say if you think there's no light in a person, pay attention to what they do not to what they say. Then you'll know. People say all kinds of things. That's beside the point. It's what they do that counts. Charlotte once told me that, and I took it on board. It's the only truth I live by.

*

I'm afraid Charlotte thinks I'm awful.

*

There's that game we played at school when we were children. You know the one. You divide up teams, they go to opposite sides, and you throw the ball at anyone not on your team. It's not a heavy ball, it doesn't do much damage, but if you throw it hard enough, it stings. Once you're hit, you go to prison. We called it hell. Either you're captured or you're dead.

The last man standing wins.

I like winning.

He didn't. He had a mole on his right cheek. I believe I mentioned that.

What kind of woman picks a man for his mole?

Mother came from a town on the line between Wallonia and Flanders, and she grew up speaking an ungodly mix of languages, a dialect, which meant she spoke neither language well. She married a lawyer. A meek, pathetic little man with a soft heart and a hard mole.

I knew he was weak. But once in a while he'd surprise and stand up to me. Mother always intervened. He should have stood up to her. That's what he should have done.

"Don't be so hard on Dirk," she'd say. "He's a good boy. It's been a bumpy road for him from the start."

I had no idea what she meant by that, but I took it and ran with it. I cried. I pouted. I acted frightened, wounded, damaged by his feeble attempts to discipline me. Sometimes, I wouldn't speak a word for days.

This frightened him, and it wasn't long before he stopped intervening.

*

You must watch people. Observe every detail. I have learned everything I know by watching. It's why I'm the last man standing in this little kingdom of mine.

*

I was six. Charlotte was in my class.

She was better than I was at reading and math. And she could draw a pig that looked like a pig, whereas I drew a pig and it looked like a ham. She had a much better set of colored pencils than mine in bright, deep colors. They didn't break so easily as my pencils did, and they didn't roll off her desk because while mine were round, hers were octagonal. Such small things as pencil design can be so clever. She kept them in a tin with the words *Faber-Castell* on it.

I was convinced Charlotte drew better because of those pencils.

On my way home from school one afternoon, I stopped in to the stationery shop where I often went with Mother, and I asked the clerk if he had any Faber-Castell pencils. I thought I would buy some with money I had taken out of Mother's purse that morning.

"Oh yes," he said. "The new tins just came in."

The clerk found the shopkeeper, who went into the back and returned with a wood crate. It was the new lot; he hadn't even unpacked them. I remember the rise in my stomach, the same one I feel when a car goes over an unexpected up and down in the road. I put my hands in my pockets so no one would see them tremble, and I waited as the shopkeeper opened the crate and pulled out the shredded newspapers on top of the load. Then he whistled. A long whistle, the kind I've heard boys do when they see a blond woman in a tight skirt. A whistle for the pencils made much more sense to me.

I could feel my whole body vibrating. I wriggled my fingers in my pockets. The money was there. Would it be enough?

He lifted out the new pencil tin, and we both looked at it in wonder. On the lid next to the words *Faber-Castell* was a brilliantly colored picture of jousting knights on horseback, but instead of swords, they held pencils. One horse was draped in a yellow caparison, the other in a red one.

The shopkeeper grinned and held out the tin. "This one?"

I took the money out of my pocket and put it on the counter.

Please God or Satan or whoever can help me now, let it be enough.

Even at that age, I wasn't above invoking both, just in case. I held my breath as the shopkeeper counted the money on the counter. He gave me back five centimes.

I released a gasping exhale. The pencils were mine.

That night, I took a creamy white sheet of paper from the desk in our living room. No one ever worked at that desk. It had belonged to my grandfather—my mother's stepfather—and it was still filled with his stationery, an assortment of good paper.

I put the paper on the small table in my room, and I took out the pencil tin. At exactly that moment, Mother called me to dinner. I was hungry—I'm always hungry—this is my burden. But for once, I didn't come right away. I wanted to draw. I wanted to draw as well as Charlotte.

You see, I have always wanted greatness. Even then, I understood that to be great, you had to be a king or an artist.

I was admiring the jousting knights, the red and yellow of the horses' blankets, when there was a rap on my door. The squeak of a hinge. It was my father.

"Please. Your mother cooked."

Mother always cooked. Couldn't he see I was busy and tell her I'd be a few minutes late to the table? Or tell me to put the pencils aside and come to the table at once. Instead, he was pleading with me. How useless.

And it made me shiver, not with pleasure, to see the mole on his cheek, the twin of my own. As I stared at the flattened ball of dark putty on the uneven surface of his sagging skin, I had the sense of looking in some future mirror. It disgusted me.

This was how I, too, would look.

Stepping into my room, he saw the paper and the pencils. "Very nice pencils," he said.

I looked down at the tin. They *were* nice pencils.

"Did you get those for him?" Mother asked.

I hadn't heard her come in.

"Where did you get these?" she asked.

I considered telling her that I had found them under my pew in the church chapel.

"At the stationer," I said.

"How did you pay for them?" she asked.

I looked at my father, who seemed uncomfortable. He wanted this to be over. He wanted to eat the pot roast that was simmering in dark beer and onions with some bread and an endive salad.

"Dirk?" Mother demanded in her shrillest, sharpest voice.

"With money."

"Where did you get the money?"

I looked her in the eye. "I found it," I lied.

Mother knew I was lying. She reached for the pencil tin, but I grabbed it, too, and we struggled a moment.

"We're taking them back to the shop," Mother said.

I held on.

"Dirk, please," that poor weak man said.

I gave the pencil tin a yank, and Mother let go with a wince. I lost my grip on the tin. The metal was slick and the shape made it hard to hold with my boy's hand. It fell to the floor and flew open revealing a perfect rainbow of colors. My god, it was a beautiful sight.

"Can't take them back now," my father said. "You see? There?" He pointed at a dent in the curved edge of the tin.

Mother picked up the tin and left the room.

I didn't eat dinner that night. After my parents went to bed, I searched the apartment for my pencil tin. I looked behind Mother's record collection, in every drawer of the desk, behind all the coats and under them, in the tall boots and the short ones, in the cheese cupboard, the pantry, in stacks of tins and baskets, under piles of magazines. She must have hidden them in my father's briefcase, which was in their room, because in the week that followed, I looked everywhere for those pencils. I know all the hiding places in these apartments. I observe things. I watch. I pay attention.

I knew she hadn't taken them back. How could I be sure? I stopped by the shop the next day on my way home from school. The shopkeeper knew my mother. He lived in our neighborhood. He asked how I liked the pencils.

"I like them very much," I said sadly. "I'll always like them."

The shopkeeper looked at me with surprise, for the answer must have seemed strangely solemn. But just then, a customer approached the counter and he turned his attention to her. Of course he did. I still remember how she was dressed—a cocoa-colored wool coat with a midnight-blue silk blouse in a floral pattern with a hint of cocoa, a combination that subtly brought the ensemble together. When I was a boy, I wished I could dress like that woman, with pattern and color. She was also wearing an enormous diamond on her finger.

Money matters, and I intend to make a lot of it. Some people understand this. Leo Raphaël does. My father didn't.

When I asked my father if my pencil tin was at his office, his face reddened, but all he said was, "You shouldn't take your mother's money."

It was his money. Mother never earned a cent of her own. Poor man, he was always stuck on the fence. He didn't have the courage to jump off and run.

At the end of that week in school, we had art class. I couldn't stop thinking about the brilliant red and yellow of the horses' caparisons in the picture on the tin. We had been at lunch and after in the chapel for prayers. I hurried ahead to the classroom, feeling in my pocket to make sure my own basic red and yellow pencils were still there. They were. I reached into Charlotte's desk, took out her pencil tin, and replaced mine with hers.

Charlotte noticed right away. She was looking around the room trying to figure out who had taken her pencils. But before she could, the art teacher asked Charlotte to please draw a red cube.

What are the chances? You ask. The moment you think there's no chance and that coincidence is too strong, coincidence will outwit you. I've seen it happen too many times. Coincidence is god.

Charlotte looked at the teacher; she looked at her pencils. There was no panic on her face. She seemed level. But my heart was pounding as I watched.

Why didn't she draw the red cube? Was she so particular that she would only draw with her Faber-Castell pencils and nothing else?

Charlotte picked up the red pencil, my red pencil, and looked at it, then she put it down and picked up the yellow pencil, my yellow pencil. And she drew a perfect cube with that yellow pencil, so pale against the white paper you could barely see it.

The art teacher, a long-nosed young nun, was writing on the board and she hadn't seen Charlotte drawing. She walked over to Charlotte's desk and stared at the cube.

Tight-lipped, she asked, "Is that red?"

Charlotte looked up at the nun and didn't say a word.

The nun picked up the paper on which Charlotte had drawn a perfect yellow cube, and she tore it in two.

"You'll stay inside when the rest of your classmates are out playing on the field. And you'll draw fifty red cubes for your impertinence," she said.

I didn't feel sick or troubled then. It was all worth it to watch Charlotte react. She had some nerve. Saying nothing, making no excuses. Silently defying the nun like that. Charlotte wasn't like the other children—rabid little beasts most of whom have doubtless grown up to be *vile adherents*. No, Charlotte was independent. Unto herself. Within herself.

Class was over and we were going outside. I hid behind the coatroom door to watch Charlotte. She had a stack of fresh paper on the table in front of her, and the red and yellow pencils. She picked up one pencil and then the other. She still looked calm, but there was a line of worry on her forehead.

She got up from the desk, went over to the trash can and pulled out the picture of the yellow cube the nun had torn apart. She took it back to her desk, and then she drew a line with the red pencil and a line with the yellow pencil.

Charlotte put the yellow pencil in her desk with the torn drawing. And she began to draw the first of her fifty red cubes.

That night at home, I took out Charlotte's pencils and saw that they were neatly labeled *red* and *yellow*.

I understood everything.

The next day, we were going out for recess and one of the popular boys lingered at Charlotte's desk. Long-lashed blue eyes, a scattering of freckles on perfect turned-up nose, he often picked teams, but he never had chosen me. It was hurtful that such a beautiful boy ignored me. I hid behind the door again and watched as he looked at her pencils.

I stepped out of my hiding spot. He looked at me and laughed.

"She can't see color. They're marked. Blue. Green. Violet—"

"Put them back," I said.

"No one likes her," he said.

We heard voices approaching—nuns. He dropped the pencils, shut the desk, and said, "No one likes you either." Then he ran outside.

That was when the other children started teasing Charlotte.

She knew I had the two pencils. She saw them and never said a word. Maybe she thought I was to blame for all of it. Maybe I was.

What I never forgot is that I had set a trap for Charlotte that made her the object of ridicule. I hadn't intended to do it, and I will say it was a life lesson. Good intentions mean nothing when you fail.

Later still, after Charlotte had endured the endless teasing questions—*what color is my hat, what color is the sky, Charlotte, what color is your shit?*—I overheard my father tell Mother that he had apologized to Charlotte's father for my behavior. The sop.

The other day, I saw him. The boy from school—a man now. All suited up. Polished leather boots. Officer's stripes on the sleeve. An attempt at a tiny moustache. Blond fuzz. Same blue eyes. I don't find blue eyes attractive, not anymore.

*

That Christmas, I opened a thin rectangular package wrapped in brown paper, and there it was, my pencil tin. Dented, but with all the pencils intact. I considered tossing them in the bin to prove a point, but to whom and for what? There was no longer any point to be made. I used those pencils. At the end of the day, one must be practical to survive.

*

My father's salary seemed to be contracting. This was before I left university. He asked me to stop taking my meals in cafés. My one wool suit was wearing thin. I needed another, but he said there was no money to spare.

Mother wasn't happy about it either. When I was home on the odd weekend, they would fight.

"Aren't they paying you? Those clients of yours?"

I told Mother that everything was more expensive now.

"Not that much more expensive," she said.

"So go to the bank, tell them you do the accounting, and you need to look at the statements."

Mother returned from the bank with a stack of papers she didn't understand. I went over them. There was no reduction in my father's income; the same amount of money was coming to his account. He was taking the same amount out. But we weren't seeing it at home.

"A woman," Mother said.

"I doubt it."

Not because I thought he wouldn't stray, but I couldn't imagine him going to all the trouble of finding some woman and hiding the fact of her.

"Then what is it?"

"I don't know. An investment of some kind? Maybe he's putting money in gold or diamonds."

Mother made a face and showed me the thin gold band she wore with a chip of a diamond. Looking at it took her right back round to the other woman.

I did need a suit. Leuven is filled with snobs. You'd think it would be intellect that mattered, but as I soon learned, the so-called intellectuals are the worst snobs. It mattered little that I was among the best students, that I could emulate my professors, sprinkling grand, obscure words in my speech as if to say, *I could use these words and only these words all the time for everything.* I learned to sit with a hand on one side of my face, a finger raised as if holding back from making a trenchant point, that finger also covering the mole.

Intellectuals are thieves. They steal to make money. Students write papers. Professors filch ideas. It happened to me. I don't blame anyone. All property is theft, and one person or another has always taken credit for having been the first to think or say it.

Money matters. What good is a mind if not to live well and show people that you are as rich as the best of them?

*

After the Nazis came, the university closed, and I returned home. Mother was still obsessing over the money my father wasn't bringing home even though we had a bit more given that they weren't paying my tuition fees.

"An old lover," she wailed.

"Pfft. Nonsense."

It turned out the money was going to my father's former clerk, who was in hiding with his wife and their four children. Living in someone's basement. The trust in that, on everyone's part. The hider, the hidden—how to keep four little brats quiet when it matters.

I don't like children and I don't want them, but I do have an imagination. I remember that clerk—a tense, slender man with a stringy neck that looked ready to snap.

So, to get a few facts straight. When I overheard my father tell Mother about the family, I felt more respect for him than I ever had. It took some guts to do what he was doing. He said he'd been helping them for over a year. They had been trying to get passage out under new names and he'd paid for those names.

I heard that and I thought, *My god, I underestimated the man.*

But Mother was furious. The next day when my father went to work, I made her sit at the kitchen table. It's next to the window overlooking our courtyard—bleak and gray. It struck me then that Charlotte sees everything that way. How completely despairing. I don't know why she came to mind so out of context, other than the gray. I'm not in love with Charlotte if that's what you're thinking. I've never been in love with a woman. Put that in your pipe and smoke it.

"The envelope's gone," Mother said.

"What envelope?"

"The one I found. Your father did something with it. Did he go out this evening?"

"He went for a walk and a pipe with the architect on the fourth floor," I said.

"He must have given it to him."

"His pipe?"

She was pacing around, mumbling to herself. And then a little after, she said, "You could have had a suit. Two suits. Or three."

"I don't need three suits," I said. "Certainly not now. Mother. Let it go."

"Why are you standing up for him? It was a mistake. All a mistake."

"I think he meant to do it."

"Marrying him," she said.

Well, I didn't like the sound of that. If she regretted marrying him, then logically, didn't she regret me as well?

"You got me in the bargain, didn't you?"

"I already had you."

I thought I had misheard. But I hadn't and this was a shock. You understand now? *The mole.* I was born with it. When she married him, the mole and I already existed. She chose him because of that mole. Don't you see? Everyone assumed I was his. That she finally married the father of her child. Because of the damn mole.

He was weak. Yes. But not so pathetic as I had always thought. And it was a shame. Because he wasn't even my father.

I wasn't pleasant to Mother. For some inane reason, I felt I needed to sort this all out, if only in my own head, and I ordered her to tell me everything.

"Who was he? My real father."

But she wouldn't.

Every day, as soon as he left the apartment, I pounced. I could see that it was making her brittle. She was always thin. She got thinner. She was starting to disappear. It happens.

I don't blame myself.

People do things. They have only so much strength. It's all on them. People can erase themselves.

*

They found the clerk and his family first. Then they took my father away.

*

Mother was dressed up. Navy-blue silk. Her best coat. She was going
out. For the first time in a week, she wasn't wailing, but her eyes were
puffy and her face looked awful. I told her to splash some cold water
on it. And maybe put on some face cream.

She looked at me with the oddest glint in her eye.

"My stepfather," she said. And she started laughing. She was laughing and laughing. She couldn't seem to stop.

"What about him?"

She laughed even harder and pointed at me. At my grandfather's
desk. At herself.

And finally I caught on. Finally she was answering my question.

And you know what? I wish to god I had never asked. I'm trying to
erase all this. I imagine myself putting the fact of my step-grandfather
and my mother in a pencil tin and shutting it very tightly. There's a
picture of knights on the tin, but they aren't jousting with pencils.
They have swords.

*

The tram isn't a locomotive; it isn't especially heavy. It's more like a
very large automobile, in terms of weight.

They called me and I went to the hospital. She was covered and
oozing through the sheets. Already out. She couldn't talk or open her
eyes. But her face was unscathed. Remarkable.

"Mother," I said.

Not so much as a flutter.

The doctor told me he could operate, but he thought it was hopeless. He was French, which suggested to me at least that he might be
less precise. The rumor was that all the good doctors had fled. But this
man looked thoughtful. He was taking time to talk to me. Maybe in his

mind he was weighing the possibility of a botched surgery against my mother's will. What she wanted.

No one steps in front of a tram like she did by accident. People were watching. They all said it looked quite intentional, and I didn't doubt them.

The doctor had fine features, small crinkles around his eyes. I wanted to talk to him over a coffee. I told him he looked like he could use some rest, and he smiled and said, "Always."

"Sorry to . . . I don't mean to . . . I don't want to put you on the spot. But I feel I must. You think it's hopeless, or you're certain it is?"

"I'm certain," he said.

"Then don't operate."

I sat with Mother until she died. It was the most peaceful we've been together. She was quiet for the first time in months but for her breathing, which was unsteady and came in gasps. I was once on a train when a pregnant woman went into labor. There was a nurse on board, and she asked me to run to the dining car for hot water. I did. But I didn't stay to see the outcome; I got off at the next stop. So I don't know if the poor woman had the baby on the train or off it. I didn't want to see that. I'm not interested in babies. And why was I thinking of that? Sitting with Mother made me think of that woman in labor. Of how you move through the world in nearly the same way when you come in and go out.

I dozed off and when I awoke, the hand I held was cold and Mother's lips were blue. How long had I slept? How long had I been holding her corpse's hand? She wouldn't let go. Her hand was locked around mine. I tried not to break her fingers loosening the grasp, as if she could have felt it. Finally pulling my hand away, I got up fast, feeling a bit faint as I did. I took a big breath and called in the nurse, who in turn called in the good-looking doctor. They confirmed all the details. Catholic burial. I asked them to put it down as an accident. And I asked the doctor if he'd like to have a coffee sometime, and he told me he'd like that very much.

MASHA BALYAYEVA, 5TH FLOOR

The trip with Harry into the unsecured territory was the last we made together. I don't know if Harry went alone sometimes after. He didn't tell me where he went when he left Paris.

We moved into a simple flat near the Invalides. Harry said it was important to be *plausibly embedded* there—his words. He even bought me a crucifix to wear, but I only put it on when he was around. He also made me read the Bible. The newer part. And he organized those first clients for me, wives and mistresses of the Nazi occupiers. Dressmaking. It was Harry who told me what to say if they asked questions—that my family had been wealthy and had lost everything to the Bolsheviks. That I was intending to study art. I had gone on to Brussels where a cousin had also fled, but he died, so I was forced to take in work as a common seamstress. But many of my clients in Brussels were people whose clothes I no longer wished to alter. If pressed, I should whisper the word. *Jew.*

"Don't argue," he said. "I see the argument coming. It's rising like steam. I read you like a cabaret poster, darling. Big red letters—arms and legs wide open. Don't make the argument. Just don't. Don't ask me if all the French are bloody anti-Semites. Of course not. But a lot of them are."

He was right, I was about to tell him that this script of his was a betrayal of myself, my family, Mrs. Raphaël. That it was a lie. But I came to understand that truth is often the ultimate betrayal. There is no bright line between lies and truth. There is, however, a bright line between good and evil.

Harry understood almost before I did when I was angry or frustrated, when I felt love or gratitude. He watches faces, you see. He has a way of looking at people so they don't know that he is. He's a great observer of human behavior. He would have made a wonderful psychiatrist. Or lawyer. Or doctor. But such was not the time. Instead, he made a wonderful spy.

*

Every night, Harry wanted me to tell him about my clients. He seemed to think I could find out more if I knew less about them in advance, but I soon learned that all the women whose dresses I was altering were married to men in Pétain's government. And these women talked, telling me of their husbands' travels, how they were disappointed not to be able to go to the opera in Berlin this season. How men were spoiling all the things women loved to do. One woman told me that she had found out her son's clarinet teacher was *one of them.*

"You know," she said.

"Oh, I do," I said. "What's his name?"

"Vive. He had us all fooled with that name. Never fooled again."

A few nights after that, Harry brought someone over for dinner, a thin young man called Alex with dark hair and a long, sensitive face—a clarinet player.

"Alex is leaving for Marseille," Harry said.

"The weather's warm, but I can't say as much for the people," I told Alex.

Rations were scant but Harry always managed to find good food. I had made a solid meal of potatoes and sausage, and Alex ate hungrily.

"When do you leave?"

"Tonight," Alex said through a mouthful.

I poured him a glass of wine, and he washed down the food and ate some more. I told him not to take any rides with goose farmers.

"I don't plan to," he said, laughing.

"Or anyone you aren't sure of."

I looked at Harry as I said it. Harry wasn't laughing. He looked at his watch.

"Time to go," he said.

They left and I began to wash up the dishes. A few minutes later, I heard footsteps running up the stairs to the flat, and the key in the lock.

"I need your help," Harry said.

"Of course." I dried my hands.

Harry had taken my coat off the hook and was holding it for me. As I slipped arms in sleeves he said, "The woman who was to have taken Alex to his shuttle—"

"His what?"

"Shut up—sorry. Listen! The next person in the chain. The woman isn't where she's supposed to be. Can you take him?"

"Yes, but why me?"

"They're expecting a woman."

"How do you know where I'm to take him?" I remembered how Harry had told me everyone knows only the direct connections to their link in the chain.

"I know . . . her. No time. He's outside having a smoke on the corner next to the laundrette. Alex." As Harry pushed me out the door, he whispered the name of the café where I was to take young Alex Vive.

And so it began.

*

Harry was exacting. So particular it sometimes hindered him.

In my early years in Brussels, I had an older client who was readying her wardrobe for the trip of her lifetime—where she would be seen by the people who mattered. She wanted everything to be perfect and she insisted on alteration upon alteration. Finally, the clothes to her liking, she set off. But early on, her luggage was lost, and all she had were the clothes she was wearing. Harry had begun to remind me of that woman.

It was in Paris that Harry began to have outbursts. They seemed to come on overnight. He wouldn't tell me why he was so tense, and I was left to conclude that he had kept his temperament well hidden, or he had new and troubling information he didn't want to share with me. Either way, he was losing his sangfroid, and it worried me.

"How am I supposed to think, with you interrupting me? And you don't listen," he chided.

He would pace up and down, ranting. And after, when he calmed, he would tell me he loved me, and he would thank G-d that I could handle his moods.

Once, he yelled at me when I dropped my papers getting off a metro car. As I picked them up, I could feel people staring. Harry knew it unnerved me.

We took the stairs up and out of the station.

"It's all part of the game," Harry said. "French husbands always yell at their wives."

"But we're not married," I whispered.

I could see a look of distrust in his eyes. They were the creeping eyes of a mink I once saw caught in a furrier's trap. I stepped onto the sidewalk and pulled away from him. It was only human of me. And it struck me then that I wasn't the first who had pulled away from Harry and maybe that was why he was so alone in the world.

*

I believe Harry loved me, but I know he never loved anyone as much as he loved his mother. He carried her photograph with him. She had large, sad eyes—dark and her hair too. Her face revealed that she viewed her life as tragedy, and she would use that tragedy to take down anyone who stood in her way—or her son's. Yes, I could see all this from the picture. And Harry's stories about her only confirmed my understanding. His father had died when he was a child, leaving Harry and his mother alone in France.

"But she isn't French?"

"She liked France," he said.

"She's English?"

"Not exactly. Some of her people came from a place east of where your people came from."

"I'd like to meet her."

"Mother would love this meal," Harry said, and then he changed the subject.

I assumed his mother was in England. He told me that if things got bad, he'd find a way to send me to the farm as well.

"I want to stay with you."

"If it gets bad," he said again, stubborn Harry, "I'll get you a job making clothes. On the farm."

"Making clothes! Who can afford new clothes?"

"The government. For men and women like me. They're English. All their lives English. Because of what they're doing, they need to look like Czechs and Germans and Belgians. They're bringing in foreign seamstresses to dress them."

"Really?"

"I swear on my mother's life."

When Harry was serious about something, when it mattered to him, and I believe I did, he swore on his mother's life.

Spies needed costumers. The more I thought about it, the more it made sense.

Another time, after that, Harry was out late in the evening and he returned smelling of perfume. Not mine. I remembered the woman in the chain who was meant to escort Alex. She had told Harry things she wasn't meant to tell. I hadn't asked about her, why she hadn't come, if she was captured or alive.

"If you're with another woman, I shall go to England," I said.

Harry blew up at me and swore on his mother's life that he hadn't been with another woman since he met me.

Later I learned that Harry's mother had died during the war. The last war. Twenty years before I met Harry.

To be clear, it wasn't Harry who betrayed me. He wasn't a cad. He would never have done something like that. Not to me. I love Harry. It burns in me. I love him still. How I love him. And I couldn't tell you why. All I'm sure of is nothing will change that.

JULIAN RAPHAËL, 4R

The attacks on London stopped over a year ago and there's been a collective breath holding since. The British ascribe the failure of the Blitz to the fact that while the Nazis leveled parts of the city, they could never destroy all of it, and the bombing didn't affect the British people's sense of who they are. The Nazis are still bombarding other parts of England and a couple months ago, they hit a boy's school in Sussex. But mostly we're fighting them across the channel, all the way to Russia and Africa and Italy. Some say Mussolini will fall before the New Year and Italy will side with the Allies. I have my doubts.

Papa took me to Italy when I was a boy. He was buying paintings, and he told Mama it was a father-and-son expedition. Some fathers take their sons fishing or shooting. But we went to art auctions.

Papa's talking about Italy now. He drove up for my two-day leave. He'd been in London where he organized the delivery of a painting in a Cadbury truck and he's reading me the letter sent to the *Times* editor that inspired this latest venture.

"'In a burned and ravaged London, we need to see beauty, and art. Might the National Gallery consider displaying one painting weekly? Which could be taken speedily to safety in case of a bombing—' We're doing it, damn it," Papa says, folding up the worn newspaper clipping. He pulls a Cadbury Dairy Milk bar out of his pocket and offers it to me.

"Try it. You're in for a treat."

"How did you choose which painting to put on display?"

"We put a questionnaire in the *Times*. You know, What painting would you like to see in the Gallery? That sort of thing. You'd be surprised how many people wrote back and voted."

"There isn't much else going on other than dodging rubble, is there?"

I'm less impressed by Papa driving paintings around in a chocolate lorry than he wants me to be. Although, I am tempted to eat the Dairy Milk bar. They stopped making them and I haven't had chocolate since I joined up. In Brussels, shopkeepers give you chocolates when you're small and everyone is handing chocolate about—your friends, your parents' friends. It's an addiction. I remember once turning down a chocolate Guy offered me after a dinner at his house. "Are you sick?" his father asked me.

I set the Dairy Milk bar on the table. Papa and I are indulging in beer and sausages at a cramped roadside pub. He's staring at me, a strange look on his face.

"Not sick. Finishing the meal first. Mum would approve," I say, misunderstanding Papa's look.

"You're so like my brother," he says.

It's not the first time Papa has told me this.

Papa blinks hard a couple of times. He unfolds the newspaper clipping, adjusts his spectacles. "As for what else is going on," he reads, "'Trustees of the National Gallery announce that *Frosty Morning* by Turner will be on display for a month.' I love it. If the museum's bombed—"

"I don't think it will be," I say through a mouthful of sausage.

"Don't talk when you're chewing. In the unlikely event that it is bombed, it will be a tragic loss of . . . only one painting. The rest are secured. But in the meantime, the painting on display reminds us of the idea, the big idea."

"What big idea?"

"Of who we are. As people."

"You're beginning to sound like an Englishman."

"That's in the works as well."

"Really?"

"There's no better country to call our own."

I tell Papa what Blake, the fellow on my crew, took to saying when I told him my family collected art. "A word is worth a thousand pictures."

We both have a good laugh at that.

"I used to think you bought paintings only so you could sell them for a lot of money."

"Sometimes I do," Papa says.

"I believe we have a painting that's worth more than everything you've sold put together."

"Clever boy, bringing us back to the auction—"

"Not intentionally."

"Take credit when it's due. And you're not mistaken. I remember how you sat still. You were not known for sitting still. When you were small and your mama was very tired, she would play the statue game with you. Do you remember?"

"No," I say, stretching my legs under the table and sipping my beer. It's good to relax.

"Your mama would say, 'Pretend you're a statue and see how long you can stay still.'"

"How long could I?"

"Thirty seconds. Tops. But at that auction, you were a statue. You had the list and you knew the numbers. You had retained the starting prices of all the paintings. At one point, you even told me exactly how much to bid on a particular painting but to stop after that. I asked you why, and you said, 'If you get it at that price, you'll be able to sell it for more. Anything else is risk.' Do you remember?"

"Maybe."

Of course, I do.

"It's valuable, then, is it?"

"It is," Papa says.

"I love that painting."

It's of a river with two figures, one in a top hat, on a grassy bank beside an avenue of bare trees. The painting hangs in our hall. Well, it did.

Papa says he wants me to go into business with him when all this is over.

"I'll think about it."

"The point is," he says, picking up the thread of the story as he always does despite his tangents, "when you got out of the auction house, which you said smelled like your grandma's attic, you started to run. It was so strange. Here you were, masterminding the auction."

"I wasn't masterminding anything."

"You did mastermind it. And then you couldn't stop running."

"I miss running. The way boys run. With no point."

"Ah." Papa adjusts his stomach over his belt. "Obviously, I don't. You ran through the whole city. Rome! I ran after you. The fountain, the Colosseum, the Pantheon."

"No."

"Oh yes you did. All the way to the Vatican. Rome in a day."

We're both laughing. This little place has grown on me. It doesn't feel so awfully cramped, and it's bright for a pub. Almost everyone here is on leave, and there are a few girls too.

Papa notices the girls.

"Not for you," I say.

"Never. Have you met anyone?"

"Not really."

"I met your mama after the Great War started."

"Then I'll wait a bit to meet someone, all right?" I start laughing again. I don't know what it is with the laughing.

Papa's laughing too. "God willing," he says.

And this makes us laugh harder.

Laughter. Perhaps a cure for war.

Without warning, Papa's crying. I've never seen him cry before, not even when his mother died.

"What is it?"

"We don't talk about it. What's happening."

"We can't."

"Why on earth not?"

"We don't need to talk about it. We're in it."

Papa wipes the tears, takes a few pound notes out of his pocket, and pays, leaving a generous tip. I push my chair back from the table and I run out of there. I hear footsteps behind me. Papa's chasing me. I run along the road. It's lined with hedges, no shoulder whatsoever, so it's dangerous. But not nearly as dangerous as taking off in a Stirling or a Boston or a Spitfire.

I hear Papa's breathing—hard and labored. I don't want to kill the man. I turn to see that he still has tears running down his face, but he's smiling.

*

This was just before a mission I couldn't talk about, not even with Papa. We're bombing targets in Belgium. I imagine Guy already there, doing reconnaissance. I like the idea of Guy going before me, figuring it out, fighting and laughing his way across the continent.

COLONEL WARLEMONT, 3L

As I put the blackout papers on my windows, I remember I haven't checked my mail. I don't get mail these days, but checking is part of my routine.

The elevator hasn't worked for a year, and I take the stairs. Everard's wife is upbraiding him as usual. What a voice she has. Funny how you can coexist with people when the world outside seems all right. You overlook their quirks and chalk up their awful traits as idiosyncrasies. But when the world turns inward, there's no tolerance. Not from me, not toward me. It's the way things go. I've seen it before.

I open my mailbox, trying to block out the shrew. Her husband turns on German radio. She shuts it off. I hear a crash and a child begins to wail.

They should return to their village, live in a house with fields around where they can make all the ruckus they want. Miss Hobert once told me something terrible happened there with Everard's father, who might or might not be alive, or in jail, or on the run. It's so terrible even she hasn't yet gotten to the bottom of it.

A few years ago, our resident notary emerged as an enthusiastic National Socialist. When Everard expressed to me his interest in Hitler and the party, I told him Hitler was a bitter and talented ideologue, but people were not as stupid as he thought, and they wouldn't be fooled into supporting him.

Everard must have flicked on the radio again. I hear the RRG—the

German radio broadcast—in the hall as I do every night. He's making sure each of us hears his version of truth.

The truth is a dangerous thing, and the people who talk most about it, in my experience, like it least. Miss Hobert, for example, loves truth.

"Why do we not value truth anymore?" she asked the other day.

When did we ever?

I might just tell her those cakes are indigestible even for dogs—who have no trouble digesting small mammals swallowed whole—bones, fur, and all.

The exterior door opens, and Charlotte appears in the frame. She looks older. Not a child anymore, that's certain. I hurry to take her bag, pulling up my trousers as I do. Need to add another notch in the belt. Those last kilos are gone and then some. Maybe it was good I came into all this with a bit of excess. Hold the line. Slow the decline.

"I'll help you upstairs."

"No need."

In my mailbox is a square white envelope addressed to me. The writing's familiar. I take the envelope out then shut and lock the box with my brass key.

"At least let me carry your bread."

I take it from her, and we start up the stairs together.

"How's Zipper?" Charlotte asks politely.

"I've been letting him into the basement to eat rats."

"Really?"

"Hold the railing," I tell her sternly, thinking of how just the other day I nearly fell on the wet stairs.

We reach the landing and both of us pause for a moment as one does on a landing.

"Are the soldiers giving you trouble?"

"No," Charlotte says, starting up the next flight of stairs.

"If they do, I can go out for your supplies."

"You can't."

"I can get your bread."

"But not groceries."

She tells me how, some time ago, Smets wouldn't give her Francois's butter ration, not without both their cards.

"I'll pound that man into his floor one of these days."

We pause on another landing.

"A Nazi officer gave me the butter."

"Charlotte!" I say sternly.

"Almost two years ago and I gave it away when I found it."

Charlotte's a soldier; she'll make it through. She takes her bread, thanks me, and continues up to the fourth floor alone.

*

That night, I make a simple meal of bread and beans, and when I finish it, I take out the letter. Zipper is resting his muzzle on my knee, and I smell his breath—ripe from vermin and foraging. Bloody breath. Poor lad.

Before I open the envelope, I hold it up to the lamp—a faint line of glue below the flap. I'm not the first reader of this letter.

It's from Masha. She writes that she won't see me for a while, but she wants me to know she's fine. She'll be at the farm. The salutation is, *Dear Uncle*. And she signs it, *Love, Masha*.

*

It isn't long after I receive Masha's letter, and there's Harry, again, at my door. He's pale and thinner than before. And something else.

"You're two years late," I tell him.

He sits on the floor with Zipper and puts his arms around the lad's neck. Zipper is aloof by nature, Bouviers aren't the warmest of creatures, but he tolerates the hug.

"Harry?"

"There's a problem, I need to . . . correct. Tardiness . . . mine."

He doesn't say more, leaving me to pick up the thread.

"I had a letter from Masha. She's at the farm—"

"In Paris," Harry says quickly.

"She wrote that she would be at the farm."

"That was the plan." Harry looks pained as he says it.

"I don't have much beyond bread to offer you. Some beer. My neighbor upstairs has taken to making—"

"Just beer, please."

I go into the pantry—it's chilly—and I pull two of Francois's beers out of the cold storage near the window and take them back to Harry. Who hasn't moved.

"Francois has outdone himself with this batch. The man is brewing up a storm." I uncap the bottles and hand one to Harry.

"He's a brewer, then?" He takes a gulp.

"An architect."

"Makes sense."

Both of us understanding that everything that didn't make sense before now does and vice versa.

"So, how is Masha?"

Harry is trying to formulate a word, a sentence. Instead, he bursts out crying.

I feel a cold dread sink into my stomach. I put my beer aside and wait.

"She wanted to help . . . She insisted that she could do more than report gossip. And she could. She was good at taking messages from one person to another, taking people across parts of the city where it's more dangerous but there's no other way."

I understand, of course.

The story comes out. I remind him to keep his voice down. I want him to tell me. And I don't.

"She was to meet a man. The contact, the shuttle. We'd used him a lot."

"Who was he?"

"Doesn't matter. But he's smart. Trusted. She had someone with her."

"Who?"

"An English pilot. RAF. Young chap, who'd escaped. And she saved him. I just got word he made it down to Gibraltar."

"Go on."

"We've been doing this without a hitch."

"You were due for one."

He took a swig of beer. "We had word of an infiltration."

"Word from whom?"

"Doesn't matter."

"Oh yes it does."

"Some thought it was Masha. The leaks—"

"There were leaks?"

"Yes. They started not long after Masha began to help. I told them it was coincidence."

"Told who?"

"Doesn't matter."

"Dammit, Harry. It always matters."

"They went to the café as planned, Masha and the RAF pilot. A kid, really. And Masha sat with the shuttle, the man they were to meet."

"Where was the kid when she was with the shuttle?"

"In the toilet, waiting. If Masha didn't go down to check on him within a certain amount of time, he was to go out the basement exit, and she was to leave out the front. We knew the place, you see. We had done it before. But then, something alerted her."

"What?"

"I don't know. She wasn't making sense when she got to me."

"What was she saying?"

"She thought she was in Belgium."

"In Belgium?"

I was delaying the end. I wanted to pretend there wasn't an end.

"She was just holding on by the time . . . by then. They shot her as she left the café."

Harry's rocking back and forth now. He knocks over his bottle—and it rolls across the floor dribbling beer. Zipper gets up, his paws sliding out in four directions on the polished hardwood, and he trots over to lick it up.

"Who shot her?"

"She ran to our meeting place. It wasn't far. She ran."

"Who shot her?"

"The RAF chap was minutes behind her. They hadn't seen him in the loo, so he got out through the basement." Harry pauses. "And I was a minute or two late. I was late."

"Late to what?"

"Our second meeting place. Another café. I got there right when the young chap did. I told him to go to church."

"What church?"

"A real church. The priest is a saint. Afraid he will be before it's over. The shuttle was sent right back to Brussels. We're worried his cover was blown. The RAF chap was trying to help Masha, but they were coming and I told him to go or he'd be killed too. They hadn't seen me yet."

"Was she dead?"

"They were coming—"

"Who?"

"Gestapo. They were coming. They were chasing her. She was dying."

"Did they get to her?"

Harry looks at me, his navy-blue eyes wild, pleading. Tears pour down his face.

"She was dead. When they got to her."

We're silent. I pick up the bottles and take them to the kitchen. That's where I do my rocking. Alone. Where no one, not even Harry, can see me.

*

Harry asks me the favor. He tells me that the RAF fellows Masha was saving are coming through Brussels and they need to change things up a bit because of the problem in the line.

How could I turn him down?

ESTHER RAPHAËL, 4R

Date: 10 November 1942

Patient: male, age 23

Clinical Record: Burns over 60 percent of his body.

Nurse's Notes: Administered salt bath.

He howled in pain, and I howled with him so he wouldn't feel bad about it. The doctor came running and I said everything was as good as it could be. The patient was getting it out of his system, that was all it was.

The salt helps. It relieves the pain in the long run. And this is a good place to come with burns as there's a talented surgeon here doing skin grafts. The last nurse who assisted him threw up and fainted. I've asked to assist in the next surgery.

*

Date: 11 November 1942

Patient: male, age 35

Clinical Record: Leg crushed in crash landing. Amputated yesterday.

Nurse's Notes: Assisted. Administered morphine.

Morphine is a saint. The only saint.

The sawing was the hardest part. Can't they cut between the bones like you do a turkey leg?

I like the way they leave a bit of extra skin to stitch around the stump. It's clever and tidy.

*

Date: 12 November 1942
    Patient: male, age 21
    Clinical Record: Shrapnel wounds on torso. Shrapnel removed.
    Nurse's Notes: Salved and bandaged wounds.
    Looks like someone dug out his flesh with a sharp spoon. He'll be out in a few days and back in service after a short home stay.
    When I bandaged his wounds yesterday, he grabbed my hand.
    "Marry me," he said.
    "I don't know you."
    "Doesn't matter."
    "It does to me."
    "I'm going to die anyway."
    "Not this time."
    Anyone in the ward who could listen was listening. Mercifully, it was a small ward, and I was the only nurse in the room.
    "My odds are seventy-five percent."
    "Your wounds are healing," I told him.
    "No. You don't understand. Live or die is fifty/fifty. Twenty-five percent I'll be captured. See? So, make my life mean something."
    I wanted him to let go of my hand.
    "Make it matter." He gripped my hand more tightly.
    "What about my life?"
    "You can go on being a nurse, whether I live or die. See the logic? It's brilliant."
    "No, it isn't."
    I searched around in my nurse's satchel with my free hand and took out an enema bag. He let go of my hand right away.
    "I don't need one of those."
    "Good."
    I gathered my things and left the ward. Today, he was discharged, and I'm relieved never to have to see him again.

Two weeks later, he's back.

Date: 26 November 1942

Patient: male, age 21

Clinical Record: Left arm amputed. Right arm broken. Lost left eye.

Nurse's Notes: Assisted. Care for stump. Administered morphine.

"You should have married me when you had a chance," he tells me.

"Why is that?" I ask. I don't have to worry about the poor boy making a grab for me because his only arm is broken and in a cast.

"Any woman who marries me now is going to have to stay on the far right."

I kiss him on the forehead.

"You have the softest lips in the world. I swear you do."

His eye is an animal eye. Needy. Urgent. Lost.

"I want to go up again. But I don't think they'll let me. What else can I do?"

I don't know what to tell him. The morphine's kicking in, and I kiss him on the lips as he falls asleep.

*

Date: 27 November 1942

Patient: male, age 20

Clinical Record: Severe burns over both legs. May have to amputate.

Nurse's Notes: Administered salt baths.

He bears the salt bath like a champion.

"Help me keep my legs. Please? Shall we do one of these every day?"

"If I can."

"Every day."

I find out the boy is in the RAF. He's been flying planes. I ask if he knows Julian.

The boy thinks for a moment. "Is he a navigator?"

I'm sitting on the boy's bed, checking his blood pressure. "It would make sense. He was doing maths."

"I think I've heard of him. Is he your fiancé?"

"My brother."

I look around the ward at the men, with their pocked, seared, torn flesh, bits and pieces of limbs missing. All stretched out in this quiet, spacious room. Green walls, stone floor. A manor house before, so the windows are wide, and they look over meadows with stone walls and tree-lined avenues. It feels suitably remote. A place you'd go with a purpose—to write or to paint—or not at all.

I release the pressure on the cuff around the boy's bicep. "Your blood pressure's perfect."

"Does it mean I'll keep my legs?"

In the end, he loses a foot. And after, he tells me, "A foot doesn't seem like so much until you lose it."

*

Date: 27 November 1942

Patient: male, age 32

Clinical Record: Severe lacerations on torso.

Nurse's Notes: Assisted in cleaning and closing wound.

His side is sewn up like a zipper. For the second time.

It was oozing green when he came in, and he had a fever.

I assisted the doctor who cut him open and cleaned out the wound, leaving it unstitched for a few days so the air could get in and the infection could drain out.

It's my job to put sulfa powder on the wound. Cool compresses on his head.

The patient babbles and rolls about and pus oozes out his side.

On the third day, his fever drops, and the doctor sews him back up.

"Freak accident," the patient tells me when he finally comes to. "We crashed and I sliced myself open like a can of beans trying to get out of the plane. Everyone else was dead. I still don't know why I wasn't."

"Where did you crash?"

"Belgium."

I nod and swallow hard, "Do you know someone named Julian Raphaël?"

"Nope. But I've been on the lam for a spell."

I'm dressing the wound. It no longer smells rotten and the yellow of it isn't pus, but iodine and sulfa.

"How were you not captured?"

"Belgians got me out. They have quite a system."

"Will you go back to fight?"

"I can't wait for it to end, but so long as the war's on, I need to be in it."

*

Date: 28 November 1942

Patient: male, age 24

Clinical Record: Severe burns. Legs and arms crushed. Possible amputation.

Nurse's Notes: Administered salt baths. Sulfa.

Legs and arms torn to shreds. Burns.

I use more sulfa than I've ever used. He's too fragile to do a salt bath.

Despite my efforts, infection sets in.

Immediate surgery.

The doctor has no choice but to amputate. The infection's deep in the flesh where the sulfa can't reach—and probably in his blood.

After it's done, I wheel his legs to the room where they will be disposed of and as I approach, I smell burning flesh from the incinerator.

I touch one of the legs on my gurney—still warm—then I push open the door. The sheet pulls off the foot as I go through, and I see dirty toenails in need of clipping, a bunion below the big toe, a longer second toe. It's a working foot that digs into the earth and curls its toes around the soil.

I leave the legs with the orderly, who asks me to come round to the pub that night where a few of them are meeting. He says this as he checks the legs for metal or tags.

"You'll come?"

"Not tonight," I tell him.

"Suit yourself, but we'd love to have you." He has a thick Scottish accent that makes him sound like he's talking through pudding.

"Thank you."

I'm holding back tears and it makes the nobs of my eyebrows ache, but I don't cry. I can't. I made a promise to Charlotte that we wouldn't cry unless it was an ending.

I hurry back along the stone-floored corridor and into the operating room.

The doctor is sitting on a chair with his face in his hands. I've worked with him a lot, another good Scotsman, married with two or three children. I forget. He doesn't cry either.

Another nurse draws a sheet over the patient's face. I had wanted to ask the patient about Julian. He was in the same division. But now he's dead.

"Hang on," I say to the other nurse.

The doctor still has his face in his hands.

I run back down the corridor to the incinerator room.

"Changed your mind?" the orderly asks, grinning.

He's about to shove a leg in the open door to the furnace.

"Yes . . . No."

He pauses. "Well, lassie?"

"I need the legs. To bury with him."

The orderly sighs. "Poor bloke."

We both look at the leg he's holding.

"Tallish, was he?"

"Not really."

"Poor bloke," he says again. "No one'll know. I'll get it back with him."

"Thank you."

"See you at the pub?" he asks hopefully.

"Maybe."

                              *

I've decided two things.

   I don't believe in any god.

   I'm not going to marry.

   I can't tell Papa I don't believe in their god.

   I can't tell Mama I won't marry.

   Maybe it's the reverse.

   I won't tell either of them any of it.

   It will kill Mama—the idea that she won't have grandchildren.

   Yet another reason Julian must stay alive.

CHARLOTTE SAUVIN, 4L

I dream of Esther's hair—thick, wavy—hair that's a mane and a tail. And then someone is shearing that beautiful hair, shearing Esther the sheep and she's standing in front of me, and we're both crying. And I'm gathering all the hair, all the beautiful hair, and I make a new promise because we've broken our old one. To make a hat of it.

*

Philippe and I met only the one time in Antwerp. It was risky, and we both knew it. Philippe wouldn't tell me anything about what he was doing. He said it was safer that way.

I visited the priest who married us, brought a satchel full of Father's beer, and then went to confession.

And after, Philippe and I stumbled into a cramped room above the rectory, a closet of a room with bare encroaching walls, and he stripped off his pants—linen pants?—his shirt, and he pulled off my dress, and we were together on the hard cot, his flesh and my flesh devouring each other, and I remembered him, the strength in his shoulders, his firm, uncompromising intent. How he is nearly out of his mind with desire.

We were not waiting to live. And this was a choice.

We met on Rosh Chodesh. Philippe said it was the birth of the new moon. And then he was gone again.

*

There's a letter in our mailbox from Mrs. Raphaël. A short, elegant letter that's warm like bread. She writes of Scotland, of Esther, of Mr. Raphaël. And Julian, who has joined the RAF.

I slip the letter in the bag with the movie camera and the films and put it under my bed—a reminder of my promises.

*

The movie camera wasn't Julian's first camera. The Raphaëls gave him a No 2 Beau Brownie for his tenth birthday. There was a geometric inlay on the front, and Julian told me the case was the color of a dark sapphire. He let me take a few of the photographs in that first roll and when it was developed, he came to me with the stack of pictures.

"Yours are better than mine," he said.

"Not better."

"The exposure's better in every one of yours," he insisted. "Something you're doing with the framing and the shutter."

After that, he insisted that I go with him when he took pictures, to help him find the angle and understand how the light falls.

*

The rations are insufficient, and we each learn what we will do for money. There are people who have food, who have found ways to buy and sell. Some are sharp men who will always figure out how to make money on other people's misery in good times and bad. But not all of them.

*

The Colonel stops in and Father pours two beers. I've taken out the fabric and the wood hat block I brought from the milliner's shop—it's adjustable—and I'm making a hat. A warm hat. I'll use my own head to measure as I imagine it's about the size of a boy's.

Father offers to share our supper, but the Colonel won't hear of it. Sitting there, so contained on his chair, soft and shriveling, sweet and bitter, he reminds me of an old parsnip. He drains his beer and sets the glass on the table with a plunk.

"Masha's dead," he says.

A hole, black, bullets my vision and moves outward, pulling all things living and not yet born into it, until there is only darkness. I drop the scissors and grab the edge of the table.

"Charlotte?" Father's voice. Far away, beyond the darkness.

A jagged arc of light appears to the right of me. I close my eyes. The arc is still there. Shimmering and flashing, it begins to float across the darkness until all I can see is a field of pulsing light. The light owns me, it controls me, until finally, it floats on and fades. I open my eyes as the darkness reorganizes itself into the intelligible—Father's face, a chair, the window.

Then the sick, the vomiting. The weight of original sin.

*

"It was a migraine," Father tells me.

The Colonel has long since left, and I am in bed, spent, with a wet cloth over my forehead.

"Your mother had them too," he adds.

"Moses."

"Moses?"

"Yes. Genesis. Darkness, light, order emerging from chaos, the sick and banishment coming from a woman's original sin."

"And what was that sin?"

"Understanding that she didn't have to obey."

Father is reflecting, his face now his own, the distortion gone. For a time in the living room when I looked at him, he had no eyes.

"You might be right," he says.

We don't mention Masha.

That night, I'm restless, turning one way and another, on my back, my side. Father's snoring in the next room. I'm thinking about the letter from Mrs. Raphaël telling me Julian is in a plane and of the shorn Esther in my dream. I hold back tears. It was a bad dream. That's all.

Masha wouldn't want me to cry. I promised Esther I wouldn't.

I get out of bed, tiptoe into the living room, and pull the blackout paper from the window so I can look out over the square.

Did I know she would be there? Maybe.

I don't feel afraid when I understand what I'm seeing. I wonder if I am asleep and she is part of my dream or if she is asleep and I am part of her dream.

The cat is in the middle of the street staring back at me. And then she moves. She's letting me understand her size, the scale of things. Her grandeur. She isn't a mere cat; she's a lioness. She yawns and stretches. And then she lies down and closes her eyes. I watch her for a long time, until I, too, fall asleep. When I wake in the morning, stiff from having slept in the chair, I look out to see that she's still there. Like me, she's waking. She yawns and stretches and crosses the square as a car speeds out of a side street. I don't know if the lioness walks through the car or the car drives through her. Either way, no one is hurt.

I want to tell Masha about her. The lioness. Is she the mystical? Or the ordinary?

*

I go back to bed. I'm remembering Philippe's warmth. The energy in his body. The sound of his breath. Was it slow and steady? I sit up, panicked. How did he breathe?

Philippe is alive.

Masha is dead.

And Julian? I think of Julian.

And Esther. Our promise not to cry.

I get out of bed and find the pair of linen trousers I have hidden in my drawer. Philippe's trousers. I wrap them around my pillow.

I'll tell Father about the baby soon. Tomorrow, or the next day.

As for the lioness, I'm keeping her to myself. There's only so much a person can tell.

MASHA BALYAYEVA, 5TH FLOOR

You want to know how I died? In good time, my dears, I'll tell you everything. Have patience. It's worth the wait.

You still want a little something, don't you?

I was murdered. There. Satisfied for now?

*

I remember Charlotte talking about time. It was before she went away to study in Antwerp. Before Harry. I was sewing a coat. In fact, I was sewing the coat I wore on that last day. Camel hair with a beautiful nap and drape. A coat that falls like water.

Charlotte told me it's all the same. Time.

"Do you see into the future?" I asked her.

"I wouldn't want to because it would take away the moment. But the future is in every moment, and so is the past."

How the rabbi would have loved that!

"Describe camel hair," Charlotte said.

"You describe it."

She touched the fabric, she examined it, holding it close to her eyes, she swung it about, watching the waterfall of movement.

"It's not heavy given the density of the fibers," she began. "And it's soft. Not itchy like wool."

"Go on."

"It has a sheen to it, but not the kind you see on the seats of pants or the elbows of a jacket when they're worn. It's different."

"Perfect."

"Is it always a particular color?"

The question melted my heart. I wanted her just once to see through my eyes. And I wanted to see through hers.

"This one is natural. Uncolored, so it is indeed the color of a camel."

"Ah."

"But sometimes it's dyed. Usually black or blue. A dark color that can cover an already tonal natural beige."

"I understand."

"And sometimes what people call camel isn't really camel hair, rather it's the color of a camel."

"Is camel hair expensive?"

"Quite. Mrs. Raphaël bought enough fabric so I could make a coat for her and one for me as well. But I could make it for you instead. What about that?"

"Father bought a new coat for me this year."

I was more than a little irked that Francois hadn't come to me to make Charlotte's new coat.

"From Italy." Charlotte smiled. She knew what I was thinking.

"Oh well, then. If it's from Italy. Is it cashmere?"

"And soft wool."

"What color is it?" I almost didn't ask, but I knew Charlotte would be annoyed if I didn't.

"Gray," she laughed.

Later, I saw her wearing the coat. It was indeed gray. And a quite becoming shade of gray at that.

It was Charlotte who suggested the princess seams. She told me I'd look elegant in something tailored.

"Very thin people can wear clothes that hang a bit. Although not too much. But you should have something that takes your shape because it's so lovely," she said.

By that last day I wore the coat, I'm afraid to say, I had grown so thin it hung on me like a curtain.

I don't know why I wore it. I think to look like a Parisian. As though I belonged in the place I lived. But the truth is I never have. Not ever.

It was a simple task. I was walking with a young man. We were to act like lovers out at a café. He would go down to the toilet while I looked for my contact, our shuttle. I would greet the shuttle as though he were my lover's friend, who I happened to see at a place I often went.

"Everything will go beautifully," Harry said.

I was told the shuttle was a Canadian living in Paris. He had flown in the RAF in the Great War.

Everything would go beautifully.

My supposed lover had mumbled something about the toilet being convenient given that his stomach was off. Poor boy—English. Couldn't have been more than nineteen or twenty.

I never wanted to know the details. Their names, their stories. I used to think the more you knew the better. But as the rabbi said, the trick of life is not knowing that you know nothing; rather, it's knowing as little as possible in a time when knowledge can only harm you.

I sat down with the Canadian man, the shuttle.

He smiled encouragingly. "Delightful to see you again,' he said in French.

He was much older than the boy I was escorting. The idea that they were friends struck me as implausible. I pushed a loose floor tile in a circle with the toe of my boot, feeling a cold chill around my neck. The waiter came to our table and the shuttle ordered three beers. His French had the slightest accent, not quite Canadian. I've always been acutely aware of these nuances in accent and language, I think because I spoke with the accent and lexicon of the place I grew up, and the rabbi had insisted that I learn to speak another way, one that wouldn't be easily identified as provincial in a city.

"Always dress and talk like the people you find yourself among," he'd said.

"You didn't," I told him. "You stand out like a tree in the field."

"There's only one tree in the field, and usually the farmer leaves it alone. But when stalks grow too tall, they're cut down."

I followed his advice. Thanks to my uncle and to Sophia Raphaël, I'm a parrot, a good mimic. I learned to speak French like a Belgian. And when I came here, I dropped my Belgian accent and took on a Parisian one, not too elevated, not classless, appropriate for a Parisian woman who might casually run into a Parisian acquaintance in a local café that smelled of stale beer and fresh coffee.

I've spent my life pretending to be someone other than who I am, and I know when others are doing the same.

The waiter brought our beers and the shuttle fumbled around for his ration tickets. I had a chance to study him. Small dark eyes, dumpling nose, cleft chin, long yellowed teeth—a few of them gold-filled. He was wearing a pair of thin leather gloves. Cheap, not the bold well-made gloves of a former airman. I knew in my stomach he was not cut of new-world cloth. He didn't have the open-faced swagger of an American, the stoic confidence of a Canadian.

He finally found his tickets and gave them to the waiter, who looked at him expectantly.

"What?" the shuttle asked.

"And three francs," the waiter said.

"How much?"

"Three tickets and three francs."

The shuttle searched in his pockets with a gloved hand, mumbling in French.

He pulled out a few coins and dropped them on the table; among them was a Belgian zinc coin.

"Don't tell me you want the *handelszink* too," he said to the waiter.

It was the way he said it—the accent he couldn't hide when speaking his native tongue. And the derision in his voice. The shuttle wasn't Canadian or French. He was Flemish.

I looked down at my coat and noticed that the seam was opening on the edge of a buttonhole. A tiny ball of fuzz had formed from the fabric wearing against the button. I picked at it. I didn't want my eyes to betray me. What I was certain I'd just figured out.

The waiter moved on to the next table and the shuttle collected the spare coins. As he did, the index fingertip of his left glove bent backward all the way. He was wearing the gloves to hide that he was missing part of a finger.

I glanced at my watch. I was supposed to go downstairs no later than fifteen minutes after we stepped into the place. If I didn't, the RAF boy was to leave through the basement exit.

"I'll check on him," I said.

"He's in the toilet?" the shuttle asked not looking up, still trying to capture a last coin with his abbreviated index finger.

"He mentioned that he's feeling off," I said.

This was when I made my mistake. I couldn't stand the way he was pushing the coin around the table. I reached over, picked it up, and gave it to him.

He looked at me. And we both knew the game was up.

"I'll get him," I said, as if by still playing my role I could erase the moment.

He didn't move. "Good idea."

I stood and walked slowly toward the toilet. I checked my watch again. Seventeen minutes. No one could be late in these situations. Fifteen minutes was fifteen minutes. Surely the young RAF fellow had already slipped away.

I was near the front door, and I could see the waiter passing the table where the shuttle was sitting. As they exchanged a word, I stepped outside and began to walk to the emergency meeting place.

There were a few people on the street, all in dark coats, and I re-gretted the camel hair at once. It was too easily seen. I stood out. In my beautiful shroud.

I heard the first shot. It was very loud, but I kept walking, thinking the strange buzzing in my head was from the sound of it. I turned a corner and tried to run, but my legs felt thick, like they were running through a custard. Why?

I stumbled along and as I did, I was conscious of a warmth on my neck and I reached up feeling a wet that covered my hand.

I looked at my hand. It was bright red.

I should have felt panic, but I didn't. All I thought was that Charlotte wouldn't have seen it as red, and it was so bright, so vivid . . . It was life.

I stumbled along to the meeting place—another café—why was no one following me? I remember worrying that the blood would ruin my coat if I didn't get hold of some cold salt water very soon.

I could see the folds of the coat moving, and I registered how grace-fully the fabric flowed around my legs. Even when I stumbled and nearly fell, the coat moved like royalty. And when the blood began to drip off my neck and spattered the front of the coat, it carried on. As did I.

I reached the café, but Harry wasn't there. The café owner rushed to call an ambulance.

"No," I said. "A glass of water. A napkin."

Where was the RAF boy? He was supposed to be there too.

I tucked the napkin in the hole in the side of my neck, took a sip of water, felt very sleepy. I heard another voice, one I didn't recognize, but I was too tired to look and see who it was.

I was about to doze off when I heard running footsteps. *They've caught up with me*, I thought. *They're here to finish me off.*

But it wasn't the Nazis, or the gestapo, or whoever had shot me. It was Harry.

He saw me and he started crying.

"For G-d's sake," I said. "Get me to the doctor. The one you trust."

But Harry was looking at me and sobbing. He couldn't stop himself.

"The doctor."

He didn't seem to hear me. Or maybe I wasn't making a sound. I felt cold. And warm at the same time. And quite distant from the whole thing. I remembered my coat.

"Salt water," I said.

"Who was it?" Harry asked.

Why wasn't he calling the doctor?

"Belgian—"

"We're not in Belgium, we're in Paris."

"A Flem . . . Doctor . . . Harry . . ."

Harry was hugging me, holding me. And sobbing. I could hear footsteps all around.

I felt the cool of the gun's barrel on the side of my head. And I think I must have known. But there was so little time between *must have known* and *known*—being alive and then dead—that I can't be sure.

I lost track of the café. I didn't see what happened next. I was gone from that place. I'm in quite another place.

I'm not certain Harry had to kill me. I don't know whose footsteps I heard. Whose voice. No one seemed to follow me into the second café. Maybe they followed Harry. I don't know if he was afraid that I would live and talk or that I would talk and live. Or talk and die. I don't know if he was afraid that I'd be tortured. Or that he would, because of what I might say. And I will never know these things.

*

I do know that I was buried in my coat. Blood and all.

*

We never married, even though Harry told people we had. Harry wanted children and I didn't. I felt I was past the point where I could have them easily, but he wanted me to try.

In the midst of a war, when everyone was starving, and my child would be Jewish, he wanted me to *try?*

I told him that was silly. And he said, "Then we can't marry because the whole point of marriage is to have children."

I can see it from where he sits. He wants his genes to go forward in time.

I can also see the hubris in that. The self-importance. He wasn't a king; he had no empire. He only had me.

I think Charlotte would have told me to leave him at once, that any man who couldn't see the future in the present with me alone wasn't the man who loved me most or best. And Charlotte would have been right.

*

I know only one thing. Life is a dream. You wake up long enough to know it's a dream . . . just before you die.

AGATHE HOBERT, 3R

I see all kinds of things, and I don't meddle. I would if I thought it would be a lie not to, but that's the only time I can imagine getting involved.

Take this evening in the square. I wished I had worn a hat on two counts. First, it was cold. And second, I can't get hold of my henna hair dye and up top is a bollix. A great white stripe down the center of my head. People were looking at me. I'm as fetching as a red skunk.

But I don't have a good hat.

I had gotten my bread; it hasn't escaped my notice that the baker is giving me smaller pieces. I don't have a scale and I can't see hers. Next time, I'll go behind the counter and look for myself.

I was hurrying to buy my paper and then tuck myself back in the safety of my apartment. I do prefer to stay home.

That was when I saw Charlotte Sauvin with the newsboy. I'm not gossiping! Who would I tell? She gave him a parcel. It was flat and wrapped in brown paper. I slowed my pace and slipped around the corner. I wasn't spying on them, but I didn't want to talk to Charlotte, so I had no choice but to wait out of sight.

The newsboy opened the parcel right then and there, and he pulled out a hat. Not just any hat. A thick wool hat that was dark gray, almost black. He put it on and for the first time, ever, I saw the boy smile.

He never smiles at me, does he? Or at anyone else. What can I say? Everyone likes a present.

"Perfect," I heard Charlotte say in that cool voice she has. The girl is as emotional as a block of marble.

Charlotte took her newspaper and handed the boy coins. I thought, *That's very odd! Why would she give him a hat and coins?* What else was the boy giving her? That's what I'd like to know. Not because I'd tell. I need to keep my guard up. Stay safe. She's in my building, you understand. Guilt by association happens. It does. I've heard the stories. My tenant in the building near the train station—Putzeis—told me of two cases where someone did something and someone else did nothing and that someone else paid the price. I'm sure there are dozens of these stories. I would hear more of them if I were a gossip or at all social. But these days, I don't have the energy. And you never know who you're talking with, do you?

Charlotte was walking away, and I hurried over to the newsboy. The top of my head was cold, and I felt my throat scratch and tickle. Belgium is no place to catch cold. Before you know it, you've got bronchitis or worse, pneumonia, and then you're done for.

"That's a smart hat," I said.

The newsboy looked at me. Not smiling anymore.

Were his eyes always that shiny? Or were those tears? I'm sure he can cry at the drop of a hat. Conniving little beggar.

He held out a copy of *Le Soir*, and I paid him for it.

"That hat must be very warm."

"I don't know yet," he said. "I've only just put it on."

Dirk was in the lobby when I stepped into the building. He looked at my hair, I swear he did, and he smiled.

"Well she didn't give me a hat," I said huffily.

I did say that. I'm normally less forthcoming, but it came out.

"Who?" Dirk asked.

"Who do you think?"

I moved around him, and that was when I slipped on the wet floor. What a time to mop! I must advise the notary's wife lest she kill us all. I didn't fall, but I might have. I might have broken a leg or cracked my skull. All it takes is one fall at my age, and you're shitting in a bedpan for the rest of your years.

I looked back to see that Dirk was checking his mailbox. He looked disappointed to see that it was empty. Who gets mail these days?

The main door to the building opened, and the notary stepped into the lobby with a man I had never seen before.

"Mind the floor if you value your life," I called out to them.

The notary and the man, a Flem—don't ask how I know, but I know—hurried past and up the stairs without so much as a glance in my direction.

Dirk shut his mailbox and followed me to the staircase as I began my ascent.

"Who didn't make you a hat?"

"It's odd, you know. A Flemish man all alone in such a large apartment. I'm sure that's why he's here. He's looking at the apartment. The man with Everard—the notary."

"Yes, I know." Dirk passed me on the stairs and waited on the landing above.

"Maybe he has a family."

"He's not wearing a wedding ring."

My lungs felt cramped and burning. My goodness. To almost break a leg and before that perhaps come down with pneumonia. I could die.

"Charlotte," I said as I planted foot on landing. "The hat!"

"Why would she give you a hat?"

"She gave the newsboy one."

Shut up, Agathe, you fool. Don't go on like that. It's none of his business.

And now Dirk is following me up the stairs.

"What kind of hat?"

"Warm and new. She's a hatmaker, you know."

"I didn't. But I find that quite funny."

"Why?"

As if you're indignant on Charlotte's behalf. You don't give a fig about that insufferable, reed of a girl.

And now I hear the Colonel talking to those two imbeciles he's got in his apartment. Did I mention? The Colonel is taking in half-wits, and he talks to them all the time loudly, as if the louder he speaks, the better they'll hear. But they can't hear. Nonetheless, he calls out incessant instructions: Put on your shoes. Take off your shoes. Slice the bread with this knife. Wash your hands. Time to put the paper on the windows.

The Colonel's obviously starved for conversation. Alone as so many of us are, not that his wife was a brilliant raconteur. I never liked her, and I always wondered if he did. She couldn't have children, and all her philanthropic work was I suppose meant to compensate. She married up, and that's the best I can say of her.

But now he's taken it upon himself—all the work for her causes. Why? It's occurred to me that he's getting subsidies for doing it. From the church? Probably. Right hand doesn't know what the left is doing. The Colonel's an atheist for heaven's sake. As for his wife, we all know what she was. One of them.

I spoke to the notary's wife about it. She's a simple woman, but perhaps I've underestimated her. I took her a slice of cake the other day and she invited me in for a cup of tea. I learned a little something of why they left their village. Everard was in business with his father, both of them notaries. But another notary came to town and took all their work. By undercutting. And do you know what she told me? The new notary was one of them too. Yes. A Jew.

Dirk has reached his apartment. I can tell he's watching as I pull myself up the last flight. I never used to be breathless on the stairs. One of these days, I'll expire, and no one will notice.

No more cakes for the Colonel. I can barely scabble one together these days. Even lard is hard to come by. Putzeis gives me a bit of lard or butter along with the rent. Very generous of him. Putzeis is a good man. Very truthful.

He's doing some work with the VNV. I don't know what and I didn't ask, but he told me about it right up front, and I appreciated that. It's unusual in these times for people to be so forthcoming.

"Look, we all do what we believe we must," I said to Putzeis. "The point is that we tell the truth. Without truth, what do we have left? Nothing!"

Oh, but he agreed. How could he not? How could any reasonable person not agree?

The phone in my apartment is ringing. I put my key in the lock. And then I take it out. It's probably about my aunt, who's been ill. I heard this through a cousin, who called to tell me I should visit her.

"I'm not sniffing after the corpse for a funeral meal," I said indignantly.

"That's not what I meant," my cousin said, and she sounded shocked.

As if that's not exactly what people do. I have another cousin whose parents had quite a lot of money before the war. They had four sons, but only the one stayed close to home. Well, they gave him all the land, didn't they? And they left him the house when they died. His wife inherited land as well, but when his mother asked him about it before she died, he lied to her and said they hadn't gotten anything from his wife's family. So, his poor mother felt sorry for him and left him even more. As for his brothers, they never spoke to him again. Money does that. And lies about money.

"Thank you for letting me know," I said to my cousin when she told me.

"Will you see her?"

"One way or another," I said.

I wait in the hall until the ringing stops. I don't want to talk to anyone.

People should think twice before they meddle. It isn't my cousin's business, whether I see my aunt or not. Who do these people think they are?

As I put my key in the lock again, I hear footsteps behind me, and I turn to see that Dirk has come up to the landing and is watching me. He looks amused.

"Can you stop playing your saxophone in the evenings?" I ask, hoping to put him back on his heels.

"No," he says, looking even more amused. He smiles at me, an obliging smile, and it gives me a moment's pause.

"Do you get out of the building much?"

"Yes," he says.

"I don't do well in the cold. I don't like to take the tram, and I'm nervous about driving these days. Checkpoints."

"Avoid the checkpoints."

"If I lose my way."

"I see."

Perhaps I've been wrong about him. Such an obliging smile. Understanding.

He could help me.

"Would you care for a slice of cake, a cup of tea?" I ask.

"Don't mind if I do."

I open the door and Dirk follows me inside.

*

The building's falling apart. Not the bricks and mortar but the atmosphere. The feeling of the place. It isn't what it used to be. This morning, the Colonel knocked and when I opened my door, I saw that he was with one of those serge-suited simpletons of his.

"I have no more cakes," I said to the Colonel.

What if he wasn't asking for a cake?

"Oh." The Colonel seemed surprised.

He wasn't asking for a cake.

"What do you want?" I asked crossly.

I was keenly aware of the white stripe that went down the middle of my head. I touched my scalp.

Oh great, call attention to it, you ninny.

"I wondered," the Colonel said, "if you might be willing to loan us a puzzle or two."

The Colonel indicated his drooling comrade and quickly offered him a handkerchief. The man wiped his mouth and chin with a grunt. I personally wouldn't have touched the handkerchief after that, but the

Colonel had no such compunctions. He folded it up and put it right back in his pocket.

"They're very good at puzzles, you see," the Colonel continued. "Being as all they've had to go by are their eyes. I saw one of them put together a puzzle at the other place, the house that burned to the ground," and here he paused.

Did he expect me to tell him how sorry I was that it had? Well, I was sorry because it meant now there were these men living across from me. I have no doubt they have impulses, and the thought of that makes me feel sick. I didn't say a word.

"Lightning fast," the Colonel added.

"If they're so fast, one puzzle won't do much good, will it?"

"Exactly why I thought of you," the Colonel said. "I know you have two dozen or so of them."

How dare he? Put me on the spot like that. The cad.

"They're very good at cleaning as well. Should you need a set of hands."

That expression, *set of hands*. Well, it set my teeth on edge, that's what it set.

"Oh no."

"Not for money. They need to keep busy."

"I'm sure there's plenty to clean in your apartment with those dogs of yours."

Enough of this being friends with neighbors.

"There's only one and he's a very clean dog."

"How could he be? He eats rats."

The Colonel had a look on his face I hadn't seen before. Steely. Not friendly. Not the Colonel I knew, but then, you never really know anyone, do you? How can you? That's why it's essential to be vigilant. Self-protective. Wary.

"If it goes on like this, we'll all be eating rats. And that's if we're lucky," he said. "I'll wait here for you to fetch those puzzles."

Cornered! What else could I do?

I gave him two puzzles. I happen to know that both have a missing piece. That's what you get when you insist on handouts.

He thanked me, but there was something unfinished in the exchange. I don't like loose ends.

"Maybe they can help Charlotte with her hats," I called after him.

The Colonel didn't look back. "I doubt it. She's a very independent girl, you know."

*

That was yesterday and last night. I tossed and turned.

What a bitch you are. Really. A complete bitch.

But I'm pleased to say that I came up with a way to redeem myself. In the morning, I marched up the stairs and knocked on the Sauvins' door.

Francois opened it. He smiled. A perfunctory smile. Trust me, I know one when I see it, one that says, *Hello, goodbye. Please leave.*

"What can I do for you, Miss Hobert?"

"Not you. Charlotte."

From where I stood, I could see Charlotte at the table. She was sticking needles into felt wrapped around a wood hat mold. Timing is everything.

Francois opened the door wider, and I stepped in.

The upper-level apartments are superior in this building, in any building. And the parquet floor is simply exceptional. I have rugs on my floors to hide all the dents in the pine.

"Hello, Miss Hobert," Charlotte said.

She didn't even look at me. She's focused on her work. Well, I wouldn't want her to look up from my hat.

"I'd like a hat. Not a large hat, more of a cap. Something I could wear . . . even indoors."

"Oh."

Charlotte stuck the last of the pins in the felt, then looked at me, at my head, at my hair. What a strange girl.

"I would pay. A reasonable amount," I said. Somehow the girl compels it out of me. I know better than to make the first overture when it comes to money.

"What is a reasonable amount?"

I named a figure that was fair, and I do know my prices. Even these days, there's a scale—overmarket and under.

"The choice of fabric is limited."

"Show me what you have."

After all, she had my offer, and now I was the client.

Charlotte adjusted a pin in the felt and got up from the table.

She's quite thin, Charlotte is. Enviably.

"A cup of tea?" Francois asked.

Well, wasn't that generous of him? We all know how scarce it is.

"No thank you. I just finished mine."

We waited in an awkward silence.

"The Colonel might ask if you want a bit of cleaning help from his new tenants."

There you go, Agathe. You can't shut up, can you?

"Tenants?"

"The deaf men he's taking in."

"I didn't know."

"They can't speak, not a word, and one of them drools, so I wouldn't recommend."

"I don't think we need any help of that sort."

Mercifully, Charlotte stepped back into the room with three bolts of cloth. One of them was red. Another deep gold, and the last pale blue. She laid them on the table, and we looked at them together.

"I need to measure your head."

"Of course."

Charlotte had an old paper tape. She measured the circumference around my forehead, from the base of my skull to the crown, between my ears. And she wrote everything down. Very precise.

"What do you think?" She indicated the fabrics.

I could see that each was labeled with a color—winter sky, marigold, crimson.

"It's difficult to know," I say.

Good lord, at your age, Agathe, you should know!

"The wool of these two is the same." Charlotte indicated the red and the gold. "Bluefaced Leicester."

"Sorry?"

"That's the name of the sheep the wool comes from. It's especially soft and dense and as such very good for hats."

"And what about the fabric that's actually blue?"

"It's cashmere."

"I see. What color do you think will look best on me?"

Charlotte held up one bolt to the side of my face and then another and finally the third. She had me turn to the window and did it again.

"Winter sky," she said decisively. It brings out your skin and eyes.

I've always quite liked blue. People say it's my color. Well, Charlotte has taste, I'll give her that. Let's see how the hat turns out.

"I can pay you a bit to start, but I want to try it on before I give you all the money."

"That's all right. I can make adjustments. We'll get it exactly to your liking."

I didn't thank her. I've never believed in thanking people one does business with. I'm paying her and that is thanks enough.

FRANCOIS SAUVIN, 4L

I was surprised to see Hobert this morning, poised on the threshold, almost losing her balance as she peered at Charlotte. I had the passing sensation that our doorway might mark a crossing to a different life for her, that this was her liminal moment, one that would cause her to change for the better before it was too late. I invited her in. It turned out she wanted a hat, not a transformation. Maybe the hat will do the job.

It was pure delight to see Charlotte describe how the color blue looked on our inquisitive neighbor. Not that any color can save that poor woman from herself.

When the fitting was over, Hobert turned to me and said, "You really should be careful about the Colonel. His newfound fascination with the underclass is a danger to us all."

"Funny. That's exactly what the Pharisees said to Pontius Pilate."

"I didn't know you were religious," she sniffed.

"I'm not."

"Well, the Colonel is no Jesus. So, be careful."

"I don't know what you're talking about, but we must all be careful. You have a wonderful day."

She made no move to leave; once again she was poised on the threshold.

"If I were you—" she began.

"And thank goodness, you're not. If life has taught me anything, it's that we need fewer men in this world."

*

This evening, our resident Jesus, the Colonel, stops in. I tell him I have a new batch of beer made in the good Trappist tradition and, given his saintly character, it seems most appropriate. I describe my first assay with the new recipe, how too much beet sugar and an overzealous fermentation turned the bottle into a rocket that shot into the top of the pantry cabinet and exploded with such a crack I thought it was a bomb.

"I should have paid more attention in chemistry," I tell him.

"I should have paid more attention. Had we been observant, we would have noticed how damnably clever Germans are, and maybe we would have been on our toes."

"I doubt it would have mattered."

I wipe down the bottle. It's sweating even though the room is chilly. I've taken to wearing thick wool hunting socks and two sweaters. Charlotte and I drink hot water all day to ward off flu. I uncap and quickly pour the dark brown liquid into two tall glasses. A brackish smell drifts up with the carbon, still the only thing that offsets the strange smell of rot.

I hand the Colonel his glass. "Moment of reckoning."

"And who better to reckon with?"

We take our beers to the living room where Charlotte is shaking out the blue fabric.

"The beer looks all right," I say.

"Looking right is half the battle. And I won't add that Hobert has lost that war."

I see Charlotte give the Colonel a sharp look. She takes a pair of scissors from a side table and kneels on the carpet, studying the fabric. Charlotte moves it in a curve, then an angle. She's making up her mind.

"Fucking Nazis," the Colonel says, lowering his voice so Charlotte won't hear. "Taking our beer. Nasty children with guns."

"We're all children."

We raise our glasses.

"To a better end than we now see."

I sip the beer. "Not perfect, not terrible."

"Oh, it's very good. No, my dear Francois, it's magnificent."

The Colonel settles into a chair. "I have a couple of lads living with me," he begins.

"I hear they're good at cleaning."

"And I hear that Charlotte is making hats."

We're both chuckling.

"You remember, the wife worked with all those deaf people," he continues.

"Did she?"

"Yes, yes. You know. Causes. Everything was a cause. Helping a who-who there and a what-what here."

I have no idea what the Colonel is talking about.

"Deaf and essentially mute. They can make sounds of course but not words. Not blind, thankfully, so they can cook and tidy up, that sort of thing, but on the street, poor souls, lost."

"Where were they before?" I ask, mystified.

"A house. Farmhouse. A bit pastoral for my taste. Rough. Not a fan of the countryside. Give me a city and I'll raise you a stand-up building and a couple of parks. Place burnt. To the ground."

"The place in the country?"

"That's the one. Nowhere for them to go, so we've arranged a rotation of places. Here a bit, there a bit. You see what I mean." The Colonel leaned forward, low voiced. "I swear, if I hadn't done it, she'd have come back from the grave and killed me. She would. The wifey."

The Colonel rests on this thought with what looks like both terror and amusement.

"That wifey of mine. Bruiser."

As the Colonel talks, I watch Charlotte work—measuring the fabric, carefully cutting it again and again. Face puckered in consternation, checking the measurements she has written down, measuring her own head. Another cut in the fabric.

"One at a time. Two at most," the Colonel is saying with that easy levity of his. "Poor lads. They really can't talk at all. And they only seem to understand a bit of French. No German, that's for sure. And I don't know a word of Flemish. Well, a few words. Do you know sign language?" The Colonel makes a helpless gesture with his big hands, "Me either. What a time not to be able to communicate."

"When the conversations stopped, that was the moment of danger," I say.

"Agreed."

"Remember how Leo was infatuated with Turkish houses?"

"I do not."

"The way they have a gathering room on each floor, for talking."

"I never heard that. Anyway, my gal would have been pleased. Oh yes, she would have been over the moon that I'm finally doing something for someone other than myself."

I remember then that the Colonel's wife had a stroke during an argument with a waiter over moules frites at a restaurant near the Place Sainte-Catherine. The Colonel was with her and later he told me with a look that somehow managed to convey both grief and mischief, "What can I say but that she was passionate about her shellfish? She died doing the two things she loved most. Eating and arguing."

The faint bray of Dirk's saxophone mixes with the RRG broadcast from the notary's apartment on the ground floor. It's only a matter of time before his wife starts screaming at him.

If I didn't know the content of the broadcast or the source of what can't quite be called music, if I didn't understand the circumstances of our lives, if my son-in-law, Philippe, were here at the table with us, and instead of my dilute, bitter, overcarbonated beer . . .

We'd be drinking a delicate burgundy and talking about Wittgenstein and Reinhart, and I would say something banal about how astonishing it is that I fought against him in the last war—Wittgenstein. Formally speaking, fought, for had we known . . . had we known . . . I'd like to think we would have raised the white flags and called off the charade.

"Dark waters, swamp of vitriol. He's quite alone." The Colonel, still talking, pulls me out of my reverie. "No one comes near him. Maybe he has no friends at all. How his parents raised a boy like that? Too much kindness."

It takes me a moment to understand that the Colonel is talking about Dirk. He carries on as I drift back . . .

I would sip my burgundy and watch Charlotte and Philippe dance, with the French doors open over the square, the sound of voices and the clink of silver on stoneware drifting up from outdoor bistro tables with the roar of an occasional engine, the cool night air, the smell of garlic and flowers—

"Both missing pieces," the Colonel says loudly, as if he knows I'm not paying attention. "I've asked the lads to get to work and make pieces to fill in. Puzzles. They're clever with their hands. Makes me proud."

The broadcast sounds louder, the saxophone whines, it's almost time for the blackout. I step over to the gramophone and put on a record. As the first strains of music reach my ears, I feel another wave of nostalgia.

"The little chicken thief can play, can't he? You know who should hear this? That big lump on the second floor. Composing dirges for frogs, that's what he's doing. Now this . . . now this," the Colonel trails off as he takes another sip of beer and closes his eyes, letting the music wash over him.

The music shifts. It's one of Charlotte's favorites that she and Philippe danced to. Impulsively, I grab her hand, and we dance, the thud and drag of my bad leg part of the rhythm, and for a moment, I forget everything but the wild, dizzying swirl. We dance until the song is over, and when it is, the Colonel claps. How such a thin man can have those meaty hands? I wipe my brow and sit in breathless exhilaration as Charlotte goes back to her sewing, a smile on her face.

*

The building has gone quiet and Charlotte is putting blackout paper on the windows. I snap on the lamp.

And now I'm seeing Django in his wife's gypsy wagon, both of them Roma, and she's making flowers, shiny paper flowers to sell at cafés, and he knocks over the lamp or does she? And the flowers—those lovely, gaudy, terrible creations—ignite like ghost money, the whole place goes up in flames, not killing him or her but burning off the ends of his fingers and giving his guitar playing a singular flavor. Like burnt toast.

"Rumor has it that the sorties are coming closer and closer to Brussels. RAF. Brave lads. God help them if they crash."

I don't look at Charlotte as the Colonel says this. She thinks I don't know about Philippe. Maybe it's better that way. I haven't decided.

"I should be getting back to my little flock."

The Colonel finishes his beer with a look of deep pleasure but also longing. It's the look of a man having one last smoke before the firing squad.

He gets up from the table, and I see again how terribly thin he is. I never thought I'd live to see the Colonel waste away. He looks like someone else; maybe he is someone else. Maybe the Colonel has been replaced by an imposter. But I know I look different too. We're all being replaced with ghosts and strangers.

*

Charlotte was ten and it was the middle of the night. The sound of her padding around the apartment woke me and I got out of bed and went into the living room to find her, a ghost in a long flannel nightgown, eyes half-closed. She seemed to be almost asleep, but I knew from experience that it was the other way around. She was almost awake.

"Charlotte?" I asked. "Do you know where you are?"

"I'm . . . here," she said.

"And where is that?"

"With you."

Oh Charlotte. My cagey sleepwalker.

I led her back to her bed and tucked her in without waking her.

*

Charlotte was eleven, and she was standing over my bed in her night-gown, watching me sleep.

"How long have you been up?"

"There are no stars tonight, Father."

"Because it's cloudy. Go back to bed."

"I can't sleep."

I sat up and looked at her. I knew from experience she wouldn't relent.

"I can make you hot milk."

"Yes."

I rolled out of bed, feeling the shooting pain in my leg. I had talked about it with a doctor, who suggested that I consider amputation.

"I don't much like that."

"The trouble is, sometimes people feel the pain even after we take off the leg."

"Then why would I consider it?"

The doctor was a complacent man, comfortable in his profession, near retirement. "Suit yourself," he said. "You have my number."

I took his card out of my pocket and tossed it in the trash.

"Not anymore," I said.

I heated up milk at the stove.

"Nutmeg?" Charlotte asked.

I had spoiled her and that wasn't the end of the world. So long as she was strong, she could be spoiled. I poured the milk into a mug, grated nutmeg over the top, and gave it to her.

"Will you wait while I drink it in bed?"

"Yes."

What a divine little monster.

She was in her bed and sipping slowly. Little sips, little breaths. It was maddening, because I sleep well in the evening, but not so well in the morning.

"Once there was a boy and there was a girl," I began.

Charlotte settled back against her pillow. She still liked my stories. I wondered for how much longer. Shame on me for feeling annoyed with her. The moment was everything.

"They were very good friends."

"Like Julian and I are?"

"Exactly like that. They ran and they climbed trees and they flew kites. But when winter came, with snow and ice and cold rain and wind, they had to stay inside and be studious and read their books and do their lessons."

Charlotte had gotten to be a better listener, but I could see a question in her eyes.

"Sometimes they ice-skated."

A little smile, a sip of milk.

"Even so, they couldn't wait for the thaw of spring, when the air would grow soft with a hint of fresh grass and salt, for, of course, they lived by the sea."

Another smile, another tiny sip.

"A wide river flowed to the sea nearby. An estuary."

"I like salt water."

"I know you do. There were tall trees on its banks that leafed out in summer to give shade, but in early spring, they were sticks letting in the sun so grass could grow—"

"You can say it," Charlotte told me between sips.

"Say what?"

"That the grass would turn green." Charlotte's eyes crinkled in an almost smile.

"When the grass was green, the boy and the girl ran outside to play at the river. They climbed trees, waded in shallows, danced in the breeze.

It was the girl who saw the hat blowing across a field. A beaver top hat so well made the brim didn't have so much as a dent when it reached them. The girl thought it had special powers."

"The mystical is in the ordinary."

"What?"

"Masha told me."

"Oh. Yes, it's true. The hat was mystical and when the boy put it on, he saw the future: people and events and creatures and vistas that weren't yet in the landscape, and he saw the girl as a woman—"

"You left out that she's dressed in trousers."

"Of course she is." I took Charlotte's empty mug. "The boy understood that what was ahead was already part of the world and if he wasn't heedful, time would move faster than he could—"

"Yes, just because you can't see something doesn't mean it isn't there."

Our eyes met, Charlotte's gray eyes—wide, uncommon eyes. Who in the family ever had eyes like those?

"And it was this knowledge that made the boy do something seemingly impetuous to those who don't understand time. He knelt and asked the girl to marry him."

"I wonder if Mr. Monet knows the hat is magical?"

"I should think so."

"Mr. Raphaël said it's worth all the other paintings put together. Because Mr. Monet painted it. He asked how I would measure the value of a painting."

"What did you tell him?"

"The one I loved most would be worth most to me."

"Did he agree?"

"No. He said Julian told him to buy it."

"Julian's quite something."

"My best friend," Charlotte said softly. And with that, she fell asleep.

*

I hear the Nazis have taken over my offices, and there are horses in the stalls again, filling them with shit. At least the fountain will be put to good use, for the beasts, the ones with fur not uniforms. It's a square fountain—suited to a space that's all rectangles and squares.

The trenches were a maze of rectangles. Wittgenstein and I were trapped in a geometry not of our making—and yes, I am convinced that had we known the other was across a field, we would have stopped shooting and escaped to talk about something worthwhile. Like architecture. Wittgenstein designed one building I knew of, built in Vienna for his sister—a stark, minimalist house, the kind of structure Belgium's own Victor Horta aspired to design in his later years. It disappointed me that Horta abandoned his garden of earthly design for all those straight lines and columns. Unlike Wittgenstein, he was no master of simplicity. I would have talked to Wittgenstein about that too.

They can't stop me, those fucking Nazis. I'm designing buildings that have no straight lines. I might never see them constructed, but I have the comfort of knowing that they exist. They have facades that are trees, windows that are flowers, staircases that curl around like snails, stalks of cornices curving up to roofs that branch out, to better watch the clouds—or the real stars—should they ever be seen again.

CHARLOTTE SAUVIN, 4L

"The world is everything, that is the case. The world is the totality of facts, not things, The world is determined by the facts, these being all the facts."

*

I've been reading the Wittgenstein book. I don't know what I'm hoping to get out of it. Comfort? A sense of knowing? I'm not getting either, only questions.

*

"The freedom of will consists in the fact that future actions can't be known now."
   Define future, please. If the future is in this moment, as I believe, and we have free will, it isn't a question of knowing the future but understanding the present.

*

"In a manner of speaking, objects are colorless."
   Obviously.
   "Space, time, and color are forms of objects."
   Obviously not.

*

I'd rather read a magical book with the illusion of a beginning and an end. Not pithy little bursts that force me to consider every damn sentence.

*

My hands tremble as I wrap the first hat I've ever been commissioned to make, the irony that it's for Miss Hobert not escaping me. The brown paper is too thick, and it doesn't take the shape of the felt as it should, but it's all I have. I've never been so nervous. I don't startle at loud noises, big storms, mice—and there are mice in this building. The Colonel claims there are rats too. I've never seen one, but I wouldn't be afraid if I did. I hear the mice at night. When I was a girl, I begged Father to get a cat.

"I'm allergic," he would say.

"To cats?"

"To cleaning up after animals."

Father is so mild, so amenable, so reasonable—other than when it comes to bringing an animal in the house—I shouldn't have faulted him. But I punished him. When I went to a friend's house, and they had a cat or a dog, I would mention it to Father as if to say, *Some families manage to have more than one child, and they also have pets*. I would talk about how that house felt like a real home and reminded me of the Raphaëls, who also had a real home despite the lack of animals. It was cruel, I know, and it pained Father. I could see that. I could see the hurt in his eyes, but I didn't relent and neither did he, ignoring notes I left on the table about a free kitten here, a stray cat needing to be adopted there. Father held firm. See, he's as stubborn as I am.

Even the loss of my job hasn't seemed to affect him. Could he hide it from me if it had? Maybe. He's acting so calm and cheerful it's maddening. I think if I walked into the kitchen naked and baked a pair of shoes, he would comment only on the temperature of the oven. Maybe it's because he was in the Great War, and anything is better than those trenches. Or maybe because the worst happened when my mother died, and he knows he can get through it. Whatever *it* is. But I'm afraid he's growing detached and we've changed places. Father was so determined, so focused, so involved in everything. He had notebooks filled with ideas and lists and plans that became homes and buildings. He used to say that compared to him, I was a pond, that I took my sustenance from some inner place he couldn't access.

"Barely a ripple. It's good, Charlotte. But don't be cold-blooded."

I know he worried I didn't have feelings. There was a time when I thought I might not, but I never worried about it.

I can be cruel, but I'm not a cruel person. It's a fine distinction, isn't it? And none of us know for sure what we're capable of until it's right in front of us.

There are ripples these days. In me. Life itself makes me restless. Unsettled. I used to love this place, this building. Now I feel trapped in it. Father doesn't. He's as level as the equator, and he spends all his time drawing in his sketchbook. I can see him now. I'm standing a few feet from him, and I might as well not be here. He's so absorbed in his sketch that he doesn't notice me. Father sits back and looks at it with that squinting self-critical eye he has, his fingers tapping in a particular pattern, thumb then pointer finger, back to thumb to pointer to middle finger to fourth finger, and again. Father's fingers tap when he's not drawing. It's unconscious, a tic or maybe a trick to stay in his flesh, lest he slip away altogether. Father looks up, his eyes taking a moment to focus and register me.

"I'm trying to remember," he begins.

"What?"

He smiles at me—looking at me, through me, beyond me, "All I can remember is that I've forgotten."

I'm worried that Father is giving up.

He goes back to his drawing and makes an adjustment as I slip out of the apartment with my parcel.

*

Her voice floats up the staircase, harsh, disembodied. I step to the top of the stairs and look down, seeing the square turns of massive stone steps flanged by the sturdy oak railing, descending to the lobby below. I can't see her, but I hear her more clearly. She must be talking to the notary or his wife.

"Strangers in the building. You're supposed to monitor. Keep them out."

The notary says something I can't quite hear.

"The mice are bad enough. One ran across my kitchen floor and I nearly fell. Breaking a bone at my age is no triviality. The idea of mice in my cupboard turns my stomach. But mice, however unsavory, won't kill me. With people, one never knows."

I hear another mumble from the notary.

"You do that," Miss Hobert says. "Good day."

I hear footsteps coming up the stairs. Parcel in hand, I dart back to the door and wait.

"You're late," Miss Hobert says to me moments later, her head appearing above the line of the floor.

Miss Hobert grimaces, or maybe it's a smile. She's one of those people who looked old before she was, has aged into herself, and will probably never change. She hasn't since I've known her. As she slowly climbs the stairs, her tall, lumpy form coming into view, I wonder what keeps her going. She never married, not that marriage keeps any of us going, she doesn't seem to have friends, she didn't travel before, and she certainly isn't traveling now. But who is? The only people traveling these days are soldiers invading, soldiers who are captured, Jews being deported, resistance fighters going out, Nazis coming in. Our lives, once beyond these walls, are now wholly within them and the streets have gradually emptied. No one wants to be noticed or stopped or, God forbid, arrested. We have made ourselves prisoners to stay safe.

Miss Hobert pushes me aside, steps to her door, and unlocks it.

"The only advantage," she says as if continuing a conversation, "is that the building will be warmer. More heat. It rises. Someone below can keep me from freezing, even from across the hall." She steps in her apartment and motions me inside, whispering, "New neighbor. In 2L. A Flem. Must watch it with those Flems. Dirk's father. Turned in by Dirk's mother. That's what I've heard. And what the notary's father did in Flanders? Unspeakable."

I follow her, the smell of camphor tickling my nostrils. Miss Hobert slams the door behind me.

I sneeze and place my parcel on the marble-topped table in the hall, realizing I have never been in Miss Hobert's apartment before. There are heavy drapes at the windows and diaphanous curtains under them. Wallpaper in the pattern of a garden trellis. A heavy wool runner on the wood hall floor. The pictures on the wall are mostly botanical prints of mushrooms and insects, the kinds of prints a man would have in a study. There are lace doilies on the arms of upholstered furniture that looks unused, but next to the table in the hall is a comfortable stuffed armchair that looks sat in, and on the table is a reading lamp and a simple glass.

"Don't stand there, let me see it."

I unwrap the hat to the rhythm of Miss Hobert's impatient toe tapping.

I sneeze again—camphor and dust.

"Are you sick?"

"No."

"Your apartment is warmer. I did notice that the other night. So many advantages to the upper floors. I freeze here. All the time."

I lift the hat—a true beauty in the shape of an inverted tulip—and hold it out for her to admire.

"Well? Put it on me."

I put the hat on Miss Hobert's head. It covers all the white hair, letting only the red fall beneath. I adjust the hint of a brim, giving it a tilt, an angle that lifts her sodden jowls.

It's the most beautiful hat I've made, and it makes Miss Hobert look cultivated, handsome, sought after.

Miss Hobert's watery eyes search my face for clues. I smile and her eyes narrow. She doesn't trust my smile. She whirls around and walks quickly to a room in the back of the apartment, the fatty humps on her shoulder blades making her back nearly indistinguishable from her front.

I wait, hearing the clump of her solid heels. Then a silence. More clumps. More silence.

She emerges from the back room wearing an expression I've never seen on her face before. If the hat weren't so perfectly suited to her, the expression might be called vainglorious, but under the circumstances, it's exactly the look she should have. The hat is a triumph.

"It'll do. Please, step out."

I'm confused.

"I have to get your money."

I resist the impulse to yank the hat off her head and some hair with it. The old bag.

I wouldn't steal her money if I was starving.

I step out of the apartment and close the door.

I *am* close to starving.

I might steal it.

If it's a question of our survival—Father's and mine and this baby that still hasn't moved, not even a flicker—if it's a question of our survival instead of Miss Hobert's, I would steal it.

I hear a heavy tread on the stairs. It's Dirk. He looks at me curiously, no doubt wondering why I'm loitering in the hall outside Miss Hobert's door. I could ask him the same question.

The door flies open, and there's Miss Hobert with an envelope in hand. Seeing Dirk, her face crumples into what must be a smile.

He holds out a package.

"What a remarkable day," she says, taking it and lifting the edge of the brown paper—the same crude paper I used to wrap her hat—to peek inside. A satisfied look settles on her face. She tucks the paper around the package and hands me the envelope. Not a thank you, not even a look my way. I make a point of taking out the money and counting it. Slowly.

"Did you make her hat?" Dirk asks.

"Yes."

I try to step around him to go back upstairs. He steps in front of me. Now what?

Dirk is not like most men I know. Most men would not notice Miss Hobert, let alone her hat. I force myself to look at Dirk, seeing his thick-featured face, the dark mole stuck on his cheek like an eraser, the deep-set eyes with a searching look that's always put me on edge. As though he wants something more from me than just pencils.

"I'd like a hat," he says as if answering my unspoken question.

"You'll have to pay her," Miss Hobert says.

Life confounds. Maybe this is her way of thanking me.

"How much?"

I don't want to make a hat for Dirk. I want to leave the two of them alone to gossip.

"Well?" Dirk asks.

I look in his unfathomable eyes and name the price Miss Hobert paid. "Plus, the cost of the wool."

"You have wool in your apartment. Why would you charge him more than you did me?"

"The wool I have isn't suitable for a man's hat."

"What's the difference?" Dirk asks.

I again try to maneuver around him. Again, he blocks me.

"The color," I say.

"Ah, well. You would know. Fine. I want you to make it right away. It's been an awfully cold fall, hasn't it?"

"The worst I can remember," Miss Hobert agrees.

"Then follow me. I need to measure your head."

Dirk looks surprised by this, but as people often do when they're caught off their guard, he does exactly what I tell him and follows me upstairs.

*

If Father is startled to see Dirk in our apartment, he doesn't say. He keeps on drawing, glancing up now and then to make sure, I suppose, that I'm all right.

I measure Dirk's head from ear to ear, seeing a small fringe of hairs on the outside of each helix.

Men who have hairy ears and men who don't.

It is the first time I have measured a man's head. The hat designer I apprenticed with made hats only for women. I had thought of it as a job I'd take during a difficult time, to earn some money until I went back to my studies. The academy closed nearly three years ago. Since the occupation, time has lost structure and dimension. It could be a day or a week, a few months, a year.

Philippe would know a clever way to count the days. I'm out of clever, that's assuming I ever had it.

I measure the crown, seeing a small but encroaching bald spot.

Men who lose their hair and men who don't.

It's intimate, measuring a head. I measured Masha's head when I made my first hat—feeling the oil on her scalp, the soft density of her hair, the tender skin on her neck, smelling sweet perfume and soap. It's a feeling of closeness I imagine I would have had with my mother or a sister.

Dirk's hair smells like Father's shoe brush, and his head is large and round, but to my surprise, the measurements are perfectly symmetrical. Like our building, each side is the same. Dirk sits like a statue as I work. And when I'm finished, he thanks me.

*

I tell Father I need more wool from his friend.

"The black sheep?" Father says with one of his sly little smiles.

"Yes."

Father puts down his pencil and surveys his drawing, "Maybe I'll be able to get some eggs as well."

*

I'm boiling wool over the stove for Dirk's hat. It's dense. The kind of wool a sheep grows in a harsh winter. Poor sheep, it must be cold now. I decide I won't make the hat too thick. I'll save some wool to make a hat for Father. But Father doesn't go out at all, and Dirk is paying me.

I'll make it thick. Warm. I imagine the hat on Philippe's head. Then I imagine it on Julian's, a match for his dark hair, to contrast with his pale skin. I want to give this hat to the newsboy and whisper, *Give this to him. Please.*

One thing I know, life will get you to do all the things you said you never would. Pleading with Smets for food. Working in a factory that makes cheap uniforms. Making a hat for Miss Hobert or for Dirk. Minor grievances. I know people have been disappeared. I know if Philippe is caught, he will be tortured and killed. I have no illusions. And I don't believe a house will ever be mistaken for a garden because a garden is without sin and no house is. Maybe in the end, this is why I'm reading the damn book.

*

It's late afternoon and I open my window, lie on my bed, and look at the sky. The icy air takes me back to the day Julian and I set out to see if any of the houses depicted in the Raphaëls' painting of the old Brussels harbor were still standing. We were six years old. Seven, maybe, but we had prepared for our journey. I had packed buttered hard rolls in a knapsack, Julian had a thermos of tea and a map, and I left a note for Father so he wouldn't worry when he came home from his office.

We took the tram, got off near the Bourse, and were walking past its ornate facade when Julian commented on how dirty and gray it was.

"Is it? I can't see color," I said.

"Yes, I know," he replied matter-of-factly.

I was dumbfounded. The shameful secret I had so carefully hidden didn't matter to Julian at all. And now, years later, I understand why. Julian, too, sees the world differently. He sees forms and shapes and relationships that might or might not have symmetry. Facts that add up or don't. He told me that the great debate in his field is whether math existed before it was discovered or rather was invented to explain what is, and that we might never know the answer.

"I didn't mean the color. I meant the grime," he said that day as we turned onto the Rue des Poissoniers. "I don't mind gray."

"Is the sky gray today?" I asked.

"What do you think?"

"Not sure."

"It's a very pale blue," he said. "A winter sky."

When we reached the Place Sainte-Catherine, Mr. Raphaël and Father were on the steps of the church waiting for us. They weren't angry. In retrospect, they seemed almost pleased that we had made it all the way there on our own. Mr. Raphaël had brought a photograph of the painting that was taken for an exhibition. We used it to see if any of the houses were still there. They were.

But I'm not thinking of the houses. I'm thinking of what it was like, being with Julian that day—and many other days.

I'm not afraid of solitude and I love being alone. I know this worried Masha. She didn't like solitude. But here's another secret: when I'm with Julian, I'm alone and I'm also complete.

DIRK DEBAERRE, 2R

There are two kinds of people, those who watch and observe and those who plunge right in and do. The latter are extremely energetic but often ineffectual as they've been so awfully busy *doing* that they fail to understand the best way to go about things.

I'm in the former camp. Obviously.

Now that I'm truly alone—please don't take this as self-pitying, I am simply describing the state-of-affairs *chez moi* in the most clear and factual way I can—I need a strategy if I'm to survive. This may sound dramatic, but remember, my parents already hadn't. Survived. To wit, you won't be hearing a peep out of them. Under the circumstances, it's best that I speak for all of us.

I'm organizing the apartment. One has to start somewhere, and the place is much more habitable since I've begun to empty it out.

Did I mention that Mother was a collector? A kind word for someone with a malady of accretion. Mother was a turtle carting a hundred shells, a snake who couldn't shed her skins. She had tables stacked on tables, so many chairs lined up that the living room looked like a theater without a stage, baskets hanging from the ceiling, stacked on wardrobes—empty baskets within baskets within baskets, waiting to be filled with paper weights and ashtrays, candle snuffers and linen cloths. Rug upon rug upon rug, each fielding its own army of crumbs and dust.

Oddly, in this time of need, it's harder to get rid of possessions than it was when everyone had enough—or rather, nearly everyone had enough, other than the *nomadic inferiors.*

In those days, you could put a box on the curb, and one of them—a nomadic inferior—would pick it up and take it home. I know, because I used to sneak things out of the apartment and leave them on a distant street, then wait to see. Not only if a nomadic inferior picked it up but if Mother noticed. Do you know, she never did. Nowadays, it's harder given that all the streets and sidewalks are to be kept clear.

I'm filling a box now. I've found someone who has a way of getting my cast-off things to the nomadic inferiors because these days, they're all in hiding.

I move my saxophone from the table. I can only play the saxophone so long before I risk going mad. Never mind that I seem to be driving the entire building mad, even though most of them are already crazy, the ones who are left, that is. With one exception. Charlotte may be a hatter, but she isn't mad. She's the sanest of the bunch.

Charlotte. I only ever wanted her to like me.

*

I began to attend the VNV meetings before my parents' untimely passings. I suspect the fact that I never came under suspicion is attributable to how I made my presence there known among the vile adherents who also attend those meetings. I was among them long before there was clear advantage to be so. My character was thus unimpeachable and the circumstances surrounding the demise of my parents but a coupling of sad accidents tainting them and not me.

I continue to attend those meetings, and they continue to be most useful. Accumulating information and making connections.

When Hobert invited me in for cake, I collected information that allowed me to connect more dots. She told me the notary's business in Flanders was ruined by a Jewish competitor, the notary's father turned to drink, and his mother died tragically soon after. Hobert doesn't know how she died, but she intends to find out and she promised to tell me when she does. Hobert also asked me to go down and check on her apartment building near the Gare du Midi to make sure everything was in good order. I did and it wasn't, and I made a list of what needed fixing: a broken window, burned-out bulbs. I also met Hobert's tenant, one Mr. Putzeis, a cheerful fellow given our times, and well-dressed given his apparent means, for he rents a not-very-nice apartment in Hobert's not-very-nice building in a not-very-nice neighborhood, leaving me to conclude that some people spend money on schlock and ephemerals instead of more lasting possessions. Mother did.

I am at this moment sitting on a box filled with Mother's schlock in an effort to close it.

I didn't judge Putzeis for his clothes, but I noticed. It wasn't the first time I'd seen him. He attended a VNV meeting last May at which an announcement was made about Jews being henceforth obligated by law to wear those ghastly yellow stars. There was applause all around. After that, I didn't see Putzeis for months, until I did again several weeks ago, thanks to Hobert. I have no idea where Putzeis was in the interim, nor did I ask, questions these days being off the table.

He has an extensive collection of spectacles. Yes, I notice accessories and yes, I always have. I remember wishing Mother had even a dash of panache. A good scarf would have done the trick, but she had no sense of how to elevate her figure. I urged her to talk to Masha, because I had seen the transformation of Mrs. Raphaël after Masha began to dress her, one of those subtle shifts that moves planets. I remember Mrs. Raphaël wearing a deep-blue dress that was the most elegant, flattering garment I'd ever seen on a woman. I would have liked that dress for myself, but that being impossible, I at least wanted it for Mother.

I have also noticed that Belgians dress in a very particular way. In the right hands—Masha's or Charlotte's, say—a Belgian can look as elegant as a Venetian, but more often, they're *drab reliables*, looking like farmers on a Sunday.

As for Putzeis, he was no drab reliable. And he changed his spectacles with alarming frequency. In my observations, most people wear eyeglasses until they break or until they need stronger lenses. Where was Putzeis getting the money for all those spectacles? Let alone the clothes. At one meeting, he was wearing a pair of round tortoiseshell spectacles that suited his face marvelously—making it look slimmer, almost chiseled—but he couldn't see a thing. He had to lift the spectacles to read our program, and when I approached him after the meeting, he didn't know who I was. Until he took them off.

That evening, he made a point of asking about my wife.

"I'm sure she's very well, but I haven't yet met her," I said.

Putzeis laughed and looked at me with a glint in his eye that I wouldn't have seen had he not taken off those spectacles. He was letting me know he might have something on me.

After that, my interest in Putzeis only grew. In a war of information, the best weapon is better information.

For example, Putzeis was topping up Hobert's rent with butter. No one can get extra butter these days, not unless they're helping the people charged with divvying it out, if you see what I mean. By helping, I mean informing—most likely.

Look, I don't think Putzeis is the most intelligent person I've met, far from it, but he's smart in that way of small mammals who live alongside big beasts and don't get eaten.

After that comment of his, I decided Putzeis was a person I must get to know better, and I started following him. I followed him from the VNV meetings to his apartment where he lived with a woman who was not his wife. I made a few inquiries and learned she had been previously in a relationship with one Mr. DeDecker, but DeDecker's own wife had reported him for embezzling party funds, and he had been disgraced—at which point DeDecker's erstwhile girlfriend moved in with Putzeis.

I followed Putzeis to a café frequented by men I had seen at the meetings and a few I hadn't. I followed him to the Nazi headquarters on Avenue Louise, the place where the man who called himself my father had presumably met his fate.

People do go there, but I would hazard that anyone who goes there by choice is, plain and simple, an informant and working for the gestapo.

Once again, I'm not judging. Just stating facts.

But who was Putzeis informing on? Had Nazis infiltrated the VNV? They feared, with some reason, that we Flems might be too nationalistic on our own behalf—not truly in support of Hitler's Germany, so it was certainly possible. Likely. What organization hasn't been infiltrated by the Nazis? I have no doubt the Nazis are spying on themselves. The führer wants a pure race, but to get it he's contaminated everyone.

This latter point in utter confidence, please. I've never talked to people about things that matter and now I talk even less. In fact, I don't talk to anyone.

That's one reason I got along with Julian. He's not big on talking either. And he always included me when the boys went out to play around the square and in the courtyard. We had an understanding quiet people share, and Julian can be as silent as the Colonel's new lodger when he wants to be. I have no doubt he's as clever as his father.

*

I had followed Putzeis for a week or two. It had gotten quite cold, and but for the hat Charlotte made me, a quite cozy hat, I couldn't have carried on. Moreover, I had begun to feel like a biologist studying an insect with a predictable back-and-forth. What was the point?

These were my thoughts as I trailed along on the rough sidewalk one evening in Putzeis's wake to no seeming purpose and ruining my poor good shoes in the process.

The fog had dropped like a skirt and it was freezing waiting outside Putzeis's apartment. I tightened scarf around neck. *Enough*, I thought. I was about to leave when Putzeis emerged from the building. Grateful to be moving again, I followed, staying a good distance behind, expecting him to go to the café or the grocer as he usually did.

He stopped a block ahead of me, lit a cigarette, and stood there smoking. Had he seen me and was pretending not to have? I felt my heart galloping about the way it used to when I walked upstairs to the apartment. Since the rationing, I've lost quite a few kilos, and I've noticed that my heart is much steadier.

A large black car pulled up next to Putzeis. He got in. I could see only that there were other men in the car. It sped off, and I realized that if I was to keep up this little sleuthing adventure, I would need an automobile.

I remembered that Hobert had one. That night I told her I needed to borrow it if I was to board up the broken window and replace the bulbs.

"No charge," I said generously. "Merry Christmas." For the holidays were a week away.

I didn't bother with the repairs. Instead, I drove straight to the café Putzeis frequents. A bold move, but if you're careful, you can do bold things. The first time, I pretended to be surprised to see him there. I had thought long and hard about my excuse for being in that café and in that part of town and it was very handy that a mechanic's shop was just down the street. I stopped in with the car, leaving it for a few minor adjustments. More money, but life is for the living.

Putzeis invited me to join him at his table. There were two other men there—one of whom I'd seen at the VNV meetings. We drank beers and talked about not much, until one of the men, the one I hadn't seen before, whose name was Piet, said the strangest thing—that he had to leave because the house had changed again. He was the kind of man who gets thick tongued after only a couple rounds, and he was sloppy drunk. I've always had disdain for that. Men should know how they hold their liquor and drink only that amount they can hold. Well, thick tongued though this Piet was, he caught himself, and told an overblown story about how he had moved recently and wasn't changing houses a ridiculous thing to do in the middle of all this holiday nonsense, and don't we all wish we never had to do it?

I let him cover the slip, but I had heard him. *The house had changed.*

I had no idea what it meant, but I could see from Putzeis's face that he had registered the comment and it meant something to him and I was determined to find out what. Piet and the other man left the café, and after a few minutes, so did I, leaving Putzeis there alone nursing the last of his beer. I walked down the street to pick up the car, drove around the corner, and waited. I felt drowsy from the beer, and the combined warmth of the car and comfort of the leather seat were lulling me to sleep, so I turned off the heat and leaned forward to stay alert.

Out came Putzeis. I let him get ahead before I drove slowly behind him. And once again, he had a smoke on the street and a large black car picked him up. I caught a glimpse of the driver. It was Piet. I followed them down a hill to the area around Gare du Midi. Once again, not a very nice area and not far from where Putzeis was renting the apartment from Hobert. I hit a pothole and the car lurched and dropped. I continued slowly, hoping I hadn't blown a tire. There are entire paving stones missing in the streets now. It's the start of the petulant revolution. By not repairing streets and sidewalks, the Belgians are quietly saying, they've had enough. Better late than never, but is it? I think it will depend. On what, I'm not yet sure.

I began to doubt myself. I might have damaged the car. I was the one who was being ridiculous. Maybe all of it was a snipe hunt.

The black car pulled in front of a house. Putzeis got out, knocked on the door, and waited. The door opened, and three younger men stepped out. All of them seemed to be drab reliables—but for three irregularities. They were too young for such stodgy clothes, the clothes didn't fit, being baggy and rolled at sleeve and hem, and the men didn't walk like Belgians. They got in the car, and again I followed at a distance along a nearly empty road to the station. The three younger men got out with Putzeis and went inside. Piet and another man stayed in the car.

Almost immediately, a car pulled up and a couple of gestapo agents got out. One of them went over and talked to Piet. A friendly conversation, nothing like an interrogation, that was sure, quick and collaborative. And then the gestapo went into the station.

I didn't wait around to see the gestapo arrest those young men— probably Englishmen. What could I have done? Unlike Mother, I don't wish to die. I drove home, the heat in the car still off, and by the time I got inside my apartment, I was shaking.

*

Everyone seemed to be staying in for the holidays, myself included. I've never liked the season, and this one seemed grimmer than usual. No twinkling lights, no music, no one was gathering. They weren't allowed. No festivities to avoid, not even a party. How dispiriting. Christmas of '42 was shaping up to be a bust. I didn't visit a soul outside the building—only one person who doesn't seem to have one. And I didn't eat anything special. Well, a ham. Don't ask how I got it. And yes, the two are connected. Everything has its price.

I knew I would be spending Christmas Day alone. Again. Not that I cared. But it did seem rather gloomy. What was the alternative? To invite Hobert in? Have a party for everyone in the building? Now there's a joke. I'd be reported as a simpleton and locked up in some awful camp.

I don't like to think about the camps. We all know what's happening. We've all heard. How the news travels? I have no idea. But the stories are the same, and so I've begun to believe them.

Here's something else. I surely would be put in a camp if Putzeis told anyone what he thinks he knows about me.

*

On Christmas Eve, Hobert knocked on my door. She was still wearing the pale-blue hat Charlotte made her. I don't think she has taken it off once, maybe not even in the bath, which is a genuinely frightening thought. And she brought me a small butter cake. Very sweet of her, really. I think she feels sorry for me now. Maybe she knows I had nothing to do with the deaths of my parents. Or maybe she thinks I killed them both and is grateful.

But what she wanted to tell me was that the new Flemish tenant had moved in on the second floor, he was unfriendly, and it made her almost as uneasy as the Colonel with those men of his parading through.

"How many men are there?" I asked, taking the cake from her.

"I don't know. One or two at a time. It changes. But they're all idiots. A danger. Doesn't anyone understand? And another thing," she continued, "I heard the notary tell the new tenant that the Raphaël apartment is to be searched and emptied."

Here was something interesting right in our own building.

"Why searched?" I asked.

"For the paintings. You know they had paintings?"

"Oh yes."

"Of great value it would seem. They're convinced the paintings are hidden in the apartment. Annick, the notary's wife—"

"I know who she is."

And I do for I've been watching Annick too. She thinks she's so clever, but she hasn't seen me watching her, has she? I've seen her take letters out of our mailboxes. And a little after, put them back. She steams them open and reads them. How do I know? I sent a letter to myself. A love letter. Steamy, intimate, quite detailed, brash. I can write a letter like that to a man, can't I? Oh yes, I can. I signed it, *Jacqueline*. The day it arrived, I watched Annick slip it out of my box into her apartment. And then a little later, she put it back in my box. When I retrieved it—which I did right away—it was still warm and there was glue below the envelope flap. Sloppy. After that, I will say that Annick looked at me differently. I've no doubt she was dying to ask about Jacqueline.

"Annick said the notary got a Christmas bonus for bringing this to the attention of the authorities," Hobert is saying.

"The new Flemish tenant?"

"Heavens no, he's a Nazi. The paintings."

"Good for him. And thank you for the cake."

I always say thank you. You'd be surprised how far that goes.

*

I tie some string around the box, put Hobert's cake plate on top of it, and pick it up. The plate slides, and I tilt the box just enough to keep it from crashing to the floor. This won't do. I go into the kitchen and find a small bag.

Hobert is lending me her car again to collect Putzeis's December rent. I might even fix the window this time, but the bulbs are too expensive. I told Hobert I need the car regularly now that it's winter because I have a condition I inherited from my poor father, may he rest in peace, that makes my hands turn blue in the cold and I can't possibly go out so far and for so long on foot and by tram.

She believed me. She thinks I tell the truth. That's her obsession. Truth. What a woman.

JULIAN RAPHAËL, 4R

We were turning around over Flanders, headed home. We'd completed the mission, and my head had that chronic vibration that sometimes lasts for days after a long sortie. Our wireless operator had been due for a leave, but a friend of his was killed in a dogfight and he'd gone back up to avenge him. I could tell he felt he had done so. Blake was making jokes and the operator had begun to relax. I won't say more than he should have. Hindsight is useless without a second chance.

I felt nervous. Call it a premonition. My unconscious understanding something I don't. Jung writes about this, but he's abstract and unscientific. Freud reduces it to parenting and defecating. All I know is there's a part of me I can't consciously access and it knows more. I used to think *it* should be in charge. Take maths. I can work out an equation on paper. But if I do something else—sweep the floor, take a walk, meet a friend for a coffee—it figures out the equation without me. I have only to write the answer. The trouble is, I can't access it all the time. I don't have direct communication to it. I had decided it was an unreliable friend I couldn't count on.

I was wrong.

In his last letter, Papa described this idea of collective dreams. That people are having the same dreams and he himself has been dreaming like a prophet, like Daniel, and he's terrified his dreams might come true. He wrote:

"People are having visions. They find themselves on dark roads, in forests, surrounded by skeletons. They escape on bicycles, they jump off moving trains, they wake before killing their own children—or saving them. We have all become artists in our sleep. It is a collective hallucination, this life. What will bring us to our senses?"

It's as unlike any letter from Papa as I would ever have expected to receive, and I wonder if he's going mad. I wonder if we all are.

I'm trying not to remember my dreams. When I do, I lose my bearings. And I'm the one who's supposed to keep them.

Maybe there's no mystery at all. It is rather the power of language in Papa's letter that kept me awake, buzzing with adrenalin and anxiety, focused on my instruments and the dark sky around me.

The boys were talking about the upcoming weekend. For once, we had two days off. They would be drinking on Saturday, finding some girls, going to church on Sunday. The wireless operator had a girl up north. She was coming down to be with him.

I spotted the plane coming in on our flank—a Focke-Wulf.

"Fuck wolf!"

I hoped my voice was level because the plane was coming at us fast. I gave its coordinates.

"Birds together flock their feathers!" Blake yelled, and from that, I figured there were more planes. There were.

Our pilot tried to maneuver out of range, but it was tight.

"Jammed," Blake shouted. I glanced over. He was dead calm.

He was the gunner, you see.

"Enemy approaching at—" the wireless operator began. This was when we were hit and he got it in the head and it cut him off midsentence. He was bleeding all over.

I grabbed the earphones off him. They were slippery with blood and smelled like onions.

"One down," I shouted.

"Goddammit," Blake screamed in fury. "Only one of us can fucking dance this tango!"

He was desperately trying to unjam the gun.

It turned out that it was both an engine and a man that were down. The plane was losing altitude.

"Still jammed," Blake yelled. Less calm.

"Doesn't matter now," said the pilot.

Looking out from our descent, I could see the breakneck moon, running up and away from us.

"Are we jumping?" Blake asked.

"I'm staying with the plane," the pilot said.

"I stay with the pilot," I said.

It was the right decision, but who knows if it was a good one. And if you've never crash-landed in a plane, I'm here to tell you I don't recommend it. We were coming down too fast, every bit of maneuvering was directed toward avoiding buildings and trees, and it was impossible to slow the descent enough to touch down anything like a landing. We hit with a crushing jolt and one of the engines flamed on impact. The plane bumped along a field and finally stopped.

"No time," the pilot said. "Everyone, you know what to do."

Blake and I unstrapped the wireless operator. I checked his pulse, tried to massage his heart into action. Gave him some air. But it was no good.

The pilot was holding back tears. Those two had been friends. But we could see lights on a road in the distance.

"Time to go. They'll be looking for us," he said.

We split up. I wanted to stick with Blake, but there was a protocol and I knew I had to forge out on my own. As I did, tears poured down my cheeks. Not for me. For our man. I thought of his girl waiting unrequited for her Yorkshire Achilles. This was when the rage set in.

You think you don't have rage? Think again. It's not a collective hallucination, Papa, it's rage, and it possesses those for whom acting or not acting are equally murderous and suicidal.

I heard motor engines and saw the flash of headlights pointed in my direction, then extinguished, and I began to run away from them, feeling that burning rage but trying to stay rational and read my own instruments . . .

Odds of stopping, turning back with my gun, shooting the bastards, as many as I could . . . *Sons of bitches* I wanted to kill them all . . . The rage impelling me to turn back and fight . . . They would take me down . . . Odds of outrunning the murderous bastards . . . *Faster! Faster!* . . . Odds of shooting myself with my own weapon before ever letting them take me down . . . *bastards, bastards, bastards.*

I could hear dogs and whistles and shouting. A voice in English. Was it Blake? The pilot? One of them had been captured. Maybe the Nazis didn't know how many of us were on the plane.

I stumbled across the unkempt field in that rage, any moment expecting to roll over a tumbleweed of barbed wire, which would have been the end of me.

But the field wasn't booby-trapped.

Then the rumble, the ground shaking under my feet, the great blast. It stopped me cold. Slowly I turned and I looked back at a spidery fireball illuminating the night sky. The plane had blown.

I waited, listening. Silence. They wanted to flush me out. I decided then I wouldn't let them, I wouldn't let them catch me, I wouldn't go back. I would outrun and outwit them.

I wasn't afraid. I was looking around, still trying to get my bearings on the ground, and I wondered if shipmen had the same trouble.

We were somewhere in Flanders. I knew that much. The field was barley or maybe potatoes, winter dormant, all stalk and scrub. Funny what you notice in a pause when running for your life.

I could see the flames from the burning plane across the fields. A whistle blew—my starting gun—and I opened my mouth to inhale that fire, to swallow it down, and I bolted, crashing wildly through brush and stubble, now an enemy and a fugitive in my own country. Were they chasing me? How could they not see me? I was a ball of flame and rage searing the field and leaving a blackened swath in my wake and I swore I would burn them too, those monsters. Those motherfucking bastards. I wanted their skin and bones to be the only columns of smoke seen from the sky. On earth, nothing left of them but soot and little ashes.

My lungs burned, I was tripping over my own feet, and this, *this,* was when I had a vision. Of Guy on that damn ledge, of Guy laughing about the book saving his life.

He had done it. He had made it out. He'd left behind his murderous rage. Maybe I could too.

I reached a canal. Not frozen, but it might as well have been. The water was skimmed with ice, and I plunged in feeling the burning cold as I waded chest deep, holding my gun over my head, water filling my boots, my trousers. The fire slowly extinguishing. How long before I would freeze? I could hear the whistles, the barking dogs. When I glanced back, I saw beams of light zigzagging the fields behind me, but they seemed to be moving farther and farther away. Until the lights flickered and extinguished and I heard a splash, and everything went dark.

*

I wake in a pile of straw with a terrible pain in my head.

I had no dreams, Papa.

Or maybe this is a dream. Daylight ventures through cracks in a wood wall of what looks like a barn.

The rage is gone, and I have that emptied-out feeling I had as a boy after a fever broke, and for a moment I'm in my room at Number 33, in my bed, feeling the rough linen of my sheets, the silky cover of my down comforter, Persian carpet, aqua wallpaper with gold cranes, leather bookbindings in green and burgundy and deep blue, the splendid chaos of pattern and all the colors Charlotte cannot see, she herself being an achromatic divinity.

Charlotte.

Dust and straw tickle my nose and I sneeze. Immediately, I'm surrounded by men. No room, no comforter. I reach for my gun. No gun.

One of the men laughs. Another tells him—in Flemish—to shut up. They question me in English. I tell them who I am and what happened. Then they switch to Flemish, and I make the mistake of answering in Flemish.

One of them wants to shoot me right away.

"Why?" I ask. "You're Flemish, aren't you?"

This gives him pause.

But then another says he doesn't know of any Flems who went over to fight with the Brits.

So, I speak to them in French, foolishly thinking it might help.

Now two of them want to shoot me.

They only know of a few Walloons who went over and most of those were avenging someone. Their view—it's always personal.

The men move away from me and argue in whispers. I look at their hands, red and rough-knuckled, gesturing. Orphic callouses. Overgrown split nails.

"I'm Jewish," I call over to them.

It's a gamble, but I know from their hands that these men work the soil. They're farmers and, as such, likely not Nazis. Their land is what they have, and they don't like other people taking it. They wouldn't have kept me in a pile of hay in a freezing barn if they were Nazis. They'd have collected their bounty and sent me on my way to a camp. No, they're farmers, simple men who seemed to have made a simple decision to be decent.

They look hard at me when I say this. I don't know what they were expecting to see that they hadn't already.

One of them comes over.

"Say something in Jewish," he says.

"Thank G-d my mama kept up traditions," I say. And I say it in Hebrew.

Not yet persuaded, they're staring at me. I half expect them to ask me to drop my pants. Mercifully, they don't. I wasn't circumcised. Papa wouldn't allow it.

"Strange fugitive . . . fugitive stranger . . . Your name, surely you got a name," the first man, salt-tongued and rough-hewn, says, lighting a cigarette. He's got lines going all directions on his face. The weight of his eyelids is such that I can't make out the color of his eyes. Charlotte would tell me it doesn't matter.

"Raphaël." For some reason I don't want to give them my whole name. Did I tell them my name before? Mama always said there is power in names, that naming is a sacred art. Maybe I didn't tell them. Maybe they forgot. Never mind that they are nameless to me.

"Like the angel, eh?" another says, the one who wanted to shoot me.

"Why were you in England?" a third asks.

"I was studying. Maths. I enlisted as soon as I could."

"You're a pilot?"

"Navigator. The maths, see—"

"Maybe you're better at maths than navigating given that we found you in a bloody canal."

They're all laughing, and the sound of it makes me uneasy. My life depends on this parley.

Once again, they step aside to discuss.

"If you're going to kill me, please, let me take a shit first. You'll have a cleaner corpse on your hands."

The first farmer likes this, I can tell. He's on my side. But I'm not sure about the others. I sit on the hay and wait.

In the end, they take a vote. It's four to three in favor of letting me live.

*

I'm given farm clothes—heavy blue pants and shirt. Wood clogs. I'll work here until it's time to make the journey Guy made. His exodus gives me solace. I tell myself, *Guy did it. I can too.*

*

That night, I have a vision of rooftops, slate and thatch and red tiled, of spired cathedrals, domed mosques, the charred ruins of temples. I'm streaking through a starless night sky when I see twinkling lights, the ones they put up in December and take down in January, and then I'm running through blackened streets following those lights. Tight-wired, and fearless.

*

The farmer with the heavy lids tells me I am to be a deaf-mute.

For a moment, I think they're going to pierce my eardrums. Cut out my tongue. Visions aside, anything is possible. This I know.

He's laughing at me. He must have seen apprehension, fear even, in my eyes.

"You'll be playacting, see, pretending. If people don't believe your pantomime, they won't throw tomatoes they'll shoot you."

Do I tell him the deaf can make sounds? No. Most people don't know this. Most Nazis probably don't know this. I go along with a plan that seems to be working.

They set me up with a pile of straw and a rough wool blanket in the barn's loft. One or another of them brings me food—simple food. Potatoes, a bit of butter, some cabbage, smoked fish. Enough.

I'm put to work on the farm. And here's the strangest thing. I like it. Dirty, underfed, mucking out pigpens, hands blistered and callusing, the endless manure—pigs shit all the damn time—and then I remember hearing that people in the camps were made to eat fish coated in feces, and if they brought it up, they had to lick their vomit. And thinking of this brings that rage again, a rising tide, surging, uncontrollable, and the one thing I know is I must live to keep fighting.

In the meantime, I learn to milk the cow. There's one, and her poor teats are sore from all the milking. But they're warm and there's a comfort in pulling them and seeing the milk squirt into the metal bucket. I like the sound. I sit on a stool with a long reach to keep from being kicked in the head. She's in pain and there's nothing I can do except be as gentle as I can. I've never milked a cow before. The cream rises. A truism Papa loves, and I'm seeing it manifest, and god but it's tempting to take a sip when no one's looking, but they're looking most of the time, and I haven't forgotten the vote. One of them changes his mind and I'm a dead man.

They're making certain I haven't duped them. And they're teaching me not to turn my head when I hear loud noises, to press my tongue to the roof of my mouth and hold it there so I'm not tempted to use it.

"Otherwise," the one who wanted to kill me second says, "we'll have to cut it off."

*

I lose track of time, moving from barn to field, from field to the pens. I'm reminded of long Saturday walks with Papa circling the ponds, watching swans, or out to the Bois and through the forest. Always on the Sabbath, Papa talking endlessly about ideas and art and religious observance being nonsense, nature being his temple.

The heavy-lidded farmer brings my food. There's a cup of buttermilk with a bowl of potatoes. It's the biggest meal I've had. *They've decided to kill me after all*, I think.

He squats down in the straw and watches me eat. "Tomorrow, crack of dawn," he begins, "you'll clean up and then be off."

"Thank you," I say.

"No time for that now. You can come back and thank me when it's over."

He tells me I'll go straight to Brussels.

"There's a snake in the grass," he adds.

I look around.

"In Brussels. Dunno who. We haven't found it yet. You'll have to take care not to be bitten. Don't trust anyone."

"My gun . . ."

"If they catch you with that. You're a goner, lad. Wishing you luck. Make us proud we didn't shoot you."

NOTIFICATION

Decree of the German Military Authority regarding assistance to British Soldiers:

Any individual who is found to harbor, assist, or in any way aid a British soldier shall be considered to have committed an act of espionage against the German army and shall be put to death by firing squad.

Any person having information regarding the above shall report promptly to the relevant municipal police authorities or be subject to fines and imprisonment and possible death.

Brussels, 15 January 1943

CHARLOTTE SAUVIN, 4L

I pick up the heavy pot of steaming water and carry it to the bathroom. Papa would be furious with me for doing it, but I must stay strong. I can't always need help with everything. I slowly pour the water in the tub. The heat makes my face drip with sweat as the wool plops onto the porcelain with a splat. My throat aches, and I feel hot.

I turn on the spigot to rinse it, then lift the dripping mass and let the water drain, my hands stinging. I put it back on the floor of the tub, pushing down on the wool, being careful not to wring it as that will damage the fibers, until the stream of water becomes a trickle and then a slow drip.

This is when I hear them. Unmistakably. Whispers.

I move closer to the end of the tub where the pipes come up from the Colonel's apartment below.

Voices.

I tiptoe into the hall and listen. The Colonel and Father are talking. They are not whispering.

"Thank you for the beer," the Colonel says.

"I've another batch coming," Father tells him.

I step back in the bathroom and listen. Nothing. I turn on the spigot and rinse the wool again, feeling what is now a stabbing pain in my throat. The water flows over the wool and I imagine it rising like the water in a story Father told me when I was young, overflowing the tub and rushing down the hall and under the door, falling down the stairs, washing the building clean.

*

"The poor Colonel, have you noticed, dear? He's a thin slice of his former loaf. I never thought I'd see the day. Those boarders of his are flesh eaters, I think." Father hands me my morning coffee.

I sip it, trying not to make a face at how weak and bitter it is—mostly chicory.

"Don't they have their own ration cards? They should."

"You look flushed."

Father gets up slowly and walks over to me. I can see how he's aged these past three years. The line of his jaw has sagged, but there's no fat for a jowl, and the pooch under his chin folds into his creased neck. He's so thin and tired. He claims not to be hungry, but I know he's as hungry as I am. Father is disappearing right in front of me. There are many ways to disappear. My mother disappeared in one way, Philippe in another—I miss Philippe—and now Father. Funny, how a life can be drawn and erased. Before the war, I would have painted my life on a wall, a mural of people and places, food and dancing, trams and automobiles and trains, country roads and city streets, starlit nights and foggy mornings. I see Professor Weiss pouring drinks in front of an enormous painting. The French and German students toasting him. Did they? They must have once. Mr. Raphaël cutting the roast. Mrs. Raphaël trying on a dress for Masha and Esther and me, I see the soft folds of her velvet skin.

But it's emptying out now, my picture is. All the people in it are becoming shadows.

Father puts a hand on my forehead.

"My dear. To bed with you."

"Don't they have ration cards?" I ask again.

"The cards aren't so useful these days, are they?"

*

When you're sick, really sick, you want to be told to go to bed. You want to be cared for, to be brought hot and cool drinks, to have your forehead checked for fever, your throat for redness. You want to be told you'll be better soon. You want to be a child. Father understands this. He takes care of me exactly as he did when I was small. He finds the metal tray with a line around the rim and a faded bouquet of flowers painted on it, and he brings me tea and a bit of bread. He puts the extra pillow under my head. He makes sure I'm not too warm or too cold.

I want to cry. I should be kind to him always. I should protect him. I must protect him. He's taking care of me now, but it won't be long before I will have to take care of both of us.

I don't tell him about the whispers I heard the other night. I have no doubt they came from the Colonel's apartment. Why does Father need to know that the Colonel's lodgers can speak?

*

That night, I'm riding my bicycle along a stone path. I'm with Julian; he's on a bicycle beside me. A man is ahead, and I pump my pedals to catch up with him. I'm sure it's Philippe, but I can't quite see his face. I see his linen pants. His head? His hair? I'm trying to remember him. Julian is saying something to me, but I don't hear him. I'm breathing hard, trying to catch Philippe. I'm hot and sweaty, my limbs are heavy, they won't move fast enough, and I'm falling farther and farther behind and then I'm alone on a tram next to a canal. The tram is filled with people. We're packed in so tightly we can't move, and at the moment I think I can't bear it, one side of the tram car is gone. It disappears and there's only a loosely fastened mosquito netting and I understand it's my turn to dive in the water. My escape. And so I jump, and the moment my body hits the water, I wake up.

*

I can't find Philippe in my dreams. He's always ahead of me. I never see his face. I worry it's an omen.

*

I've slept half the day, I can tell by the light, which is as even and flat as the horizon, light this time of year being fugitive. January in Brussels.

The sheets are damp, my fever broken, but Father insists I spend the day in bed. He tells me the wool is dry and clean and I will be up and working with it in no time. I can see the definition of bone on his cheeks, the hollows under his eyes. He's losing his flesh, becoming a shadow. I'm sure I am too.

"Did you sleep?"

"I was afraid you might sleepwalk."

"Father. You need to sleep."

"Soon enough. I'm not happy with my sketch. Maybe when you're up, you can look at it."

"I could now."

"Later."

*

I touch my stomach. I don't think about the baby as often as I should. I never talk about it with Father. He's afraid for me; that much I know.

Maybe I'm imagining it. I haven't bled for months. But then, I'm not eating enough to bleed. I'm not eating enough for one, let alone for two.

Maybe the baby will survive, but I won't. If we all starve, none of us will survive. I need to get up. I can't waste a precious day. Is it a precious day? If it isn't, how can it be wasted?

*

I open the window and feel the cold, fresh air. My window is directly across the courtyard from Julian's, and for a moment I expect to see him there.

In my dream, Julian was trying to tell me something, but I couldn't hear him. I worry he might be dead. But I feel shame and ingratitude for being able to see Julian and not Philippe.

*

I drink hot water and snooze again, waking in the late afternoon. Mercifully, I don't remember my dreams. Sadly, I don't remember them. The dreams being more vibrant and alive than anything else. How quickly an existence can shrink. I once had a life of unimaginable possibility.

I get out of bed and find the book in a stack of books on my dresser.

*

"If a lion could talk, we wouldn't be able to understand it."

What does Wittgenstein mean by *understand*? There's a question of words and then there's experience. The lion wouldn't have lost a mother—or at least not my mother—nor gone to school with Dirk, been friends with Esther, loved Julian and then fallen in love with Philippe, seen Smets refuse to give us our rations and Father reduced to a shadow, the Colonel to a thin slice. How could the lion truly understand me without knowing all this? Or conversely, how could I understand her? But if my lioness could talk and I could understand the words—her language—and could extrapolate from my own experience, my own sadness and joy, to empathize with her, why couldn't I understand?

*

"The picture agrees with reality or not, it is right or wrong, true or false. The picture represents what it represents . . . what the picture represents is its sense."

I beg to differ. Whether the picture represents reality is not what makes it true or false. It is the picture's sense that makes it true or false.

*

I read as much as I can and I set the book aside and put my hands on my stomach, feeling the taut skin over the swell of my abdomen.

Things unseen that are real and things seen that don't exist.

The baby? The lioness?

I saw the lioness. I have no doubt she was there. I don't know if anyone else saw her, and I don't care. I feel I could talk to her. I would like to talk to her.

I'm not feverish and I'm not losing my mind. And I haven't changed my view of philosophy, not a bit.

I want to paint again. I love painting. Maybe, when I'm better, I'll get out the canvas and the oils, and I'll try.

*

I'm remembering Philippe. His hair, how it's rough under my fingertips. The strange light in his eyes, how intense it is. How he's curious about everything and everybody, but he keeps it all to himself.

I almost can't bear the remembering, but I think it's worse to forget.

There's been no news of Philippe, Julian could be anywhere, and the baby still hasn't moved.

*

"If there are objects, there can be a fixed form of the world."

The book holds a key, and it makes me think of something other than my circumstances, which is worth the pain of reading it.

I put tiny potatoes in the sink to wash them. Humans aside, I don't see how the world could have a fixed form. Nothing seems fixed.

If a bomb drops on this building, the form of our little world would change from fixed to anything but fixed.

You look back or ahead and everything is different. But it's all in this moment. Nothing is fixed in time. Didn't Wittgenstein understand this?

The potatoes are sprouted. I pick off the sprouts. If we had a garden, we could plant them.

I chop the endive and put it in a pan of water to boil.

And people change from day to day, minute to minute. You can look in the mirror and see a stranger. Philippe is so changeable I have trouble remembering him. At times, I thought him more handsome than any man I'd ever seen. Other times, his eyes were prominent, his nose crooked, his jaw square and pronounced. A question of light? Miss Hobert said her face collapsed overnight. Father in his trench had a leg that worked one moment and didn't the next.

Look, either there's a fixed form of the world, which makes no sense except in the abstract as an ideal, or the form of the world is fixed only until it shifts, which it does all the time being in constant motion, in which case, what is the point of this statement? For it's a statement that is no longer true the second before it's uttered.

"Charlotte?"

Father steps in the kitchen, and for a moment I don't know if it's Father or his shadow. He blinks in the light from the harsh bulb—the bags under his eyes and his drooping mouth and nose combining to make him look sad and comical.

"I asked if you should see the doctor. You haven't said. About the baby."

"I don't know."

I've never mentioned the pregnancy to Father, but of course he's aware. I eye a piece of brown paper on the counter. I find a pencil on the shelf above the stove; there are pencils stashed all over the house. Father draws all the time, he carries that notebook everywhere with him, but he leaves his pencils behind. Father, soldier, architect, brewer, shadow.

I put my finger to my lips. He waits as I ignite the stove. I write, "Philippe alive and parachuting."

"I know," Father whispers. "I know everything. I made him tell me before he left."

I start laughing. I can't help it. Father is laughing too. The whole situation seems funnier than anything I've ever heard or seen and we're standing in the kitchen laughing like idiots at my needless note. We laugh about nothing and everything. We're drunk with laughter. And in that moment, we're free.

I dip the edge of the note in the fire and watch it burn. Then I extinguish the stove, sweep the ashes into my hand, and rinse them down the sink.

I hear the grunt and squeal of Dirk's saxophone and I feel another giggle rising.

*

"Notes must have some pitch."

*

What would Wittgenstein do if he were trapped in this building and forced to listen night after night to notes with no pitch at all?

SOPHIA RAPHAËL, 4R

When Leo finally tells me, I tear my clothes, and for the first and I hope the last time in our lives, he chastises at me.

"Would you rather he was a coward? Sitting safely in England while our people are being gassed and tortured and shot and clubbed to death?"

I am sobbing. Leo calls it wailing, but it isn't. Wailing is theatrics. This is grief, heartbreak.

"Stop it. Stop it now!" he says.

I wrote a letter to Charlotte, telling her Julian was flying in the RAF. And that I worry about Masha and never trusted that Harry or what he and the Colonel might be doing. But mostly I was writing about Julian. I know how Julian cares for Charlotte. He loves her. I thought she should know. I haven't heard anything from her. I hope she's all right.

Leo has no idea I wrote that letter. Do I write again to tell her Julian's plane was downed and he's missing?

"You don't want to have a stroke," Leo is saying.

"I'm fine."

I'm not fine. What mother wants to give birth to a son, to feel the slippery little eel, compressed bones, wrinkled skin, slide out of her, to nurse him into human form, to love and teach and feed him—only for him to be killed? By men. It's all men.

"Don't look at me that way," Leo says.

He's lost weight, grown a beard. He looks strong. Determined. Feisty. Angry. When Leo loses his temper, which is rare, it takes a while for him to recalibrate. I haven't seen him like this since I met him. Well, at least someone's thriving. Most of our relatives are still in Russia and only G-d ever knows what happens there. But we've had no word. For a time, we had letters from cousins in Denmark—they would write notes under the stamp. I steamed off the stamp from their last letter and saw written under it in tiny print, "Help us, we're starving." Leo's been trying to get food through to them. He's bribing anyone he can, crimes these days as often being life-saving decencies.

"I would be disgusted if Julian were here. Sitting in this comfortable house, moping and useless," Leo says.

I want to argue. I want to tell him there's nothing comfortable about this house and that sounds like a not-so-subtle dig at me. I would also remind him that I've been helping at the infirmary on the new base. I'm no nurse, but I can help, and I do. The English are only allowing in women immigrants to stay if they're nurses or domestics. The work is also a way to hedge my bets. We have papers, but who trusts papers these days? Leo isn't the only one who has taken off those extra kilos. I'm thinner than I was when he married me. All my clothes hang on me. I need Masha.

I wrote Masha too. I'm worried she's gone off with that Harry.

"Sophia?"

"Don't yell at me."

"Not yelling." Leo paces, calming himself. "He's not dead."

"You don't know that."

"And you don't know that he is, so stop acting like it."

I put on a coat and step outside into a wet wind that goes right to my skin. That's humidity for you. I'd rather stand in the snow than in a cold rain any day, but then, like Leo I was born in Russia, and I've always believed you're most at home in the climate you're born into.

Julian is at home in Belgium. G-d willing, that will help him.

I look across the sea. Some sanctuary. There are U-boats in these waters now. It's one reason they built a base up here.

Last night I dreamed that men in gas masks burst into the house and dragged Esther out of bed by her hair.

Today, I called Esther and told her to cut her hair into a bob.

"I already did," she said. "Too much bother otherwise."

That was a relief.

I feel an arm around my shoulder, Leo next to me.

"Julian is the smartest boy I know," he says.

"Yes. But not a boy, not anymore."

We're silent a moment as we listen to the wind billow, the sound of the waves.

"What happened to the others?" I ask.

"The gunner is missing, another crewman dead from a direct hit, the pilot was captured and is in hospital—"

"So strange. They're trying to kill him one moment and they treat him in hospital the next. And then I suppose after they'll put him in some kind of camp and try to kill him again."

"I suppose," Leo says.

"Who told you?"

"I telephoned the base."

Leo is being clinical. Factual. Pushing out the emotion. I'm not good at that, and Leo knows it. He knows me better than anyone. He has been by my side through so much—births of our children, deaths of our parents, the stock market crash, and the aftermath when money paid for a fraction of what it had.

"Men have escaped the camps for officers and soldiers," Leo says. I know he's been thinking about what it would take to escape from a place like that, or from the worse kind of camp Julian might be sent to if anyone finds out who he is, the kind of bravery you'd have to have. "Guy did it," he adds.

"Guy? How do you know that?"

"Julian saw him. On the base. Guy had been captured and escaped, made it out through Spain, although he was caught again in Spain. But he talked his way out of that too."

"Guy has always been a good talker."

"Yes."

"Unlike Julian."

"True. Anyway, he made it to Gibraltar and back to England. Right away had his nose bobbed."

"Julian doesn't need a nose bob," I say, as I start to shiver. "How did Guy look?"

"I didn't see him."

"How did Julian say he looked?"

"He didn't. Come on, let's go in. No sense getting sick now."

I'm seeing Leo in a new way. He's so vibrant against all this churning gray. He's pure energy. Whoever said a cold wind is invigorating didn't know what they were talking about; it's human energy that's invigorating. We're not meant to be alone.

"Julian looked wonderful when I saw him. Our son."

Leo knows me so well. He knew I was afraid to ask. He holds the door for me, and we go inside, the sound of surf and wind fading.

DIRK DEBAERRE, 2R

There are soldiers all around, more than before. Brussels in winter is the glummest city on earth even without the barricades and occupiers in their gray uniforms. Everything is gray. I don't know how Charlotte hasn't given up with an outlook like hers. I find myself thinking about how I can kill them all. Soldiers, pedestrians—everyone.

Last week, a Belgian woman shot and killed a German officer at dusk. I've heard they put her in front of a firing squad that wounded her on the first round. "I'm a better shot," she said before they killed her on the second. Since then, there's been a curfew. No one is allowed out past seven. It's a prison.

I do appreciate the car. It has lifted my spirits to drive about, and it's created a distance, a wall between me and the misery of my confederates. Although naturally, after I'd gone to the trouble of talking Hobert into letting me take it out nearly every day, Putzeis went back to his old pattern of doing little and talking much. And I'm paying for the petrol. With all the driving back and forth, it's a real kick in the wallet.

*

Hobert was right about everything, and she was wrong.

The new tenant who took over the apartment across from mine—Mr. Van Cauter—is civil enough, to me. I've seen him at the meetings. He knows my face and is tolerating me, for now. Notably, I haven't played my saxophone since the New Year rolled around.

And the Colonel's apartment has indeed become a way station for misfits. I've been puzzling over how he's managed to pull it off with Everard, the notary. There must be money in it for them both.

I began to follow the Colonel just after Christmas, mostly out of boredom. I was surprised to find it was more challenging to follow the Colonel than to follow Putzeis. I had always thought of the Colonel as the drab reliable who tempers all our idiosyncrasies.

Think again, Dirk.

The man is shockingly aware of his surroundings, and at least twice he turned and gave me a hard look when I was trailing him. He retrieves the deaf men—the *holy innocents*—from a baggy-faced woman, a real Belgian farmer. The Colonel brings the holy innocents to his apartment where they stay a few days before he returns them to a man with a truck, perhaps the woman's husband, who presumably drives them back to whatever godforsaken place in the Belgian countryside they're coming from. I'm not sure what the point of it all is, but according to Hobert, no one can afford to keep them long—or wants to. She has taken to referring to them as deplorables.

One of the holy innocents stays on as the Colonel's permanent lodger, and I suppose that's part of the bargain. He's called Jacques.

All seemed on the up-and-up, but I had a suspicion I wanted to test, so on New Year's Eve I set off a firecracker just as Jacques and the Colonel stepped out of the lobby. The Colonel dove for cover, but Jacques was already at the corner waiting to cross. Stone-deaf, he hadn't flinched. I was around the flank of the building behind an empty flower box, watching as the Colonel got up and dusted himself off. He headed straight to me, shook his finger, and said, "When will you grow up, Dirk? Your father had such hopes for you. Poor Jacques might have walked into traffic."

I didn't bother to tell the Colonel that Martin DeBaerre wasn't my father. "Jacques isn't blind," I said.

"No. But he needs a new pair of spectacles, and they're impossible to come by these days."

The Colonel marched off to retrieve Jacques, and I picked up the remnants of the firecracker, thinking of Putzeis and his spectacles, for I had concluded that the Colonel's activities with the holy innocents were exactly that. Wholly innocent.

*

Until this afternoon when I went up to Hobert's for the car keys. Her door flew open. She was wearing the blue hat of course, and she looked wild-eyed. She pulled me into her apartment and shut the door.

"They've gone in!" she announced.

"Who?"

"Gestapo."

"Where?"

"The Raphaël apartment. I told you, they're tearing the place apart, tearing holes in the walls to find those paintings and making a terrible racket right above my head. And that's not all."

From the look on Hobert's face, something horrible and delicious was about to be disclosed.

"Annick, the notary's wife—"

"Yes, I do remember who she is." I was losing patience with Hobert. I wanted the information.

"We must all be careful of Everard. Violent tendencies run in families."

This was unexpected. Everard is mild mannered, controlled. Not a man who inspires fear. "What sort of violent tendencies?"

"Annick found her mother-in-law on the floor, head split like a cut egg. Lengthwise so there was an eye on each half, but the nose on one side. Annick said she wouldn't have thought it possible, but she saw it herself and assured me it was. And ever since, she has been unable to eat pâté."

"Goodness." I was for once almost wordless. "When?"

"Years ago and not here."

Just then, we heard footsteps. Finger to lips, Hobert moved to the door and listened. We heard a key in the lock, the creak of the Colonel's door.

Hobert flung open her door again. The Colonel and Jacques were stepping in his apartment and as they did, I caught a flash of a man in the Colonel's hall—thin, short-cropped black hair, blue eyes, a pale face, one I would know anywhere. He quickly moved out of sight. As the Colonel shut the door, he caught my eye. We both knew what I had seen, but I didn't say a word, and neither did the Colonel.

"Was there another man in there?" Hobert asked me. "Someone new?"

"No."

"I think there was. I'm sure of it. I saw a shadow. And do you know what? The other night I heard voices."

"The Colonel talking in his sleep."

"I don't think so."

"Oh well, that and a *handelszink* will get you exactly nothing these days. If you don't mind, the car keys, please."

She took the keys off the hook in the hall and handed them to me. I looked in her eyes and she looked away.

"Don't go mad like the rest of them," I said sternly. "You're better than that. Good evening, Miss Hobert."

*

I pull up next to the café. I can see Putzeis through the window with his friends. It all looks very jolly, but I picture how these same men led the three young Englishmen into the station with gestapo officers ready to pounce, and I hear the quickened beat of my pulse flutter in my ear as I get out of the car and go inside to join them.

I'm not afraid, but I'm aware of the danger, and I don't know if any of us are truly unafraid of dying. Let's think about this a moment. We wouldn't say we were afraid of being born. But dying—dying makes grown men shit their pants. And yet, we all die. I've decided that the way we die matters. Take Mother's passing. She had an admittedly unpleasant incident preceding, but from what I could glean watching her, a pleasant death.

And why am I obsessing about morbidity? Because of what Putzeis just told me. One by one, his friends have left the café. The last to go was Piet, the sloppy fellow. Putzeis and I are alone at the table. He's wearing gold-rimmed spectacles, new ones that aren't as flattering, but at least he can see me, and now that the men are gone and Putzeis has taken off his gloves, I notice his hands are sweating. And also that he's missing the end of a finger.

"Never try to fix your own car," he says, indicating the missing finger.

I think he's telling the truth about how he lost it.

"Look," he says, "I trust you."

"Thank you."

"I may need to ask your help with something."

"Well, I'm honored."

"There's someone I thought I trusted, but I'm no longer sure I should."

"Such are the times."

"It's Piet. He's made mistakes lately, one almost cost me everything. But when I called him to task about it, he told me something about you."

Putzeis is looking hard at me.

"Really."

"Something he'd heard. Through the grapevine. About why you're not married."

"Find me the woman I can marry, and I will." I laugh, hoping the heat in my cheeks doesn't show.

This seems to reassure Putzeis. "That's what I thought. I told Piet, I said, 'Not every man will marry a cow like you did.'" Putzeis's looking in my eyes as if they will reveal the truth. "I may need you to keep a lookout in your building."

"My building?"

"The network is operating in your building. The resistance. The *line.*"

"I didn't know."

"There's a delivery tomorrow."

"A delivery?"

"Don't be dense."

"Apologies, but I really don't know what you're talking about," I say.

Of course, I do know exactly what Putzeis's talking about.

He leans forward, so I smell his sour yeasty breath and see his large-pored nose. Blackheads. He should scrub it better. "A fugitive," he hisses. "Posing as a deaf-mute, a half-wit."

"Ah." I nod as if I'm just now putting together the pieces.

We sit there in silence.

"If I ask this favor, you can't fuck it up."

"What is it exactly that you want me to do?"

"Make sure the delivery is made. That I'm not double-crossed."

I push my beer away and make a face. I'm not fond of beer. Give me a good glass of Pommard, and I will be a happier man. With some change in my pocket, I might afford a bottle.

"Double-crossed by the Colonel?"

Putzeis looks relieved. He was beginning to think I, too, might be a half-wit.

"I would pick up the package myself. Normally, that's what I'd do. Walk right into the building and leave with the package, no middleman. Colonel Warlemont thinks I've been in Brussels only a few months. Paris before that. And Canada prior. Miss Hobert knows better. I'm afraid if she sees me, she'd say something."

"Oh, she would. She'd blow your cover in a heartbeat. She's quite the quidnunc."

"I thought so." Putzeis sips his beer contemplatively.

"It's not an easy thing you're asking," I say. "There may be complications."

"Always. Like what?"

"Oh, well, our resident Nazi for one."

"Who's that?"

"I'm sure you've seen him at meetings. Van Cauter. Face of an embalmed pear. He'll have to be managed."

"Managed?"

"Kept occupied during the delivery. You wouldn't want to compete with him for the prize."

"You're right. Damned Nazi would want to call the gestapo straight away and cut me out."

"And the notary's wife . . ."

"What notary?"

"Everard. Lives on the ground floor. Also rather active in the party."

"What's the trouble with his wife?"

"Spies on everyone all the time. I don't know who she works for, let alone how the Colonel has pulled it off under their noses."

"He hasn't pulled it off under my nose," Putzeis says with no small pride. "Well? How about it?"

"The trouble is—"

"Yes?"

"It's hard to get my mind around why I'd do it."

"There's money in it," Putzeis says slowly. I can see him making calculations. It's so obvious. I tell you he's turning into an abacus before my eyes.

Many of my classmates in Leuven were Communists. Went about in moth-eaten sweaters. Never washed behind their ears let alone in them. Wax. Such silly people. How could they not see that we're all greedy shits, them included. When no one has money, it's straightforward—share and share alike. Everyone's the same until someone has a chance to be the same only better. Ten times out of ten, they'll take that chance. Look at Putzeis. His clothes. His eyeglasses. Why should he be better off than I?

"How much?" I ask.

"I'll give you a cut of my fee."

I can see this pains him.

"A cut."

"Twenty percent. You'll be helping with the first ten percent of the job so it's a generous offer. Most of the work is on me. I thought up the scheme. I get the information out of them. And then I turn them over."

"I see."

"I didn't share my money in Paris with anyone. I made the connection there, got inside. Stirred the pot."

"The pot?"

"Created uncertainty in the line."

I can see that Putzeis knows he's talking too much and should stop. But he's decided he trusts me, and he needs me to trust him—or at least to fear him—and he senses I don't.

"I told them someone in their organization was a snake, playing a double game."

"Did it work?"

"The fear of being tricked is worse than the knowledge that you have been."

I'm not sure this is true, but I'm being agreeable.

"Why did you come back from Paris?" I ask.

"One of them was on to me. I told the gorilla—"

"The *gorilla*?"

"Never mind. But I told him she was the snake. The woman." For a moment, Putzeis lets himself look self-satisfied. He gulps his beer.

"My god," I say admiringly. "Paris has become quite the jungle."

I'm staring into his eyes. Putzeis is carrying a lot of skins.

"You need to tell me now if you'll do it. Otherwise, I'll find someone else," he says.

I shrug and nod. "Why not? I could use the hard currency."

I must say I'm enjoying this little drama. I'm thinking of it as a play of sorts. The kind Mother could have put on in our living room if she had the vision to use all those chairs instead of keeping them empty and waiting.

Who's to say I won't divert that package and collect the money my-self? I've said it before. Away from the front it is a war of information, and I have more information than Putzeis. I know who the package is—the man I saw in the Colonel's apartment this afternoon. Julian Raphaël.

*

Men talk about women. They keep dirty pictures in drawers under piles of socks, hidden in books, behind their shaving soaps, even the man who called himself my father had a picture or two tucked away. They dream of reaching down and touching that soft undercarriage up the skirt between the legs and there it is. Well, I don't. I'd like to find something a bit harder down under.

Putzeis trusts me. To what? And why? I trust people to be them-selves. I trust them to cut off my testicles. I trust Piet to stab me in the neck. I trust Hobert to push me down the stairs. As for me? I don't trust myself. Not one bit.

COLONEL WARLEMONT, 3L

Dirk knows Julian is in my apartment. And that I know he knows this.

I considered having Julian leave in the night and might have done but for the recent curfew. More likely than not, Julian would have been seen and captured. This was my reasoning. But having him stay wasn't much better in terms of odds, and I didn't sleep, not a nod.

*

It was a monumental bungle—Julian being shuttled to my little safe house. Once I'd gotten him inside without being seen, I knew we had to get him away from here as soon as possible. The likelihood that he'd be recognized was too great. But there's a whole process I'm not part of in moving these men—identification papers to be gotten, transport, and so on—and I was reminded of what Harry had said about each of us only knowing the next link in the chain. It wasn't a simple one, two, three he's out. Far from it.

I had been given the name of a gentleman to contact should I need to move one of the chaps quickly for some reason—a fellow named Captain Anderson, whom I rushed out to meet yesterday at a café in Anderlecht near the abattoirs. Fittingly, the Nazis have taken over the slaughterhouses. I found it unsettling to meet in their shadow but courageous in a Machiavellian, keeping-the-enemy-close sort of way. I will say, it's the nearest I've been to a hunk of meat since the Nazis took the city.

It was a cold day, but we sat outside so as not to be overheard. A rank smell drifted over from the slaughterhouses, and the beer was watered down. As I drank it, a seasick feeling came over me. Anderson himself struck me as an odd fellow. He kept his gloves on. I've never had a beer at a café, indoors or out, with a man who kept his gloves on. Even in the cold. Not once. Canadians can be odd, I'll give them that, but it didn't sit right. I couldn't shake my sense of unease, and because of it, I didn't explain who Julian was or why we had to get him out, only that it was urgent we do so. Anderson was annoyed I wasn't more forthcoming.

"If you tell me exactly what the problem is, it would be most helpful."

I shook my head ruefully. "That's not the protocol I was given," I said, a bald-faced lie because in truth, this never came up.

The sour look on Anderson's face put me off even more, but I agreed to meet him with Julian—the package—in front of the pharmacy in the square at five o'clock the next day. What other option did I have?

"I'll have a car waiting on the side street," he said. "It will be a quick exchange provided you make a timely delivery. I'll handle everything personally."

The waiter passed by our table. Anderson held up his hand as I reached for money. "Please, allow me," he said.

As he dug through his wallet, a French railway ticket fell out onto the concrete. I picked it up and handed it to him, and it was on the tip of my tongue to ask if he knew Harry. I didn't ask and Anderson didn't have enough money for both beers. I paid the waiter for mine and left.

*

When I returned to the apartment, Julian was outwardly calm, but I could see his jaw working and a determined look settle in his eyes. As for me, the sense of unease I felt at the café lingered.

"I don't like this Captain Anderson," I mouthed to Julian.

Jacques nodded—all empathy—when I said it.

*

Julian needed provisions for his trip, so this afternoon, Jacques and I headed out for the shop. When we reached the ground floor, Everard—the notary—appeared in the lobby with the new tenant, Van Cauter, a lifeless fellow who looks like someone extracted his flesh and stuffed him with eggshells. I had tried to contact Harry when Van Cauter moved in, but Harry's been MIA since he told me about Masha and proposed the current scheme. That was over two months ago. I remember asking then if there was a chance he'd been followed to my apartment.

"My dear man, there's always a chance."

Thanks for that, Harry.

"I've had a complaint from one of the building residents," Everard said.

Van Cauter made no move to step aside and let us have a private conversation.

Bugger me. Everard and I had made a deal. We shook hands on it. We had commiserated—genuinely, at least on my part. I told him I have guilt for not having silenced my wife's tirade in time to prevent that stroke. I feel empathy for Everard, who is no doubt hoping his wife, too, will have an over-the-top jeremiad that does her in, so he can live with his guilt rather than with her. But that's where truth ended and fabrication began. I lied when I told him my guilt compelled me to take in men I never would have. This was when he in turn felt sympathy for me. I've always said truth is overrated.

"We're all in a tight spot these days, with no place left to stand," Everard said.

He seemed less enthused with the Nazis than he was two years before. They hadn't welcomed him to their inner circle, and I understood what his wife wanted. What he thought he'd get from the Nazis and hadn't. I made it worth his while. Everard was grateful for the money.

He's not the most sympathetic chap, our notary. His handshake is a dead trout, but he lives by the rule book. And that's how Hobert got to him. She'd made it clear the rules weren't being followed. Stormed in waving the banner of truth. Give me a liar and a thief and a whore, and I'll show you God's army.

"I have a complaint about Hobert as well," I said. From the look on Everard's face, I knew I had guessed the identity of our resident complainer. "She's getting black-market butter and terrorizing building residents."

Van Cauter took a small notebook out of his breast pocket, flipped it open, and wrote something down.

"How is she terrorizing residents?" he asked.

"With bad cakes."

Van Cauter wrote that down too. I'd forgotten how humorless they are, these Nazis.

"Now then, if you'll excuse us, Jacques and I have our shopping to do."

Van Cauter snapped his notebook shut and looked hard at Everard.

"You need to register Jacques at the town hall. He must be registered. Assuming he's staying," Everard said.

"Yes. For the time being."

"Is there anyone else staying with you?"

"Not at the moment."

Did I hesitate too long before replying?

Jacques was trying to understand what was going on. I'm sure he had some inkling that it had to do with him, only it didn't, not really. I steered him toward the door.

"We'll go immediately. The town hall."

Van Cauter said something to Everard in a low voice.

"We need to look in your apartment," Everard said.

"Look in it? Or search it?" I asked.

"Miss Hobert said she heard voices. And she saw someone else in there yesterday afternoon."

"Miss Hobert has a rabid imagination." I about-faced Jacques and we stepped back in the lobby.

The thing about contingency plans. You don't want to resort to them, ergo the name, but we were going to have to implement ours and right away.

We walked slowly up the stairs, Jacques leaning on me as though he needed my help. I tried not to think of how inadequate our plan was or the other times I had been forced to implement contingency plans. They had always gone badly. You're in a corner and you must get out of that corner and it's impossible. Enter the contingency plan.

"I have a dog," I said to Van Cauter as Jacques and I reached a landing and took a pause to catch our breath.

"You needn't register the dog, obviously," Everard said.

Was this his attempt at humor?

"Just warning you. He's gotten less friendly in his old age."

"How old is he?" Van Cauter asked.

"Four and a half."

We began to climb stairs again and I tried to reassure myself. The plan would work. It had to, and it was better to get Julian out sooner than not at all. Dirk had seen him. Hobert might have too.

Jacques and I paused midflight.

"Why are you stopping again?" Van Cauter asked.

"Jacques's heart isn't strong."

Jacques has the heart of a draft horse and with luck, he'll outlive us all.

We continued up and soon we were at my door.

"I'll have to deal with Zipper," I said loudly.

"That's your dog?" Van Cauter asked.

"Yes. Zipper!"

Right away, Zipper began to bark frantically from behind the door.

With a look of what I alone knew to be beautifully studied terror, Jacques stepped back and indicated that Van Cauter should go ahead of him. Jacques would have made a brilliant actor on the silent screen.

"Jacques doesn't like to be left alone with Zipper," I said.

At the sound of his name, Zipper barked and growled and snarled even more viciously.

I'm not saying all Nazis are stupid, but I can't say I've met any brilliant ones. I'm sure at the highest levels there are men and women who are smart enough in a diabolical way, but the people below are not, and this is another reason not to give up.

Key in lock.

"Stand down, Zipper! And you! Don't move!" I said to Van Cauter.

I opened the door. Seeing Zipper, teeth bared, ruff up, a mass of muscle poised to pounce, Van Cauter stepped back. Of course he did.

"Back, Zipper!" I shouted.

With that, Zipper leapt forward from the doorway, grabbing Van Cauter's ankle, yanking his foot out from under him and knocking him on his back. Teeth sinking in with an awful crunch, jaws locking, Zipper shook Van Cauter's foot back and forth.

Van Cauter screamed in pain, his arms flailing.

"I told you not to move."

"Call him off."

"Why did you bloody move?"

"Call off your dog," Everard shouted.

"Zipper, release!" I finally said.

Zipper released the ankle and backed away growling. I grabbed his collar and held him.

Van Cauter sat up, face white, eyes narrow slits, and breath coming fast through his mouth as he stretched forward to look at the ankle, but only a hole in the fabric of his trousers suggested anything amiss. He rolled up his pant leg to reveal the bite—clean, deep punctures, no torn skin. Tidy. At first, the holes looked white too, but they quickly began to fill with blood.

God, I was proud of the old boy, doing such excellent work in a pinch.

"Perhaps you should go downstairs and take care of that? Unfortunately, dog bites tend to infection," I said.

Van Cauter glared at me and slowly got to his feet. I made no effort to help him, and I noticed Everard didn't either.

I was still holding Zipper, who was growling in a low steady drone. Jacques had already gone inside the apartment and disappeared from view.

"What's he doing? Jacques!" Van Cauter shouted.

"He's deaf," I reminded him.

A flushing sound quickly answered the question.

"Zipper makes him nervous," I added.

Van Cauter was seething. "Keep that fucking dog in the hall," he said.

He limped into my apartment, and Everard and I followed. I hadn't felt such gut-clutching anxiety since the last war.

By this time, Jacques was sitting on the sofa looking out the window. He seemed despondent, and I understood why. It's a lonely game, and so few of the fellows who've passed through have been as kind to him as Julian.

I followed the two men through the apartment. They were very thorough, searching the pantry, the utility closet, the bathroom, inside both wardrobes, under the bed, behind the bedroom curtains. There aren't a lot of places for a grown man to hide, but they searched them all and then they searched the drawers, I'm sure looking for a gun. I don't have one here. I keep it buried at the farm of the lovely woman who has been ferrying these chaps my way.

"Can you fix the window latch?" I asked. "I tried, but it needs a new part."

Everard was peering out at the courtyard. "I'll look and see if there's one in the basement."

"Much appreciated."

I could tell he was feeling badly about all this, that he thought he had betrayed my trust, and he had. But I wasn't holding it against him. He turned to Van Cauter.

"Shall we?"

They made a rapid exit, Van Cauter leaving a trickle of blood on the terrazzo.

"I would wash that ankle," I called after him.

Everard turned back. "Keep the dog in your apartment."

I followed them to the hall and watched them go down the stairs.

"Register Jacques immediately. This afternoon," Everard called behind him. It was his way of making amends. Everard knows that men like Jacques are also being deported and if he's properly registered, that's less likely to happen.

*

At best it was always a long, slow day when you had to get something done at city hall, but the war has made the place a purgatory. Everyone waiting endlessly and often for nothing. Ahead of me, I heard request after request being turned down. It seemed no one was getting what they wanted or needed, and there was still a line of people, each hoping their fate would be different, us included. I used to be able to peg my compatriots by their clothes, the roughness of their hands, but these days, we're all badly dressed and worn out, and anyone who isn't should be avoided.

Seeing this, it was impossible not to be reminded of Julian dressed in those crude farm clothes they'd given him to wear. Even here, he'd stand out in those clothes. Jacques did.

The clerks were slow moving, and many were on their lunch breaks. I could see them eating sandwiches in the back while we waited, smelling mildew from inside and street tar every time the door was opened. Soldiers use the road as a thoroughfare, so unlike most it's oiled. The smell was pungent. There was an elderly couple with darker skin behind

Jacques and me. Gypsies? They shouldn't have risked it if they were. Gypsies were being deported to camps.

Julian's fate hung heavy on me.

A pregnant woman ahead of us stepped up to a window. She'd been on her feet too long, and she made me think of Charlotte. I had wanted to offer the woman a seat, but there was no chair.

Just when I thought Jacques and I should call it a day and hope for better luck in the morning, another window slid open, and a man called out, "Next in line!"

I pulled Jacques forward.

"Name?" the clerk asked.

"He's Jacques Goffin," I said.

"Let him speak for himself."

"He's deaf."

"What's your name?" he asked Jacques.

"His name is Jacques Goffin, and he's deaf."

"Why are you talking for him?"

"Because he can't hear a word you say. And he doesn't speak, not really."

"Where's the proof?"

"Proof of what?"

"That he's deaf!"

I gave the clerk a telephone number I had been given to use in an emergency.

"Jacques's mother," I said.

The clerk placed the call and a woman picked up. The clerk held the telephone receiver so I could hear as he asked about Jacques—if he was indeed her son and if he was truly deaf.

"Yes, yes," she said. "Yes he is. I should have drowned him when he was a baby, as soon as I knew what he was." And with that, she hung up.

The clerk might not have been the sharpest arrow on the stick, but he had the good sense to be shaken by the call, so much so that he processed Jacques's registration right away. The chap can't read or write, so I had him sign with an X and the clerk accepted it. A small miracle in a series of what I hoped would be bigger miracles.

*

As we took the tram back to Number 33, I understood that it was out of my hands. I had done what I could, and we all know Julian isn't stupid. All I can say is thank God Zipper is now the best-trained beast in this tiny former Kingdom of Belgium.

JULIAN RAPHAËL, 4R

Odds of being hidden in my own building.

Odds of the Colonel hiding me.

Odds of being seen by Hobert . . . actually, quite high.

Odds of ever seeing Charlotte again.

I didn't tell the farmers where I lived in Brussels. It was a shock when I saw the Colonel at the exchange point. For him as well—I could tell, though it was just a flicker on his face. How the poor man had aged, I noticed that, too, but only when I stopped shaking. Or maybe he was shaking. This was disaster. We both knew it, but it was too late. My escort left the moment the Colonel arrived. There was nothing but to get me inside the building without being seen—and out again with dispatch. We went directly to Number 33.

The Colonel had one RAF pilot already staying in his apartment—and Jacques—who was truly deaf. The pilot was from a different crew that had crashed on a beach where he'd been picked up by fishermen. He was to leave the Colonel's a couple days after I arrived, and we exchanged a whispered word in the bathroom. I wanted him to let my parents know I had no regrets, should he get back and I not make it.

The Colonel was edgy. He knew there was a problem in the line, and he didn't feel right about Anderson.

Never underestimate anyone. It made me laugh to think I wanted to live if only to tell Papa that the Colonel is an absolute brick, Zipper is a genius, and Jacques has a heart of gold. In the short days Jacques and I were together, I taught him to read a few simple words—cup, car, gun. Another reason to live—so I can help him after the war.

Not long after Jacques left with the Colonel, I heard footsteps on the stairs and the Colonel's warning signal. The one he would give should all be going south.

"I'll have to deal with Zipper!"

I grabbed the fish knife, ran to the Colonel's bedroom, pushed up the window. The night before, the Colonel had broken the latch. I'll never forget the sight of those strong hands of his pulling apart the metal latch to make it look like it had given way from years of use. I stepped out onto the ledge, the one I had studied so carefully all those years ago when Guy was inching along it. And I slid the window shut.

I wasn't afraid. There was no time for fear. I dug out the mortar with the knife, though it took me longer than it had taken Guy to get out a chunk. But I did. And then I was sliding along the narrow building ledge, hoping it wasn't crumbling, too, edging myself toward the Colonel's kitchen balcony. I could hear men searching the apartment. The Colonel was speaking to them in that booming voice of his, so I would have a map of exactly where they were—in the living room just beyond the kitchen. The balcony was the most dangerous place for me as I would be fully visible through the window, so I had to wait out of their sight on the ledge until they were gone. But then what?

There was no way to get out of the building by going down. Van Cauter would see me. It was too risky to slip back in the Colonel's apartment after they left it as they'd be watching his every move. And Hobert would have heard all the racket and be lurking. These were the thoughts swimming in my head when I spotted him looking out the window at me—Dirk. He had an amused expression on his face, and he didn't say a word. He just watched. The Colonel gave the signal that the men were out of his apartment, and I quick climbed up onto the Colonel's balcony and then hoisted myself up to the fourth floor and onto Charlotte's balcony.

CHARLOTTE SAUVIN, 4L

At first, I think the tapping is Father's pencil. But when I look over, I see Father slumped in his chair, the pencil having fallen into his lap. I jump up and hurry to his side, but he's only sleeping.

And still, I hear the tapping. Maybe it's the heat pipes, I think as I follow the sound down the hall and into the kitchen. I look out on the balcony, and I see him.

He puts a finger to his lips and quietly, so quietly, I slip off my shoes, tiptoe over, and open the door.

I let Julian in and shut and lock the door behind him. "I kept my promise," I whisper. "I think of you all the time." He takes me in his arms and kisses me.

He has changed—of course he has. He's gaunt, his hair cut close but still with the serious look on his face. My dear Julian, for this moment with me. It takes all my control not to cry. For as soon as I see him through the glass, I understand a terrifying thing. I cannot remember Philippe, but I will never forget Julian. I have always known him. I can't live without him.

*

Father and Julian and I are writing frantic notes. Burning them on the stove as we go. Julian is determined to meet this man, Anderson, at the pharmacy, but there's little time to get him there. Father leaves the kitchen and comes back with a suit and hat, motioning at Julian to put them on. We agree that I'll escort Julian, Father's hat pulled low over his face, and he'll cough if anyone approaches. I will tell them my father's sick, and I'm taking him to the pharmacy. That will keep Hobert away and hopefully the notary too. They'll know I would only resort to the pharmacy's outcast medicines in desperation.

I can see the anxiety on Father's face. He doesn't like the idea of me going, but he knows he can't stop me.

I won't lose Julian again. I can't.

When Julian's ready, I tell him to wait in the kitchen. I put on my coat and crack the front door to make sure all is clear. Dirk is standing on the other side. He pushes into our hall and we struggle with the door a moment before he overpowers me and shuts it.

"Anderson's a snake," he whispers. "You can't trust him."

Julian is still in the kitchen. Father has stepped into the hall and seen Dirk and, for a moment, we are frozen. I imagine Julian is too. And now there really is no time.

I'm looking in Dirk's eyes, searching his face, trying to know. But I can't read those eyes. His face tells me nothing. He's so good at protecting himself, at not letting anyone see what he's thinking. I understand that.

"It's a trap," Dirk insists. "I'm telling the truth."

He fumbles in his pocket, puts something in my hand. A chipped and worn stub of wood, not quite a cylinder, that familiar eight-sided shape. I stare at it. I don't need to read the label to know it says, *RED*.

"I owe you," Dirk says.

*

Father and I step out to the square. A cold, damp January day.

Dirk told us the man Julian was to meet would fittingly be wearing a red scarf and waiting in front of the pharmacy. Indeed, Captain Anderson has a blood scarf around his neck. And he smells like a burnt fish. He is so surprised to see me with Father—and not Julian with the Colonel—that it takes him a moment to recalibrate.

I don't rush him. We are counting on this moment. It is everything.

Anderson's sharp eyes dart from Father's face to mine. I see him contemplating his next move from behind tortoise-rimmed spectacles.

"And so, you have no hat," I say.

Anderson touches the bald spot on the back of his head and makes a face revealing overlong teeth that give him the look of a malicious rabbit.

"I was expecting someone else," Anderson says.

"So sorry to disappoint," I say, as though I take it personally.

"No offense intended. I—"

"Black or gray?" I interrupt, circling around him, so he's forced to turn his back to the square.

"I'm sorry?"

"It's the best I can do under the circumstances."

A figure in a bulky dark coat and a new felted hat steps out of Number 33 and walks quickly to the bakery.

"I don't understand," Anderson says.

"Your hat."

"But I'm not wearing a hat."

"Exactly!" Father says, catching on.

"Eigengrau, then?" I ask. Anderson doesn't know what it means, and he doesn't like not knowing. "It's the color you see in the absence of light. A gray that looks good on anyone."

"Oh yes," Anderson says. He still doesn't know.

"Brim? Or no brim?"

"My hat has a brim," Father says, helpfully.

"No hat," Anderson says in exasperation.

"But isn't that the point?" I ask.

"What point?"

"That you need a hat!"

"A hat?" Anderson is looking at Father now as if he might yet be a downed crewman disguised as an older Belgian gentleman.

"I make hats."

In spite of himself, Captain Anderson is intrigued. Although fashionably dressed, he is, indeed, hatless.

"Did you make his hat?" he indicates Father's.

I notice Father's eye twitching, the corner of his mouth fluttering. "Sadly, no."

Captain Anderson looks like a man who is hard to corner, harder still to befuddle, but we have.

"No hat," he says decisively. "And now, I must be on my way."

As he says it, I see the truck that delivers grain to the bakery every afternoon at five pull onto the avenue and drive off.

"Good day," Father says politely, as a strangled choke erupts from his throat and rises into a tortured fit of coughs. "Apologies . . . bit of a cold."

Captain Anderson backs away from Father, who's hacking and gasping, and walks quickly to a side street where he gets in a black car that pulls out from the curb with a screech.

Father suppresses another giggle and reaches for my hand. I help him stumble back to Number 33, and we hurry up the stairs to our apartment. It's over. Julian is gone.

*

"The events of the future can't be inferred from those of the present."

I can't stop thinking of Julian. I remember that day in the darkroom, years ago now, in another life. How his face revealed something I didn't then understand. How I mistook my deepest feelings for mere familiarity. How Julian did not make that mistake. He knew all along.

JULIAN RAPHAËL, 4R

I noticed right away that she was pregnant.

She looked beautiful. Pale. Strong. She was in a word, fearless. This is how I saw her.

She was thinking fast. She handed me Francois's suit, and I put it on. It was baggy on me—and doubtless on him. What can I say? It was a time of disappearing. If you didn't watch yourself, you'd be erased like a pencil mark.

We all waited in the silence, and it reminded me of how Charlotte and I used to work in the darkroom. I didn't have time to think about whether I had treasured those moments as I should have, of how you only appreciate what you have when you're losing it, or you've lost it, of the perversity of living.

When Charlotte opened her front door to find Dirk, she must have thought we were cornered, I was lost, and that she and Francois might be too.

I waited, unable to make out their whispers in the front hall.

Charlotte appeared again in the kitchen doorway, her face bloodless and still.

"Take off your clothes," she said.

It's all a question of time and place, isn't it?

I had imagined Charlotte saying those exact words to me. I had spent long sleepless nights thinking of what it would be like to hold her naked. Needless to say, I had not imagined Francois there too. Let alone Dirk.

I took off the suit and Francois put it on with a hat that he pulled low over his face. Charlotte ran into her bedroom and came back with something she pressed into my hand.

"Go to the bakery," she said.

And then they were gone, leaving me standing there in my underwear not knowing what the hell to do and that was when Dirk reappeared. He handed me a bulky coat, a hat, and a suit—his own—motioning me to hurry. As I dressed, he took his shoes off and gave them to me. The shoes were too small, the suit enormous. I had to tie the belt around me to keep the pants from falling down, and that was when I remembered that damn argument between Turing and Wittgenstein.

Dirk has always been a liar. So if Dirk told me he was a liar and not to trust him, I would be forced to conclude the opposite. In that moment, I wanted him to tell me he was a liar and that I couldn't trust him. But, of course, he didn't.

The fact was I had no choice but to trust him.

In stocking feet, Dirk ran silently downstairs to his apartment. I pulled the hat low over my head as Francois had done and stepped in the hallway.

It was open—the door to our apartment. Across the hall, I could see into the place where I grew up, where I had lived all my life. A tarp was on the floor with a stack of broken picture frames that Papa and I had hidden in the walls that last day, and there were great holes in the plaster. I boiled with fury again. My family wasn't there; it was a shell of a place where I would probably never live again. Still, my hands were fists and I stepped toward the open door.

I heard a man clear his throat and looked down to see Dirk on his landing, wearing the sternest expression I've ever seen on a face.

What would have been the point of going in our old apartment? This is where Papa and I have some difference of view. I'll tell him if I can that it's not about the buildings or the paintings or the statues. It's this moment with these people. And if we all lived like that, I'm confident there would be no more wars. If I had gone in the apartment, I might not be alive. As Dirk understood too well, there was no time.

*

I was hidden in the bakery truck under bags of grain and a blanket on the drive out of Brussels. I had a slit of a view, and through it, I could see the grayness of the city, the gray sky, the gray stone of the buildings. A drizzle began to fall. It was comforting. I felt I was seeing as Charlotte did. That we were somehow one.

CHARLOTTE SAUVIN, 4L

Today, I go to the bakery where I pick up our small loaf of sour rye. Maryanne puts the bread in a bag along with a man's felt hat. She smiles and leans in so close I can see the crisscross of lines on her face, the wisps of hair escaping her bun.

"He said Dirk might want it back," she says softly. Maryanne straightens up as she takes my tickets. "The rationing is killing us, isn't it? But I have some beet sugar for your father. Delivered yesterday."

I return home with a lightness in my heart. But as I approach the building, I see that the doors to Number 33 are wide open, and two big black cars are parked in the square. I cry out when I see a gestapo officer ushering a small figure toward one of the cars. I know the cap, the shape of it, I know it by heart, and without thinking, I hurry toward him as the officer opens the car door.

The newsboy sees me, and he shakes his head furiously—too late—the officer has noticed me too.

The newsboy spits at me. "Nazi lover," he snarls as he gets in the car.

Brave boy. Champion. Little hero.

I force myself to turn away and hurry inside. No crying. It isn't an ending. Not yet.

*

Miss Hobert is pacing in the lobby, her face puckered. She's sliding a ring on and off her finger. It catches on her knuckle, and I can see that the knuckle is swelling.

She's going to pull her finger right off if she doesn't stop it.

"Oh! They're going up, floor by floor. I can't bear it. I can't. I won't be in my apartment for this. What will they find?"

But I notice her eyes are dry, and I wonder if she's enjoying this, her moment of high drama.

"What will they find?" she asks again, knuckle cracking as she wrenches the ring over it then pushes it down.

"The rat I hope." I hurry across the lobby to the stairs.

"I only told them that I heard something in the Colonel's apartment."

I stop and I turn to look at Miss Hobert, seeing her shifting collapsing face, her caterpillar lips. She's still wearing my hat.

"What did you hear?"

"Oh . . . Voices. And not the Colonel's. And I would swear on a Bible that he had another man in there. Besides the one who drools."

Now tears spill out her eyes, finding paths along the horizontal crevasses of her wrinkles.

I turn away from her and continue up.

"I had to tell the truth, didn't I? About whom I thought he might be? The other man."

I pause on the stairs, but I don't look at her. I can't.

"The truth is they already searched the Colonel's apartment, and they only found Jacques," I say.

*

"Where were you this morning?"

"Getting our bread," I say.

An SS officer and a Nazi army officer sit at the table with Father and me, much as we sat here with Julian and Esther on a morning a few years ago in that other life, but instead of a sweet loaf of challah, there's a gun in front of us—Father's old rifle.

"Beer." The SS officer writes a note. "Isn't that against regulation?"

"What regulation would that be?" the other officer asks.

I've seen him before. He's Schmidt, the man who slipped butter in my bag over two years ago.

The Germans exchange glances—hard, questioning looks—as if they've never encountered a situation like this. And maybe they haven't. I can tell that Schmidt admires Father for his cheerful calm. And indeed, it's a quality that should be admired in a time like this, even when it is found in the soul of an enemy.

Gestapo are searching the apartment. I can hear the opening and shutting of drawers, the clink of toiletries on glass shelves. One of the gestapo emerges from the back hall with the rolled canvas and box of oil paints Mr. Raphaël left for me.

"Those are mine," I say.

I can tell the gestapo wants to take them.

"You paint?" Schmidt asks.

"Yes. Yes, I do. I paint."

"Leave them," he says to the gestapo.

The gestapo looks at the SS officer, who opens his mouth to object, but seeing the unyielding look on Schmidt's face, shuts it.

"Put them back where you found them," Schmidt orders.

The gestapo takes the paints and canvas back to my room.

When they've finished searching the apartment, the SS officer turns to Schmidt and begins speaking in German. I understand a little. Enough. The exchange is heated, and I glance at Father who is still waiting calmly.

Schmidt looks troubled.

The SS officer has a triumphant look on his face. He turns to me and says in his imperfect French, "The rifle is forbidden. No one is to have firearms."

"It isn't a functioning gun," Schmidt interjects. "There's no bolt."

"Firearms of any sort are forbidden. We are required to arrest him."

"This isn't sensible," Schmidt says.

"It is required. The sooner we leave, the sooner he will be back. If there is no problem as you insist."

"He'll be back by evening," Schmidt says to me. "Maybe earlier."

Father bends down to tie his shoes, and I see that he's shaking. Schmidt turns away, giving us privacy. He must think Father's sobbing. But he's not. Father's giggling again. He unties and reties his shoes, struggling mightily to suppress the laughter. And he's smiling as he gets up from the table. I run to find his overcoat with the pockets and cuffs I mended a month or two ago, and I help him into it. He hugs me tightly and tells me to put the beet sugar in the kitchen.

"Something to look forward to," he says, holding his voice steady. "Perhaps you'll try a glass when the time comes?" he adds, with a bold nod to Schmidt. "I know you've been spending time in the apartment across the hall."

Now I understand that these are the same men who are tearing apart the Raphaëls' apartment.

Father holds up a hand, warning me not to speak or move, to wait. *Please, Charlotte, wait.*

And then the SS officer is taking Father downstairs. I run into the hall and watch them go, Father's hat getting smaller and smaller as they move down the stairs. At the bottom, he looks up and gives me a little wave.

Without a word, Schmidt steps into the Raphaël apartment. Incarna, the cleaning woman, is waiting for him there. She looks at me, gives a defiant jerk of her chin, and follows Schmidt into the living room. The Raphaëls' hall, once lined with paintings, now has jagged holes in the plaster. A stack of picture frames sits on the floor.

"Jewel under stove when go on vacation. And living room wall.

Replaster and paint. Maybe . . . three years? Silver . . . ?" I hear Incarna say in her broken French.

I run back into our apartment and to the balcony overlooking the square. Through the window, I see the SS officer and Father getting in one of the black cars. Father glances up and, seeing me, tips his hat. The doors slam and the car drives away.

JAN EVERARD, NOTARY, GROUND FLOOR

Briefing of Events

Date: 19-20 January 1943

Location: 33 Place Brugmann

A search was made of apartment 3L at which residence lives one Colonel Warlemont and a Bouvier dog called Zipper. For the past two months, the Colonel has been running a halfway house for deaf-mute Belgians, this in the aftermath of a fire that destroyed a home for the infirm in the Ardennes. Acting upon the complaint of one Miss Hobert in apartment 3R, who felt her security was threatened by the presence of the Colonel's lodgers and who questioned whether they were in fact deaf and thus without speech, I conducted a thorough search of apartment 3L in the company of Ivo Van Cauter, a city administrator who has recently taken up residence in apartment 2L.

We found only one individual living in apartment 3L with the Colonel, and such individual, whose name is Jacques Goffin, is quite clearly Belgian and a deaf man who is unable to speak. At my request, Mr. Goffin has been registered in the town hall in the Commune d'Ixelles and is now legally authorized to live in this building.

Further, there seems to be confusion about a meeting between one Felix Putzeis and the residents of apartment 4L, namely Francois

Sauvin and his daughter, Charlotte. At approximately 16:55 hours, Mr. Van Cauter saw Miss Sauvin and her father leave the building for the square. For reasons unknown to me, Mr. Van Cauter followed them. In the square, the Sauvins encountered Mr. Putzeis. At approximately 17:00 hours, I personally witnessed the resident of apartment 2R, one Dirk DeBaerre, leave the building and walk across the square to the bakery to fetch his daily provision of bread.

At 10:00 the following morning, the gestapo arrived to search the entire building. They found:

1. Mr. Sauvin in apartment 4L drinking tea and sketching.
2. Colonel Warlemont and Jacques Goffin in apartment 3L repairing a jigsaw puzzle.
3. Miss Hobert in apartment 3R reading a book in her foyer.
4. Mr. DeBaerre in apartment 2L eating his breakfast.

Mr. Van Cauter participated in the search.

Only one item of contraband was found in the building. A rifle missing its bolt, consequently unusable, dating to the previous war and owned by Mr. Sauvin.

Mr. Sauvin has been taken in for questioning as there are four reports on file calling into question his loyalties:

1. Mr. DeDecker, a former senior member of the VNV who managed a clothing manufacturer where Charlotte Sauvin worked for a brief time, claims that Mr. Sauvin has refused all work since May 1942. However, Mr. DeDecker is now in jail for embezzlement, so his claims should not be given weight unless corroborated by others.
2. Mr. Smets, a grocer on the Rue Berkendael, reports that Mr. Sauvin has consistently attempted to defraud the government by manipulating ration tickets.

3. Mr. Christophe Wolters, a former partner in Mr. Sauvin's defunct architecture firm, claims that Mr. Sauvin is a Jewish sympathizer who actively resisted carrying out government edicts regarding Jews.

4. A former resident of the building, Mrs. DeBaerre, claimed that Mr. Sauvin helped her husband deliver identity documents to a Jewish family. Mr. DeBaerre was being questioned by the authorities at the time and denied that Mr. Sauvin knew anything about the matter. There was no evidence to support the claim. Consequently, the report was filed but never investigated as both Mr. and Mrs. DeBaerre died shortly thereafter.

Yesterday, at 14:00 hours, Zipper, the Bouvier dog owned by Colonel Warlemont in 3L, viciously attacked Mr. Van Cauter, causing him to seek medical attention at a local hospital. The gestapo informed Colonel Warlemont that his dog would be shot on suspicion of rabies. The Colonel asked to do it himself, stating that he knew how to make sure it was done so the beast wouldn't suffer. The request was denied.

Lastly, a comprehensive search of apartment 4R, previously inhabited by Leo and Sophia Raphaël and their children, Esther and Julian, is underway.

33 PLACE BRUGMANN

BUILDING RESIDENTS

5th Floor Maid's Room
~~Miss Masha Balyayeva~~, ~~refugee—Nansen Passport, seamstress~~
deceased, unconfirmed

Apartment 4L:
Mr. Francois G. Sauvin, architect
Miss Charlotte E. Sauvin (daughter), student, Royal Academy of Fine Arts,
Antwerp

Apartment 4R:
~~Mr. Leo Raphaël~~, ~~fine art dealer~~ in Britain
~~Mrs. Sophia Raphaël~~ ~~(spouse), housewife~~ ditto
~~Miss Esther Raphaël~~ ~~(daughter)~~ ditto
~~Mr. Julian Raphaël~~ (son), ~~student, Cambridge University~~ RAF

Apartment 3L:
Colonel Herman Warlemont, Belgian Armed Armed Forces (widower)
Mr. Jacques Goffin, deaf/nonverbal, unemployed

Apartment 3R:
Miss Agathe Hobert, former café proprietor

Apartment 2L:
~~Mrs. Mathilde Boudrot~~, ~~(widow)~~ **deceased, 13 April 1939**
Mr. Ivo Van Cauter, city administrator

Apartment 2R:
~~Mr. Martin DeBaerre~~, ~~attorney~~ deceased, 29 June 1942
~~Mrs. Katrin DeBaerre~~ ~~(spouse), housewife~~ deceased, 5 July 1942
Mr. Dirk DeBaerre (son), student, Katholieke Universiteit Leuven

Ground Floor
Mr. Jan Everard, notary
Mrs. Annick Everard (spouse), housewife
(two children below age of mandatory registration)

All residents are Belgian citizens unless otherwise noted and are duly registered
in the Commune d'Ixelles.

20th day of January 1942
Sworn and attested, this 2d day of April 1939

IVO VAN CAUTER, 2L

I shot the fucking dog, and that's all I'll say about the matter.

JACQUES GOFFIN, 3L

X

FRANCOIS SAUVIN, 4L

My little bird, my dear one, my only.

Please, bear with me. My thoughts scatter like seeds.

How proud I am that you of all artists will become celebrated for your inventive and ravishing use of color, and I know you will say when it happens that it's no achievement at all, rather a question of science that you talked about endlessly with Julian. Color is light and you see it differently. But that's only part of the story. You have vision.

*

I've always admired how strong you are. When I see that cold gaze you sometimes wear, I know you'll survive.

There's no other way. We can pretend our world is a kinder place, but those who believe that will be caught short and cut down. Sadly, they won't be the only ones.

*

You'd be pleased to know that I no longer smell the rot. I know what it was now. Your theory of time is no theory. It is truth.

*

I remember four years ago, at almost exactly this time of year, you painted a picture of the square. I wanted to call it *Red Square,* but you said that was misdirection and title matters, because it is the only color that you and I both see. It was a strange thing to say, and it reminded me of how singular you are. The picture is unusual too. It made anyone who saw it think of hope and death. It reminded me of something Bosch might paint were he to live in these times. Leo insisted on buying it from you, but you told him he couldn't have it yet as your professor intended to show it at a gallery in Antwerp. Unless the Nazis have taken it down, it's still there. *Dream of the Blood Moon.* It is a work of art, and I'm not the only one who understands this.

*

There once was a square with a seducer of a garden that lured with incantatory charms—lush, aromatic trees and flowers of unearthly delicacy. People did not merely fall in love with this garden—although many lovers came there—they yearned to be near it always. And so they surrounded it with dwellings large and small and they came there to live a dream of a life.

But the time came when people around the world were divided. We could talk about waves of history, how kindness and decency give way to cruelty and obscenity, how the fruit of one vicious war was not lasting peace but fear and suspicion giving rise to a new war. People began to look at their neighbors and see everything that was different. It was as if you saw only shapes of petals, lengths of stems, openness of blooms, forgetting they were all flowers with petals and stems and blooms. It was a disease.

The disease didn't infect the garden right away or the people who lived around it. They still gathered and talked and argued and agreed— or agreed to disagree. Until one night when all the flowers were ripped out of the soil and the trees were cut. People awoke the next morning to see a Golgotha of stumps and holes in place of their garden. It was devastating for all but especially for one young woman, who had been born into that place. She saw and sensed things others couldn't, and it was as though her insides, too, had been torn out.

This was the beginning.

In place of the garden, a monstrosity of a church was built. At first, a generous oblate was appointed there, and he opened the church doors to all people. But the disease infecting the world sickened the church too. The good oblate was banished and replaced by a succession of thin-nosed men who shut the doors to all but a chosen few.

The young woman ached for her lost life in the square. Did she abandon all hope? No. But she lost sight of her future and began to live only in her memories. She didn't understand that the garden was still alive in her soul.

The people comforted themselves with the idea that things were as bad as they could be and could not get worse. How wrong they were. Wretched sentries surrounded the square and the people skirted it, avoiding the church at the center of their misbegotten world.

One dark evening, the young woman was walking home. She crossed the square, though she sensed soldiers watching her from the shadow of the church. But when she looked, she saw the church doors burst open and the hideous brick walls collapse. Blood poured off the altar into the streets, deep-red blood, flooding the square, and in it, bodies and limbs and heads and demons.

Around the square, skeletons hurried home, none noticing they were wading through blood. None seeing the carnage.

How strange, she thought, that I am the one who sees.

On the steps of what once was a church stood a great beast looking upward.

If you were to interrupt, Charlotte, as you always did, you would correct me and say that beast is a lioness.

The young woman followed the beast's gaze to the black-lacquered sky. The stars had fallen. Only the moon illuminated the sea of blood below. And evil trembled. It was a picture of life and death and the young woman understood that at last she could see the world rightly.

MASHA BALYAYEVA, 5TH FLOOR

Harry had fallen asleep. It was before the occupation, and we were in my Brussels attic. He slept a bit, then stirred and woke, pulling me to him so my head rested on the warmth of his chest, the hair tickling my ear. Harry was hairy, and this was why they called him the Gorilla.

We lay there for a time in silence.

"Can't sleep," Harry said.

"Me either . . . What do we do about it?"

"When I was a boy, I had a trick to fall asleep. It had to do with rain."

He trailed off. I had the feeling he was deciding whether to tell me.

I didn't say a word. Even then, I knew that if Harry thought someone was too interested, he got suspicious. It didn't matter if that someone was me. Harry had trouble trusting, and I wanted him to trust me. I never wanted him to be suspicious of me.

"I would imagine that I had gone on a long journey in the rain. A cold, driving rain. I was walking into a strong wind. Like the rain I walked through that first time we . . . That first time . . ." He trailed off again.

"I remember. But why rain?"

"It was part of the conceit. That helped me sleep."

"The rain?"

"Not only the rain."

"Did you like rain as a child?"

"It rained all the time in England."

"I thought you grew up in France."

"In both places. I would walk and walk in that rain. In my imagining. Endlessly. Tired and cold, up a hill. Down a long road, gravel I think, with nothing along it. No houses, no buildings. Nothing but rain and wind. Until I reached a castle made of stone. It looked cold, inhospitable. Still, I would go inside."

I was watching Harry's lips as he talked. They barely moved. I had thought it was a trick he had, not to move his lips much, but that night I realized it was his natural way of speaking. It made him seem as if he were afraid of saying things or of having people know he had said them.

"What was in the castle?"

"Nothing."

"A rather empty dream."

"It wasn't a dream, not exactly. I would climb the stairs. They curved around and around and looking down from the top, with the dark railing, it was a snail. I'd never liked snails, not much. But that snail was beautiful. And then finally, I would reach a door—"

"And?"

My body was trembling. I couldn't help it. I couldn't believe what I was hearing.

"A girl would open it . . . Don't look at me that way."

"Darling, I can't look away."

"I'm magnetic."

"To me, and apparently to her, the girl."

"I know what you're thinking."

"Trust me, you don't."

And he didn't. Harry had no idea.

"I do know. But it wasn't sexual, not at first. I was still a boy, at first."

Now it was me and not Harry who was deciding if I wanted to tell. I was staring up through the skylight, at swirls of clouds, my hand in his hair. I felt the smooth weight of Harry's curl twirl in my fingers and thought of the stairs that were a snail.

"What did she look like?"

"I don't know. Well, I do know, but in an abstract way. How she seemed. How she felt." He pushed my hand away and sat up. "What is it?"

Harry might have misunderstood before, but he did know me, and he knew I was holding something back. "Tell me." He was holding my hand too tightly. I tried to pull away, but he wouldn't let me until I told. As always, I gave in to him.

"When I was a girl, I was restless. It was hard for me to sleep. I would imagine I was in a tower. With a staircase that curved around itself."

Harry tightened his grip on my hand.

"I would hear footsteps climbing the stairs."

"You heard them, or you imagined you heard them?"

"Does it matter?"

"Yes."

"I'm not sure it does. The footsteps would stop at my door, and I would open it to find a boy standing there. A boy who had gone on a long journey to find me."

I was watching Harry's face. His eyes glittered in the moonlight. I could see he doubted me.

"You're lying," he said.

"I never lie."

And I wasn't lying. It was all true.

"We'll have to change that," he said, pulling me closer to him.

"Do you believe me?"

"Does it matter?"

"I think it does."

"I believe you to the end."

"The end of what?"

"Everything."

It was the moment I understood that Harry was my fate.

Should I have paid more attention? Darlings, one thing I know is that it wouldn't have mattered.

*

I never met Philippe, but even if I had, I don't think my view of him
would change.

It isn't that he doesn't love her. He does. But he doesn't love her
enough or in the right way. Charlotte will always be second to his ambition, his parents, his work, maybe a child if she's able to bear it. I won't
elaborate on that. It isn't my story to tell.

*

Charlotte had come home for the holidays. This was shortly after she
met Philippe. I knew something was afoot because Charlotte mispinned
a seam, and she never made mistakes like that.

When I pointed it out, she was dismayed. I told her it's not the
mistake, it's how you correct it.

That was when she told me about him.

I could tell how attracted she was to Philippe, but the trouble with
love is that you need the one thing and also another. You can't be in
love or stay in love without first falling in love. But you can fall in love
with the wrong person. I would know.

"Philippe's an architect," Charlotte said.

She'd pricked her finger with a pin and there was a spot of blood
on the cloth. Charlotte didn't notice it at first.

"He's talented. There's something spare and emotional in his drawings, and they're lean. Not like Father's. And he paints."

I blotted the blood off the wool with my handkerchief.

"Does he like your paintings?"

Charlotte hesitated. "He was brutalized in a critique of his painting.
It's one of the reasons he's doing architecture. He thinks the academy's
full of philistines. Fakes."

"I see. But your paintings, does he like them?"

"He isn't sure I should paint." She pricked her finger again.

I quickly blotted the wool. "Why not?"

"He worries I'll always be thwarted out in the world beyond the academy."

"And why is that?"

"Because I don't see color."

We were silent for a moment. I was surprised to see a blush rise in Charlotte's cheeks.

"The thing is, he asks my opinion."

"About what?"

She briefly hesitated.

"Color. What color to use. It's funny, isn't it?"

Charlotte looked at me again, her eyes searching.

"Not really."

I wanted to say more, but I stopped myself and Charlotte looked disappointed. I wish I had said more, about how she needed to create family, a circle, a wall of protection. I knew too well how you can end up alone or with someone who doesn't protect you in the way he should.

*

The lioness has a different way of seeing. This is what I know.

JULIAN RAPHAËL, 4R

I'm crossing the mountains in Spain. We had a couple of close calls through Belgium and France but, having gotten this far, I'm optimistic even though it's rocky and icy, the paths sometimes barely there. I have a guide who is risking his life to save me, and every day I ask myself if I would do the same for him, and I tell myself I must. This is how I must live my life now and for whatever time's left.

Each night, when I'm able, I read a little from the book Charlotte gave me. How did she know it would be such a comfort? During the day, I keep it over my heart in my breast pocket, just in case.

*

"The world is everything, that is the case. The world is the totality of facts, not things. The world is determined by the facts, these being all the facts."

*

I told Charlotte I love her. Every word we spoke was dangerous, but there's danger everywhere and I would have always regretted it if I hadn't told her. As Blake would say, "Nothing comes to those who wait."

What I didn't tell Charlotte was that while Papa and I had hidden the empty frames in the walls, my family's paintings are all tucked under that new parquet in her front room—Monet, Boudin, Delvaux,

Van der Ast, and all the others. It was a clever plan Francois came up
with; a section of the floor was of a piece. You couldn't tell and once
Papa and Francois and I had slipped all the canvases under it—while
Charlotte was out shopping with Mama and Esther—and Francois had
nailed it into place, it looked exactly like the rest of the floor. Because
it was exactly like the rest of the floor. Papa paid for the installation.

*

I reach Gibraltar and start asking after the rest of my crew. The pilot
has been sent to a prisoner's camp after a brief stay in hospital, and
Blake is on his way back to England, God bless. He got ahead of me.

I also ask about Guy. He is unaccounted for but for reasons unex-
plained, he is presumed to be alive. Then I ask about Philippe, Charlotte's husband. He is missing and presumed dead. His plane was shot
down before he had a chance to parachute out. Don't think I felt joy
or relief or vindication when I heard this. I cried, for Charlotte's sake.

"Whereof one cannot speak . . ."

CHARLOTTE SAUVIN, 4L

"Thereof one must be silent."

*

The Colonel is banging around and shouting in his apartment. If I didn't know better, I would think he'd been drinking. Jacques can't hear the shouting, so I think the Colonel is doing it to punish Miss Hobert and the awful man on the second floor. Good. Someone should punish them.

It's dark out, and I put the blackout paper on the windows and light a candle, noticing by the flicker of the match that my hand is trembling. I'm too restless to sit.

I hear footsteps in the hall, and I run to the door and open it, only to see Schmidt standing there, holding a bundle wrapped in linen. Behind him, the Raphaëls' door is open and their ravaged apartment lit.

"My father . . ."

"Still not back?" Schmidt asks.

"No."

I'm looking in Schmidt's eyes, and I have to say they aren't the eyes of a monster. They're the eyes of a young man who hates his situation and is doing what he can under the circumstances, maybe the best he can.

"I'll go to the headquarters and check on him."

Schmidt looks nervous, and I feel a chill. Maybe he knows something I don't? He shifts the bundle he's holding, and a piece of silver drops to the floor with a clatter. It rests there glinting in the faint light.

Mrs. Raphaël called it Etruscan, an American pattern that reminded her of Egypt, a place she said she liked. The fork is long tined and could stab you in the throat if you weren't careful.

"I'll check right away," Schmidt says, making no move to pick up the fork. "I've no doubt he's fine. I'll make sure he comes home."

"Thank you." It pains me to say it.

Schmidt steps around me and continues down the stairs with the Raphaëls' silver, leaving the fork on the floor.

I pick up the fork and take it inside.

*

I wait. Alone in darkness. The night is so still I could almost convince myself we had imagined the war.

*

The sound is faint at first, foam on the edge of the surf, a seashell's roar. But it grows, filling the silence. I would swear it's the roar of one engine, one small plane, but I must be imagining it. I must be imagining everything.

Philippe.

I try to picture him at the controls speeding down from the dark to save us all.

The roar grows louder and closer. I'm not imagining anything. It's deafening, thundering. Passing low above Number 33 and beyond. And then there's a shrieking shatter followed by a booming explosion that rattles the windows and makes the ground reverberate.

Sounds erupt in the building, footsteps and voices and doors banging open.

I throw off the blanket and run up the hall, hearing the slap of bare feet on polished stone. I open the door to see the Colonel looking worse than he did after his wife died—and I remember that Zipper was shot. From below, we hear the notary shouting, "Go back in your apartments, everyone, in your apartments! Our building wasn't hit. Go back in your apartments!"

I tiptoe to the railing and lean over the descending squares of staircase to see Dirk peering up at me. I look into his eyes for a moment before he steps back in his apartment and slams his door.

"Not back yet?" the Colonel asks.

I shake my head.

"We'll know soon."

"What will we know?"

"Everything. And hopefully, everything will amount to nothing at all."

We hear more doors shutting downstairs and the faint sound of sirens in the distance. And then silence.

*

In the middle of my white night, I get out of bed and tear the black paper off all the windows. The glow of the waxing moon fills the apartment, making it a new and strange world of shadow and mystery. I look out the window and the square below comes into focus and I see her at the top of the church steps. My lioness. She's vibrantly awake, and even from my aerie, I sense her energy. I feel a quiver through my body, as she leisurely walks down the steps, muscles rippling with possibility. She crosses the square, holding for a moment below my window. Looking up at me, she leaps, flying toward me with perfect control and power, then she's here, staring at me through the pane, her eyes filled with spirit. I see how thick and lustrous her fur is. I want to touch it. I want to feel her strength. I open the window and let her inside. I'm not afraid. How could I be?

*

"There is indeed the inexpressible. This shows itself as the mystical."

*

It is the next morning, the twenty-first day, a day of transformation. A number marking endings and beginnings. Twenty-one is the weight of a soul, and I leave the apartment for Avenue Louise before dawn with this knowledge.

The tram isn't running yet, only faint glowworms from bakery windows relieve the gloom, but as I walk and walk through the heavy mist on this dark January morning, I feel a strange and prodigious energy. Reaching the corner, I turn left and continue three blocks more toward the gestapo headquarters as, gradually, the empty avenue fills with people, most of them Belgians. There is a buzz of conversation, the mist floats low on sidewalk stones, we are all walking on fog.

Up ahead, the street is cordoned off, and there are soldiers everywhere. I make my way through the crowd.

"Excuse me," I say. "Please, I need to see my father."

*

But he isn't there. Nothing is there. And as I stare at the hole where a plain art deco building once stood, I feel stunned and empty. It must be a dream. Please let this be a dream of not finding Father, a dream where I have almost reached the place I'm going, the place where he is, and something keeps me from it.

As I stand there, numb, voices filter in and I piece together the story as I would a hat.

"It's Longchamps who's done it."

"He's mad!"

"Brilliantly!"

"A mad bomber!"

"Who the hell is Longchamps?"

"He's a Belgian!"

"From Brussels, no less."

"An aristocrat!"

"RAF."

"His father was tortured in this very building."

"To death."

"Nazi bastards."

"Shhh."

"Enough of that."

"Bold Longchamps."

"Enough of all of that."

And indeed, it is Longchamps who has bombed the Nazi head-quarters, the building where so many Jews and Belgians have been interrogated and killed—Father and the newsboy now among them. I don't know if Schmidt checked on Father. I don't know if he was in the building, too, and I don't care. I don't know if Father was dead or alive when the bomb hit, and I don't know what to do or who to talk to. I ask one of the soldiers, but he tells me in French that he doesn't speak French. I try another and another. Finally I find a gestapo officer.

"Please," I say. Am I screaming? "My father was there. In that building."

"Go home," he says. "You will be informed in due time."

"Informed of what?"

I am screaming.

"Of whether he's dead or alive."

"No one in there is alive," I scream.

"Then why are you asking? Now move along!" The gestapo officer turns to a soldier. "Break up the crowd and arrest anyone who refuses to leave," he orders.

Whistles blow, the crowd swirls and disperses into the mist, and I with them. For what I do know is that it is an ending.

*

I'm still numb as I walk. My hand is tingling. Is it tingling? I hold it up, seeing long-tapered fingers, the slightly crooked pinky finger, lines over knuckles, pale nails. Is it my hand? It is a hand that hasn't held a paintbrush for years. I think of the paints and the canvas Mr. Raphaël left me and a picture forms in my head of a place where people eat and dance and sing in the light but cast no shadows. I intend to paint that picture.

*

I look up at the houses, rows of doors and windows pressed up to the street watching me pass. I am alone now.

It's colder, the mist has dispersed, and there isn't a cloud in the sky. But for a moment, I think it has begun to rain.

How strange, a cloudless rain. A deluge pouring down my face.

And then I feel it. At first, I think I'm imagining the sensation. It's so faint, so fleeting—an eyelash, a butterfly, a flicker of a spark, a drop of water skipping across a hot stove. I must be imagining it. But there it is again. I'm not imagining it. The baby is moving.

I stop crying, rest my hands on my stomach, and look up at the perfect cloudless sky and then down at the blur of paving stones slicked with winter-scarred leaves, understanding I must watch my every step as I make my way up the avenue and across the square to Number 33.

*

The apartment is so quiet I can hear the clock ticking, and I follow the sound to Father's office, seeing the disembodied face looking pale and lost in its forest of brass, a fitting clock for today. Everything is exactly as Father left it. I would never know his study, too, had been searched. I look out over the courtyard where Julian made his way along the ledge and Guy did before him. Below, the ripple of a curtain in Dirk's apartment window catches my attention. *Later, I'll talk to him, later.* I turn my back to the window, my gaze drifting to the walls of shelves bearing Father's considerable collection of books, punctuated with mystical totems accumulated over the years—broken seashells, oddly shaped rocks, misfit beach glass, a jade Buddha, a lidless cherrywood box, a tiny bronze llama—and then to his drafting table on which sits the closed sketchbook with the drawings that took so much of his time and attention in the past two years. *It is the book of retreat and surrender*, I think.

I'm very tired. I put a hand on my stomach, trying to remember that it's worth the effort, living. I sit down and stare at the closed sketchbook, on the cover written in Father's elegant script:

"The picture agrees with reality or not, it is right or wrong, true or false. The picture represents what it represents . . . what the picture represents is its sense."

I open to the first page.

"The world is everything and that is the case."

I see a drawing of Number 33, the geometry of it, the lines and symmetry, but this Number 33 is different. Father's version of it reveals light as a master photographer would.

I turn the page.

"The world is the totality of facts."

Below the text is a cutaway drawing showing rooms and windows and stairs and halls, but again this version is unlike the Number 33 I know so well. Father's is a building that a wise king would grow in a garden.

I turn page after page.

"The possibility of facts is form."

I see unmortared stones sealed with moss—thick walls that Father has noted are "soundproofed"—and tree trunks with branches of light extending from the walls and ceiling in place of sconces and chandeliers.

"Form is the possibility of structure."

Ceilings open to the heavens and bare floors grow carpets of grass and on every level instead of a modest landing, there is a spacious gathering room with low sofas and long tables where Father has noted "conversation not eavesdropping" and he has drawn all the people who have lived in this building. There's Julian and me and Esther and Masha and Mr. and Mrs. Raphaël and Miss Hobert wearing my hat, and Dirk and his parents, and the Colonel and his wife and Zipper and Jacques with some other men in serge suits, and the notary and his wife and their children, and the woman who used to live on the second floor and even Van Cauter. We're seated on those sofas and from the way we seem to be talking, lounging even, I feel our conversations will go long into the night . . . But Father isn't there.

"A logical picture of facts is a thought."

I turn to the last page and see him—in our apartment, seated exactly where I am now, is Father. It is a perfect likeness of a man who each morning woke up and created possibility. It's also a picture of Father as he wanted to be, with two perfect legs, his body slim but not gaunt, an almost smile on his lips below the thin aquiline nose and capacious and serene brow. In his hand, he holds an olive branch that is also a pencil. I look more closely and see that in the drawing there is a sketchbook on the drafting table that's open to the page I'm looking at and on that page is the self-portrait drawn in miniature, an endless recurrence of Father creating and hoping, and below it is written:

"What is thinkable is also possible."

I close the book and sit there listening to the clock. It's an effort to get up, but I do. I walk to the living room, my footsteps echoing on the polished parquet floor, and I look out over the square at the familiar buildings, the brick and stone and stair-stepped gables, the cupolas, and domes, and tiles and square panes and arches, and beyond at the grand boulevards, the meandering streets leading down to the great square, modestly encircled, only the tallest tower truly pointing to heaven, the gray city of underground rivers, and a thousand dirty secrets, of fog and mist, and forgotten dead, a place the Romans took and discarded, the Spanish took and discarded, the French took and discarded, the Germans took and lost, and now have taken again, a city claimed and abandoned, steeping in its own brew of time and failure. It is the city I have known my entire life, and like Number 33, its hideous secrets have been revealed, its everyday failures and misdeeds, and fatal betrayals, but also a mad, glorious bravery I would have once thought impossible. Father never gave up on this place. Why should I?

Acknowledgments

Number 33, the place I was fortunate to call home for some years in Brussels, and Mesdames Goldschmidt and Warlemont. Jean de Selys Longchamps and Guy Pevtchin, and all those who risked their lives to save people and art. Ludwig Wittgenstein, whose preface to *Tractatus Logico-Philosophicus* is a touchstone. Alan Turing. The painters: Eugène Boudin, Balthasar Van der Ast, Claude Monet, and especially, Paul Delvaux. The National Gallery.

Thanks to—

Dorian Karchmar, blessed champion. Laura Bonner and the WME team: Sophia Bark, Anna DeRoy, Ryan Feldman, Perry Weitzner.

Elisabeth Schmitz, oracle. Peter Blackstock, Morgan Entrekin, Laura Schmitt, and my team at Grove: Justina Batchelor, Natalie Church, Judy Hottensen, Paula Cooper Hughes, Gretchen Mergenthaler, Margaret Moore, Mike Richards, Rachael Richardson, Deb Seager, and Kelly Winton.

Allegra Le Fanu, torchbearer, and all the fine people at Bloomsbury.

Geoff Shaevitz, litmus tester.

My heroic readers: Linda Davis and Yelena Veisman.

Abettors: Carson Becker, Brian Sidney Bembridge, Michael Blumenthal, Joe Dapello, Claudette Groenendaal, Kate Kramer, Pete McCabe, Kirill Mikhanovsky, Barb Paulini, Marie Thérèse Rainey-Meade, Hillary Richard, Matt Sartwell, Russ Tutterow.

And ever grateful: Seamus Heaney, Ken Kesey, Ralph Salisbury. My mother Frederica, the painter. My father Douglas, the storyteller. Louise Fiedler, wartime nurse. My dearest inspirations: Benjamin, Ecem, George, Max, and Daniel, wordsmith and pencil box knight.